P9-BYR-602

Praise for
STARFIST I: FIRST TO FIGHT

"CAUTION! Any book written by Dan Cragg and David Sherman is bound to be addictive, and this is the first in what promises to be a great adventure series. *First to Fight* is rousing, rugged, and just plain fun. The authors have a deep firsthand knowledge of warfare, an enthralling vision of the future, and the skill of veteran writers. Fans of military fiction, science fiction, and suspense will all get their money's worth, and the novel is so well done it will appeal to general readers as well. It's fast, realistic, moral, and a general hoot. *First to Fight* is also vivid, convincing—and hard to put down. Sherman and Cragg are a great team! I can't wait for the next one!"

—RALPH PETERS
New York Times bestselling author of
Red Army

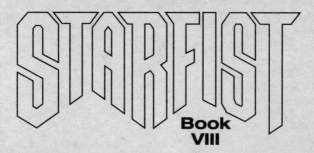

STARFIST

Book VIII

KINGDOM'S FURY

DAVID SHERMAN AND DAN CRAGG

BALLANTINE BOOKS • NEW YORK

A Del Rey® Book
Published by The Ballantine Publishing Group
Copyright © 2003 by David Sherman and Dan Cragg

www.delreydigital.com

ISBN 0-345-44372-1

Manufactured in the United States of America

First Edition: January 2003

10 9 8 7 6 5 4 3 2 1

Dedicated to
Major Edward Stalker, United States Air Force

We Americans owe everything to men like Ed Stalker, whose
courage, dedication, and patriotism guarantee the survival
of our precious rights and liberty.

STARFIST

Book VIII

KINGDOM'S FURY

PROLOGUE

Almost loud enough to drown out the crash of thunder in the middle distance, the raindrops spattered on the leaves. They slid and rolled down twigs, aggregated into dribbles and flowed into runnels, some of which reached major branches and flowed to tree trunks, where they sluiced to the ground below. Or they fell onto the heads, shoulders, and backs of Fighters who slip-walked stealthily through the sodden forest. The Fighters didn't mind the rain; they were genetically accustomed to being wet. Now and again one of them got so wet that the gill slits on his sides opened to extract life-giving oxygen from the water.

This, the Fighters minded. There wasn't enough water running over their bodies for their gills to function properly, and their lungs cut off when the gills began working.

The Leaders and Masters with the Fighters wore coverings over their gill slits so rainwater couldn't tease the slits open. But the receptors that lined their sides were exposed on all the aliens, so they easily sensed the listening posts the defenders of Haven had established.

In columns of twenty Fighters each, each column headed by a Leader, four hundred Fighters penetrated the outer line of listening posts. A Master followed every fourth column, and an Over Master was in overall command. The Over Master didn't expect to have much to do on this raid. It was well-planned, and he had drilled his Masters thoroughly. Their first task was to assemble the columns of fighters behind the line of listening posts, in front of a section manned by the regiment of the Army of the Lord that was led by

Earthman Marines newly arrived on the mudball they called Kingdom. The Great Master in command of the Kingdom operation sought to instill fear in the newly arrived Marines. The Army of the Lord was already terrified. The Earthman Marines who had been fighting for months were sorely wounded, with many casualties, and their morale suffered.

The Over Master listened with satisfaction to the splash and thunder of the storm; so much noise totally masked the sounds made by his Fighters.

"Acting Colonel Deacon, sir?" Second Acolyte Burningbush, assistant intelligence officer for the 842nd Defense Garrison, stood in the doorway of the garrison's situation room. He darted an apologetic glance at Colonel Deacon Hosanna, the proper commander of the garrison.

"Come." Ensign Wolfe, commander of the second platoon, Company B, 26th Fleet Initial Strike Team, Confederation Marine Corps, didn't look up from the situation reports he was reviewing with the officer whose command he held.

"Sir, the LPs are reporting anomalies." Burningbush hesitantly held out a thin sheaf of papers, not sure whether to give them to his real commander or to the infidel usurper.

Hosanna's face was expressionless as he inclined his head, meaning Burningbush was to give the papers to Wolfe.

"What kind of anomalies?" Wolfe muttered as he took the papers. He skimmed them quickly, then read again more slowly. "Full alert," he said halfway through. "All hands. Everybody awake and in fighting positions."

"Why?" Hosanna demanded. "Don't you know what this is?" He read the papers over Wolfe's shoulder. He saw the anomalies, small figures moving toward the city, and assumed they were lizard- or small mammal-like animals moving to higher ground from flooded-out burrows, and he said as much.

"Colonel Deacon, have you ever seen the recordings of the traces made by those creatures?" Wolfe replied, looking at the Kingdomite commander.

Hosanna blinked. Of course he'd seen the electronic signs of migrating animals.

"I have. It was part of the orientation for all officers and noncommissioned officers of 26th FIST when we first arrived. The Skinks have a lower body temperature than humans, they give infra signals just like smaller animals." He looked directly at Second Acolyte Burningbush. "Why haven't you passed the order yet? *Do* it. *Now!*"

The junior Kingdomite officer jumped at the shouted word. He cast a fearful glance at his rightful commander as he darted out of the room.

"You may be right," Wolfe said harshly to Hosanna, "but I'd rather be embarrassed by ordering a full alert over a lemming run than be caught sleeping by a Skink attack."

"As you wish," Hosanna said, his face expressionless.

"If I'm right, I hope your men know how to fight," Wolfe growled. He checked to see that he had a fresh power pack in his sidearm as he strode from the situation room to the command center.

Alone, Hosanna allowed an expression to fix on his face. It was a combination of hatred and fury. Archbishop General Lambsblood had a great deal to answer for, putting the off-world infidel junior officers and swords in command of units of the Army of the Lord over more senior officers, officers pure in their faithfulness.

The Over Master transmitted a halt command to the Masters, the Masters relayed the command to the Leaders, the Leaders, in turn, halted the advance of the Fighters and moved them out of ragged columns into a staggered line facing the defensive positions.

The Fighters couldn't see the positions, and the receptors on their sides could not pinpoint the bunker locations; they weren't close enough. But they knew there were many camouflaged a short distance ahead because their Leaders had told them they would form on line when they were just out of firing range.

On command, the Fighters lowered themselves to the ground, elevated the nozzles of their weapons enough to keep them from getting clogged by anything on the ground, and began slithering forward through the muck. Very soon the largest bunkers became visible, hulking black-on-black out of the stygian darkness. After the Fighters entered their weapons' most extreme range, their side receptors began to detect minute electrical impulses radiating from the bunkers.

Suddenly, their receptors overloaded by massive electric discharges all along the defensive line, the Fighters were disoriented. Lights as brilliant as a small sun lit them up. Then surprised shouts came from the bunkers, followed quickly by fléchette fire studded with plasma bolts from the blasters of the few Confederation Marines positioned among the soldiers of the Army of the Lord.

The Over Master shrieked orders, Masters shrilled them in turn, Leaders screamed them out. The Fighters damped their receptors and regained equilibrium. They pointed the nozzles of their weapons at bunker apertures and fired. Many streams of a viscous, greenish fluid spattered harmlessly against bunker walls, but some disappeared though the apertures. Agonized cries echoed out. But attackers were quickly being shredded by fléchettes or flashed into vapor as the Fighters wriggled deeper into the mud and returned fire.

The Over Master transmitted an order; a half-dozen Large Ones on the right flank rose to their feet and charged a silenced bunker. One flashed into vapor when a plasma bolt grazed his shoulder. The flame that flared from him ignited a Large One who ran by too close. The other four made it past safely and ran around the bunker to its rear. They peeled off, two to one side, two to the other, and headed for the rear of those bunkers that still fought. One pair was quickly pulped by long bursts from fléchette machine guns in the second line of bunkers. The other pair made it into the entry tunnel of a bunker. They burst into the bunker room behind the soldiers firing through the apertures.

As he heard trampling behind him, a Marine spun around,

brought his blaster to bear, squeezing the firing lever when he saw the color of the huge figures. The nearer one flashed up, but as fast as the Marine was, he wasn't fast enough. The nearer Large One had been swinging a sword at him even as the Marine spun about. After the Large One flared up and ignited its partner in the closed space, the sword completed its arc, chopping deeply into the Marine's neck. The heat from the two flaring Large Ones singed the defenders, sucked the oxygen from the air, and immediately burned their lungs.

As more of the defenders obeyed the commands of the Marines and opened up on the attackers, the rate of fire from the bunkers increased despite those no longer in the fight. The fire from the attackers slowly ebbed as their numbers dwindled under murderous fire from the bunkers.

On the attackers' left flank a Fighter with a genetic defect that afforded him more intelligence than Fighters were bred for realized that he and his mates would all be killed if something wasn't done about the lights. He understood that the Earthmen needed instruments to detect them when they couldn't see. It was time for him to take a risk. He raised his head and shoulders high enough to allow him to aim carefully, then fired a deliberate spray into the aperture of the bunker almost directly in front of him. Screams immediately came from the bunker, and fire ceased. He sprayed another, longer stream. The screaming stopped.

Pleased, the Fighter slithered to where he'd last known his Leader to be and came upon his body. He rooted through the Leader's belt pouches, found what he was looking for, stuck it into the waistband of his loincloth, and returned to his position.

"Fighters, to me!" he called out, his voice a raspy gargle.

Fighters to his left and his right looked at him uncertainly. He was a Fighter like them, not a Leader. But their Leader was dead, along with half of their mates. And this Fighter did call to them in the voice of a Leader. So, uncertain or not, they edged closer to him to hear and obey his next order.

"With me!" the Fighter shouted when he saw seven Fighters ready to follow him. "Between the two dead bunkers. *Now!*"

He leaped to his feet and sprinted forward. Seven Fighters ran with him. Fléchette fire took down one. He skidded to a stop with his back against the nearer bunker, next to the aperture, and signaled one of the other Fighters to do the same at the other dead bunker. When that Fighter was in place, the Fighter who had taken charge signaled again and waited until he saw him spraying acid into the bunker. Then he stuck the nozzle of his own weapon through the aperture of his bunker and sprayed from side to side.

Satisfied that they'd truly killed anybody who might have been left alive, he signaled his remaining Fighters to lower themselves to the ground and spread out in the space between the dead bunkers. The low humps that were the second line of bunkers were just out of range. More important, he could see that the lamps were mounted on spindly towers between the two bunker lines.

He shouted, and the Fighters slithered forward until they were within range. He shouted more orders, and his six remaining Fighters began spraying two by two at three of the bunkers in the second line. He didn't fire with them; instead, he slithered toward the nearest lamp tower.

Withering fire converged on the Fighters he left behind, but one second-line bunker stopped firing, then another. No fire came near him, and soon he was in the dark, below the outward-pointing cone of the lamp's light. He found a thick cable lying on the ground, parallel to the line of lamp towers. Directly beneath the tower a cable ran upward from the cable on the ground. Emanations from it tingled his receptors. Slithering as low as he could, he followed the cable to the left until he reached a junction that led toward the second bunker line. He briefly pondered the situation, and decided it might be where to kill the lights. He backed off out of splashback range, then sprayed toward where the cable lay. Almost immediately, the changes in the discharges he sensed told him the acid was eating away the cable's insulating covering.

Without further warning, lightning flashed and deafening thunder cracked. When the Fighter who had taken charge could see again, the lamps were out. He smiled grimly and slithered as fast as he could back to where he'd left his companions. One of them was still alive, whimpering, one arm almost torn off. Hastily, he tore the breechcloth from a Fighter corpse and wrapped it around the arm to stanch the flow of life fluid.

"Go back," he ordered.

The wounded Fighter whimpered again, but crawled away.

The Fighter drew his dead close to each other, then got out the fire maker he'd taken from his Leader's corpse and touched it to one of the dead Fighters. Jumping up, he ran as fast as he could before the flare could catch him. Between the first two bunkers, he paused to flash the Fighter who'd fallen there. By the time he got back to his own position in the line, more flares were lighting the night. Masters and Leaders ordered the flaring of the dead and the withdrawal. Moving quickly, the intelligent Fighter flamed all the dead from his section, then joined the exodus. Three times before the attack force was safe from pursuing fire, he had to stop again to flame more of the newly dead.

The Over Master in command of the raid reported more than thirty bunkers killed, at least six of which held Earthman Marines. He further reported more than 250 Fighters along with seven Leaders and two Masters died gloriously in the great victory. He did not report the Fighter who assumed the role of a Leader. He didn't know what to make of that; a Fighter assuming the role of a Leader was unheard of.

CHAPTER ONE

Captain Conorado, just returned from his court-martial on Earth, nodded when his officers and senior noncommissioned officers finished bringing him up to date. "All right. Mac," he said, addressing Lieutenant Rokmonov, the assault platoon commander, "you take over third platoon. Wang," to Staff Sergeant Hyakowa, acting platoon commander of third platoon, "you're back to platoon sergeant again. Top," First Sergeant Myer, the company's top kick, "you've got the roster of replacements. Let me know how you assign them. Some of your Marines are going to move into billets above their rank. As soon as I have your new rosters, I'll pass the names up to Battalion for promotion. And make sure Souavi gets those new uniforms issued.

"In the meanwhile, 26th FIST is relieving us on the line. Tomorrow we begin kicking some serious Skink ass!"

The officers aye aye'd and headed to their platoons. The platoon sergeants followed the first sergeant to get their replacements and find out what the "new uniforms" were about.

"Siddown," Myer growled when he and the platoon sergeants reached his desk. They pulled up chairs and sat close. "Wang, remember that sample of acid third platoon brought back from Society 437?"

Hyakowa nodded. "Yeah. That doctor we had with us thought it had a phosphoric base with some sort of organic solvent."

"Well, someone at Headquarters, Marine Corps, came up

with a good idea for a change. They figured sooner or later Marines would run into the Skinks again and we'd need some defense against that acid. They analyzed the hell out of that sample until they knew what it was. Then they sent it to Aberdeen to develop an antidote and a retardant." He shook his head. "They haven't managed to come up with an antidote, so we're stuck with the old ways of dealing with the acid on flesh: small doses are to be cut out of the flesh before they eat all the way through; larger amounts will eat flesh and bone until they kill, unless you immediately amputate the limb. If it's a trunk or deep head wound . . ." he paused, and shook his head again. "Aberdeen did manage to develop a retardant, an impregnator for the chameleons. It won't protect flesh, but it will stop the acid from eating its way through the chameleons so a Marine wearing an impregnated uniform is protected."

"Does it really work?" Hyakowa asked. The other platoon sergeants had the same question. Almost anyone with combat experience knew that more than half of the "technological advances" or "improvements" in weapons or equipment didn't work the way they were supposed to when they were subjected to the harsh realities of combat.

Myer shrugged. "Who the hell knows? The retardant was tested against acid the chemists at Aberdeen cooked up, but nobody knows if that acid is the exact same as the Skinks'. We aren't going to know until a Marine wearing impregnated chameleons gets hit by the real thing."

"What effect does it have on the chameleon effect?" one of the other platoon sergeants asked.

Myer glared at him. He didn't like being asked questions he didn't have answers for. "What'd I just say? The damn things haven't seen combat yet. But they claim it has no effect, the chameleon effect still works." He shook his head. "Not that chameleons seem to give a hell of a lot of protection against the Skinks. Maybe they can see in the infrared like those bird-creatures on Avionia. Maybe they have some other sense that allows them to sense us some other way."

"Whatever." Myer sat back and slapped a palm on his

desktop to end the discussion. "Twenty-sixth FIST brought an extra thousand sets of chameleons, enough for everybody left in 34th FIST to get one, with some extras." He shook his head sadly; he hated losing Marines. "We had more casualties than they realized. Anyway, send people to Supply this afternoon, Sergeant Souavi will have them in stock. Your people can pick up one for each of your Marines. The new men already have theirs. Speaking of which—" He picked up a few slips of paper from his desktop and handed them out. "—these are your new men. Don't spend them all in one place, it's liable to be a long time before we get any more."

He took them outside to where the new men waited and called them out to join their new platoon sergeants. Rokmonov was waiting for Hyakowa. As long as he'd been with Company L, he was a new man too, with third platoon now.

The general mood in 34th FIST was, if not jubilant, at least relieved. After months of combating an implacable enemy who was hellishly difficult to find, and suffering the heaviest casualties most of them had ever experienced, they were finally reinforced and had replacements for their losses. Not that the new men could fully replace their dead. Close friendships had ended with the lost lives. Although new friendships can grow just as close as old ones, the new friends can never truly replace those lost.

The mood in Company L of 34th FIST's infantry battalion was perhaps higher than anywhere else. Captain Conorado was back. Lieutenant Humphrey, the company's executive officer, was well-liked and had filled in admirably during Conorado's absence, but nearly everyone in the company had been through multiple operations and deployments with Conorado. Nearly every man in Company L trusted their company commander to a degree they trusted no other officer.

So it was a jocular third platoon that greeted its newcomers when they assembled in the shell of a building that had been nearly demolished by the Skinks' antiarmor weapon.

The shell was a couple hundred meters inside the perimeter. Even though they were surrounded by evidence of how far the Skink weapons could reach, just being off the defensive line made them feel they were out of danger, at least for the moment.

The men of third platoon took the assignment of Lieutenant Rokmonov as their new commander with equanimity. If lost friends could never be fully replaced, neither could their late platoon commander, Gunnery Sergeant Charlie Bass. But they all knew Rokmonov. The grizzled officer had been a gunnery sergeant before he was commissioned. If they didn't think he was going to be as good a platoon commander as Charlie Bass had been, well, *nobody* was that good, but Rokmonov was probably as good as they came. Like Charlie Bass, he'd been filling a platoon commander's billet on a semipermanent basis. Rokmonov finally broke down and accepted an ensign's silver orbs when 411th FIST, which he was then in, had a sudden influx of company grade officers, one of whom got his platoon. He didn't want to ever again lose his job to a man who had probably recently been junior to him in rank—most Marine officers were sergeants or staff sergeants when they got commissioned.

Third platoon didn't get enough replacements to fill all of its eight vacancies so maybe Sergeant Bladon and Corporal Goudanis would return. For some men of third platoon, the arrival of the new men was cause for celebration.

"Rat," Rokmonov said to Corporal Linsman, the acting second squad leader since Sergeant Bladon was evacuated, "the paperwork goes in today to get you your sergeant's stripes."

"Welcome aboard, Rat," Sergeant Ratliff said. He slapped Linsman's shoulder with his left hand while flexing his right fist.

"Thanks, Rabbit." Linsman grinned, but cast a wary eye at Ratliff's fist. The Confederation Marines still "pinned on the stripes," so every newly promoted man was punched in the shoulder once for each chevron by any enlisted man who held the same or higher rank.

"Way to go, Rat!" Corporal Dornhofer called out.

"Ya mean I got to call you 'Sergeant' now?" Corporal Pasquin cried.

The others added congratulations, even Corporal Kerr. Linsman was the second corporal in the platoon to make sergeant who had been junior to Kerr when Kerr was almost killed and had to spend nearly two years in recuperation.

"We need a new gun team leader," Rokmonov said when he thought the congratulations had gone on long enough. "Taylor, you don't have to hump the gun anymore, your new corporal's chevrons will be enough weight."

Lance Corporal Taylor grinned widely and happily accepted congratulations for his promotion to gun team leader.

Rokmonov looked at Hyakowa and nodded for him to take over.

Hyakowa stepped forward and studied the platoon roster for a moment. "This is a sad day for third platoon," he finally said. "We need two fire team leaders, but nobody thought to give us experienced corporals." He shook his head morosely. "What I'd really like to do is make Schultz a fire team leader, but we all know how he'd react to that." Schultz was a career lance corporal; if anyone tried to promote him, he'd turn it down—angrily and, some feared, violently. "As hard as it is to believe, the only other lance corporals we have in the blaster squads are Claypoole and Dean." He looked apologetically at Ratliff and Linsman. "I'm really sorry to have to do this to you, but do you think you can manage if I give each of you one of them as a fire team leader?"

Ratliff grinned wolfishly as he waited for the hooting and laughter to ebb slightly, then said in a parade-ground voice, "Gimme Dean. I'll break him in or break him."

Dean's face was a flickering mix of joy and indignancy.

"What?" Linsman squawked. "You mean you're going to stick me with Clay— Wait a minute. If Rabbit gets Claypoole, that means I get stuck with Dean." He worked his face into a grandly overacted fury and shouted at Hyakowa, "Are you trying to ruin my promotion?"

Claypoole first beamed, then shot a furiously offended look at Linsman, which set off fresh gales of hoots and laughter.

Hyakowa looked at the second squad leader blandly and said in a calm voice, "Corporal, soon to be Sergeant, Linsman, may I remind you that you are a Marine noncommissioned officer? As such, you are supposed to do more with less than anybody else in Human Space. And make it look easy. I fully expect you to take Claypoole and turn him into just as good a fire team leader as . . . as . . ." He shook his head again. "What am I saying? No, it's not possible to turn him into as good a fire team leader as Kerr, or even Chan." He nodded sagely. "But you *can* turn him into a reasonable facsimile."

Claypoole glared at Hyakowa; *he* didn't think that was funny.

"Rabbit," Hyakowa returned to Ratliff, "I have full confidence in your ability to turn Dean into . . ." His eyes went distant and he shook his head again. "I'll talk to the Top. Maybe I can get him to give us a corporal from one of the other platoons."

It was Dean's turn to glare and endure the hoots and laughs.

"As you were!" Rokmonov shouted after a moment. "We have some new people." He nodded toward six Marines who stood slightly apart from the platoon and hadn't joined in the laughter. "I'll let Staff Sergeant Hyakowa introduce them to you while I give the promotion recommendations to the Skipper. Staff Sergeant, the platoon is yours."

"Sir, the platoon is mine. Aye aye." Nobody bothered to call the platoon to attention; they weren't even standing in formation. Not when at any instant they might have to bolt back to fighting positions on the defensive perimeter. Hyakowa watched Rokmonov head for the company command post, then turned back to the men.

"We have one new lance corporal, name of Zumwald." He gestured for the gangly, redheaded new man to identify himself. "Lance Corporal Zumwald was in the security company at Headquarters, Marine Corps, when he got pulled for this assignment." He glanced at the roster. "So were PFCs Gray and Shoup." He looked back at the platoon. "Don't let their ranks and latest assignments fool you. All of these Marines have a couple of combat deployments with FISTs under their belts. No cherries here. Rabbit, you've got those three. Put one in each fire team."

"Roger," Ratliff said, nodding. He crooked a finger at his three new men.

"I'm giving you Longfellow as well. Sorry about that," he added to Linsman.

"Good," Ratliff said. Longfellow hadn't been with the platoon long, but Ratliff had seen enough to know he was a good Marine. Linsman merely shrugged at losing Longfellow.

"Linsman, you get Little and Fisher."

"Right." Linsman waved his two new men over.

"Hound," Hyakowa said to Sergeant Kelly, the gun squad leader, "move your a-gunners up. Sorry I only have one humper for you, but that's all they gave us. His name's Tischler.

"One more piece of business," Hyakowa said when Tischler moved to the gun squad. "We've got new uniforms coming. I want one man from each squad to go to Supply to pick them up. They're chameleons that are supposed to be impervious to the acid in the Skinks' shooters. From now on you *will* wear them." He looked at the men to see if anyone had a pressing question. None seemed to.

"That is all," he finished. "Squad leaders, let me know how you reorganize your squads."

The squad leaders took their men aside.

"Now I've got all my troublemakers together where I can keep an eye on you," Sergeant Ratliff said when he gave Godenov to Dean.

Linsman said the same thing when he assigned MacIlargie to Claypoole.

Claypoole's expression showed he was a bit put out. Not because he had MacIlargie, whom he liked, but because he *only* had MacIlargie in his fire team.

Corporal Kerr didn't show it, but he wondered why he retained Schultz and Corporal Doyle instead of getting a new man. Did Hyakowa and Rokmonov really think Chan could do a better job of integrating two new men into the squad than he could?

Nobody but the new men wondered why Corporal Doyle wasn't given a fire team.

Both as the more senior brigadier and as the man with the local experience, Theodosius Sturgeon, commander of 34th Fleet Initial Strike Team, was in overall command of planetside operations on the Kingdom of Yahweh and His Saints and Their Apostles, more commonly called "Kingdom." As such, he wanted to get 26th FIST involved as quickly as possible and gave it patrol duty its second day planetside. Brigadier Johannes Sparen, commander of 26th FIST, was relieved he didn't have to ask Sturgeon to give his FIST a mission beyond the defensive perimeter they were fed into as soon as they debarked from the Dragons that had ferried them from the orbital shuttles.

"Jack, the Skinks may have an innocent sounding name," Sturgeon said, "but they're exceptionally dangerous. They have horrible weapons, and they're unpredictable. I want you to put out patrols in force tomorrow, platoon size. And I want them in constant radio contact with Battalion. My staff is very familiar with the situation here." The situation here on Kingdom was unlike any he'd been in before. "Until you're familiar enough, I'll instruct my Infantry Two and Three shops to give any assistance yours request. Just until your people are familiarized with the situation. My infantrymen will relieve your platoons on the line before dawn tomorrow so your people can get an early start."

"You're in command, Ted," Sparen said. His calm voice belied the excitement he felt at getting into combat with an enemy alien sentience he'd only learned about on his way to Kingdom.

"Do this thing, Brigadier."

"Aye aye, Brigadier!"

Once outside 34th FIST's headquarters in Interstellar City, Sparen had to restrain himself from running to his HQ.

The honor of 26th FIST's first contact with the Skinks fell to first platoon, Alfa Company. The platoon was strung out in a line about two hundred meters long in a moderately dense forest along the edge of a marshy area when Lance Corporal Ransfield, the platoon comm man, said softly, "I have movement."

"Hold up," Ensign Cainey, the platoon commander ordered into his helmet comm's all-hands circuit. "Where?" He asked Ransfield.

Ransfield didn't look up from the UPUD Mark III's display as he pointed to his right front. "About two hundred fifty meters."

"Right front," Cainey said into the all-hands circuit. "Anybody got anything on infra?" Nobody did. He projected his preloaded situation map onto the inside of the chameleon shield of his helmet. The map confirmed what he already knew—no friendly forces within two kilometers of first platoon's position.

"Send a report to Battalion," Cainey ordered Ransfield. "And get an updated sitmap."

"Aye aye," Ransfield murmured. He requested the map and showed it to the platoon commander when it downloaded. No friendly forces where the UPUD picked up the movement—nor did it show anybody else in that area. Movement by people undetected by the string-of-pearls was ominous; all the briefings the Marines of 26th FIST had about the Skinks told them the creatures were almost impossible for the surveillance satellites to detect. Now what should he do? He could call in artillery on the movement, but what if it was some farmer's gaggle of geese? That would be bad for relations with the locals. But if it was Skinks, they didn't know a Marine platoon was here and he could ambush them.

"Tighten up," Cainey said, giving the all-hands order. "Echelon right, on me." Immediately, the first platoon

Marines began to close their interval and move on an angle—those behind Cainey swung in an arc to his right rear, those ahead of him to his left front. He knelt, facing the right front. The ground was damp under his knee.

"Closing," Ransfield said. "Two twenty-five." He kept his attention on the UPUD, a device that combined satellite communications, geoposition locator, and motion detector. It also could receive a variety of data, including real-time situation maps such as the one he'd just downloaded.

"How many?"

"Not sure. Twenty, twenty-five."

"Keep me posted at twenty-five meter intervals." He listened for vagrant noises, but all he heard in the direction of the movement was the gentle sloshing of water. He saw a fish jump in the marsh and heard the splash as it fell back. He saw tiny light reflections off flitting insectoids over the water.

"Aye aye," Ransfield replied.

Cainey quietly issued orders to his squad leaders on the command circuit. "Fire teams, close to contact. Ten meters between teams. Gun teams second from end. Get behind something."

"Two hundred," Ransfield murmured.

"Full shield rotation," Cainey said into the all-hands circuit. In each fire team and gun team the Marines obeyed; one man used his infra shield, one his magnifier, one his light gatherer.

"One seventy-five."

"Anything from any other direction?" The platoon was now closed to a line little more than a hundred meters long.

"Negative." Ransfield wasn't as certain as he sounded. There was still too much movement toward the ends of the platoon, which might interfere with the UPUD's ability to detect movement farther in those directions.

"One fifty."

"How many?"

"Same, twenty, twenty-five. Can't be positive. The movement flickers in and out."

"Anybody have anything visual?" Cainey wasn't concerned when none of his Marines reported seeing anyone—or anything. Sight lines in the lightly wooded marsh hardly ever reached a hundred meters. He looked to his flanks. He could see his Marines only when he used his infra shield. All of them appeared to be behind cover, so they should be safe even if the approaching Skinks had that other weapon he'd heard about, the thing that turned trees into kindling and men into shreds of blood and gristle.

"One hundred."

"Heads up, they should be entering visual range." Should be, but still nobody reported seeing them.

"Seventy-five."

Something was very wrong. "Is that thing working?" If the Skinks were that close, he should see them in the marsh. Twenty or twenty-five people couldn't move that well-concealed in an area that semi-open.

"Diagnostics say yes."

"Run the diagnostics again. See if you pick this up all right." Cainey spoke into his helmet comm, "Two-three, make a move for the UPUD."

Second squad's third fire team was the farthest to Cainey's right. "Roger, Six Actual," Corporal Ascropper, the fire team leader, replied. He rolled onto his side and hefted his blaster into the air.

"I got that," Ransfield said.

"Secure, Two-three."

"Aye aye."

"Tell him to stop moving, he's confusing the signals," Ransfield said a few seconds later.

"Two-three, secure from movement and stand tight."

Corporal Ascropper blinked. He'd lowered his blaster and resumed his position as soon as Cainey told him to secure. "Roger, have done," he answered.

"I'm still getting movement from his direction," Ransfield said.

"Two-three, check your three and your six. We're picking up movement from your location."

A moment later Corporal Ascropper reported, "Flank and rear secure."

"Movement to the front?" Cainey asked Ransfield.

"Negative. Front movement stopped." He paused as he studied the UPUD display. "Movement to the right stopped."

"Any movement anywhere?"

"Negative."

Ensign Cainey lay lost in thought for a moment. He'd heard scuttlebutt, rumors, that the UPUD Mark II had been so sensitive it picked up gnats in the air in its highest setting and burned out. The Mark III hadn't been around very long, maybe that bug hadn't been completely worked out.

"What's your sensitivity setting?"

Ransfield flicked his eyes at the settings. "Mid-range," he replied.

"Have you changed it since we stopped?"

"I haven't touched the settings since we left the perimeter."

"Run it up to most sensitive."

"I'm getting movement right here!" Ransfield had to force himself to keep his voice low instead of shouting.

"Show me." Suddenly pumping adrenaline sounded in Cainey's soft voice.

Ransfield looked up from the UPUD's display for the first time since he first spotted movement 250 meters to the right front. "Great Buddha's balls," he murmured. He rapidly looked back and forth between the display and a point less than two meters away. "It's picking up that bug." He pointed.

Cainey looked where the comm man pointed and saw something that resembled a small dragonfly wafting about in the breeze. He breathed a deep sigh. That did it; there had to be something loose inside the UPUD that made the sensitivity of the motion detector change.

"Damp it back down to normal." Then on the all-hands circuit, "False alarm, equipment failure. Prepare to resume patrol."

"Sir?" Ransfield said as Cainey stood. "The UPUD showed that bug at less than two meters. It showed the first movement at two fifty."

"The UPUD has a history of failures in the field," Cainey said. "This is another failure. On your feet, we're moving out."

Ransfield glanced at the display again before standing, and that probably saved his life. "Movement right!" he shouted.

A high-pitched whine, like that of a buzz saw, came from beyond the right end of the Marine line. Seven of the dozen Marines who had already reached their feet were knocked off them: one had an arm torn off just above the elbow; two fell with most of their torsos blown away; one, sideways to the line, stared down in horror at where his abdomen had been before he fell dead; another tried to take a step and collapsed when one leg detached itself at the hip; the Marine closest to the whine flopped legless to the ground, his feet up to mid-calf still standing. Ensign Cainey's head erupted in a mist of pulverized blood, bone, and brain.

The skull-splitting whine continued. Dirt gouted, rocks shattered, and saplings splintered as the weapon's projectiles hit, but the Marines were safe below its trajectory.

"First squad, maneuver right!" ordered Staff Sergeant Groap, the platoon sergeant. "Stay behind cover! Second squad, use your infras. Return fire but make sure who you're shooting at." *Damn!* He realized that most of the casualties were from second squad and its attached gun team. "Second squad, report."

Before all the fire teams of second squad could report, they were hit from the marsh. Small, dun-colored figures with tanks on their backs and hose nozzles in their hands rose from the water and sprayed streams of viscous, greenish fluid at the Marines who were trying to return fire at the weapon that had just killed half of them. Two of the seven Marines remaining in second squad and its gun team shrieked in agony as the acid hit exposed skin and began eating flesh and bone. The other five were either well enough protected by rocks or trees or the topography, or the acid only hit their chameleons.

Ransfield dropped the UPUD and pulled his blaster into his shoulder. He brought it to bear on one of the Skinks in the water and fired. Even though the Marines of 26th FIST had been briefed on the phenomenon, he was still startled when the Skink vaporized in a brilliant gout of flame. Quickly, he shifted aim and flashed another Skink, and a third. Staff Sergeant Groap, only a few meters away, was also firing and flaming Skinks in the water. The high-pitched whine continued from the right but didn't seem to be hitting anyone.

The Skinks in the water became aware of the two Marines firing at them. Their Leader barked out shrill commands, and they leaped out of the water and charged, wildly spraying green acid as they closed into range. Five more of them went up in flame as they ran.

"Move!" Groap ordered Ransfield. The two scuttled backward, firing at the more than a dozen Skinks that were still charging and spraying acid.

The *crack-sizzle* of a blaster came from their right. The Skinks had come in sight of one of the survivors of second squad, and another Skink flashed brightly into vapor. At a shrilled order, three attackers veered toward him. One of them got close enough to drop a flow of acid across that Marine's back. His uniform saved him.

Suddenly, so many *crack-sizzles* came from farther right they almost blurred into one, and the whine of the shredding weapon shuddered to a stop.

A shrill voice barked out commands, and the remaining Skinks spun about and raced for the water. Groap and Ransfield snapped off more plasma bolts at them, and only three Skinks managed to reach the water and disappear under the surface.

The blaster fire from the extreme right stopped.

"Squad leaders, report!" Groap snapped into the all-hands circuit.

A moment later the first squad leader reported in—no casualties, enemy on the flank defeated, no enemy wounded or prisoners. Second squad's report came in piecemeal. Five of the thirteen Marines were uninjured, five were wounded, three were dead.

Groap organized a defensive position and saw to the care of the wounded while Ransfield called in a report. Minutes later the Alfa Company headquarters ordered them to hold tight while Marines came out to help them collect the bodies of the dead and escort them back in.

As near as could be determined from the debriefings, first platoon had killed between twenty-five and thirty Skinks. The Marines had lost three dead and five severely wounded, and held the ground at the end of the firefight. By any conventional measure, it was a victory. But the way the Marines of first platoon, Alfa Company, 26th FIST saw it, they'd just gotten their asses kicked.

CHAPTER
TWO

"Father? Shall we ever be able to go home?"

Zechariah Brattle shook his head sadly. "Not as long as evil lurks out there on our land, Samuel." He nodded toward the hills above the Achor Marshes on the shores of the sea of Gerizim. "New Salem anymore, son, is as far away as—as Earth."

None of the families that had somehow survived the massacre of their camp above the sea wanted to think about the horror of that night. Only two weeks in the past, it was too fresh in their minds. They were concerned now with simple survival.

"Why did God allow this to happen to us, Father?" The question was not an accusation, just a young boy asking someone he respected for an explanation of something monstrous: Why had a decent and righteous people been destroyed?

Zechariah massaged the back of his neck for a moment. "It is not given to us always to understand why the Lord does things, Sam. This is not the first time our people have suffered woe. I believe God is punishing us now for allowing our ministers to lead us into sin." He sighed and gazed silently at the far-distant bluish smudge for a brief instant, remembering that dreadful night. He shook his head to clear it of those memories. "But Sam, instead of dwelling endlessly upon what happened back there," he nodded toward the distant blue line on the horizon, "we should ask what lesson is in all this for us. We have been spared for a reason. We must be brave now and face the future."

23

But Zechariah was ashamed of himself, ashamed of the way he and the other survivors had fled the scene of the massacre pell-mell, stumbling through the darkness that night, concerned only for their own survival. Neither he nor any of the other men among the survivors had mustered the courage since to go back to the site and search for survivors.

The Brattles, Hannah Flood and her children, and five other families—forty souls in all—had made it to some caves on the south end of the Achor Marshes and had remained hidden there for a week now. During the day, they could barely make out the dark line on the horizon that was the hills above the sea, the place where the City of God sect had been wiped out by . . . None among the survivors was sure who had slaughtered their friends and neighbors, but they all agreed that the killers could not be of this world.

The Brattles and Hanna Flood's family were among the several that departed the City of God camp the night it was revealed how the sect had commissioned an act of terrorism—the destruction of the deep-space starship *Cambria*, its crew, passengers, and cargo—to focus attention on the sect's persecution by the rulers of Kingdom and, they believed, the Confederation of Worlds. The terrorists called themselves the "Army of Zion," which to Zechariah and other faithful communicants smelled of blasphemy. Murder was not a tenet in the beliefs of the neo-Puritan sect that called itself the City of God. In fact, as the survivors now knew, the removal of the sect to the Sea of Gerizim had been a preventive measure, engineered by their leaders to avoid retaliation when their sponsorship of the deed became known. The only good thing to come out of the attack was that, presumably, Minister Increase Harmony and his cronies perished along with the thousands of innocents.

The Brattle family had only proceeded a few kilometers along the road back to their home in New Salem when the attack took place. None of them would ever forget it. An earth-shaking roar had suddenly descended upon them from the night sky, a tidal wave of noise so powerful that their clothing and the flesh beneath it vibrated from the concussions. At first Zechariah thought the Angel of Death had come to punish the sect for transgressing the Word, but he soon realized that a fleet of aircraft was passing directly over where they stood. The machines swooped down on the encampment, trailing blinding streams of flame, and then, abruptly, all went dark and unnaturally quiet.

Instinctively, Zechariah reached for his wife Consort's hand, and in the dark he put his free arm around his son and daughter and drew them close to his side. It was so quiet they could hear one another's breathing. After a few moments Zechariah's hair stood on end as a low groaning sound reached the group over the several kilometers that separated it from the plateau where the body of the sect had taken refuge. The sound came in undulating waves, not loud but distinct—the unmistakable expression of thousands of voices raised in a merging scream of primal fear. It reminded Zechariah of some old paintings he had seen illustrating the tortures of the damned in Hell. That terrible moaning would have been the perfect audio accompaniment to those frightening scenes.

In a short while the sound died away completely and total silence and darkness enveloped the small group.

For what seemed a long time—but was no more than ten minutes—the group stood there silently, waiting for the machines to come for them. But nothing happened. Zechariah glanced to the south. In the bright starlight he could easily make out the narrow outline of the road leading back to New Salem and their homes and fields.

"We must get out of here," he whispered to Consort. His words seemed to break the trance the others had fallen into.

"Back to New Salem!" a man standing nearby with his family whispered.

"No!" Zechariah whispered vehemently. None of them dared talk above a whisper lest whatever had attacked the camp hear them and come their way. "No," he repeated. "For all we know, the fliers came from there and will go back there. Aren't there caverns in the hills a few kilometers to the southwest of here? I say we leave the vehicles here, load up with what supplies we can carry, and strike out on foot for the caverns."

There was a brief whispered conference, but it did not take much convincing for everyone to agree that Zechariah was right. "What of, what of . . . ?" a woman asked, nodding her head back toward the plateau.

"When they leave, we will come back and search for our brethren, but now we must save ourselves," Zechariah answered. "Let us gather our things and depart this place. Everyone, maintain the utmost silence until we are far away from here."

The "few kilometers" to the caves turned out to be closer to a hundred, and the trek took them four days. They covered the distance at night and hid in the brush during the daytime. Meanwhile, nobody came after them, and the aircraft were not seen again until they had reached the precarious safety of the caves.

"Keep watch, son," Zechariah told Samuel. He patted the boy on the shoulder and left him sitting just inside the cave entrance, scanning the far horizon for any sign of life or activity. Two days earlier aircraft had been spotted. From so great a distance the refugees could not tell whose they were, but the machines moved so fast, Zechariah was convinced they were not Kingdomite or Confederation craft. It had been some years since the City of God had been involved in any of the sectarian wars that plagued life on Kingdom, but Zechariah was familiar with the standard military fighter-bomber aircraft in use by the armed forces, and what they had seen were not of those types.

The sight of the machines struck animal fear into the survivors, and most of them rushed far back into the interior of the caves and covered their heads, crying out to the Lord for mercy. But Zechariah had remained steadfastly on watch, following the craft as they disappeared rapidly to the south, toward New Salem. But he had quaked as he crouched there, perspiring, limbs weak with fear.

That had been two days ago. Now, Zechariah arose and walked back into the cave. "Rise up!" he shouted at the people crouching about their cook fires. "Let us seek Divine guidance." Slowly the others gathered around him. When they were assembled, he began, "I am reminded, friends, of the 119th Psalm of David, Verse Ninety-two, 'Unless thy Law had been my Delights, then had I perished in my Affliction.' We have been sorely afflicted, friends." Murmurs of agreement arose from the others. "We have been afflicted because we strayed from the Law and allowed vain and foolish men to lead us into evil.

"But friends, we must have a clear and strong persuasion of a future state. We must be heartily willing to wait for the fulfillment of all the promises of the Covenant of God until our arrival at that world, where we shall have all the spiritual blessings of the heavenly places bestowed upon us. We should be content and patiently and cheerfully allow of it that we are willing to let our crucifixion go on with a perpetual succession of pains without any prospect of any relief, but at and by the hour of our death."

Zechariah looked at the faces around him in the flickering firelight. There were tears in some eyes. "Let us pray." He bowed his head. Silently and earnestly, he begged God to favor him with a Particular Faith, a sign of prophecy granted to the faithful, an intimation perhaps transmitted by an angel, that a particular prayer would be answered. He begged the Lord to give him some sign of what they should do.

After a full two minutes of silent prayer, Zechariah raised his head and looked around the cave. "Well?" he asked, looking into the assembled faces to see if the Lord might have favored someone else with a Faith. Some smiled, some nodded their heads, but there was no Faith there today.

"That was a fine sermon, Zechariah," one of the men said.

Zechariah felt better. Prayer, even prayer that was not answered immediately, was good for him. The small cooking fires glowed dimly. The survivors had managed to salvage much of the personal belongings they'd taken with them after the schism on the night of the disaster, so they were not without some food and clothing and tools. To reduce the volume of smoke from the fires, they used a native plant whose roots burned slowly and generated little smoke. Their meager food supply was supplemented with the small lizardlike creatures that abounded in the caves.

Silently, Consort ladled Zechariah a small bowl of thin stew, which he sampled halfheartedly. But he finished the stew quickly, more hungry than he had thought, and set the empty bowl down. "We need some salt to cover up the taste of this grit."

"And running water," Consort added. Since they did not have a running water supply in the caves, their eating utensils had to be cleaned with sand from the floor, so all the food was gritty. The water they drank came from a tiny, intermittent trickle far back in the depths of the cave. The flow was precarious, and the spring water had had to be rationed. No one had bathed in a week. "Zach," she continued contemplatively, "I never knew how 'rich' we were, back in New Salem. We had good food, a roof over our heads, running water . . ." her voice trailed off.

"And the Lord was with us," Zechariah added automatically. Then he started and a strange expression came over his face.

"Zach! What is it?" Consort reached out a hand and laid it on her husband's shoulder.

Zechariah stood. "Connie, it is time for us to go back to the camp." He turned from his fire and strode to the center of the cave. "Listen, everyone! Come to me. I am going back to the camp. Who will go with me?"

The others shuffled into a rough semicircle around where Zechariah stood. All remained silent for a moment, the firelight casting huge shadows upon the cavern walls and flickering over their impassive faces. "The Lord will go with us, as He always has," Zechariah added quietly.

They were all afraid, he could see it in their eyes. Then: "I will," Hannah Flood announced loudly. She looked at the others.

"As will I," Amen Judah volunteered, nodding at his wife Abigail, who involuntarily held out a restraining hand but then took it back immediately. She bit her lip to hold back her tears.

"And I too, Father," said Comfort Brattle, Zechariah's daughter.

Zechariah started involuntarily. "You are too young," he protested.

"I am twenty, Father, and strong and not afraid . . . well, not afraid to go with you," she added.

Zechariah hesitated. It would not be fair to the others if he rejected his own blood for what would appear to be the sake of saving it. He had always advocated a person's responsibility to the community. If Comfort had the courage to volunteer, then he would take her. "That's it, then. The four of us will go," he announced. "There are enough elders to remain behind to take care of the children, if we don't . . . don't . . ." his voice trailed off. It seemed the other members breathed a sigh of relief as they came forward individually to wish the party well.

"Zach," Amen said, "I suggest we leave tonight."

"Yes," Hannah added. "Let us go as we came, in easy stages, moving in the darkness. We can get water on the second day, at the pond we passed coming up here. We won't need much food."

Zechariah put his arm around his daughter and drew her close as he talked to the other two. "Good. Let us take with us whatever tools we can use as weapons. We have some knives among us." He knew perfectly well that the few knives they had would be useless if whoever had attacked the camp returned, but knives were all they had, and the possession of even those useless tools might give them some slight confidence.

"Father! Let me come too!" Samuel shouted. He had come back from his post at the cavern's mouth, attracted by the sound of the meeting his father had called.

"No!" Amen Judah shouted. He looked at Zechariah.

"No," he continued more softly, "you must stay with the rest. We cannot spare all our manpower on this venture."

"You have left your post, Samuel. Get back to it at once," Zechariah said. When Samuel made no move to return to the cavern entrance, his father stepped up to where he stood, seized him by the arm and dragged him back. "Boy, you are a watcher! You watch. You observe. You report what you see out there. You *do not* leave this spot until relieved by another watcher. The next time I give you an order, dammit, you will obey it, understand?" Zechariah breathed heavily as he spoke.

Samuel looked up at his father in astonishment and with a twinge of fear. He had never heard him speak that way before. The tone of command was a dimension to his father's personality he did not know. "We are like soldiers now, son," Zechariah continued in a gentler voice. "Like those Confederation Marines you admire so much, we obey our orders."

Zechariah looked at his son. He will grow into a handsome man, he thought. "You are my only son. If Comfort and I do not return, it will be on you to continue the Brattle name, Sam." He put both hands on the boy's shoulders. "Until we are all out of this trouble, I am counting on you."

Back with the others again, Zechariah suggested that since it was hours before sundown, they should get some rest to prepare for the long night's trek. He took his place on a pallet beside his daughter. As he was about to fall asleep, Comfort nudged him. "Father?"

"Yes, daughter, what is it?"

"Father, this idea to go back to the camp now, did it come to you as a Particular Faith?"

Zechariah sighed resignedly. He recognized that tone in her voice. Sometimes Comfort's orthodoxy was questionable. "Daughter, don't bug me now, okay?"

The campsite was a vast shambles. Flesh-eating scavengers had fed sumptuously on what remained of the dead, but there was enough left to . . .

"No power of our world could have done this," Amen

whispered as the four stood, awestruck, on the sea edge of their old camp. The huge meeting tent was collapsed, its prefabricated plastic sections looking as if they had been melted. Vehicles lay overturned everywhere, and the ground was littered with clothing and personal possessions. Everywhere lay evidence of human remains—not the complete bodies of recognizable persons, but piles of bones and desiccated flesh that had once been human beings. Flying things that had been feeding when the quartet arrived hopped and scrabbled away as the humans moved forward, clutching their knives fearfully.

"Do not be afraid," Zechariah whispered. "If the Lord did not want us to be here, we could never have come this far."

"Is anyone alive?" Hannah shouted. The others started at the sound of her voice but then they all took up the call. Their voices echoed eerily through the deserted groves and among the abandoned equipment. Flocks of scavengers took flight at the sound, swirling upward to perch in the trees, releasing rivulets of varicolored excrement in their excitement. Zechariah shuddered as he realized what that stuff had once been.

"Thank God, we must be alone," Comfort whispered.

"Thank God for a lot of things," Hannah replied.

It was nearing dusk when they finished searching the camp and the underground bunker. If there had been survivors, they were long gone. But they had found two ground-effect vehicles that were still drivable, and loaded them with tools, utensils, and supplies they knew would be useful. The cars were the newest models, formerly the property of a prosperous congregation several hundred kilometers to the northwest of the New Salem settlement. Best of all, they had infrared guidance systems that permitted them to drive in the dark without artificial light.

Zechariah and Comfort sat in the dimly lighted cab of their vehicle, drinking from lukewarm bottles of beer they had found. "I never much liked this stuff—before now," Zechariah commented.

"Father, what is this?" Comfort held up a belt she had

found under her seat. In the dim interior lighting, Zechariah recognized it as a military-style gun belt. He took it from her, popped open the holster flap and withdrew a large pistol. It looked just like the one he had carried when he was in the wars. He pressed a stud on the slide. The energy pack was at full power. "An M2411 A1." Zechariah Brattle let out an admiring whistle. "Those folks from up there believed in being ready. This is government issue," he mused, examining the gun more closely. "It is illegal for civilians to have anything like this." He shrugged. "But the Lord giveth, and I ain't about to question the Lord." He strapped the belt on. The former owner was right-handed, as was Zechariah. "Now, Comfort," Zechariah smiled, "*that's* what is called a Particular Faith!" They both laughed as Zechariah patted the holster.

"What now, Father?"

Zechariah punched a button on his console. "Hannah? Amen? How do you read me?"

"Five by," Amen Judah answered. Like Zechariah, Amen had been in the wars.

"Follow me. We're going to get our people and we're going home." Zechariah put the car into forward.

"Home?" Comfort asked excitedly.

"We are. Home to New Salem." Zechariah casually tossed his empty bottle out the window, something he would never have done two weeks ago. "Daughter," he turned to Comfort, "pop me another of those beers, would you?"

CHAPTER
THREE

The Great Master sipped from the delicate, handleless cup and rolled his eyes with contentment. He sighed, the sound of gravel tumbling through a narrow cut in a mountain stream. He wore his ceremonial robe with its rectangles of golden metal plate. A ceremonial sword lay across his lap. Sheathed in precious wood that curved elegantly with the curve of the blade, the sword was as nonfunctional for combat as his armor.

The Over Masters and more senior of the Senior Masters of his command sat cross-legged in their rows in front of him. Their armor was equally ceremonial but less splendorous than that of the Great Master. They bore no swords or other weapons, ceremonial or otherwise. The only functional weapons in the room were those carried by the five Large Ones who sat or stood around the Great Master, and those shielded from sight behind screens on the room's periphery. At the Great Master's sound of contentment, they bowed low over their knees and touched their foreheads to the matting before their ankles.

The diminutive female who knelt at the Great Master's knee poured fresh, steaming liquid from an exquisite pot. The Great Master glanced lovingly at the single flower, imported at great expense all the way from Home. It stood in a fluted vase on the low, lacquered table on which he placed his cup before he lifted it, refilled, and sipped anew.

As though that was their signal, more diminutive females entered the room. Their feet shuffled softly over the matting in the tiny steps that were all their narrow ankle-length robes allowed. Each carried a tray with a finely decorated steaming pot and two handleless cups. These females knelt with breathtaking grace at low tables set between the Over Masters and more senior Senior Masters. With equal grace and in near perfect unison, they poured from the pots into the cups. When the cups were full, the females gracefully turned about on their knees and bowed low to the Great Master.

He flicked languid fingers, and all the females save the one who served him rose liquidly to their feet and quietly shuffled away. The Over Masters and more senior of the Senior Masters reached to the low tables and lifted the cups to their lips. They sipped, and sighed with pleasure, the sound of rain falling on a forest canopy.

The Great Master grinned so his teeth showed. It was the grin of a predator that has pounced and borne its prey, struggling and squealing, to the ground. His breath rasped through gill slits almost fully atrophied from lack of recent use. When he spoke, his voice was high tide crashing against a volcanic cliff.

"Phase two of this operation has begun well," he began. "At the slight cost of fewer than three hundred Fighters, we have achieved two glorious victories! In one raid we devastated the morale of the Earthman pond scum in their defensive positions by demonstrating that we can breach their lines anytime we wish. In another fight we slaughtered the Earthman Marine reinforcements. Their morale is now as shattered as that of their cousins who have already learned they will lose to us."

He swiftly drew his sword and thrust it into the air above his head. "Now, while they are dazed and bleeding and know not where we will strike again, it is time to launch Operation Rippling Lava!" His voice crashed and sizzled, a lava river falling into the ocean.

The Over Masters and more senior of the Senior Masters roared their eagerness for Rippling Lava, the sound of a monsoon storm crashing down on an unprepared village.

*   *   *

Brigadier Sturgeon sat front and center in the briefing room. On his right was Brigadier Sparen, commander of 26th FIST. Colonel Ramadan, normally 34th FIST's chief-of-staff but now acting commander, sat to his left. Sturgeon now commanded what was called "Marine Expeditionary Forces, Kingdom." Commander Daana, 34th FIST's F-2—intelligence officer—who was pulling double duty as F-2 for the MEF, stood at the lectern in front of the room. Behind the three top commanders, the other section chiefs of their FIST staffs sat in rows of folding chairs, as well as commanders of major subordinate units and their number twos. A few officers from the CNSS *Grandar Bay*, observers more than participants in the briefing, sat in the last row of chairs. The Army of the Lord was noticeably absent.

"The Skinks are still defeating the string-of-pearls," Daana said. "The *Grandar Bay* has its surface reconnaissance analysts using the same technique to study the satellite data that was developed when an infantry platoon from 34th FIST first encountered the Skinks on Society 437. So far, nada." This was the first mention the officers from 26th FIST had heard of Society 437; they made notes to remind themselves to find out about it. "Even when planetside forces are in direct contact with the Skinks and the analysts know exactly where to look, they're damnably hard to detect unless they're using one of those long range weapons—those things kick out a clear enough signal so the string-of-pearls has no problem spotting them. Navy forensics wants us to capture one of those weapons. They haven't been able to figure out what it is from the scrap we captured after the fight in the Swamp of Perdition." He glanced at the navy officers in the back of the room to see if they had newer information. They didn't.

"They always withdraw underwater," Daana went on. "So far they haven't returned to the surface anyplace we have surveillance devices. Which suggests they don't resurface, but enter underwater caves. Or at least, caves with underwater egress. The upshot is, we have no idea where they might be based."

"Has the *Grandar Bay* searched for caves?" Sturgeon asked.

"Yessir." Daana tapped a command on the lectern top. A color-coded topo map appeared on the wall display behind him. It showed the land around Haven and Interstellar City to a distance of a thousand kilometers. "As you see, sir, there are a lot of rivers, canals, and wetlands in the vicinity." Indeed, the map was riddled with the blue lines and blobs that represented rivers and lakes, along with the iconic green-fronds-on-blue that meant marshes and swamps. "Finding caves was easy." He tapped another command, and a dense spattering of deep red splotches and squiggles was overlaid on the map. "This region is absolutely riddled with cave systems. Navy estimates that if the army sent in an entire corps of cave specialists, it would take them five years to explore just the caves shown on this map." He looked back at the commanders. "Of course, sirs, the army doesn't *have* an entire corps of cave specialists."

That elicited brief but appreciative laughter, as loud in the back of the room as the middle. No matter how frequently or severely the Marines and the navy were at odds with each other, they held a mutual disrespect for the army.

Sturgeon hadn't laughed, though a slight crease that could have been a smile crossed his face. "Are we deploying more surveillance devices?" he asked.

"Yessir. As fast as 26th's Four gets them in, I get them out." He tapped a third command. The map behind him morphed into a time lapse schematic of surveillance device deployment. It began when 34th FIST set defensive positions around Haven and Interstellar City, with merely a scattering of symbols for surveillance devices. The scattering slowly thickened until the arrival of 26th FIST, then rapidly became denser.

"I have one other item, sirs. The assault against sector India Delta during the storm the other night may have left something we can use. In all previous contacts with the Skinks, they always either carried away their casualties or their casualties were vaporized. It is possible, though not yet certain, that a Skink was killed by fléchette fire in that action and its remains left behind. At any rate, a small amount of organic material was found after the storm let up. Neither the Confederation biologists in Interstellar City nor the navy med/sci people aboard the *Grandar Bay* have the proper equipment to fully analyze it. It has been sent back to Earth by courier for analysis."

Sturgeon nodded, then stood. "Please continue. I have other matters to attend to."

"Attention on deck!" Ramadan snapped as he stood and came to attention. There was a brief rattle of chairs as the other officers gained their feet and stood at attention.

"As you were," Ramadan said when Sturgeon was gone. The officers resumed their seats, and the briefing, which was designed primarily for the benefit of the commanders and staff of 26th FIST, continued. Sparen remained. He needed the briefing as much as his officers did.

Soldier of the Lord Prudence didn't know whether the long hours he spent watching the surveillance display board were penance or an indulgence. If he was committing the sin of spying as he watched the blips and images, listened to the sounds, and saw the other symbols that meant nothing to him, then this service was a penance. If, on the other hand, his superiors in the Army of the Lord knew he was true to his name and worthy of being entrusted with privy knowledge he should not normally have, then he was being rewarded and the hours were a blessed indulgence.

One source of Prudence's unsettlement about his assignment was a thought that he kept carefully tucked away where he wouldn't have to consider it: The devices that fed their surveillance data to the display board could be of great use to the Collegium. It was the sacred responsibility of the Collegium to root out heresy wherever it attempted to germinate. Surveillance devices such as these could help the Collegium catch heretics before they became firm in their apostasy. They could also be used to spy on and capture, for punishment, anyone who might challenge the Collegium. Prudence had heard rumors that the Collegium did not restrict itself to finding heretics. Although he praised the Lord for the necessary and soul-saving work the Collegium did, he also feared its potential for evil. That a sacred instrument of the Lord could be used for evil was something he could not bear to think about, so he kept that reason for discontent tucked away where he wouldn't have to examine it.

Soldier of the Lord Prudence was startled from his reverie by something he realized had been on the display for a time, unnoticed by his wandering mind. Whether this job was penance or not, he would have to do penance for this neglectful conduct. But later, now he called out: "Lesser Imam Macque, I have movement on sensor seven!"

Sergeant Macque, gun squad leader, second platoon, Charlie Company, 26th FIST, and off-world infidel who had been granted command of Dominion Company of the 811th Sacred Fusiliers of Kingdom's Army of the Lord, came from behind his desk in the garrison's command bunker. He leaned forward to look over Prudence's shoulder at the surveillance display board.

Prudence pointed at white blips on the display.

Macque reached past him and hit a control. The red lines that appeared around the blips were thin, indicating that whatever they represented were small. "Could be Skinks," he said softly. "They don't give off much of an infrared signal."

"Demons in the middle of the afternoon?" Prudence believed that demons only appeared at night, when men were weak and their faith could be more easily tested.

Macque snorted. "They might be creatures out of somebody's hell, but they aren't demons." He also was surprised at the possibility of Skinks moving so close to the perimeter during the day, but said, "Maybe they show up better in infra at night and they're moving during the day to mask their signals. Got some over here too." He pointed at another group of red-rimmed blips. "Come on, baby," he murmured. "Come to mama." He tried to will the moving blips to get in range of a visual sensor so he could make positive identification. "There's more," he said, pointing at a fresh grouping of blips. He picked up the handset of the hardwired comm unit. "We've got a lot of movement in sector Delta Hotel Seven," he said to the battalion ops duty NCO as soon as the recognition and acknowledgment exchange was over.

"You got that Charlie Six?" the battalion duty NCO asked.

"Roger," replied the Charlie Company duty NCO. The battalion order was for all surveillance reports to go directly to Battalion, and for the relevant company headquarters to listen in. Each Marine company was integrated into a Kingdomite regiment, with the Marines in all command billets. The FIST's infantry battalion controlled an entire Kingdomite division.

A new voice came on the comm—that of the Marine duty officer. "All hands, listen up. We have multiple reports of movement to the division front. All units, stand to and be prepared for company. Acknowledge."

"Roger, Foot Six. Charlie standing to."

The other two company headquarters also acknowledged the alert order. The entire 82nd Division of the Army of the Lord was moving into position.

Macque slapped his helmet on and toggled the squad all-hands circuit. "Up and at 'em," he said. "Look alive, we might have company in a couple of minutes."

Seconds later high-pitched buzz saw whines came from beyond the perimeter and *things* with speeds too great to be deflected by the slanted faces of the reinforced ferrocrete bunkers shattered against them, gouting holes in their surfaces, sending chips flying, and raising dense clouds of dust.

The 82nd Division and its commanders from 26th FIST were bunkered into Heaven's Heights Ridge and two hills, Hymnal and Psalm, that guarded the northeast approaches to Haven. The entire ridgeline and Hymnal Hill came under simultaneous assault. The dust clouds blocked the vision of the defenders—not that many of the Soldiers of the Lord were willing to look through their bunker's apertures.

More of the buzz saw guns opened fire, not at the bunkers, but on the ridge and hillsides in front of them. At the same time, sappers moved purposefully on the flat below the heights. One by one, symbols blinked out on displays as the sensors feeding them died. The defenders were doubly blind—from the dust clouds they couldn't see through and the displays that no longer showed movement.

Skink Fighters wearing full body armor with interlocking helmets had been infiltrating all day, crawling under the trees slowly and quietly enough that neither the motion nor the audio detectors picked them up. Sappers had already noted the positions of the visual detectors, and the Skink infiltration routes avoided them. Also, the creatures showed poorly on infra. Now, with most of the detectors dead, the Over Master in command of this phase of Operation Rippling Lava gave the command, and ten thousand Fighters rose to their feet and trotted in orderly lines to the foot of the ridge and the hill that were under attack. There, they awaited the order to begin mounting the heights.

The Over Master gave another order, and his guns raised their aim from the slopes of hill and ridge to impact with devastating effect on the slopes of the bunker faces.

"I want artillery on those guns, and I want it now," Commander Van Winkle ordered.

"But Archbishop General, those guns are not firing at our defenses," Archdeacon General Crucifix, commander of the 104th Division, objected. "We must preserve our artillery fire to defend our own defense sector!"

"Go to your quarters and stay there!" Van Winkle said coldly. He was not going to waste any time arguing with the man whose position he was filling. The Haven defenses were under heavy attack, and the attack had to be repulsed *now*.

Ignoring Crucifix, who stood sputtering, he turned to the Marine artillery observer. "Sergeant, send that fire order to FIST artillery. Tell them they'll have proper authorization by the time the guns are ready to fire."

"Aye aye, sir." The artillery observer was smiling as he began to speak into his hardwired comm unit.

"Get him out of my sight before I have him clapped in irons," Van Winkle ordered.

"Certainly, sir," replied Gunnery Sergeant Hu, the battalion's assistant personnel officer. He turned to Crucifix and gestured toward the command room door. "After you, sir."

"Bu-Bu-But . . ." Crucifix sputtered.

"Sir, I do believe he means it."

Crucifix looked around the command center. His own soldiers outnumbered the Marines, but none of them were armed. All of the Marines were—and they looked ready to use their weapons. Gathering as much dignity as he could, he turned and marched out.

Gunnery Sergeant Hu followed closely, to make sure Crucifix went to his quarters as ordered. As he walked he spoke into his personnel comm unit and gave orders for a supplyman to meet him with tools and a padlock. Hu had been around long enough to know that a lot of generals thought orders didn't apply to them; he was going to make sure Crucifix stayed in his quarters as ordered.

Van Winkle didn't see Hu escort the Kingdomite division commander out of the command center. He was too busy ordering the Kingdomite artillery liaison officer to relay the fire order to his regiment, and contacting Brigadier Sturgeon to get authorization for the artillery fire mission he'd just ordered.

Within the bunkers no one could tell what was happening outside. The crashing and battering impact on the bunker faces reverberated inside with a din so loud it allowed for awareness of nothing beyond itself. The sonic overload beat men down, opened their mouths in silent howls, bled them from their ears. On the entire twelve-thousand man front, only the 350 Marines whose helmets were able to muffle the noise were capable of fighting—if they could see through the thickening clouds of pulverized ferrocrete dust.

The Over Master spoke a command, and his ten thousand

armored Fighters, urged on by Masters and Leaders, began their climb.

Brigadier Sturgeon didn't hesitate to issue authorization for the fire mission Van Winkle had ordered. It arrived at 34th FIST's artillery battery seconds before the guns were ready to fire. The six guns of the battery finished locking their guidance systems into the string-of-pearls and fired. The string-of-pearls, which had so much difficulty picking up infrared signals from the Skinks, had no problem seeing their horrid weapons. Seconds after the guns of 34th FIST's battery fired, six canisters of scatter munitions burst open above six Skink buzz-saw weapons. The hundreds of sub-munitions the canisters expelled spread over a wide area and exploded before they reached the ground. Shrapnel tore the crews of the weapons to shreds. The crews of six other weapons had died moments earlier, when the guns of 26th FIST's battery fired. Both batteries fired again, and twelve more weapons fell silent.

The twelve dozen guns of the two Kingdomite divisions also fired. But they couldn't tie into the string-of-pearls guidance system, and their fire wasn't as accurate. They didn't have scatter munitions either, so rounds that hit more than a hundred meters from Skink positions had no effect on the devastating fire, and most of the Kingdomite rounds landed more than a hundred meters away. The Skinks had two thousand weapons firing at the defensive line. They held more buzz saws in reserve.

"Each of you, get two Raptors in the air," Brigadier Sturgeon ordered Brigadier Sparen and Colonel Ramadan. "I want Jerichos on those weapons."

"Aye aye," the FIST commanders replied. They contacted their squadrons, gave orders. Ramadan told his air people to instruct 26th FIST's air wing on the tactics they'd developed to use against the Skinks.

In moments two Raptors from 34th FIST's squadron lifted off and headed for Heaven's Heights Ridge, staying well below the ridge top. They hovered a kilometer behind Heaven's Heights and locked their Jerichos onto the string-of-pearls guidance system. One at a time, four Jerichos belched out from under the wings of each Raptor, swooped up over the ridge, and hit their targets. Each Jericho wrought the destruction of a tactical nuke, leveling an area half a kilometer in diameter. Their areas of destruction overlapped. A three-kilometer-long swath of forest and wetlands was cleared of the monstrous Skink weapons.

The pilots from 26th FIST's squadron had to wait a few minutes before taking off because they needed extra briefing in the tactics. They headed for their firing position behind Hymnal Hill and locked in. One of them wasn't tucked behind the hill well enough. His Raptor had just fired its second Jericho when the threat warning shrilled in the pilot's ears, just before his Raptor disintegrated. The other Raptor got off all four of its Jerichos, then dropped altitude and sped back to base less than fifty meters above the ground. The Skinks knocked three of those six Jerichos out of the air before they reached their targets.

The Over Master issued two prearranged commands. One command halted the fire against the bunkers, began the withdrawal of those weapons, and led the ten thousand Fighters who were just short of the heights—still undetected by the dazed and blinded defenders—to close the final gap and begin their killing. The second order sent sappers along the line of killed weapons, to set fire to the corpses and fragments and to retrieve the weapons.

Silent until now, the Skink Fighters shrieked and barked as they charged the final twenty-five meters. They jammed the nozzles of their acid guns into the apertures of the shattered and cracked bunkers and let them spray.

The stunning, ear-ringing quiet that fell when the Skinks stopped battering the bunkers lasted only seconds. It was replaced by the screams of Kingdomite soldiers whose flesh was being eaten by the acid.

All along the line, Marines began firing back. The flashes

of dying Skinks lighted the bright afternoon even more brilliantly. Enough of the Marines had the presence of mind to radio reports to their command elements that they were being overrun, so Brigadier Sturgeon and his staff recognized the severity of their situation. In moments new fire orders were issued, and all the artillery began firing on the defensive line. The Marine cluster munitions mowed Skinks down by scores, but more of them survived because of their body armor and helmets. The Kingdomite artillery, by dint of numbers, killed just as many. But shells from those guns also hit bunkers already weakened by the Skink fire and collapsed them, wounding or killing the defenders inside.

"Regimental artillery, cease fire!" Sturgeon barked as soon as he realized the Kingdomite fire was killing Marines. The rumble of the Kingdomite guns slowed and stopped. There weren't enough Marine guns to do the job on the ridge and the hill, and he didn't dare send any Raptors up. What could he do to stop the Skinks from taking Heaven's Heights and Hymnal Hill?

"Cooks and bakers?" he asked Sparen.

"I can have them on the move in five minutes," Sparen replied.

"Ram, can you get anybody there sooner?"

"Van Winkle's been rotating his line companies off the line," Colonel Ramadan replied.

"Have whoever's available hit Hymnal Hill."

"Aye aye." Ramadan picked up the comm to his infantry commander.

"Who else is available to move?" Sturgeon wanted to know. "We need to get more Marines up there."

Meanwhile, the Marine artillery kept pouring its scatter munitions on the high ground.

CHAPTER FOUR

"THIRD HERD, SADDLE UP!" Staff Sergeant Hyakowa bellowed as he raced into the park where the Marines of the platoon waited tensely, watching the fight on the heights above the city.

"Fall in," Hyakowa shouted as he skidded to a halt.

In seconds the Marines were in formation, all with their weapons and gear, though the new men were still shifting everything into place.

"Squad leaders, report!"

Sergeant Ratliff looked to his side. "First squad, all present!"

Sergeant Linsman didn't pause; he'd taken stock as he ran into formation. "Second squad, all present!"

"Guns, locked and loaded," Sergeant Kelly sounded off.

Hyakowa pointed at the nearest height, Hymnal Hill. "We're going up there," he said, "as soon as some Dragons get here."

A muffled roaring came from behind a nearby building.

"That's probably them now." Hyakowa looked toward the sound in time to see two of the armored, air-cushioned, amphibious beasts slip around the corner of the building.

The drivers reined in their mounts and reared about so the ramps faced the Marines when they dropped.

Lieutenant Rokmonov poked his head out the rear of one of the Dragons and called out, "Mount up!"

"Ah, shit," Ratliff muttered, and glanced toward the hill. He remembered too well the Dragons that had been killed in the Swamp of Perdition, and the Marines whose lives were lost when they erupted. Hymnal Hill was close enough so they could reach it in ten minutes or less if they ran. But orders were orders.

"First squad, move out!" he shouted, and led the way onto the Dragon Hyakowa pointed him at.

Less than a minute after they stopped in front of third platoon, the Dragons were loaded and headed for the rendezvous point to meet the Dragons carrying the rest of the company.

There was no time for planning. A squad and a half of Marines were on top of Hymnal Hill fighting for their lives against hundreds of Skinks. Commander Van Winkle relayed the order from Colonel Ramadan as soon as he got it, immediately ordering six Dragons to pick up Company L. Captain Conorado linked into the string-of-pearls and began studying the situation even as he pulled on his sidearm and gear.

"All hands, listen up," Conorado said on his all-hands circuit. He could tell by changes in pitch in the faint rumbling that came through the Dragon's armor that the six vehicles were on line, speeding toward the reverse slope of Hymnal Hill. He transmitted the sitmap to his platoon commanders and platoon sergeants.

"Some Marines are going to die up there if we don't get to them right now," he said. "The little bad bastards that are overrunning them outnumber us by at least ten to one. "We'll off-load just below the topological crest and go over it on line. Volley fire downslope as soon as we reach the top crest. Everybody, chameleon shields in place, shirt necks closed, sleeves down and cuffs tight, gloves on. *No exposed skin.* I don't want any casualties because someone let that acid get inside his uniform." He hoped the new uniforms really were impervious to the Skinks' acid sprays. "And plasma shields up. We're going to have a lot of fire up there, let's not have any Marines killed by Marines! Make sure your Marines understand. Do it!" He plugged into the vehicle's comm to give orders to the Dragons.

In the Dragons, the platoon commanders and sergeants transmitted the sitmap to the squad leaders, who in turn projected them for their men to study. They relayed Conorado's orders while the Marines examined the projected maps. But they listened more than they looked; the maps only showed the slope of the hill and the line of bunkers thirty meters down the hill's opposite slope. Adrenaline coursed through every Marine in the Dragons and sweat bathed them. Most of them had fought the Skinks more than once, and most of them had lost friends to the Skinks' ghastly weapons. Some had suffered wounds at the hands of the Skinks. They were going up against better than ten to one odds! Were even Marines that tough? Those who held belief in a deity prayed to whatever god they believed in.

For a moment before the Dragons reached the infantry jump-off line, the Marine artillery concentrated its fire on Hymnal Hill's defensive line. Then the Dragons stuttered to a stop and their rear ramps dropped. The Marines bolted off, and even before they were all on line, Conorado gave the order to advance, and they ran uphill. The Dragons rumbled behind them. Taller than the running Marines, the Dragons would be seen by the Skinks first if they were with the line, and Conorado wanted his entire force to make contact simultaneously. He didn't want the Skinks warned by the Dragons that his infantrymen were coming. He radioed for the artillery to cease fire, and the artillery shifted its fire to Heaven's Heights.

Half a minute after the Dragons dropped their ramps, the Marines surged over the hilltop, and their momentum sent them crashing into Skinks, bowling the nearest ones over.

"Volley fire, point-blank!" Conorado screamed.

The Marines of Company L were lucky that the Skinks had not begun to organize a defense against a counterattack. They were stunned and totally disorganized. The pummeling they'd taken from the artillery was devastating, even though body armor had kept most of them alive. As many as had been slaughtered by the Marine scatter munitions and King-domite artillery, there were still far too many of them to take cover in the bunkers.

The Marines who could opened fire into the thick mass of enemy. Others were in physical contact and used their blasters like quarter staffs, battering the Skinks, breaking their bones, smashing their flesh into bloody pulp. The near-est Skinks shrilled and tried to back off far enough to bring their acid guns to bear on the Marines. Some a little farther back saw the counterattack and sprayed acid in the direction, but little of the fluid reached the Marines. Most of it spat-tered against their mates and tumbled them to the ground, screaming their death agonies.

A clear lane suddenly opened before the Marines, and they opened fire with their blasters. Along their front, Skinks flashed brightly into vapor—the body armor gave no defense against the plasma bolts. The Skinks were so tightly packed that each bolt flashed at least three of them. Hundreds flared in the first few seconds, but there were still many left. The brilliance of the flashes blinded the Marines and the heat of the flares stopped the Marine advance. A Skink barked a command, and hundreds of Skinks charged.

"Back off!" Conorado shouted. "Get down. Fire prone!"

The Marines withdrew a few meters and fell into prone positions. Their fire resumed, even heavier than before. Plasma bolts slashed into the Skinks.

Now, with the infantrymen out of their line of fire, the Dragons opened up with their guns, gouting huge streams of fire. The six guns of the blaster platoons and the heavier guns of the assault platoon were set up, and their fire, added to that of the Dragons, put up a plasma wall that vaporized most of the attackers. The blastermen picked their targets and fired. The flashes from the dying Skinks were dazzling, even to them.

The Skink charge staggered against the wall of fire and broke. Those nearest the fighting turned and ran panic-stricken at the Skinks behind them, trying to force their way through them to flee to safety. Marine fire—Dragons, guns, and blasters—pursued them. In seconds the mass of Skinks on the hilltop realized they were about to be wiped out, and nearly all of them ran. Masters and Leaders ran about, shrilling and barking orders for the Fighters to turn around and fight, but the Fighters were too shocked by the carnage they'd suffered to obey.

"To the bunkers," Conorado commanded as soon as he could see again. The Marines leaped up and sprinted, expecting the Skink buzz saws to open up on them before they could get under cover in the bunkers. They didn't know the Skinks had already withdrawn the buzz saws.

Conorado saw the Skinks in flight across the flats below Hymnal Hill and called in an artillery fire mission on them. The 82nd Division's artillery regiment responded faster than it had to its previous fire missions. Hundreds of Skinks died before they reached the safety of the wetlands and waterways.

A couple of the Marines of second platoon, Charlie Company, 26th FIST, had been killed when plasma bolts they'd fired at Skinks crowding in with them ricocheted off the walls and hit them. A couple more had been overwhelmed and killed by the sheer number of Skinks who crammed inside their bunkers. But most of them, though injured, were still alive.

Company L had no time to rest after beating off the attack on Hymnal Hill—Heaven's Heights was in imminent danger of being overrun, and they were the closest Marine infantry to the ridge. After checking for casualties, they scrambled back into their Dragons and roared off, relieved that their worst injury was a broken arm suffered by one of the new men in the mad melee when they first crashed into the Skinks.

Conorado got good news en route to Heaven's Heights.

"Twenty-sixth's cooks and bakers will meet you," Brigadier Sturgeon told him. "They're under the command of the security section commander. You have operational command."

"Cooks and bakers." Half a millennium earlier, in a war that had engulfed most of Old Earth, the expression had been literal. It soon came to mean all rear echelon personnel. The Confederation Marine Corps believed, as had the United States Marines and the Royal Marines to whom it traced its ancestry, that every Marine was a blasterman first and a "cook and baker" second. The understrength company of clerks and supplymen, cooks and messmen, who met Company L at the bottom of the south end of Heaven's Heights were well-trained as infantry, even though few, other than the twenty Marines of the headquarters security section, had experience in combat.

The Dragons carrying the two companies didn't pause. They got smoothly on line and began their ascent of the ridge, Company L on the right, the cooks and bakers on the left.

"Lieutenant, it's down and dirty," Conorado said as soon as he established communications with the commander of his reinforcements. "There's no finesse involved, no tricky maneuvers. We dismount just before the Skinks come into sight, line up, and charge. It's the same kind of frontal assault armies have been using since the time of the Sumerians. Align on me and keep up. That's all there is to it. Questions?"

"Sounds pretty straightforward." The lieutenant—Conorado didn't know his name—sounded nervously excited. Conorado assumed that the man hadn't seen action in a while.

"One more thing." The captain examined his latest sitmap. "They're still massed so densely it's hard to believe the artillery had any effect on them. You've never seen so many live bodies on a battlefield at one time before."

He'd barely finished speaking when the Dragons lurched to a halt and their rear ramps dropped. The Marines flooded out. Squad and fire team leaders shouted their men into line ahead of the Dragons. Conorado gave the order, and more than two hundred Marines ran on line up the slope. They clearly heard the din raised by the Skinks, even through the continuing explosions of artillery rounds.

The artillery, after firing a brief concentration over the southern end of the ridge, shifted its fire to the northern end before the infantry reached the top.

This time they didn't smash into the Skinks. The nearest were seventy meters away when the Marines came in sight of them. There were so many, it seemed all the Skinks in the universe were swarming over the defenses of Heaven's Heights.

"Volley fire, seventy meters!" Conorado shouted over the all-hands circuit. "Advance . . . Fire! . . . Advance . . . Fire . . . Advance . . . "

The fire from the right side of the Marine line was smooth. The Marines of Company L fired in unison, took two steps forward and fired again on command. Their volleys went true, a wall of fire slamming into the Skinks, vaporizing them by the score. The line's left side, the "cooks and bakers," was more ragged. Except for the security section, they weren't on a good line and their fire was uneven, with many bolts flying high. Still, by the time the Marines cut the distance to the first Skinks in half, they'd obliterated nearly all of the closest enemy soldiers.

The Skinks on Heaven's Heights, though, weren't as disorganized as they had been on Hymnal Hill. Even though the vastly outnumbered Marines in the bunkers fought valiantly, the twelve guns of the two FISTs' artillery batteries couldn't pound the ridge as intensely as they had the smaller hilltop, and the Skinks had suffered a much lower casualty rate. It didn't take long for the Skink commanders of the nearest units to organize a defense against this new threat. Commands were barked out and hundreds of Skinks charged the Marines.

In response, Conorado stopped the Marine advance and had his men fire volley after volley into the charging Skinks. The flashes from flaring Skinks were dazzling, but the foe kept coming until, just under fifty meters from the Marines, they dropped to the ground and began firing acid. Hundreds of streamers of the greenish fluid arced out over the ground between the opposing forces and splashed to the ground around and on the Marines; almost all of them were hit. The retardant that impregnated their chameleons worked, but some of the Marines in the cooks and bakers company screamed when the acid found its way inside improperly closed uniforms. With the Marines flat on the ground, the Dragons that had carried them up the ridge moved forward and added the fire of their big guns to the fray.

"Fire in front of them," Conorado shouted over the all-hands circuit. "Hit the dirt in front of them, go for ricochets! FIRE! FIRE! FIRE!"

The ridge top strobed with flashes as the devastating fire put out by the Marines hit Skinks. Again, the fire from Company L on the right side of the Marine line was more effective than fire from the left. But there were thousands of Skinks, and only two hundred Marines. Every Skink in range of the Marines who was killed was almost immediately replaced by Skinks from the mass behind the line. The greenish fluid continued to stream unabated.

The Skink Senior Masters had space, and space gave them time to maneuver. The Marine artillery couldn't fire too closely to the southern end of the ridge top for fear of hitting the counterattacking Marines. The Senior Master in command of the forces at the northern part of the ridge ordered his Fighters south, out from under the artillery bombardment. The Senior Master in command of the central portion was caught in a squeeze and decided to aid the southern unit in dealing with the counterattack. Horrendous as their casualties had been, there were still thousands of Skinks left to move toward the ferocious fighting at the ridge's southern end.

More than two hundred blasters *crack-sizzled* at the nearby Skinks. Conorado ordered the ten Dragons to pour their fire into the mass of Skinks behind the line. Still, the streamers of acid floated at the Marines. The mass of Skinks behind the line drew rapidly closer. They reached the line of shooters and charged through it. The infantrymen and the Dragons shifted their aim to meet this new threat, and so many charging Skinks flared that the shooters were hidden behind a wall of strobing light. But there were too many Skinks, and some survived to close with the Marines.

Silhouetted against the flashes of their dying comrades, six Skinks emerged directly in front of first squad's third fire team. Corporal Joe Dean swung the muzzle of his blaster at one and pressed the firing lever. The Skink flared. Then Dean had to roll out of the way as another clubbed at him with the nozzle of his acid weapon.

"On your feet!" Dean shouted into his fire team's circuit—his first command in combat. He used the momentum of his roll to gain his feet. Another Skink was on him before he could shift aim. He swung the butt end of his blaster at the Skink and knocked him thudding to the ground. He shot it, and the flare when it vaporized sent him reeling back, which caused the strike from a Skink armed with a long knife to miss him. He recovered his balance in time to block a second knife chop, and followed through with the motion to slam the Skink across the chest. While the thing was staggering, Dean stepped back and blasted it. This time he was ready, and the flare didn't take him by surprise.

To Dean's left a Skink managed to knock Lance Corporal Izzy Godenov's blaster from his hands, then it leaped at him and tried to wrap the hose of its weapon around the Marine's neck. Godenov slugged the Skink in the chest—he'd meant to hit him in the stomach, but the thing was shorter than he realized. The Skink's body armor was hard enough that the blow stung Godenov's hand. Still, the Skink staggered back. Godenov pounced and bore him to the ground, straddled him and wrenched the Skink's helmet off. The Skink tried to bite Godenov's hands, but the Marine clamped one hand under the Skink's jaw to hold it in place, then gouged out his eyes with the other. The Skink shrilled in agony and clamped hands over its damaged face. Godenov jumped away, found his blaster, and vaporized his wounded opponent.

A few meters away, on Dean's other side, PFC Quick lived up to his name against two Skinks. He slammed the butt of his blaster into the juncture where one Skink's helmet met his body armor. He spun to his other attacker before the first one hit the ground and jabbed hard with the muzzle of his blaster. The Skink jumped backward to avoid the jab, and Quick pressed the firing lever. Instantly, he turned back to finish off the first Skink, who was still writhing on the ground.

"Buddha's balls!" Corporal Claypoole shouted as a group of Skinks appeared just meters in front of him and Lance Corporal Wolfman MacIlargie. He skittered backward and leaped to his feet before three converging Skinks managed to swarm him. He blasted one of them before the other two bowled him over. But Claypoole, a man of average height and strength—for a Marine—was much bigger and stronger than the Skinks. He let go of his blaster and used his size and strength to fling one Skink away from him, then twisted around on top of the other. Shoving down hard on the creature's head and chest, he pushed himself to his feet and stomped on it, but before he could do any real damage, the first Skink grappled with him. The Skink had lost its helmet when Claypoole threw him off, and now it tried to bite with sharp, triangular teeth. Claypoole grabbed its head and jerked as hard as he could. The Skink's grip broke. He flailed with his fists, trying to beat Claypoole's arms. The Marine ignored the blows and swung the Skink like a sledgehammer at the other one, which was just rising. The Skink's scream stopped abruptly when its neck broke. The other collapsed heavily from the collision, and Claypoole leaped on him. He tore the Skink's helmet off and slammed the palms of his hands against the creature's ears. The Skink screamed and his eyes bulged as he went into convulsions. Claypoole dove for his blaster and rolled back to his feet, looking for more Skinks.

MacIlargie jerked back when he saw the rushing Skinks

and rose to a kneeling position to fire at them. He got three, but a fourth closed and swung the nozzle of its weapon at his head. The nozzle hit hard enough to stun him and he fell over. The Skink leaped on him and dropped the nozzle to draw a long knife. MacIlargie recovered enough to bat the stab away, but he didn't have enough control of his body to wriggle out from under his smaller attacker. The Skink shrilled and thrust again with his knife. MacIlargie grabbed the Skink's arm and managed to deflect the thrust so the point of the blade jammed into the ground. The Skink struggled to pull the knife back, but MacIlargie held on hard enough to stop it. He struck at the Skink with his free hand, but was still dazed enough that he couldn't put enough force into the blow to knock the Skink away. The Skink fended off a second blow, then used both hands to yank his knife free. Reversing his grip on the knife's hilt, the Skink grasped it with both hands to bring it down into MacIlargie's chest. The Marine drew on all the strength he could muster, slammed upward with both fists and propelled the Skink backward. Instead of embedding itself in his chest, the downthrust blade sliced along MacIlargie's arm, the sharp pain and gushing blood startling him. Sitting up, he grabbed the Skink's knife arm with both hands and twisted. The Skink screamed and dropped the knife, but MacIlargie kept twisting. There was a sudden snap, and the arm in MacIlargie's hands flopped. He pushed the Skink off and picked up the knife, then slid it under the apron of the Skink's armor and into his belly. Momentarily free from attack, he looked around for his blaster.

Miraculously, no Skinks came through on the far right side of the thin Marine line. Corporal Kerr saw peripheral movement and looked to his left. His throat went dry when he saw Skinks closing on the Marines there. For an instant he flashed back to the Siad horsemen who had swarmed into Tulak Yar, the village on Elneal where he was almost killed. He shook himself angrily. This isn't Tulak Yar, he thought. Those aren't the Siad. "Fire left," he ordered, and put action to words.

Lance Corporal Schultz looked and his skin crawled. He'd fought the Skinks several times, but never in such numbers. The sight of so many so close for the second time in fifteen minutes made him feel like maggots and other tiny beasties were crawling over him, burrowing into his flesh. He rose to a knee and started picking them off.

Corporal Doyle held the extreme right side of the line. Ever since the Marine advance stopped, he'd been terrified that the Skinks would flank them, that all the Skinks on Kingdom would attack the Marines through his position. His first reaction to seeing a frontal assault that didn't come directly at him was profound relief. The relief didn't last. As soon as he tried to aim his blaster, he realized that in order to have a field of fire clear of Marines, he'd have to move forward, closer to the larger mass of Skinks he'd been shooting at. In that instant every fiber in his body screamed *Run away! Run away!* But he knew he couldn't. He was a Marine corporal in the middle of a firefight. No one would ever talk to him again if he ran away. Everybody else might die if he ran away. He'd live in disgrace for the rest of his life if he ran away. He crawled forward, closer, so he could blast at the Skinks charging the Marine line. He didn't notice the wet and foulness that abruptly filled the crotch of his trousers.

All along the line, Skinks closed for hand-to-hand combat. With the infantrymen grappling with their attackers, only the Dragons still fired at the oncoming Skinks. Marines began to fall before the overwhelming numbers.

The crew of one of the Dragons had been killed when Skinks converged on it, sprayed enough acid onto the vehicle's ramp to eat through the thin armor, and broke in. The other Dragons were maneuvering to prevent the Skinks from doing the same to them; the effectiveness of their fire was reduced. The flashing of dying Skinks no longer dazzled the killing ground. Skinks were making it across the killing zone in larger numbers.

Claypoole and MacIlargie stood back-to-back. Each had his combat knife in one hand and a long-bladed knife wrested from a Skink in the other. Skink body armor was designed to stop projectiles but was less effective against bladed weapons. Half a dozen Skinks lay around them, bleeding from wounds—a couple of them were no longer moving. But others, too many others, were circling the two, wielding knives of their own, tightening their circle. And more were rushing toward them. The scene was repeated all up and down the line.

Then several of the circling Skinks flared up from plasma hits. An instant later, Marines bowled into the Skinks.

"Kilo Company to the rescue!" shouted one of the newly arrived Marines. He lifted his blaster and flamed another Skink.

The loud *crack-sizzle* of Dragon guns behind the line increased, and Skinks in the killing zone flared into vapor. More *cracks* of blasters and the louder *sizzles* of Dragons came from the left front.

When Brigadier Sturgeon asked who else was able to move and said he wanted more Marines in the attack against the high ground, each FIST in his command ordered an infantry company out of its defensive positions. When the new, stronger counterattack struck, the Skinks broke and ran. Once more the Kingdomite artillery regiments fired on the flat below the heights.

CHAPTER
FIVE

The blood-flecked thing that had once been a woman screamed horribly as an almost fatal surge of electrical current coursed through her broken body. He depressed the button for several seconds, causing the woman to writhe against the restraints in uncontrollable spasms. Dominic de Tomas, Dean of the Collegium, lifted his thumb, and the current abruptly ceased. The woman lay on the table semiconscious, struggling for breath. The interview, as de Tomas called such sessions, had been going on for over an hour, and he was beginning to lose interest since his victim was nearing the end of her endurance.

"Primitive, but effective," de Tomas remarked to a black-uniformed guard standing nearby at rigid attention. It was not often the Dean of the Collegium himself participated in the sessions, and the guards and technicians were impressed. De Tomas smiled amiably at the woman panting and gasping on the bloodstained rack. She had been a minister of the Anabaptist Sect, in fact one of the last of the Anabaptist leaders on Kingdom, thanks to de Tomas's unflagging pursuit of dangerous thinkers. The few remaining Anabaptists had converted to more politically correct sects, but the dying woman on the rack stubbornly refused to recant. That was all the same to Dominic de Tomas because the minister would die no matter what she promised to do under his torture.

De Tomas walked over and stood looking down at the minister, who was slowly recovering the power of speech. "We have modern and humane methods to make people do what we want," he said. "But in your case I decided to use electroshock because . . . well, it's more painful, and because I have no further use for you, and, to be perfectly honest, because you are impossibly ugly."

The guards and technicians present chuckled at his banter. They were all loyal members of de Tomas's Special Group, an organization of highly trained and dedicated armed men, rivals in many ways of the Kingdomite Army of the Lord. He had built their strength to well over one thousand members, and had even given them military ranks and titles, as well as the latest weapons. It was they who enabled him to enforce his will as the Dean of the Collegium. They were handpicked men who had completed a rigorous course of indoctrination and training, after which they had sworn a blood oath of total loyalty to de Tomas.

Unlike de Tomas himself, who believed in nothing, they had been indoctrinated into a military cult based on the twelfth-century Germanic Order of Teutonic Knights. Their icons of military virtue were the German prince of the Cherusci tribe known as Hermann Arminius, who destroyed Quintilius Varus's legions in 9 A.D. in the Teutoburger Wald; and Heinrich I, "the Fowler," who was elected king of the Germans in 919. In fact, the logo of the Collegium, which de Tomas had designed shortly after becoming dean, was a silver goshawk symbolic of Heinrich, wings spread, perched on two golden lightning bolts—representing Arminius's victory over the Romans. De Tomas artfully, but not overtly, encouraged the belief among his followers that he was the reincarnation of Heinrich. Whether his men believed this or not, they did believe that Dominic de Tomas was their leader, for whom they would gladly sacrifice their own lives. They also believed that anyone who opposed the work of the Collegium, and especially those brought before it for heresy, were enemies of the state who deserved death, and were unfailingly rewarded with it.

The fact that Dominic de Tomas himself was not of Teutonic origin had no bearing on his status as the leader of the Special Group, or what amounted to chief priest of the order.

*   *   *

De Tomas beckoned to the technician in charge of the interrogation lab, a stormleader, the equivalent of a lieutenant in the Army of the Lord. "I've had my amusement for today," he said. "Into the furnace with her . . . slowly and feet first. Revive the bitch periodically. Put it all on a vid, so I can watch later. You know the procedure." He shrugged. "I have an important meeting to attend now." He gestured at a Shooter, one of four handpicked bodyguards who accompanied him everywhere, "Theodor, if you please."

The jackbooted guard snapped to attention and handed him a cape, black, with a bright red lining, a silver goshawk and golden lightning flashes emblazoned on the back. De Tomas donned it with a practiced flourish. He saluted the stormleader smartly and swirled to the door.

Behind him the Anabaptist began to scream as she was wheeled slowly into the maw of a raging blast furnace. Shrieks accompanied them all the way to the elevators.

Dominic de Tomas had risen to the presidency of the Collegium, the disciplinary body of the ruling theocracy on Kingdom, through guile, ruthlessness, and considerable talent as an administrator. A failed poultry farmer, he had emigrated to Kingdom as a member of the now defunct Rochester branch of the Scientific Pantheist Sect.

The Scientific Pantheist movement had been founded by two brilliant eccentrics in the city of Rochester, New York, in the year 1956. Rochester was famous as home to various crackpot sects, most notable the Spiritualist movement that flourished there in the nineteenth century. The Pantheists had their first falling out in 1958 over whether to call their system of beliefs Scientific or Universal Pantheism. The founders became martyrs over this question, killing themselves in a fight on the steps of the public library on July 18, 1958. But the profound schism occurred shortly before the Second American Civil War. The Rochesterians maintained that nature was dominated by a polarity of life or a unitary intelligence, but they kept the freethinking creed of social responsibility espoused by the original founders of Scientific Pantheism. This put them at odds with what became known as the Philadelphia branch of the sect. The Philadelphians believed in the unity of life force in nature but denied that it represented an intelligence incorporated in the essence of a Supreme Being.

The Philadelphians were quite numerous and prosperous on Old Earth, where they ridiculed the Rochesterians mercilessly and succeeded in making them the laughingstock of the religious orders, derisively calling them "SciPans," a term the Rochesterians abhorred. So they emigrated to Kingdom, where they'd been assured there would be the guarantee of freedom for them to practice their beliefs as they wished while living in harmony among themselves and with their neighbors.

De Tomas had joined the sect because he sensed their weaknesses and because a man like himself, with no core belief in anything but his own destiny, would be free to pursue his own goals unnoticed. As a requirement for emigration, the Pantheists had been required by Kingdom's theocracy to nominate a member to sit on the Collegium. De Tomas saw that as his opportunity and volunteered. He was accepted because nobody else in the libertarian sect wanted anything to do with a body they considered positively medieval. De Tomas assured them his membership would be pro forma only. How wrong they were. The SciPan sect had speedily become defunct on Kingdom, thanks primarily to de Tomas's persecution of his former "coreligionists"; the Kingdomites did not particularly like freethinking, socially active congregations. Many sects were allowed to practice on Kingdom, but only those that practiced a strict orthodoxy, did not proselytize, and did not ask questions.

The Collegium was originally formed to enforce orthodoxy among Kingdom's many sects. As such, it possessed extraordinary police powers over virtually anyone suspected of heresy. The Collegium's decision in any case was final, and it could impose the death penalty without resort to other civil courts. The dean's office was permanent, but he was advised by members of the various sects appointed on a rotating basis. They advised him on the finer points of sectarian orthodoxy, but over the years, de Tomas was able to dispense with their counsel, securing for himself a free hand to conduct investigations and impose punishments.

Originally the civil police in the various communities had been charged to cooperate with the Collegium by apprehending and bringing heretics before its tribunal. But under de Tomas's leadership, he persuaded the Convocation of Ecumenical Leaders to allow him his own enforcement arm, and he had then created the Special Group. They were feared everywhere their jackboots marched.

But de Tomas's influence among the sects on Kingdom ran much deeper than the police functions carried out by his Special Group. Over the years, he had also created numerous administrative bureaus that conducted constant surveillance of the sects' members to ensure that the arts, entertainment, and the news media complied with guidelines he published and updated constantly, in the name of the Convocation but actually on his own authority. The objective of his strict control was to ensure that the activities of the Convocation were always portrayed in the most favorable light and that nothing was allowed to adversely influence public faith in the Convocation or the sects' leaders. The leaders were content to let de Tomas act in their name. But maintaining public morale was proving difficult in the present crisis since the Army of the Lord had taken such a terrific beating at the hands of the invaders. Even so, de Tomas's propaganda experts had put the best possible spin on the military defeats. The citizens of Haven were led to believe that the Army of the Lord, with some minor help from the Confederation Marines, had stemmed the invaders' advance on the capital and was soon to launch a devastating counterattack. Sects surviving in the outlying cities and towns were being told to hold fast, that relief would soon be on its way. So far it was a great propaganda victory.

In addition to the propaganda activities created to ensure the Collegium's control over public opinion, de Tomas had quietly and efficiently created a Security Bureau with a wide-ranging system of informants. Very little went on in the sects' territories that de Tomas was not aware of. In short, he had created a government within a government, and his version was infinitely more efficient than the loose control managed by the cumbersome and fractious Convocation of Ecumenical Leaders.

And finally there was the Young Folk League. Since each sect on Kingdom conducted its own schooling, it was not possible for the Collegium to control educational activities beyond basic curriculum oversight. So the ingenious Dean of the Collegium had established the Young Folk League, Kingdom's version of the scouts, for young people of age eight to eighteen. Branches thrived in all the towns and cities on Kingdom. Most parents were delighted when the league's monitors took their children on weekend camping trips and other outdoor activities. The league had been in operation for more than twenty-five years and was de Tomas's most fertile recruiting ground for the Special Group. It was also a useful tool for surreptitiously playing on young people's natural rebelliousness against adult authority and undermining their faith in the sects.

But de Tomas's actual investigations of reported heresy had become almost perfunctory over the years. His real interest lay in maintaining himself in a position of power which he could exercise from behind the scenes. He used his authority carefully, to eliminate potential rivals or, as in the case of the Anabaptist just fed to the flames, people who might ask questions or demand government accountability. Meanwhile, he discovered enough real heretics to make it look as if the Collegium was doing its job. Most were given prison sentences. Real heretics were useful to de Tomas because anything that divided the sects weakened them and diverted their attention from matters of importance to him personally, such as the small slave-labor industries he had created using the prisoners in his custody. One of the many such enterprises, for instance, was a porcelain factory that produced exquisite and highly profitable items for sale in markets throughout Human Space. The export company he created under a front was to all appearances a legitimate business venture, but its profits went directly into de Tomas's off-world bank accounts.

The current disaster was just what he had been waiting for. The Kingdomite armed forces were severely weakened in the disastrous battles with the invaders, and best of all, even the vaunted Confederation forces were on the defensive. Whoever these mysterious invaders were, de Tomas was quite sure they would be beaten; the Confederation would not allow its forces to be mauled like this. And once the Marines were gone, the Kingdomite army's morale destroyed and its forces weakened, he would emerge perfectly secure, ensconced as the Richelieu of Kingdom.

But just then Dominic de Tomas had been summoned to attend an important meeting of the Convocation of Ecumenical Leaders at Mount Temple, and he was late.

There they all are, the fat pigs, de Tomas thought as he sat on the dais just behind Ayatollah Jebel Shammar, the current chairman of the Convocation. And there sat the superannuated Cardinal Leemus O'Lanners of the Fathers of Padua, in his bright red robes, and also that disgusting pea brain, Bishop Ralphy Bruce Preachintent, who had just passed his chairmanship to Shammar. De Tomas hated the way the man shouted and perspired when he talked, as if he really believed in all his fundamentalist crap. The furnace is too good for that fool, he told himself. All of them were absolute zeroes to de Tomas, and as he sat there he dreamed of putting them all into the furnace someday. It would serve them right, he thought, the doublespeak theocratic rabble.

The meeting hall atop Mount Temple had been reduced to rubble by the constant bombardments, so the Convocation was sitting that day in spacious subcellars where the participants were relatively safe from the Skink weapons. Obviously the invaders thought Mount Temple, because of its elevation, was being used as an observation post.

The main topic of discussion that afternoon was the invasion crisis. The ministers were frightened. Their capital city, Haven, and International City, where off-worlders were confined, were both surrounded and under siege. From what remained of the hall on the surface of Mount Temple, one could see the defensive lines around the cities and even observe the surrounding ring of enemy positions some kilometers farther out. Communications with the outlying colonies had been reduced to radio traffic or the occasional atmospheric shuttle or drone lucky enough to get through the besieger's antiaircraft system. But the word from the outlying congregations was not good: many towns and cities had been wiped out.

And the Confederation's potent Marine Expeditionary Force, even with the help of the entire Army of the Lord, had not been able to break the siege. Over and over again a minister would stand up and ask why God had allowed them to fall into such disaster. Had they sinned? And if so, was it just punishment for their sins?

"I CALL upon ALL of my brothers to get down on their KNEES and beg the LORD to give us a SIGN! Tell us, O LORD: HOW have we TRANSGRESSED against thy WORD?" Ralphy Bruce Preachintent had thundered at one point. Ralphy Bruce stood there, face streaming with tears (or perspiration), his arms raised beseechingly to heaven. The other ministers were used to his histrionics, but many of them, especially those from sects that did not believe in charismatic preaching—which was most of them—were embarrassed by his outburst.

Ayatollah Shammar called for order after giving Bishop Ralphy Bruce sufficient time to regain his composure. "Brother Ralphy Bruce is right," Shammar intoned. "We must consider what to tell our congregations, those we can still talk to, those that still exist, why this evil has been foisted upon us by deities we all believe to be just and loving. But now I think it is time Archbishop General Lambsblood gave us an update on the military situation."

Archbishop General Lambsblood was the commander in chief of Kingdom's armed forces. "In brief, brothers, if this Brigadier Sturgeon would listen to me, we should mass our forces at the invaders' weakest point and launch a breakout. But he has rejected my advice and, under the circumstances, I am powerless to compel him to do what any sensible commander would realize is necessary." Lambsblood sat down heavily. De Tomas smiled to himself. Excellent! he thought. Morale is low, combat efficiency is weak. And what did that old fool, Lambsblood, think this brigadier was? De Tomas had met Sturgeon several times and knew he was the kind of commander who could fight. He would attack the invaders when he was ready; de Tomas understood that, it was what he would have done himself. And this Sturgeon would attack them where they least expected it. Were I he, de Tomas thought, I'd launch an attack on their rear, destroy their logistics bases, command and control elements, and only then attack across the lines, using the Army of the Lord incompetents as a diversionary force. No, he would steer clear of these Marines. But once they were gone, things would go back to normal. Old Lambsblood, he thought, the damned fool! But—de Tomas was feeling good now—he'd feed the old bastard into the furnace *head* first, and spare him a bit of agony.

"Brother de Tomas?"

De Tomas looked up, startled. His reverie had been a bit too deep. Apparently Ayatollah Shammar was asking for his report. At the meetings, de Tomas always brought the Leaders up to date on his efforts to ensure orthodoxy among the sects. Although nobody seemed enthusiastic about apostates at that stage of the military crisis, de Tomas was prepared with a lengthy list of names, heresies, and punishments. "Unfortunately, she died during interrogation," he told the leaders when he got to the case of the Anabaptist.

"Dean de Tomas," Shammar said, ignoring the fact that

the Anabaptist had died—and nobody else in the group seemed to think it particularly noteworthy either—"what of the City of God?"

Several days before, the Convocation had requested de Tomas to look into reports that the City of God had removed itself from its settlements to a new location in the remote wilderness. Because the Army of the Lord was stretched thin supporting the Marines on the perimeter, the Collegium's help had been requested to look into the matter.

"They have been wiped out, Ministers," de Tomas replied shortly. There was a collective gasp from the assembled ministers, followed by a short silence and then quiet murmuring as they whispered excitedly among themselves.

"How do you know this?" the Venerable Muong Bo, the leading Buddhist, asked.

"My informants told me they had removed themselves to somewhere along the shores of the Sea of Gerizim. I dispatched a drone, and their camp was found and surveyed. The destruction was total and there was no sign of life. Their towns are deserted too. Of particular interest, however, is activity at New Salem, which I think may have been taken over by the invaders."

A huge screen blinked into focus along one wall of the conference center. It showed in graphic detail the destruction of the camp in the hills above the Sea of Gerizim. The recording included sickening close-ups of the bodies.

"It was *them*!" someone shouted. Many of the leaders present had witnessed this form of destruction among the towns and villages of their own sects. Archbishop General Lambsblood resignedly verified that what they were seeing was indeed the work of the alien invaders. The leaders were clearly shocked, but it was the shock of recognition, not of sympathy, because privately they all despised the self-assured holier-than-thou attitude of the neo-Puritan sect.

"Do you know why they removed themselves into the wilderness like that?" Nirmal Bastar asked.

"No, Swami Nirmal, I do not. But now I suppose that is, ah, 'academic,' shall we say?" De Tomas dared not smile at his remark, but to him it was hilarious. Nobody seemed to notice.

The lights dimmed suddenly and the ground trembled. The leaders shifted uncomfortably in their seats. The invaders had launched a salvo at the mountain, or at some nearby target. The hall went quiet for a few moments, and then someone asked, "Did any of them survive at all?" referring back to the City of God.

"I do not think so," de Tomas answered. Many heads nodded gravely. It was apparent to de Tomas that the assembled leaders thought the destruction of the City of God was good riddance to a potential thorn in everyone's side. Privately, de Tomas was as delighted as the others at the fate that seemed to have overtaken the neo-Puritans. They had always been a problem, since they were so hard to infiltrate and control. They eschewed entertainment of all types—for them, work and making families was "entertainment" enough—had no interest in news of the outside world, and considered illustrated Bibles the only form of art worthy of attention. Worst of all, they did not believe in public education but schooled their children at home and absolutely forbade them to participate in the Young Folk League.

The meeting dragged on for another hour. It was finally concluded that Archbishop General Lambsblood should seek a meeting with Brigadier Sturgeon and ask him to communicate his plans for breaking the siege to the members of the Convocation, although none thought he would.

Outside the meeting hall, as de Tomas was hurrying to get back to his headquarters, he stopped to greet Jayben Spears, the Confederation ambassador to Kingdom. He did not like the way Spears always looked at him, with a faint expression of disgust. De Tomas passed it off as the ambassador's unspoken hatred of the Collegium and what it stood for, which he could accept. But sometimes . . .

"Ah, Mr. Ambassador." De Tomas smiled and bowed politely.

"De Tomas." Spears nodded slightly, keeping his expression neutral.

"You missed a very interesting meeting."

"Yes?" Spears said.

"Yes. Are you here to see anyone in particular? May I get him for you, escort you there?" De Tomas smiled again.

"Don't bother. I know where I'm going," Spears answered. He brushed by de Tomas, avoiding his outstretched hand, and headed for the chairman's office.

De Tomas stood looking after Spears, a sardonic smile on his face, his unshaken hand still outstretched. He lowered it to his side. "Come see me sometime," he called after the ambassador. "Sit in on one of my interrogations! We'll have lunch after!" Spears hunched his shoulders and did not bother to acknowledge the invitation. De Tomas laughed outright. Just then, the arrogant fool was beyond his reach. "But you just wait, you bastard," de Tomas whispered aloud, "you'll deal with me one of these days." He flexed his powerful arm. De Tomas was a legend among his minions because of his enormous physical strength. "I could end you with a blow," he whispered at Spears's receding back, "but honor and arms scorn such a foe," he added.

The leaders flocked into the elevators that would take them to a series of tunnels through which they could disperse throughout the city without danger from the enemy bombardments. De Tomas watched them for a moment and smiled. Geese! he thought. Goddamned geese! They all belonged on a platter.

"Brother de Tomas!" Ayatollah Shammar called as he held an elevator door open. "Are you coming?"

"No, Holy One," de Tomas replied, bowing slightly, "I think I shall take in the air." Shammar shook his head in consternation. As the doors closed the ministers gawked at de Tomas, wondering where he got the courage to walk about openly on Mount Temple during a bombardment.

De Tomas's guards fell into step beside him as he briskly mounted the stairs to the ruins on the surface. They carefully threaded their way through what had been the main entrance hall to the front of the building. Outside, the air was thick with smoke. Debris lay everywhere. His escorts' uniforms began to reveal smudges and dust, but they neither flinched nor hesitated as they surrounded their leader, ready to use their own bodies as shields. All over the hillside ruins and craters smoldered, stark evidence of the recent bombardments. In the distance clouds of smoke from other sites that had been hit rose lazily into the air. The infernal weapons the invaders were using seemed to operate on an unknown principle that prevented detection from the string-of-pearls satellites in orbit and the counterbattery fire from Marine artillery. De Tomas thought, These invaders are pretty tough customers. Maybe if they win, I can reach an accommodation with them. . . .

Then a thought struck him and he stopped in mid-stride. His escort stopped too and looked at him questioningly. He shook his head and smiled. Dominic de Tomas continued walking, head held high, apparently oblivious to the destruction, and unconcerned that in the next second a salvo might vaporize him and his men.

Having established himself as a hero and a leader, he was finally being forced to act the part.

CHAPTER
SIX

"Sir, we recovered a Skink body," Commander Daana, 34th FIST's intelligence chief, reported. Following the successful counterattack against the Skinks, the staffs of both FISTs were briefing Brigadier Sturgeon.

Sturgeon cocked an eyebrow at Daana and waited for him to say more.

"It's not intact, sir. Just the lower half; pelvic structure and legs."

A corner of Sturgeon's mouth twitched. He knew the Confederation's xenobiologists could get a great deal of information from half a body, but he wished the recovered part were the upper half. The head, thorax, and upper abdomen would tell more about the biology of the creatures than just the lower abdomen and legs. Not least of which would be information on how to more easily evade and kill them. The upper half probably held whatever sense organs the Skinks had that allowed them to "see" chameleoned Marines.

Sturgeon didn't ask if the remains were properly preserved—as though anybody knew how to properly preserve the alien flesh. Instead he asked, "How soon can it be lifted to the *Grandar Bay*?"

"It's already being loaded onto an Essay. It should be in a drone on its way to Earth by the end of the day." He left unsaid, *Unless the Skinks have moved one of those damnable guns to a position where it can hit the Essay.*

Both FISTs had already given him their casualty reports, including the Kingdomite casualties. It felt to Sturgeon as though the battle in defense of the high ground to Haven's northeast was a pyrrhic victory. The trigger-pullers of the Army of the Lord's 82nd Division had been killed almost to a man, and 26th FIST had lost more than fifty Marines, dead or severely wounded. Heavy losses, but maybe not too heavy. The Skink casualties had also been horrendous. Sturgeon had no idea how large the enemy force was, but no army could easily afford to lose soldiers by the thousands, as the Skinks had in that fight. And he suspected the Skinks had even less chance of getting replacements for their losses than the Marines did—unless more were already on their way. Still, as badly injured as the Army of the Lord was by the loss of the best part of an entire division, the rest of the army was intact, and there was still a population base in the tens of millions from which to draw replacements and reinforcements. And without a local population base from which to recruit, the Skinks had to be reeling at least as badly as the Kingdomites.

"Four?" Sturgeon asked, moving along.

"Sir," Captain Shabel, 26th FIST's logistics officer said, "food is still making its way into Haven and Interstellar City unimpeded. The Skinks don't seem to be interested in disrupting the food supply." He shook his head—if he was commanding a siege, cutting off food and water to the defenders would be one of his top priorities. "More important, the engineers from the *Grandar Bay* tell me they expect to complete the blaster power pack replenishment facility tomorrow. We won't have to worry about running out of power for our weapons."

That was another point in favor of the Marines and Kingdomites—the Army of the Lord had its own arsenals. As soon as the replenishment facility was in operation, ammunition for the Marines wouldn't be a problem either. The Skinks had a finite supply of munitions with no replenishment. Unless more of them were on their way.

No matter how pyrrhic Sturgeon felt the counterattack victory was, he knew the best course of action was to aggressively follow up on it, to pursue the Skinks while they were trying to lick their wounds.

He didn't ask for a report from the operations chiefs; he knew they wouldn't have anything to say. Instead he said, "Threes, your commanders will brief you on what I want. Everybody but the FIST commanders, dismissed." The officers quickly gathered their materials and exited the briefing room.

Brigadier Sparen and Colonel Ramadan leaned close to their commander as soon as the door closed behind the last staff officer.

Brigadier Sturgeon wasn't the only commander who felt the Marine victory was pyrrhic.

The Great Master showed his teeth in a grin as he looked out over the Senior Masters and more senior of the Masters assembled before him. Graceful females had already served the steaming beverage to them and departed, save for the one who knelt by his knee.

"The Earthmen Marines believe they have achieved a victory over us by defeating our attack against the northeast portion of their defensive ring." As his voice rumbled, his breath rasped through his atrophied gill slits; the sound of an ice dam on a mountain rivulet breaking on a spring morning. "They think they won, but they are wrong. We killed an entire division of the local pond scum soldiers, as well as many Earthmen Marines. The lives of eight thousand Fighters were a small price to pay for so great a victory.

"I have observed this Earthman Marine commander. He is a brave commander, but also a cautious one. A bold commander—" He lifted a hand in a gesture that suggested he humbly counted himself as a bold commander. "—would follow that 'victory' by pursuing the 'defeated' foe into his lair. This Earthman Marine will not. Instead, he will attempt to pin us in the territory he and the pond scum have already conceded to us."

His grin broadened, the smile of a large shark about to devour an injured dolphin. "He does not know the extent of the land under our control, or the number of paths we have to move out of his way undetected by his surface surveillance devices, or the Earthman navy's 'string-of-pearls.'

"This Earthman commander will send his Marines out in small units, units which we will individually entrap and destroy!"

The assembled Over Masters and more senior of the Senior Masters rapped the tiny cups on the lacquered tables and roared their approval of the Great Master's plan.

"You're shitting me, right?" Corporal Claypoole demanded.

Sergeant Linsman jumped on the straight line he'd just been handed. "I'd never shit you, Claypoole. You're my favorite turd. Besides," he shrugged, "that really is our orders."

Claypoole looked at Corporals Kerr and Chan for help, but they looked at their squad leader like it was just another day at the war.

"Me and Wolfman," Claypoole continued. Hey, he was a Marine. If no reinforcements were coming, he'd fight the battle by himself. "Me and Wolfman, just the two of us. You want us to take a platoon of Kingdomites who haven't worked with Marines out there and get them killed."

Linsman slowly shook his head. "It's not what I want, Rock. It's what the brigadier wants." He stepped close to Claypoole and jabbed a finger against his chest. "The brigadier doesn't want you to get the local boys killed!" He emphasized his words with more chest jabs. "He wants you to take them out and teach them how to kill Skinks." Jab. "And the last I heard," jab, "what the brigadier wants," jab, "the brigadier gets!"

"All right, all right!" Claypoole sputtered, backing away from Linsman's finger. "But why us?"

"It's not just us," Linsman shouted, becoming frustrated. "It's both FISTs. Every fire team and gun team in both FISTs is taking command of a platoon of local yokels and taking them out to find, fix, and fuck the Skinks! Do you understand me?" He leaned forward so his face almost touched Claypoole's.

Claypoole wished he were wearing his helmet. If he were, he'd slide the chameleon shield into place and move away from his squad leader. But he wasn't so he had to stand there and take it.

Staff Sergeant Hyakowa came by before Claypoole could voice any more objections.

"Listen up, people," Hyakowa said. All the Marines of second squad, third platoon, turned their attention to their platoon sergeant. "As of yesterday, everyone in this platoon has gone up against the Skinks at least once—and beat them. Most Marines in this platoon have gone up against them several times—and beaten them. About half of you met them on Waygone. We beat them there too." He paused and looked each of them in the eye. "They've never beaten us. They gave us a hell of an ass-kicking once, but we came out on top that time too." He neglected to mention that if 34th FIST's Air hadn't come up with a defensive tactic that saved them from the Skinks' buzz saws, that fight might have ended differently. Nor did he mention the ambush that killed Gunnery Sergeant Bass and the men with him.

"The Kingdomites don't have that advantage," he went on. "They've lost too many battles and too many lives when they've gone up against the Skinks. There aren't enough of us to win this war. We have to show the Army of the Lord that the Skinks can be beaten. And we, third platoon, Company L, 34th FIST, are the best people to show them that. Because we've done it more often than anybody else. Most of you also have experience leading Kingdomite troops. Many of you have led other indigenous troops. Those of you who don't have the experience, Lieutenant Rokmonov and I will help your squad leaders and fire team leaders teach you.

"I expect this platoon to take that battalion—" He paused to remember what it was called, shook his head when he did. "—the Lancelot Guardians of the Faith, and turn them into the best Skink-killing battalion in the entire army. They'll be joining us within two hours. We begin operations as soon as we integrate with them." With, "Sergeant Linsman, carry on," he left to visit the gun squad.

Linsman watched Hyakowa walk away. When the platoon sergeant was far enough away, he turned back to his squad. "You heard the man," he said to all of them, though he looked at Claypoole. "We will do this thing."

Claypoole silently hung his head.

Corporal Claypoole was furious. Just the two of them to take that platoon out and get it killed. Claypoole knew he was a good Marine, a good infantryman. He knew he had leadership abilities and that he'd demonstrated them in the past. He also knew that Wolfman, Lance Corporal MacIlargie, was a good Marine infantryman. Give the two of them a platoon of well-trained, well-armed, indigenous troops with high morale, and he knew he and Wolfman would acquit themselves well and kick ass on any similar-size unit they ran up against. But these Kingdomites had been hurt so badly by the Skinks, they were afraid of them. Not the individual fear of personally being killed—all soldiers faced that fear—but the fear of knowing they were going to lose any fight they got into. When troops have that fear, they're *going* to get killed. It just wasn't fair to make him and Wolfman, just the two of them, take the platoon out and get those soldiers killed. Not counting the fact that he and Wolfman were going to get killed too!

Sure, they were going to get killed. This terrain was exactly the kind that favored the Skinks. It was marshy, channeled with tiny rivulets and larger streams, slowly flowing water that skimmed over most of the ground that wasn't channeled. Stalky things that looked like reeds lined the streams and nearly filled the rivulets. Lightly flooded ground was studded with tufts of something that resembled grasses. What passed for high ground carried trees whose droopy foliage was too wet even to be called scraggly. It was nothing short of Skink heaven.

Mother Corps wasn't treating her Marines right. Nossir! If Gunny Bass was still around, Claypoole thought sourly, I bet he'd have talked the brigadier out of this!

The Kingdomites didn't have any morale, and probably didn't have any unit cohesiveness. When Claypoole met Second Acolyte Priestly, the platoon commander, he didn't seem to object to taking orders from the very junior Marine noncommissioned officer. And when Claypoole and Wolfman gave orders, none of the Kingdom soldiers looked to their own leaders to see if they should obey.

So there they were, he and Wolfman, just the two of them, and a platoon from the—Claypoole shook his head at the ridiculous name—Lancelot Guardians of the Faith, way the hell and gone out here, ten klicks from the Haven–Interstellar City defenses, two klicks or farther from another patrol, looking for Skinks who, if they deigned to be found, would kill these soldiers. And most likely kill him and Wolfman into the bargain.

This was a *seriously* messed up situation.

Well, he was a Marine. Marines were expected to do more with less than anybody else. The merely difficult we do immediately, he thought, the impossible might take a little longer. And if anything was impossible, it was this situation.

Claypoole got out his UPUD Mark III and examined it. Its infra display didn't show anything larger than a smallish dog within a kilometer of the platoon's position. He called up the caves download from the string-of-pearls and saw they weren't in easy striking range of a known or suspected cave outlet either.

"Hold up," he said into his helmet comm. The platoon stopped, accordioning by squads as the squad leaders relayed the order to their men. Claypoole muttered, off circuit, about the stupidity of the Kingdomite high command in keeping comm units out of the hands of the troops. As if a small unit leader being able to communicate directly with all his men would promote heresy. "Assemble on me." He raised his helmet's chameleon shield and rolled up a sleeve so the soldiers could see where he was. He watched as they listlessly moved into a rough formation in front of him.

"You out of whatever excuse you've got for a mind,

Corporal Rock?" MacIlargie asked on their private circuit. What he said might be insubordinate, but he said it with proper military courtesy.

"Shut up and cover my Six," Claypoole said on the same circuit.

"The platoon's assembled, Acting Second Acolyte," Priestly reported with a dull voice when the ranks were formed.

"Thank you, Second Acolyte." Claypoole nodded at the Kingdomite officer. To all he said, "Listen up. Rear rank, about face. Get into prone positions and keep watch. The rest of you, sit in place." When they did as he ordered, he moved close to the front rank so everybody could hear without him having to yell.

"Look at you," he began. The Kingdomites looked anywhere *but* at themselves. "You call yourselves soldiers, but you look like a bunch of criminals headed for the gallows. I'll bet you think you're going to die today." The soldiers, even the prone watchers, seemed to fold in on themselves. "Well, let me tell you something. The Skinks can be beaten. I know that. Acting Platoon Sword MacIlargie and me, we were in the Swamp of Perdition when we killed more Skinks than we could count. Sure, they killed a lot of Marines, but we got all of them." In fact, he wasn't sure all the Skinks in that battle had been killed, but that was beside the point. "We were out in the countryside, working with your defense garrisons. The defense garrisons, working with Marines, routinely beat the Skinks every time we fought them. We went onto Hymnal Hill and Heaven's Heights after the Skinks overran the high ground and we kicked them off it.

"Here's something else: a couple of years ago, Acting Platoon Sword MacIlargie and me, with the rest of third platoon, went to an uninhabited world called Society 437 to find out why the scientific mission there had stopped reporting. What we found was Skinks. Nobody had ever heard of them before. They had weapons we'd never heard of. They could do things nobody was supposed to be able to do; they could see us, somehow, in our chameleons, and they could breathe underwater. And they were fearless.

"You know what happened? I'll tell you what happened. We killed all of them. They killed *one* of us. That's it, just one.

"Are you listening to me? Do you hear what I'm saying? I'm telling you that Acting Platoon Sword MacIlargie and I are accustomed to beating the Skinks every time we fight them. And I'm telling you that Kingdomite soldiers working with Confederation Marines also beat the Skinks."

"They wiped out an entire division on the heights," someone, Claypoole couldn't see who, said. "There were Marines with that division."

Damn! Claypoole had hoped nobody would mention that. "That's true," he agreed. "They did it because the 82nd Division was relying too much on surveillance devices the Skinks were able to get around, and the Skinks used all those buzz saws to cover their attack. They aren't going to do that to us. Now, let's find us some Skinks and kill them."

"Acting Second Acolyte?" A soldier looked at Claypoole, the first sign of attention he'd seen from the platoon. "Do you think it's possible the Lord will allow us victory?"

Claypoole looked at the soldier for a moment before replying. "I can't speak for the Lord," he finally said, "but a few good Marines insist on it." He looked about for other questions. A couple of soldiers seemed to be considering what he'd said and looked less dull, more ready. It wasn't much, but it was an improvement.

"On your feet, soldiers. We've got Skinks to find and kill."

When the Kingdomites reformed into their patrol formation, they were a bit less listless than before.

Claypoole wasn't the only Marine convinced he was on his terminal patrol that day. Corporal Doyle knew profoundly that he and everyone else was going to get killed on his patrol. He shook so badly he had trouble holding onto his blaster. He remembered vividly the heavy casualties 34th FIST had suffered in the Swamp of Perdition and was fully cognizant of the fact that only the strike by the FIST's Raptors had saved the infantry. He hadn't gone into any of the bunkers on Hymnal Hill, but he had on Heaven's Heights, and saw the Kingdomite soldiers the Skinks had killed there. And he knew the marsh was perfect Skink country. He was convinced that he and Corporal Kerr and Lance Corporal Schultz were going to die that day. The pending deaths of the soldiers from the Lancelot Guardians of the Faith whom the three Marines were leading didn't cross his mind; their fate was a foregone conclusion. Why had he let Gunny Bass talk him into becoming a blasterman instead of letting First Sergeant Myer court-martial him and send him to a nice, safe brig somewhere far, far away from the Skinks?

Doyle's conviction of impending death was so strong that, surprisingly, it saved his life.

Schultz, on the point in front of first squad as usual, even though he was nominally the platoon sergeant, froze and lowered himself to a knee in the muck. Behind him the platoon accordioned to a stop and the soldiers also lowered themselves, though they were reluctant to kneel in the water and muck. Schultz raised his shields and scanned the swamp with his naked eyes; he held down a shiver that wasn't caused by a chill. He sniffed the air and listened carefully, seeking whatever it was that made him stop. He stuck out his tongue and nervously tasted the air.

"What'cha got, Hammer?" Kerr asked over the Marine circuit from his position with second squad in the middle of the platoon column.

Schultz didn't notice the tremor in Kerr's voice. He sucked on his teeth to work up enough saliva to say one word: "Dunno." He kept searching with all his senses.

Closer to the rear of the column with third squad, Corporal Doyle, who was too distracted by thoughts of how he was going to die to pay attention to where he was going, tripped over a crouched soldier. He landed with a loud splash in a pool of standing water.

The sudden noise startled everyone, and they threw themselves down, ignoring the water and muck they landed in. Several of the startled soldiers, thinking they were under attack, fired their rifles. Those few shots set off the rest of them, and the entire platoon started firing randomly into the surrounding reed- and grasslike foliage.

Before Kerr could order the Kingdomites to cease fire, a streamer of greenish fluid shot over first squad. He gasped, momentarily stunned by their good fortune, then found his voice and shrilled out, "LEFT FRONT! FIRE! Second and third squads, hold your fire."

He fumbled for his UPUD, found it, gave the command for a real-time infra overlay of the close-up view of his position. During the seconds it took the string-of-pearls to process his request, locate the current data, and download it, he scanned what he could see of the action in front of him. The fire from first squad was wild, fléchette rounds chaotically ripping through the foliage, most of the shots too high—and the volume of outgoing fire was decreasing as screaming men were hit by the acid streams. Only the plasma bolts from Schultz's blaster were skimming the surface of the ground and water. Kerr saw a flash of light as a bolt hit a Skink. The UPUD shook in his hand. It took another second or so for him to realize the shaking in his hand was from the instrument, not his nerves. He looked at the display. The only red it showed in the platoon's vicinity was the red of the soldiers; either the UPUD was malfunctioning or the Skinks were disguising their already faint infra signals even more.

Now what should he do? He had no idea whether all of the Skinks were involved in the firefight or if there were more of them waiting patiently for other squads to move into their killing zone. He looked at the display again. It showed what might be a waterway that meandered toward the platoon, closing to about forty meters from first squad, within the fifty-meter range of the Skink acid guns. If the Skinks were in the waterway, it would explain why the string-of-pearls hadn't picked up any infra signals.

I'm a Marine, Kerr reminded himself. When in doubt, act decisively. He took a deep, shuddering breath and spoke into his helmet radio.

"Doyle, take second squad and move up to support first squad. Now." He heard a faint noise, but not an acknowledgment. "Doyle, do you hear me?"

"Second squad, move up and support first. Aye aye." Doyle's voice was high-pitched and squeaky.

"Do it. Third squad, stay in position until I reach you." He slithered backward, in the direction of third squad. He slid his infra shield into place and looked to the side. He picked up the movement of man-size bodies—second squad moving forward to support first squad. He rose to his feet, turned about, and double-timed to third squad. "Come with me," he ordered, and led the way into the marsh to the side of the platoon's route.

The soldiers followed. None could have said whether they were more nervous because they were heading into battle or because they were following the disembodied arm Kerr exposed and held behind his back for them to see.

Corporal Doyle could easily tell where first squad was from the firing of their rifles. Fearfully, convinced that the Skinks were aiming at him and waiting their chance to shoot at any exposed skin, he slid his left sleeve up and used his bare arm to direct second squad into position.

"Fire as soon as you're in position," he said. He had to say it a second time because his voice caught in his throat the first time. In position himself, while he gratefully rolled his sleeve back down and sealed its join with his glove, he checked to see where the Kingdomite soldiers were firing. Most of them were shooting high. Even he, who until this deployment had spent his entire Marine career as a clerk, knew their fire was thoroughly ineffective. Doyle worked his mouth to make saliva, cleared his throat, and tried to breathe slowly instead of hyperventilating.

"Low . . ." he squeaked. He cleared his throat again. "Lower your aim!" he shouted, little louder than a croak. He cleared his throat once more. "Lower your fire," he shouted more clearly. "Aim low! You're shooting over them."

The fléchette rounds began shredding foliage closer to ground and water level; the stalky plants that resembled reeds and grasses suffered more of the shredding. Satisfied that most of the Kingdomites had adjusted their fire, he took a surface-skimming shot himself. His jaw dropped when he saw an answering flash.

"Great Buddha's balls," he whispered. If one random shot flared a Skink, they were probably densely massed. He started hyperventilating again.

Kerr stopped forty meters from the platoon's route and faced toward the waterway the UPUD had shown, where he suspected the Skinks were. He used his bare arm to signal the squad to line up on either side of him. As pale as their faces were, he was glad he had his chameleon shield down so they couldn't see the fear he was sure was on his face. He knew his soldiers were terrified, convinced they were going to be killed by the Skinks. He wondered what kept them from running.

He pitched his voice so every man in the squad could hear him and said, "We're going to hit them from the flank. Move fast. Walk, don't run, but move fast. Let's go." He stepped off and was relieved to see the Kingdomites move with him.

They didn't run, but walked briskly, passing to the left of second squad's flank in little more than a minute. Kerr shifted third squad farther to the left and resumed the advance. Twenty meters beyond, he saw a stream of greenish fluid arc toward first squad.

"FIRE!" he shouted, and sent three rapid plasma bolts where he thought the acid came from. Foliage shredded from the Kingdomite fléchettes, most of it low enough to be effective against a foe laying low. A bright flash answered one of Kerr's bolts.

"Keep moving," Kerr shouted. "Fire as you move. Fire low!" He spoke on his helmet radio's command circuit:

"Doyle, get second squad up here with us. We're going through them." There was another flash as another of his bolts hit home. Deeper into the foliage he saw another flash, a Skink hit by Schultz.

Third squad reached the streamlet. It was just wide enough to have a space in its middle that was clear of reeds. Kerr saw a few Skinks in that space, just enough of them showing above the surface of the slowly moving water for them to point and fire their acid guns.

"Halt and fire!" he ordered, then raised his blaster and flared the nearest Skink. He shifted aim and another flashed into vapor. Third squad fired wildly. Most of their shots missed visible Skinks, but few of their shots were too high. The surface of the water looked like it was being pelted by rain. The rain-battering increased to a storm as second squad moved up. Two more Skinks flared.

Suddenly aware of the attack from their flank, the surviving Skinks ducked under the surface.

"Keep shooting!" Kerr roared. Schultz led first squad up at a run and they added their fire into the streamlet. The water surface roiled with the fléchettes hitting it. Red stained the boiling water and steam rose where plasma bolts struck it.

After a moment Kerr ordered the platoon to cease fire and the shooting trailed off. No streamers of acid broke the sudden stillness.

"Casualty report," Kerr said when he was sure the Skinks weren't going to counterattack immediately.

Second and third squads reported no injuries. First squad had three dead. The Kingdomite medic with them was struggling to save the lives of two others who'd been wounded by the acid.

Kerr raised his shields to make his face visible and turned from side to side, looking at the Kingdomites. It took a strong effort, but he got his breathing under control and swallowed the lump that had grown in his throat.

"You see that?" he said loudly. "You beat them. The

Skinks set an ambush to kill you. They set it on their ground, and you beat them. You beat them once, you can do it again."

Several of the Kingdomites smiled weakly; they wanted to believe him. A few cheered weakly.

Their morale was rising, they weren't as frightened. Maybe, if the Kingdomites could regain confidence, Kerr thought, he could defeat his fear as well.

He got on his comm and called company headquarters with a report. Acting Lesser Imam Sergeant Linsman ordered him to bring the casualties in.

CHAPTER
SEVEN

Despite what Corporal Claypoole thought, the Marines given leadership positions in the Army of the Lord and sent out on patrol that day weren't simply to take the Kingdomite soldiers out and get them killed; they were to search for isolated groups of Skinks and kill them. They were also to locate entrances to caves used by the alien, and plant sensors around them. Corporal Dean's platoon of the Lancelot Guardians of the Faith had the good fortune to traverse farmland lined with woody windbreaks, the kind of terrain in which the Kingdomites, not the Skinks, had the advantage. So, though terribly frightened, Dean's soldiers weren't absolutely convinced they were going to lose an encounter with the Skinks. As it happened, they made their way to their destination—across fifteen kilometers of farmland, mostly patrolling along treelines—without seeing any sign of the strange invaders.

Their destination was a rift, an area of risen ground with a fast-running, boulder-strewn creek bed at the bottom. At that season, the creek filled only half of its bed.

Lance Corporal Godenov, with the lead squad, said into his helmet comm, "Let me check it out."

"You got it, Izzy," Dean replied. He turned his attention to deploying the rest of the platoon into a defensive perimeter. It only took a few seconds before he noticed he had the entire platoon, not just two squads. He flipped his infra screen into place and saw one red splotch nearing the creek bed in the bottom of the rift—Godenov hadn't taken first squad the way Dean thought; he'd gone alone.

"Dammit, Izzy," Dean said into his helmet comm, "you already proved the answer is yes. Take your squad."

All his life Isadore Godenov—now Lance Corporal Izzy Godenov—had been plagued by the question, "Is he good enough?" The question followed him when he joined third platoon, where he finally answered it with an emphatic "Yes!" on several deployments.

"No can do," Godenov answered. "Too many bodies. One man can do this recon better." He moved upstream, stepping from rock to rock along the side of the creek bed.

"Quick, take over the platoon and get them into defensive positions," Dean ordered. "You," he indicated half a dozen Soldiers of the Lord, "come with me." PFC Quick aye-aye'd. Muttering to himself, Dean led the frightened soldiers down to the creek bed.

Water had run through the rock long enough to cut a three-meter-deep channel into it. Above the rock the ground rose steeply, but not so sharply that it couldn't be plowed and planted; grain covered the slopes. At any other season, the cut would have been a deadly place to be caught in a flash flood; just then, the creek's shallow water burbled in the middle half of its bed, pooled here, eddied there. Fishlike creatures swam in the water. Occasionally one broke the surface to snatch an insectoid.

Godenov paid the swimmers and their prey no attention, his constantly moving gaze fixed on the walls of the cut. Somewhere, there should be the mouth of a cave, according to the string-of-pearls. Finding it wasn't easy. The rock walls were pitted in many places with openings that only went a meter or two into them—and every opening had to be checked.

Godenov grunted his way over a boulder as tall as his waist and peered at yet another opening in the wall. It was partially blocked by a boulder about the size of the one he'd just climbed over, but enough still showed above for a man to easily slip through. He picked his way to the side of the opening and slid his light-gatherer shield into place before looking into it with his blaster at the ready. The hole seemed to be only a few meters deep, but an irregularity at its end caught his eye. Blaster first, he slid over the boulder into the cave. The overhead was high enough for him to stand crouched over. Pointing his blaster where he was going, he moved inward. In a few steps he saw that the irregularity was a sharp turn in the tunnel. Leading with his blaster, he eased around to where he could see where it went.

He pressed the firing lever on his blaster and jumped back just in time to avoid three streams of acid that flew at him from the clot of Skinks he'd seen. The flash from a flaring Skink almost blinded him and he blinked frantically to clear his vision as he rapidly scooted backward. Harsh jabbering from around the bend grew rapidly louder, and he fired three more rapid shots to keep the Skinks from charging him.

As he followed Godenov, Dean stopped here and there to plant a sensor behind a rock or under a shrub. Still, he and his half-dozen soldiers had almost caught up with Godenov when the Marine crawled over the boulder into the cave mouth.

"Wait here," Dean told his soldiers, and followed Godenov. He was almost at the cave's entrance when there was a quick flash of light in the darkness and Dean heard the *crack-sizzle* of a blaster. He dove toward the opening and poked his blaster over the top of the blocking boulder. His light-gatherer shield showed Godenov backing rapidly toward him while firing.

"Izzy!" he shouted. "What is it?"

"Cover me," Godenov answered, and spun about to race from the cave. As he was scrambling over the rock a Skink appeared out of the side of the cave. Dean fired, the Skink flared.

"It turns back there," Godenov said breathlessly. "That's where they're coming from."

"How many?"

"Damned if I know. A bunch." He and Dean simultaneously fired at another Skink as it turned the corner.

Dean considered what to do. The tunnel was narrow enough that he and Godenov could hold off any number of

Skinks for as long as their power packs held out. But there could be more openings nearby. They had to withdraw. But first Dean used the UPUD to register the location of the cave mouth. He thought about a way to slow the Skinks down when he and Godenov pulled back, and turned to the King-domites he'd left behind, seeing only four of them.

"Come here," he shouted. "Stay to the side." He exposed his arm and signaled where he wanted them to go. The soldiers reluctantly stood and moved forward until Godenov fired again and a Skink flared. Two of the soldiers began to bolt, but Dean threw his blaster into his shoulder and fired a bolt at the rocks in front of them. They skittered to a stop.

"Up *here*!" he shouted. They came, keeping to the side of the cave mouth.

"Yessir," one of them gasped when they arrived, looking fearfully at where he thought Dean's face was.

"Grab some boulders and shove them into this opening, I want it blocked." Seeing how frightened they were, he added, "The Skinks are around a bend. They can only come around it one at a time, and the tunnel's narrow enough that we can't miss. We'll keep them off you. Now move, like this." He hefted a flat rock almost a half meter across and plunked it heavily on top of the boulder in front of the entrance.

The Kingdomites picked up rocks and stacked them in the opening. Godenov shifted to the side, then back from the cave mouth as the opening shrank.

"Let's go," Dean ordered when the last rock went into place. It wouldn't take the Skinks long to knock the barrier down, but it would hold them long enough.

"Izzy," he said, "you and me, leapfrog and keep it covered. If it looks like they're trying to push it open, blast away to move them back. You go first."

"Right," Godenov said, and headed back downstream. The Kingdomites were already gone.

Dean remained by the blocked opening, ready to fire through any chink that began to appear.

"They're running away!" Quick's excited voice came over the command circuit.

"Who?" Dean asked, confused. How could Quick know what the Skinks in the cave were doing?

"The platoon!"

"Fire a warning shot, tell them you'll flame anyone who doesn't stop." Damn cowards! he swore. He heard a distant *crack-sizzle*, then Quick's voice again.

"They stopped." He snorted. "You gotta see this. They're squatting with their hands on their heads like prisoners."

Angry, Dean snapped, "Good! Keep them like that until I get there."

"I've got you covered, Corporal Dean," Godenov broke in.

Dean slid his infra into place and turned around. Godenov's red splotch was fifty meters away. Dean found a way that kept him out of the other's line of sight to the blocked cave. Fifty meters beyond Godenov, he took a position and told Godenov to back off. Just before the Marine passed him, Dean saw one of the rocks shift.

"Keep going," he said to Godenov, then snapped three bolts at the barricade. The rocks stopped moving.

As they approached the platoon, he checked his UPUD. The real-time infra download from the string-of-pearls showed faint splotches of red that could be many bodies moving a hundred meters to the north, on the other side of a treeline windbreak. A quick glance told him the Kingdomites were still squatting with their hands on their heads.

"Quick! Get the platoon in position facing north," he ordered on the command circuit. "Company's coming."

"Roger." Quick shouted orders to the platoon. They were in position in a windbreak by the time he and Godenov reached them. Dean checked his UPUD again. This time he didn't see any movement to the north, nor did a real-time download from the string-of-pearls show any particular infra signal, though the windbreak treeline had a slight pinkish cast.

"They're in there," he said on the command circuit. "We need to flush them out." The Skinks were far enough away that their acid guns couldn't reach the Marines and their

Kingdomite platoon, but if they had a buzz saw with them it was all over—the tree line wasn't old enough to have built up a thick berm. He shouted for everyone to hear, "Take aim on the tree line to the north. On my command, open fire on it. Shoot at the base of the trees, into the brush . . . Take aim, FIRE!"

The three Marines started putting out disciplined fire, shifting their aim after every shot. The Kingdomite fire was ragged. Only about half of the fléchettes went where they might do some good; most of the rest were high, some so high they went over the tops of the opposite trees. A couple of flashes of light in the tree line met the Marine fire—Dean had been right, the Skinks were there. If there were few enough in the tree line, they had no chance of getting close enough to fire their acid guns; all they could do was withdraw.

But what if they have a buzz saw? he wondered. He couldn't get that possibility out of his mind.

"We can't stay here, honcho," Godenov said, breaking in on Dean's thoughts. "Those Skinks we left behind are going to break out soon."

Damn! Dean realized he'd forgotten about the Skinks at the cave mouth. "Izzy, do you have the map?"

"Affirmative." Godenov had the HUD map of their assigned patrol route stored and could bring it up on command.

"Lead the platoon out, follow the assigned route. Quick and I will cover your withdrawal and catch up. Drop a few sensors on your way."

"Aye aye," Godenov replied. He began shouting orders at the Kingdomites. By force of voice—and one warning bolt from his blaster—he managed to keep the withdrawal from becoming a rout.

"Quick, we'll give them five minutes," Dean said.

"Five minutes, right," Quick muttered. He'd followed Dean and Godenov's withdrawal from the cave mouth on his helmet comm. He wondered if they had five minutes before the Skinks they'd left behind broke out of the cave and reached them. He kept up the fire on the tree line, shifting his aiming point between bolts, looking toward the cut between shots.

Only two minutes passed before a line of Skinks crested the lip of the cut.

Dean saw them first, twisted around and fired. His initial bolt missed, but the second flashed a Skink into vapor with an audible *whoosh*. Quick heard the change in Dean's fire and looked. He snap-fired and got another, but his second bolt missed. About twenty Skinks ran screaming toward the Marines, trying desperately to get in range of their weapons. Three more flared up before they got close enough to open fire. The streams of greenish fluid mostly fell short of Dean and most were wide, but he knew it would be mere seconds before they started hitting close. Whatever sense they had that told them where chameleoned Marines were had a short range—and they were almost within that range.

"Quick, cover me," he ordered, and scooted back a few meters, firing as he went. When the two nearest Skinks were flared, he jumped to his feet and sprinted past Quick. He heard the repeated *crack-sizzle* of Quick's blaster and the *whoosh* of more Skinks going up. Twenty-five meters beyond Quick he stopped and began firing offhand at their pursuers. The casualties the Skinks took didn't slow them down; they kept running at the two Marines.

"Quick, got you covered. Leapfrog."

Quick spun around and started running. The closest Skink splashed him, but the protectant in his uniform protected him from harm.

He stopped twenty-five meters beyond Dean to cover him. The first wave of Skinks was down to five, but another, larger wave was closing in behind them. Half a dozen of them were huge and carried swords in their hands, and the nozzles of acid guns banged against their hips. Dean blinked. Swords? Who the hell carries swords? he wondered. The Skinks all wore khaki uniforms. Thirty more Skinks, the ones they'd had pinned down in the tree line to the north, were charging across the field toward Godenov and the Kingdomites.

"How fast do you think they can run?" Quick cried into his helmet comm.

"How far is more the question," Dean snapped back. "Let's find out." He dropped his blaster from his shoulder and ran. Quick bolted ahead of him.

Two hundred meters ahead they saw Godenov trying to organize the Kingdomites into a fighting formation in a tree line. He wasn't having much luck. About half the platoon refused to stop and kept running. The others milled about and had to be physically pushed into position.

So much for the Lancelot Guardians of the Faith, Dean thought. It always seemed to him that the fancier name a unit had, the poorer its fighting ability.

No acid streamed toward Dean and Quick as they ran. The Skinks still weren't close enough to detect them, Dean thought, or maybe they were outrunning the Skinks, who didn't think they were close enough to fire. He risked a glance back, and what he saw almost made him stumble. Most of the Skinks had dropped back, and three of the huge ones outraced their companions and had cut the distance between them to about thirty meters. They seemed to be running straight at him, crashing through the grain like a man running across a lawn. If they kept up that pace, Dean knew they'd catch him before he reached Godenov and the platoon. He put on an extra burst of speed. His heart thudded wildly in his chest and his breath came in gasps. Even if it was fast enough to outdistance the huge Skinks, he couldn't maintain this pace long enough to reach Quick and the remaining Kingdomites.

Abruptly, Dean stuttered to a stop and spun about, raising his blaster to his shoulder. The three Skinks were even closer! He sighted on the nearest one and pressed the firing lever. The huge Skink went up in a monstrous ball of light. The other two didn't hesitate, but arrowed straight at him at impossible speed. Dean flashed one of them, but the other was on him before he could shift his aim. He dove at the racing feet of the Skink as it swung its sword in a two-handed arc from above its head. The impact drove the air from Dean's lungs and spun him about. Groggy, he shook his head to clear it and looked for the Skink. The collision had tripped the great thing and its momentum tumbled it ten meters farther. It was already halfway back to its feet and turning toward him. Dean started to aim at the Skink before he realized he didn't have the blaster in his hands. Manically, he looked around for it, but couldn't spot it in the knee-high grain. The thudding footsteps of the monster were almost on him. He jumped to the side and rolled, unaware of the *crack-sizzle* of blasters and the sharper cracks of fléchette rifles.

The Skink's sword flashed and Dean felt a searing pain where it sliced through his side. He felt an odd irregularity under his body as he rolled and grabbed it. He didn't know what it was, but anything could be used as a weapon. It was the sword of one of the Skinks he'd flared. He didn't know how to use a sword, but it was the only weapon he now had.

Dean saw the flash of the Skink's blade above him and instinctively threw up his own sword to block the strike. The Skink's swing was so shockingly powerful it almost jarred the captured sword from his hands, but he managed to deflect the blow and the sword struck the ground just above his head. He curled in an attempt to gain his feet and move away, but the Skink kicked out and landed a glancing blow on his kidney. He went with the kick and rolled several meters away. Struggling to regain his breath, he scrambled away and jumped back to his feet. The Skink was almost on him again, and Dean slashed out one-handed as he dove to the side. He felt the blade slow as it hit the Skink.

The Skink, silent in its attack until now, roared out a bloodcurdling bellow. Dean leaped back to his feet and sprinted away. He changed direction then and tightly circled around to face the Skink. It came toward him, limping slightly. Bright red blood stained its trouser leg from a cut in its thigh.

Dean turned his left side toward the Skink, extended his left leg and angled back, the sword in both hands above his right shoulder.

The Skink gave out a surprisingly human laugh and came on. It stopped three meters away, legs wide, left foot forward, arms extended with both hands on the sword's hilt, the blade almost vertical. It smiled and softly said something that sounded to Dean like it should be, "Your move."

Dean stayed motionless; he had no idea of what to do. He saw how well-balanced the Skink's stance was, how it could move in any direction, block any swing he made, or make a thrust or cut of its own. Then, in his peripheral vision, he saw that he was closer to a tree line than the Skink was to him. He shifted forward, as though about to move toward the Skink, then lifted his back leg and pushed off with his front. In two backward bounds he was in the trees, with the Skink rushing toward him.

The Skink swung its sword horizontally. Dean ducked behind a tree, and the blade sank deeply into the wood. As the Skink yanked at it, Dean came around the tree's other side and jabbed at it. Without letting go of its sword, the Skink jumped back and to the side, but didn't get far enough to completely avoid the thrust. He roared as the tip of the sword stuck several inches into its abdomen, and then finally jerked the blade free. He came at Dean in a rush, and the Marine barely managed to scramble behind another tree— the Skink was far more agile than he'd thought someone that big could be.

They danced about, zigzagging among the trees. The Skink matched Dean almost move for move. But loss of blood was weakening Dean faster than the Skink was weakening from its two wounds. Then he remembered his training: if you get into a fight with someone a lot bigger than you, get in close—if you're inside his swing, he can't hit you with his full power. The next time the Skink swung at him,

Dean dropped his sword and dashed in close, drawing his fighting knife as he moved. He grabbed the neck of the Skink's shirt and pulled himself tight to its chest. He realized then how big the Skink really was—his head didn't even reach the creature's throat.

The Skink cried out in rage, and slammed the hilt of his sword into Dean's back. The pain was bad, but Dean thrust upward with his knife. The blade went deep into the Skink's abdomen, into his chest cavity. Dean twisted the blade around, sawed it from side to side. The Skink screamed in agony and beat on Dean's head and shoulders with his sword hilt and free hand. Dean stabbed again. Warm blood gushed from the holes in the Skink's abdomen, washed over the Marine's front and splashed up onto his helmet shields, almost blinding him. He stabbed again, and the Skink staggered backward. Dean held on for all he was worth and moved with the Skink. He stabbed again. The Skink shrieked and fell backward. Dean landed on top of it, pulled himself forward and sliced the thing's throat. The Skink's sides heaved as it tried to breathe through its gills, and Dean repeatedly jabbed his knife between the Skink's ribs, hoping to hit its heart.

The Skink spasmed, then lay still.

Breathing heavily, Dean waited a moment, then rolled off. Warily, he rose to his feet and backed off. He looked at the Skink, whose glazed-over eyes stared unseeing at the treetops. The giant was dead.

Dean remembered the other Skinks then and dropped to a knee, looking wildly around. He saw none, but infra showed a man-shaped red splotch approaching. He lifted the infra shield and saw Quick's face hovering in the air, coming toward him.

"You okay, honcho?" Quick asked.

"I think so," Dean answered as he stood up again.

"You don't look like it. How much of that blood is yours?"

Dean looked down at himself. His entire front was stained the deep red of spilled blood. He shook his head.

"None, I think." At that point, the loss of blood combined with an adrenaline crash and he collapsed.

Later, after he was carried semiconscious back to base, Dean learned that Quick and Godenov and the half platoon that remained had managed to fight off the two-pronged attack. Two Kingdomites were killed in the battle, and three more wounded. Quick had recovered his blaster.

CHAPTER
EIGHT

General Anders Aguinaldo, Assistant Commandant of the Confederation Marine Corps, sighed and leaned back in his chair. The back-channel message he'd just received from Brigadier Sturgeon about the military situation on Kingdom was painfully terse and direct: the 34th FIST, now reinforced by Jack Sparen's 26th FIST, was holding defensive positions around Haven, the capital city of Kingdom, and preparing a counterattack. But what got Aguinaldo's attention was Sturgeon's recommendation. It was his considered opinion that the Skinks were present in force on Kingdom and constituted a major military threat to the Confederation. Therefore, he urged Aguinaldo to inform the commandant of these facts and ask him to recommend to the Chairman of the Combined Chiefs (so he could tell the President) that it was now necessary, *immediately*, to lift the cloak of secrecy surrounding their existence. Furthermore, he recommended every resource be devoted to finding their home world and destroying them before they could launch further attacks on humanity. He concluded by stating that in his opinion it was not fair to the member worlds to keep them in the dark any longer about such a deadly menace.

"Ah, Ted," Aguinaldo whispered to himself as he read, "you let this out and you'll really be stepping on your dick."

Fortunately, Sturgeon's comments were contained in a back channel, a secure and very private means of communication between flag officers that gave them a means to frankly and honestly say what they really thought about issues. What even generals would never dare say in public was generally safe in a back channel. While Sturgeon's comments and recommendations in his message were blunt, he was forwarding them through an approved channel, even if it was not through his direct chain of command, which would have included at least one Fleet commander. Sturgeon's information was just too sensitive and requested emergency measures too important to be bogged down in normal Fleet communications channels.

Aguinaldo transferred the message to a crystal—he might need that to cinch his argument—then leaned back and considered the situation.

He knew that Ted Sturgeon never, *never*, got excited. This recommendation was not a hasty call for help from Chicken Little. If Ted Sturgeon said the sky was falling, Aguinaldo knew they better get under cover quick. The Skinks—the name had stuck from Charlie Bass's first encounter with them on Society 437—had wiped out an entire scientific mission on Society 437, and they'd now wreaked havoc with the local armed forces and the Marines on Kingdom. They were a powerful and, on some levels, very deadly alien force of unknown origin. And they were on the move—so far, only on the fringes of Human Space, but . . . well, he thought, they first showed up on the very fringe, Society 437, and were now well within the explored and settled regions. Kingdom was out there, but not *that* far out. Next could—probably would—be a populated mainstream world. And if that happened . . .

"Jesus' dirty toenails," Aguinaldo whispered. Then he said to his calendar, "Gladys, get me in to see the commandant, ASAP!"

"Not only no, Andy, but *hell* no!" General Dov Tokis thundered at his ACMC. He glared silently at General Aguinaldo for a moment. "Do you have any idea what news like this would do to the morale of the civilian population, General?" When Aguinaldo did not respond immediately,

Tokis rushed on: "I'll tell you. People would be so spooked, the stock markets would crash immediately, send us into a Confederation-wide depression! And the first thing the governments would want to know is why we didn't tell them sooner! Goddammit, tell Sturgeon to get off his ass and whip these things *now*! What's he waiting for anyway? Christ's macerated nuts, we've given him another goddammed FIST to back him up, and he's got the entire armed forces of this—this—"

"Kingdom of Yahweh and His Saints and Their Apostles," Aguinaldo answered tiredly. "Sir, would you at least read Brigadier Sturgeon's report?"

"Right, Kingdom. 'Yahweh and His Saints,' " Tokis muttered, shaking his head. "Who ever heard of a place with a name like that? Nah," he waved away the crystal that Aguinaldo was offering, "I don't have the time to read such goddammed crap."

"Sir," Aguinaldo began—he had long ago stopped calling the commandant by his first name, although they were both generals—"what will the member worlds say if the Skinks get onto one of the mainstream planets and begin to slaughter the population there? They'll wonder why we didn't get off *our* asses up here and do something to prevent it. They'll want someone's neck for not warning them in time."

Tokis shook his head. "Andy, I can't go to the Chairman with a request to alert the entire goddammed universe based on the report of one field commander. I almost had to get down on my knees and beg to get authority to reinforce Sturgeon with the 26th. I go into the Chairman now, with this wild story about these, these things . . ."

"Skinks, sir. Amphibians of some sort. No one's ever taken one alive or dead so we don't—"

"Yeah, yeah." Tokis waved his hand impatiently. "But if I go in there with this wild-assed story, I'll come out thinking God had just shoved his dick up my ass. Has Sturgeon gotten shell-shocked or what?"

Aguinaldo bristled at the insult to a proven combat commander but kept his silence. He also didn't much care for the commandant's language. The man constantly used the crudest language because he thought it made him appear tough. He had never liked Tokis, an officer who had somehow risen to the top Marine's job—a position traditionally held only by infantry commanders with combat experience—through a variety of rear-echelon, staff specialist assignments. His only commands had been in peacetime. Normally that would not have bothered a man like Aguinaldo, who never considered his own combat awards significant. But it was altogether too obvious that Tokis actually resented his combat decorations and felt nervous around him when he was wearing them.

But the clincher came when Aguinaldo had learned by chance that Tokis was a big buddy of Fleet Admiral Wilber "Wimpy" Wimbush, another rear-echelon officer. Wimbush had been in charge of the Diamunde Incursion, which, because he knew nothing about ground operations and trusted his army commanders, had gone awry. He'd been forced to turn to Aguinaldo to take over the combat operations and save the day. Wimbush's career had been ruined. Apparently, he and Tokis had been friends since their days together at the War College, and the admiral had put a bug into Tokis's ear shortly after Aguinaldo's confirmation as assistant commandant. Otherwise, he would never have been nominated for the number-two position in the Corps. There were many, however, who thought he should be number one.

"Ted Sturgeon is one of our finest field commanders, sir," Aguinaldo answered sharply.

Tokis realized he was on thin ice and backed down. Not only was he jealous of his assistant commandant, he was afraid of him. The ass-chewing Aguinaldo had given the army three-star who bolluxed the Diamunde operation had become legend in the Corps, akin to the legendary tantrum thrown by Lieutenant General Holland "Howling Mad" Smith in 1943 when he'd been forced to relieve a dilatory army division commander. "Well, sure, Andy, I didn't mean . . . well, from what you told me it just sounded like . . ." He made a vague gesture of apology.

"I trust Ted's judgment, sir. I recommend we take this matter to the Chairman."

Tokis leaned back in his chair. "No. I don't think it's politically or militarily wise to make any announcements right now. Let's wait to see how Sturgeon handles the situation."

"But, sir, the force on Kingdom could just be one of many these Skinks have dispatched into Human Space. For all we know, there could be vast invasion fleets on the way."

Tokis remained leaning back in his chair, regarding Aguinaldo through slitted eyes. He is becoming part of the problem, he thought. "Again, no. Now, Andy, we have to move on to another more pressing matter."

Aguinaldo started. Another "more pressing" matter? What the . . . ?

"Senator Barbara McSchroeder and the entire delegation from Dacowitz has signed a letter to the President complaining that there are not enough opportunities for women in the Corps. McSchroeder herself called me only this morning. She maintains women are unfairly prejudiced by promotion boards because we don't allow them to serve in the combat arms, blah blah blah. I know, I know." Tokis held up a placating hand as Aguinaldo started rising out of his chair. "Our Deputy Chief of Staff for Manpower is a two-star female. But Andy, let's give her a bone, okay? I'm having DCSM prepare a list of specialties we can open to female Marines. I want you to go over it and make recommendations." He paused. "One thing about that McSchroeder you've got to admit," he said. "She's got a great pair of tits."

Back in his office, Aguinaldo felt deflated. Now what? He could not, he *would not*, sit by idly while two of his FISTs were engaged in a deadly fight with an inimical, sentient alien force. It was unconscionable how Tokis had just sat there and airily brushed Sturgeon's concerns aside. Aguinaldo felt his blood coming to a boil. "Gladys," he said to his computer, "please get me the Chairman's office."

"General, this is highly irregular," Fleet Admiral Rafe Rackstra, Chairman of the Combined Chiefs of Staff, intoned, bidding Aguinaldo to take a seat. "Is General Tokis on travel or sick or something? I did not notice any travel projected on his calendar for this week."

"No, sir, he is in his office. He does not know I am here."

Admiral Rackstra's eyebrows rose. "Well, this *is* irregular, General. Why ever would you presume to come to me without going through the commandant?"

"We disagree over the matter I wish to discuss with you, sir. And I must come to you because you can go directly to the President."

"Oh?" Admiral Rackstra leaned back in his chair and regarded the Marine officer over the bridge of his nose. Aguinaldo knew it was the only bridge the admiral had seen in over forty-five years of naval service. "And that matter is?"

Briefly, Aguinaldo explained Sturgeon's concerns about the Skink activities on Kingdom. "I know we all thought when 34th FIST was deployed to Kingdom it was to quell another schismatic war that had gotten out of hand. But Brigadier Sturgeon believes what he is up against there is only an advance element of what could be a full-force invasion by these Skinks. I think it's time we went on full alert and briefed the Council of Worlds on the threat. Sir . . ." He offered the crystal containing Sturgeon's report. "I suggest you read this for yourself."

Rackstra took the crystal but only toyed with it for a moment before shaking his head and passing it back to Aguinaldo. "I don't have time to read this stuff. It should have come through channels anyway. Never have liked these back channels. Cut out intermediate commanders who should know what's going on. Does the President already know about the Skinks?"

Aguinaldo did not bother to point out that Sturgeon considered his situation so grave he dared not slow it down by sending it through intermediate headquarters. "Yessir, I presume she does, from the events on Society 437, but I do not think she knows about them being on Kingdom. But I just ask you to bear in mind that so far none of us here, none of us in charge, have gone up against them. Brigadier Sturgeon has, and I trust his judgment. I am asking you to take me with you to her office. I believe it's time we put the matter before her."

Admiral Rackstra was silent for a long time. He thought, This is the upstart bastard who got Wimbush fired and made a big name for himself in the process. "General, you go over the commandant's head and you come to me with the *opinions* of a field commander—a mere brigadier at that—that we're about to be invaded by bug-eyed monsters, and expect me to march into the President's office and ask her to start a goddammed panic? Do you have any idea what information like this, especially if it's ill-founded, would do to the economy of the Confederation, not to mention the psychological health of trillions of people throughout Human Space?" As he went on his voice began to rise. "You are insubordinate, General! You have committed a serious breach of military discipline, coming in here over General Tokis's head like this! *No,* I repeat, NO." Now he was screaming at Aguinaldo. "I will NOT refer this matter to the President! It can wait until the next regularly scheduled meeting of the Combined Chiefs! Now get out of here!"

Back in his office, Aguinaldo considered his options. As he sat there, the vidscreen on his console blipped. It was the commandant. Aguinaldo sighed and activated the screen. "Yessir?"

Tokis's face filled the screen. It was a bright red. His lips quivered as he spoke, "General, Fleet Admiral Rackstra has just informed me about a meeting you had with him a little while ago. Did you discuss Brigadier Sturgeon's message about events on Kingdom with him?"

"Yessir, I did."

"Why did you dare to go over my head on this, General?"

Aguinaldo sighed. That fishing lodge of his up in the mountains would be a good place to hang out in for a year or two. "Because, General, you are a goddammed fool."

With great difficulty Tokis controlled himself. "General, I want your retirement papers on my desk first thing in the morning." The screen went dead.

"Well, shit!" Aguinaldo said aloud, and smiled. I should

have known Rackstra was going to call whistledick as soon as I was out the door, he thought. He shrugged. I did what had to be done, he reflected. If I can't stand the fire, he told himself, I shouldn't be wearing this gold Nova. He thought: Tokis and Rackstra represent the fraternity of the REMFs, rear-echelon—well, rear-echelon officers who have not earned the right to command my Marines. So I guess it's time now to call upon the fraternity of fighting men. He turned to his computer. "Gladys, get me Marcus Berentus."

"And so," Marcus Berentus, the Confederation Minister of War concluded, "I decided General Aguinaldo's information was important enough to warrant a meeting with you on such short notice."

Madam Chang-Sturdevant, President of the Confederation of Worlds Council, regarded the two men sitting across from her. "General Aguinaldo," she began, "if it weren't for Marcus's intervention in this matter I'd never have agreed to see you under these circumstances. I expect you know what a serious breach of military discipline this is, your coming here over the heads of your superiors? You don't need to answer that question, I know very well how the chain of command works, General. Well, let's hear it, gentlemen."

Quickly, Aguinaldo summarized the contents of Sturgeon's message. He handed the President the crystal. Without a word she popped it into her reader, and for the next ten minutes they sat there while she read Sturgeon's report. "Whew," she said at last. "Sturgeon. Sturgeon? I've heard that name before. What kind of commander is this Sturgeon?"

"One of the best we've ever had, ma'am. I think Ted can handle the situation on Kingdom, but very frankly, I think his fear that what he's up against is merely the thin edge of a general invasion is fully justified, and we would be taking a terrible chance if we waited any longer to prepare for it."

"Marcus?"

"Ma'am, speaking as an old fighter jock, never underestimate the opposition. Both Andy and Ted are old hands at commanding combat operations. If they see an elephant in any of this, we'd better start looking for his trunk. I recommend we alert the member worlds' armed forces if not the general civilian population."

Madam Chang-Sturdevant reflected. "I'm well-aware of the threat the Skinks pose, gentlemen. I was advised, and I agreed at the time, to keep what happened on Society 437 quiet, at least until we could find out more about these creatures." She paused. "I'm going to take a big hit on this if we go public, gentlemen. Politicians can't afford to get caught withholding information from the people who elected them." She paused again, thinking. "But," she sighed, "if I didn't want to take the fire, I shouldn't have run for this office."

She turned to her console and called up her chief-of-staff on the vidscreen. "I want the entire Combined Chiefs in the conference room in one hour," she told him. "It will last no more than thirty minutes. Half an hour after that, assemble my cabinet for a full session. If the ministers are away, have their deputies sit in for them."

She turned to Aguinaldo. "I want you there with me, General."

Aguinaldo cleared his throat. "Well, ma'am, you should know that I have been asked to turn in my resignation and—"

"Why doesn't that surprise me, General?" She paused. "We'll address your future later. Marcus, take our trouble-making Marine to the cafeteria, and you two be back here in my office in forty-five minutes, so we can all three of us walk in on the chiefs in one grand entrance." She laughed. "I'm a woman and the goddammed President, so I got to have grand entrances—the more spectacular the better."

In the corridor outside Berentus turned to Aguinaldo and said, smiling, "Andy, this is the last time I'm going to bail your ass out of trouble. I'm getting too old for this close-air support role." When Berentus had been a hotshot fighter pilot, he'd flown a mission in support of a Marine platoon pinned down by hostiles during a peacekeeping deployment on a godforsaken piece of junk known as Nyongnassa. His ordnance had been right on target, and the Marines, who'd been on the verge of getting overrun, were saved. Berentus was too late to save the Marine platoon commander. It was the platoon sergeant who'd taken over and called in the strike. That platoon sergeant had been Anders Aguinaldo.

Madam Chang-Sturdevant's entrance into the conference room was spectacular indeed, flanked as she was by her Minister of War and the Assistant Commandant of the Marine Corps in his dress reds. No one in the room was more astonished than Fleet Admiral Rackstra and General Tokis, both of whom looked at one another nervously. "That bastard's gone over our heads!" Tokis hissed into Rackstra's ear. The military representatives from the member worlds' armed forces, permanent members of the Combined Chiefs of Staff, looked at one another in surprise and then to Admiral Rackstra. Both he and Tokis experienced severe sinking sensations in their guts.

Chang-Sturdevant sat at the head of the table, flanked by Berentus on one side and Aguinaldo on the other. "Admiral Rackstra, Commandant Tokis," she nodded at those officers, "I fully realize that by coming to me over your heads, General Aguinaldo has committed a grave breach of military discipline. But that is neither here nor there. We have a situation on our hands. Gentlemen, I am going to have a message flashed onto your screens. Read it and then we'll talk."

Admiral Rackstra cleared his throat. "Madam President, I advise proceeding with extreme caution. We cannot make any definitive decision on this matter until we have confirmation that this so-called 'invasion' is in fact not some hoax sponsored by a group of religious fanatics. We all remember the destruction of that container ship some time ago . . ." The other chiefs muttered their assent. "I recommend a fact-finding mission to this place, so we can see for ourselves what's going on out there."

"Madam President," Tokis spoke up. "Whatever we decide

to do, I recommend against warning the general civilian population at this time. News of this sort, if it's genuine, would result in a panic of unparalleled proportions."

Chang-Sturdevant allowed the discussion to go on for a few more minutes. "Gentlemen," she said at last, "I thank you for your frank comments and advice. I agree with Commandant Tokis that giving this information to the general population at this juncture would be a bad idea. A fact-finding mission would be a good idea if we could act on it swiftly, but we cannot. Therefore, to act on the possibility that Brigadier Sturgeon is correct in his assumption that events on Kingdom are a precursor to a general invasion of Human Space, I want you to alert your Fleet commanders at once. Summarize Brigadier Sturgeon's message. Order them to put their forces on alert immediately, but ensure a strict need-to-know about the reason for the alert. Otherwise our forces are to be told only that I have directed the creation of a task force to deal with a serious threat to the, shall we say, 'stability' of the Confederation. They are to remain in a high state of readiness until the crisis is past or until they are told to stand down." Chang-Sturdevant whispered something to her Minister of War.

"Madam, who is to command this task force?" the Army Chief of Staff asked.

"General Aguinaldo." She turned to Aguinaldo, but as she spoke she gestured at the assembled chiefs, indicating her orders to him were orders to them as well. "First order of precedence: Brigadier Sturgeon gets from you whatever he needs to resolve the current crisis on Kingdom. Make it clear to him that he makes the tactical decisions as the man on the scene and we back him up. I think he already knows this, but I want *you* to emphasize that *we* understand he and his Marines are on the very tip of the sword between these creatures and the rest of humanity."

Rackstra and Tokis said nothing, waiting for the ax to fall. Now it did:

"Admiral Rackstra, I know I have your full cooperation. I want you to put your entire staff behind this effort. Marcus," she nodded at the Minister of War, "will give you all the assistance you need, including emergency funding."

Rackstra was almost perspiring with relief. "Yes, ma'am! You have it!"

"General Tokis, I know you will support General Aguinaldo in every way possible. As far as his mission is concerned, there is no chain of command. He will confer with you as needed but his appointment is presidential and he reports directly to me, the same as Admiral Rackstra. But in all matters relating to these aliens, General Aguinaldo is the supreme commander."

Tokis silently breathed a long sigh of relief. "Yes, ma'am! Fully understood! Brilliant decision! Excellent choice!"

"General Aguinaldo, is there anything you want to say right now? Anything you can think of on such short notice that I can do for you?"

"Yes, ma'am. I want to ask Sergeant Major Bambridge if he'd like to be assigned to my staff. He's the Sergeant Major of the Marine Corps."

Chang-Sturdevant looked at Tokis, who happily nodded his assent. To his way of thinking, the entire situation was turning up roses. He was getting rid of *two* troublemakers, one a flag officer and the other the Marine Corps' senior enlisted man, both recalcitrant "warriors" who could never grasp the big picture of life above the worm's-eye view of the infantryman.

"One more thing, Madam, gentlemen," Aguinaldo said. "It'll be weeks before we can get this show on the road. Weeks before Brigadier Sturgeon even knows there's a show coming. In the meantime, Sturgeon and the two FISTs he commands on Kingdom are on their own. I have faith in Sturgeon and his men that they can hold out. But as potent as this alien force is, I just hope we aren't too late."

Chang-Sturdevant nodded. She understood very well the problems of communicating over the vast reaches of interstellar space. So did everyone else in the room. "All right, gentlemen." She stood. "Go do it. Marcus, I believe you want to have a few words with General Aguinaldo before our cabinet meeting." She walked into her private chambers to prepare for the meeting.

Berentus took Aguinaldo aside. "Andy, you know the only reason she didn't relieve those stuffed shirts on the spot is because she does need them until this crisis is over. As we used to say in the old 97th Tactical Fighter Squadron, 'Why change shovels in the middle of the shit?' Besides, they're holdovers from the previous administration, and since those appointments run for five years, they both still have some time to go before they become eligible for retirement. You know, military officers are supposed to be political neutrals, and it doesn't look good for a new President to fire the chief appointed by a predecessor.

"But I only have one thing to say that you don't already know. When the time is right, Madam President is going to advance your name as the next commandant." Berentus smiled and extended a hand.

"Well," Aguinaldo began, shaking Berentus's hand vigorously, "this morning my career was over, and now . . . I'll tell you one thing, sir, I'm moving my task force headquarters way the hell out there, because with a few notable exceptions like yourself, I don't think I much care for the people I have to work with down here."

CHAPTER
NINE

In a corner of the operations center of the Marine Expeditionary Forces, Kingdom, Brigadier Sturgeon stood quietly, arms folded over his chest. He wanted to watch the situation map develop as the patrol reports came without interfering with the work of the staff. He didn't like what he saw. Nearly all of the Army of the Lord platoons, each under the command of a Marine fire team or gun team, made contact with Skinks. In many cases the contact was so severe the patrols had to pull back before they reached suspected cave outlets they were sent to salt with surveillance devices. Kingdomite morale was even lower than he'd thought; about half of the soldiers broke and ran, or tried to, when they made contact with the Skinks. Stragglers would probably continue to dribble in for the next couple of days. Meanwhile, the Skinks continued to probe and raid the defensive positions around Haven and Interstellar City.

The situation was untenable. Despite their very high losses in the assault on Heaven's Heights and Hymnal Hill, the Skinks still seemed to number in the tens of thousands. On his side, Sturgeon had two understrength FISTs—fewer than two thousand Marines—and the Army of the Lord. His command of the army was shaky. Archbishop General Lambsblood, the Kingdomite commander, was only reluctantly under Sturgeon's command and couldn't be relied on to obey orders. Even though the forces available to him had to outnumber the Skinks several times over, Sturgeon could only count on his own Marines to aggressively take the fight to the foe. The Skinks were always aggressive. The Marines and their allies stood to lose this fight. Unless . . .

Unless he could find a Skink center of gravity and hit it hard enough to hurt them—and spectacularly enough to give heart to the Army of the Lord.

He quietly slipped out of the operations center and returned to his office. There, he called for the FIST commanders and their intelligence and operations chiefs to join him and his own intel and ops chiefs.

"Gentlemen, I'll make this short and sweet," Sturgeon said when the eight officers crowded in. "I want to find a Skink COG—Center of Gravity. Headquarters, logistics hub, communications center. Anything that will give them a major hurt when we take it out." Nobody questioned his use of the word "when." They were Marines, they *expected* to give a major hurt to anybody foolish enough to go up against them.

"Put out all recon teams. Have your battalions reorganize their scout-sniper teams into recon teams. As long as we're in this static position, the infantry can spot for the big guns, so reorganize the artillery forward observer sections into recon teams and send them out as well. That'll give us fourteen recon teams. I want them all out there tonight. They will stay out until they find a target.

"We haven't lost any UAVs, so maybe the Skinks are buying their camouflage. Put your birds out, all but one company-level team per FIST. That team will cover the entire FIST defensive front. I know that'll put a crimp in your close-in surveillance, but finding a COG has top priority." His mouth twisted sourly. "The way the Skinks are hitting the lines, we can get by without the teams fairly easily; we're getting more use out of the surveillance devices outside the perimeter.

"I want to see your operations and coordination plans in three hours. Questions?"

There were none.

"Do it."

The commanders and staff officers left, and Sturgeon settled back in his chair. Nobody had said anything, but they all knew the recon teams would probably have to go below-ground to find a Skink COG. By the same time tomorrow, sixty-four of his Marines were going to begin entering the caves. That would cause many, probably most, of them to lose communications. It was likely that some of them wouldn't come back and that nobody would ever find out what happened to them. Sometimes a commander had to send men to probable death. That was when being a com-mander was the hardest job a man could have.

Two days later Staff Sergeant Wu, 34th FIST's recon squad leader, lay burrowed into the muck and detritus under a dense bush overlooking a cave mouth on the high, steep bank of a small stream. His hands held no weapon. Recon's job was intelligence gathering. If a recon Marine had to fight, that meant his mission had failed. Like his men, Staff Sergeant Wu carried a hand-blaster and a knife, purely defensive weapons. He'd been on site for nearly four hours watching that hole in the ground. According to the string-of-pearls landsat data, the hole led into a cave com-plex. In six hours of observation he'd seen a score or more of smallish local animals poke their way into the cave, and more or less the same number come back out. He'd watched with interest a brief panic among the local fauna when a feral Earth pig went into the cave—that was the only enter-tainment he had in an otherwise boring watch.

The animals were the only activity he saw. None of the sensors the team had aimed at the cave detected anything other than those animals. The same had been true during the four-hour shifts of Corporal Steffan and Lance Corporal Sonj. Twelve hours' observation combined with lack of sign of human usage—Wu brought himself up short. What was he doing thinking of the Skinks as human? The lack of any sign of Skink usage, he corrected himself, meant that the cave mouth probably wasn't used for entry into the subsur-face complex. Maybe the Skinks didn't know about it. Maybe it didn't lead into the complex. Maybe. Or maybe it was mined. Or it was a bolt-hole and was guarded inside. It probably wasn't guarded—not close to the surface, at any rate. If it was, he doubted so many animals would move in and out so casually. Whatever the situation was, there was only one way to find out.

Wu radioed in a report, then slithered out of the muck and joined the three recon Marines in their tight defensive position.

"We go in," he murmured just loud enough for them to hear.

"Send a minnie first?" Steffan asked.

"No need," Wu said. He looked toward the others. None of them had questions. They all knew they'd have to go underground to find anything important to the Skinks. "Go," he said softly.

Steffan led the way downstream. He paused on the stream bank and probed with all his senses and sensors for danger before entering the water and cleaning the accumulated mud and debris off his chameleons. Muddy water drifted off on the current, away from the cave mouth. They were all filthy, even Lance Corporal Zhon, who hadn't taken a turn watching the cave. They had to wash off because the dirt made them visible. Cleaned, Steffan moved into cover on the stream's opposite side. Wu went next, followed by Sonj. Zhon brought up the rear.

They moved inland and circled around to approach the cave from upstream. Their chameleons quickly dried as they walked, and they were again effectively invisible to the human eye.

Steffan approached the cave while the other three kept watch from inside the forest. The cave didn't look like much from the outside, just a split in a rock face that had been revealed by erosion of the high, steep bank. Steffan used his HUD to check the sensors still in place across the stream. They showed just the four Marines and some small animals. The split was wide enough for a man to sidle through, but low. Steffan angled his torso and started into the split but jerked back out when something skittered across his feet. He let out a breath of relief when something resembling a hedgehog scampered away. He bent again and slid into the cave.

A meter or so inside, the cave widened enough so he didn't have to sidle. His infra showed a few small animals hiding behind rocks or in corners of the cave's irregular walls. With his light-gatherer he saw rubble on the uneven floor—fallen rocks, scattered bones, droppings, a couple of nests. The dirt on the cave floor had been disturbed by the feral pig that visited recently, but showed nothing that resembled a Skink footprint. A few meters ahead the walls spread out, the floor rose, and the roof dropped so the cave was less than a meter high and nearly two shoulder widths wide. He lowered himself and looked through the narrow place. A wall was some distance beyond it, but he couldn't tell whether the cave ended there or turned before the wall. As he duck-walked forward to see through the narrowing, he was aware of someone entering the cave behind him. He had to lower himself to hands and knees to get close enough to see beyond the narrowing. Beyond it, the floor dipped, then rose again before the tunnel turned to the left.

He shifted aside to allow Staff Sergeant Wu to squeeze in beside him.

Wu touched helmets and asked, "Ready?"

"As I'll ever be."

"Go." Wu slid back to let Steffan pass, then followed. Sonj and Zhon trailed without having to be told.

Two or three turns in from the entrance the cave was pitch-black and their light-gatherer shields were worthless. So they used infrared torches to see by. The cave twisted and turned, rose and fell. In one place there was a sheer four-meter drop, in another a climb nearly as high. There were a couple of spots they only squeezed through with difficulty.

At least the big ones can't get through here, Wu thought. He shuddered at the memory of a close encounter he'd had with one of the giant Skinks earlier in the campaign.

Four hours later, after following three kilometers of twists and turns, they began to see farther than their infra lamps should have allowed. Steffan stopped and raised his infra shield. Yes, there was a faint red luminescence up ahead.

Wu looked over his shoulder. The light didn't seem to have a source, it simply was. To the best of Wu's knowledge, Kingdom didn't harbor any life-forms that generated red luminescence; the light had to be artificially generated.

Touching helmets with Steffan, he said, "Careful," then added over his helmet comm to everyone, "Lights off." The recon Marines turned off their infra lamps.

The Marines resumed their advance, stepping carefully. All senses at peak, they moved much slower than before, stepping with what naive observers would have thought as theatrical slowness.

The faint luminescence grew to a dim glow when Steffan went around a bend in the tunnel. Ahead he saw that it seemed to emanate from the cave wall. Voices and the whine of a motor began to echo in the cave. Ever so cautiously, he approached the light source. It came from a narrow chink in the tunnel wall. Stepping carefully so he didn't kick the chips of rock below the split, he looked through it and whispered one word into his helmet comm: "Paydirt." Then moved forward so Wu could move up and see what he'd found.

The hole Wu looked through was only as wide as a man's hand, but the rock was a thin wall at that point. Beyond it was a huge cavern dimly lit by a few red lights strung overhead. A stack of crates next to the split blocked his view in one direction, but as far as he could see in other directions, the cavern was filled with rows of similar stacks, wide passageways between rows. A Skink stood on top of one stack directing two others who were maneuvering vehicles to move stacks. They moved three stacks out of a row, then maneuvered into the space they'd cleared and lifted two stacks that had been behind the three they'd moved and moved them out of sight, then came back and replaced the three they'd moved out of the way. They disappeared again in the direction in which they'd taken the two stacks and paused. The changing pitch of the motors told Wu the mover picked up the stacks. The supervisor clambered off the stack he stood on, mounted a smaller vehicle, and drove in the direction of the removed stacks. The others sounded like they followed him with their burdens.

Wu listened to the whine of the motors diminish into the distance until he couldn't hear them any longer. Then he watched and listened for another fifteen minutes without seeing any motion or hearing any sounds other than his own breathing. He slipped his hand into the crack and slid it up and down. The wall was irregular on his side but smooth on the other—obviously, the cavern had been enlarged and finished. In no place was the wall more than four centimeters thick. He probed for a thin spot, grasped it tightly, and snapped off a small piece which he carefully put in a pocket of his trousers. He picked up another piece from the pile below the crack and put it in a different pocket. He suspected that when the Skinks enlarged the cavern, they'd made this split and didn't notice it.

"Minnie," he whispered into his comm. Zhon reached into Sonj's pack and withdrew the minnie—in the tight confines it was easier to get the miniature recording robot from someone else's pack than from his own. He passed it forward.

Wu took the robot. It was eight centimeters high, six wide, twelve long, and camouflaged to resemble a rodentlike animal native to Kingdom. He keyed instructions into the minnie and reached through the crack to put it down next to the stack of crates. He watched for a few seconds as the recon robot scuttled along the base of the stack. If he hadn't known what it was, he would have thought it was a rat. Then he whispered, "Continue" into his helmet comm.

A few hundred meters farther, the tunnel was completely blocked by a rock fall. The fall wasn't recent. The Skinks probably didn't realize the tunnel existed. The recon team reversed direction. They stopped again for a few minutes at the crack to retrieve the minnie.

Brigadier Sturgeon allowed another day after the team led by 34th FIST's recon squad leader reported in, but none of the other teams reported finding a target. Orders went out for the other teams to come in, though the disguised UAV birds stayed out on their surveillance flights. By the end of the fourth day of intensive reconnaissance, all but two of the fourteen teams were back inside the defensive lines. Contact had yet to be established with one of those two, and the other had walked into an ambush on its way back and was wiped out. It was time to begin to strike back.

"We have no hard data—" Captain Landou, 34th FIST's psy/ops section commander began. He cleared his throat and began again. "We have no *specific* data on how the Skinks will react to an action taken against an area they must consider secure. Nonetheless, it's probable that they will react defensively to a strike against what is most likely a major supply depot. We know they have not gotten resupply or reinforcements since the *Grandar Bay* arrived in orbit. This means they necessarily have a finite store of supplies. If we can destroy a significant part of their supplies, it must have an effect on how they conduct operations in the future, an effect that likely will be of benefit to us. Psy/ops concurs in the recommendation for a strike."

He looked at the commanders and staff assembled in the MEF briefing room, but nobody had any questions; not that he'd expected any. They had heard the report on what Staff Sergeant Wu had found in the cave and intently studied the vid made by the minnie. They were itching to act. "Thank you, sir," Landou said to Brigadier Sturgeon when he finished his report and stepped away from the lectern.

"Three?" Sturgeon said.

Commander Usner, MEF operations officer, stepped up to the lectern. His face bore an expression that could be described as a grim grin.

"Sir, we believe we can conduct a successful raid on the supply depot discovered by Staff Sergeant Wu and his patrol. It will take a minimum of one infantry company and a sapper section." It only took two minutes for him to describe the raid Brigadier Sturgeon had already approved. He could tell by the way they listened that both FIST commanders and their respective infantry commanders wanted the mission— just as Sturgeon had predicted.

When he finished, Sturgeon took the lectern. The Marine Expeditionary Forces commander also looked grim, but his grimness bore resolution.

"Gentlemen," he said after looking at the assembled officers and senior noncommissioned officers, "we will call this 'Operation Doolittle' and do it. Jack, Commander Usner and his people will work with your staff to help them draw a plan for Doolittle. I want the plans on my desk at dawn. Ram, I'm sorry," he said to Colonel Ramadan, "but 34th FIST has been getting most of the action. I wouldn't want Jack to think I'm playing favorites.

"If there are no questions, that is all." He paused a second, then stepped from the lectern and marched from the briefing room.

"Attention!" Brigadier Sparen shouted, and everybody leaped to their feet.

"Commander," Sparen said to Usner as soon as Sturgeon was gone, "if I may see you for a moment?"

The others took that as their signal to leave, and returned to their duties.

The plan for Operation Doolittle that Brigadier Sturgeon approved first thing the next morning called for one infantry company, reinforced by one platoon and an assault platoon from another company, plus the sapper section from the FIST's engineer platoon.

CHAPTER
TEN

"Lord." The Over Master knelt on the matting and bowed his head to the floor before his commander. "I have troubling news." The Over Master quivered with fear in anticipation of the outburst he was sure would come. But to suffer the Great Master's anger now would be preferable to what would happen if the news were withheld.

"Our battle plan is proceeding according to plan, is it not?" the Great Master rumbled, his deep-throated tones cutting the Over Master like a whiplash.

"Operation Rippling Lava is most certainly proceeding as planned, Lord," the Over Master replied. "The news concerns the Earthmen pond scum by the great sea that we wiped out recently. Not all were eliminated in our attack. I seek your permission now to finish off the survivors."

"How did they survive?" the Great Master asked.

"We believe they were some distance apart from the main camp and were missed by the assault force, Lord."

"And who was in command?"

The Over Master named the Senior Master who had command of the attack on the City of God's encampment in the hills above the Sea of Gerizim. The Great Master wheezed angrily through his nearly atrophied gill slits. The Over Master cringed, anticipating an explosion. But the Great Master merely grunted. "Have him die, at once," was all he said.

"Yes, Lord, at once." It was apparent that the Great Master was in a good mood this morning. Were he not, he'd have ordered the deaths of all the officers involved in the City of God raid, not just the one in overall command.

"You will join me in a cup," the Great Master said, a certain sign that he was in a good mood and that the Over Master's life was safe—for the present. The Great Master signaled to one of the females stationed in the far reaches of the room. She shuffled to the Great Master's side, bearing a tray with a gracefully shaped ceramic pot and two delicate cups. After the preparatory ritual was completed, they sipped the steaming liquid gratefully, their lips making wet smacking noises; deep, satisfied, guttural sighs issuing from their throats.

The Great Master leaned back and stroked the pommel of his sword contentedly. "Of the ones who survived," he said, "do not worry about them for now. Operation Rippling Lava must proceed, and our entire effort shall be devoted to its success. We cannot afford to waste time and effort on these ridiculous barbarians. When we have destroyed the main body of Earthmen pond scum," he spit the word out like poison, "we shall deal with the others who remain. Those we do not kill we can use in our various enterprises. What of the prisoners?"

"They are being interrogated, Lord, but thus far our efforts have not been very successful. Most of them know nothing of value to us. But one whom we think does know important things, he is proving very resistant to our methods."

The Great Master indicated silence. "It is of no moment. Let the interrogations continue, if you want, but we know all we need to know to make Operation Rippling Lava a success." He signaled to one of the female attendants. "Lie with him," he commanded, pointing at the Over Master.

That unexpected reward was indeed a sign that the Great Master was in a particularly good mood and that his own courage in reporting the bad news had raised him slightly in his commander's estimation. One never knew with the Great Master which way his mood would fluctuate. Ahhh, the Over Master reflected as he let the female guide him to her mat in a dark corner of the room, things were going well, very well!

Traveling only by night in two landcars, it took Zechariah Brattle and his small party two days to reach the tenuous refuge of the caves they'd used on the way out. During the trip, as her father carefully guided the landcar using the on-board navigation system and infrared sensors, Comfort watched him closely. Her father had changed since they embarked on this foray. Always before he had been a serious man, not without a quiet sense of humor once you got to know him, but somewhat dour to the world at large. Now, especially since they found the landcar, the weapons, and the beer, he was different. Zechariah, whose every personal trait she thought she knew intimately, was now like a man who had suddenly found a new interest in life, something he'd been searching for unsuccessfully for years but never knew he wanted until it was unexpectedly presented to him. She realized it was the present emergency that had changed him. Her father was right. God often acted in very strange ways. She hadn't quite made up her mind yet, but she was beginning to think she liked the change in her father.

"Daughter," Zechariah began, but the bouncing of the car over the rough terrain made him pause briefly to concentrate on his driving. "Comfort," he tried again, "those folks from New Dedham sure came prepared." He slapped the hand-blaster that was now a permanent attachment. His teeth flashed redly in the dim glow of the vehicle's console as he grinned at his daughter.

"Father, have you ever killed anyone?"

"No. Not even in the wars, when I was mobilized. And I don't want to now, daughter. But there comes a time—you know this very well from your scriptures—when men must turn their hands to war. This is one of those times." He concentrated on his driving again, slowing the vehicle in order to take a forty-percent grade down a rock slope into a deep arroyo. It was nearing dawn and they were still a long way from the caves, so they would have to find a place to hide when the sun came up. They had used the very same spot on the way out.

The car following behind braked on the lip of the ravine, until Zechariah had successfully made his descent, then it came on cautiously. "I'm going into a slide!" Amen Judah shouted over the two-way communication console. "My brake proportioning system warning light is flashing! Get out of the way, we're coming down!"

"Hold on!" Zechariah advised Comfort as he gunned the engine and their car jumped forward, out of the way of the descending vehicle. Amen applied his brakes, but that just cut off the inertial braking system designed to negotiate steep grades without interference from the driver. When his vehicle hit the floor of the ravine, it bounced and rocked heavily before coming to a stop in a swirl of dust. "Are you all right?" Zechariah asked.

The other vehicle began moving toward them. "We're okay. A little shook up, Zach, but we're all right," Amen reported. "Sorry." He paused and then laughed. "The console was telling me, 'Check with your dealership's service department as soon as possible!' But the warning light's out now. I'll just be more careful taking grades."

Zechariah smiled. "Okay. I guess we'll have to check in at the nearest dealership." He laughed. "The Lord will provide." Switching off, he turned to Comfort and muttered, "I just wish the Lord would *provide* until He provides!"

"Father!" For her father to have said such a thing was tantamount to his taking the Lord's name in vain, which she had never heard him do.

"Daughter, even our Savior must have had to laugh once in a while during His time among us." Comfort stared at her father. She said nothing because she did not know how to respond to such a remark.

Zechariah maneuvered the vehicle up under a rocky overhang, brought it to a stop, and shut down its power plant. It was the same spot they'd camped in on the way out. They would be safe from surveillance during the day.

"Daughter, let us dine and then rest." Given the circumstances, the emergency stores they had found in the vehicle—concoctions they wouldn't have fed to their animals in ordinary times—seemed nourishing and very tasty.

They'd also discovered two Remchester 870 Police Model shot rifles, 1.27mm shoulder-fired weapons using shells 7.62 centimeters in length, each loaded with five tungsten-steel pellets weighing a total of approximately 7.76 grams. Each rifle had a tubular magazine fitted under the barrel that would hold three cartridges. One in the chamber gave the weapons a maximum load of four rounds. They were fed into the firing chamber by working a slide, forward from the open breach position, to seat a round; pull to the rear to extract the fired casing; and so on until all four rounds had been fired. They were designed for killing men at close quarters, precisely the type of weapon Zechariah had trained with in the militia.

The ballistics information printed on the ammunition boxes indicated the velocity of the tiny projectiles exceeded four hundred meters a second at one meter downrange; at ten meters downrange each pellet would strike its target with approximately seventy-two kilos of energy. Zechariah had seen what similar loads would do to a paper target, but he wondered what they would do to a man at ten meters—or one meter, for that matter. He shuddered. Well, he thought, Satan, get thee behind me 'cause you get in front and I'm going to put a hole in your ass big enough to drive this land-car through! Mentally, he slapped himself on the forehead. He was thinking like a soldier again!

It had been a while since he had fired one of these weapons, but Zechariah remembered that since the bores were open-cylinder, there were no chokes to constrict the shot patterns, so the loads would disperse 25mm for every meter fired down range. Zechariah considered this information carefully. "We can make some use of these," he said aloud as he carefully replaced the weapons in their compartments. He noted twenty fifty-round boxes stacked up in the compartments and gave a low whistle. Some of the boxes contained slugs. They would be devastating out to fifty meters, even without rifled barrels, which the Remchester 870s did not have; they were smoothbores.

After eating, they lay on pallets in the cargo compartment. None of the survivors had slept well over the last days, and Zechariah did not expect to sleep much now, but rest was still essential.

"Father, what are our chances of surviving?" Comfort asked as they lay there.

Zechariah did not respond immediately. "They are not good, Comfort. We are almost defenseless, even with the weapons we now have. And we are threatened by a vast and inimical force which you can be sure has advanced methods of destruction. Where it came from, what its intentions are, I do not know. Perhaps somewhere people are resisting. But we are too small in numbers and too weak to fight back."

"Shall we ever see home again?"

"Yes!" Zechariah answered immediately and with considerable feeling. "Yes, Comfort. As soon as we get back to the caves I'm going to load up everyone in these cars and we're going back to New Salem, to reclaim our homes."

Comfort smiled. Something else was new about her father. Before, he would often speak at public gatherings, but he was never the type of man who would step forward to lead. In fact he had always been a bit suspicious of men who volunteered to run things. But now he was talking as if he'd already made the decision to return home without consulting the others. And she knew they would follow him.

"Daughter!" Zechariah exclaimed, sitting up. "Let's go outside for a minute." He grabbed one of the rifles and some ammunition. "Get the others and have them join us outside, and bring the second rifle," he said over a shoulder as he slid the car's pneumatic door open and stepped out into the deep shadow of the overhang. The sun was well up above the horizon, but its rays had not yet reached down into the arroyo where the vehicles were parked. Still, it was light enough to see.

Then Amen and Hannah of the other vehicle joined Zechariah, expressions of alarm on their faces. "I want to have some target practice," he announced. "You never know

when these might come in handy. We found two of them."
He showed them the rifle. "Gather 'round."

Zechariah explained the nomenclature and operation of
the rifles to the others. He showed them how to inspect them
to make sure they were in working order, how to load them,
unload them, make them safe when loaded, how to adopt a
proper shooting stance, how to aim and fire and reload in
combat. He guided them through these exercises without
ammunition, to get them used to working the actions. Then
he set up targets, several empty drink containers, against the
opposite wall of the arroyo, about ten meters away from
where they stood. The more he made them practice, the
more his own training of many years before took over.

Finally, he loaded one of the guns with four rounds of live
ammunition. "I will demonstrate, and then I want each of
you to come up here and fire four rounds." He took up a
good shooting position, left foot slightly forward, knees
slightly bent, leaning into the gun from the waist, safety off,
trigger finger extended along the receiver until ready to
shoot. He placed the tip of the butt in the hollow of his right
shoulder and pulled it in tight. He put the bead of the front
sight on a bottle, and when the rear of the receiver inter-
sected the middle of the bead, he squeezed the trigger.

The rifle went off with a tremendous blast. Zechariah was
momentarily stunned. He'd forgotten how loud such
weapons were—and how heavy the recoil! The bottle was
still there! "Hit in front, Zach!" Hannah shouted. She was
enjoying this. They all were. He worked the action and fired
the second round. This time he was ready. The bottle flew
into the air, sieved with holes. He hit the other two in rapid
succession. "That's how it's done," he told the others, gently
rubbing his shoulder and smiling ruefully. "Comfort, you're
next."

They spent the next hour practicing. Then he showed
them again how to do combat reloads, holding the weapon
steady with the strong hand and loading the rounds into the
open breach over the top of the receiver with the weak hand.
He gave one rifle to Comfort and the other to Amen. "These

are yours now," he told them. "We three—and Hannah, if one of us goes down—must be alert always from now on, in case we have to use these."

"Will we have to?" Hannah Flood asked.

"We must be prepared to," Zechariah answered. "And if the devils come back, we must kill them. And now," he drew the hand-blaster, "we are all going to familiarize ourselves with this little baby."

The sun was just peeking over the wall of the arroyo when they finished. They retreated into the deep shadow of the overhang and rested.

"Zach," Amen said after taking a long drink, "how can these weapons be effective against devils?"

Zechariah paused before he spoke. "You know the devil never catches souls without the full cooperation of his victims. And he never appears in his true form because if he did, why, nobody'd have anything to do with him. So he works his evil through flesh and blood creatures. So whoever or whatever slaughtered our friends, they're mortal, and if we run up against them, we are going to do our level best to kill them before they kill us.

"Now," he got to his feet and stretched, "we've lost several hours' valuable rest. I'm going to retire, and when it's dark we'll rejoin our families. And then we are going home."

CHAPTER ELEVEN

So we are what are left of our once proud church, Zechariah thought as he surveyed the miserable group of refugees crouching and squatting in a rough semicircle about the fire. How doth the Lord chastise us. He looked into the faces. These were people he had known all his life—the Floods, Judahs, Sewalls, Dunmores, Maynards, Rowleys, and Stoughtons—all that was left of the City of God, forty pitiful survivors. The lineage of their church stretched back eight hundred years, and now they were all that was left.

But the people looked back at him with hope in their eyes. When Zechariah and Judah had driven up in the landcars a short while ago, they had gone wild, loudly praising the Lord like charismatics, dancing like savages, wild with happiness, wild with anticipation of news from the outside world, wild with joy that the party had made the trip and survived, and wild with the hope that some remnants of civilization and their old lives—the landcars—had survived.

When the travelers passed out the provisions they had brought with them, Zechariah could not stop the people from gorging themselves. They were all on the point of starvation, after all. Comfort looked at her father questioningly when he gave the order to share the provisions, but he just shook his head and passed them out into the eagerly waiting hands. He kept the beer hidden. The City of God was an abstentionist sect, but the people were desperate for any kind of nourishment and the effect of alcohol on empty stomachs would not have been a good thing.

"God bless you, Zechariah Brattle!" old Sam Sewall shouted, slurping the last sweet juices from the bottom of a can of fruit. Sam had turned 102 the previous fall and was the oldest member of the group. But he was spry and had his wits about him still. Zechariah smiled inwardly. Always, since before he himself had been born, Sam had been the picture of neatness in personal dress and of probity in conduct. He was a sharp businessman, and he and his wife Esther, only ninety-eight last spring, had run their hardware store to show a handsome profit every year for the seventy years Sam had been in business. So had his father before him. Now he squatted before the fire dressed in rags, his chin stained with fruit juice. He wiped it off with a forefinger and then licked the digit eagerly.

The others took up Sam's praises, and Zechariah was embarrassed. But there was no doubt about it: they looked to him for leadership. Whether he wanted it or not—and he did not!—he had become responsible for the people. Zechariah loved them, they were his community, his friends, and his own family. But watching Samuel, reduced to a crouching scarecrow savoring the dregs of a can of fruit, Zechariah realized they were all too human. Now he understood how the Children of Israel, wandering in the desert, could have been tempted into idolatry despite the leadership of Moses, who spoke directly with God.

Zechariah raised his arms for silence. "Thank you, friends, but I—that is, Amen, Hannah, Comfort, and I—did only what you would have done for us. And remember what the Lord said to Moses: 'Thou shalt take no gift: for the gift burdeneth the wise, and perverteth the words of the righteous.' And I'm no Moses," he said with a smile. Several people laughed. They were all feeling comfortable by then, their long hunger diminished.

"Friends, the news is terrible. So far as we know, we are the only survivors of our—" His voice cracked.

"There there." Judah stepped up and laid a comforting hand on Zechariah's shoulder.

He shook his head. No time for emotion now. "Friends, in short, the camp on the shores of Gerizim was wiped out and all who were left behind are slaughtered. I think we are the only ones to have escaped."

"Wh-Who did it?" Consort asked the question that was on all their minds. None would ever forget that terrible night on the road outside the camp at Gerizim.

Zechariah looked at Hannah and Judah. "We did not see them or their machines, and there was no trace of the killers. But the weapons of destruction they used were—were horrible beyond description. . . ."

"How did our brethren die?" Esau Stoughton asked.

"They—They were—it appeared to us that they were—*dissolved*, eaten up by some kind of acid," Amen Judah responded.

"It was the wrath of the Lord!" Abigail Judah shouted. "It was the vengeance of God upon the brethren who had sinned!"

"Possibly," Zechariah said. "But I think it more likely was the work of Satan's minions, the same minions who have been inflicting such punishment upon the Army of the Lord and the other sects, the same minions whom the Confederation Marines can't seem to beat. It was just our turn, is all. And they struck with terrible vengeance."

Mehetabel Stoughton began to weep loudly.

"Mehetabel! Everyone!" Zach shouted. "You know that nothing happens without the Lord's will! Mehetabel, Esau," he addressed the Stoughtons directly, "you live! Your sons and daughters live! I see them here—Shuah, Reuben, Tamar, Benjamin, Levi, Elon." The children looked up as Zechariah called their names. "Paul," he said, addressing Paul Rowley, who sat with his arm around Sharon, his wife, "I see you there with your daughters, Amana, Leah, Adah, and Timna. You live and your family lives!" Young Benjamin Stoughton, just turned twenty, felt a strange sensation of excitement and pride when Zechariah called out his name. He stood and remained standing. The other men and quite a few of the women experienced the same reaction as Zechariah addressed them. Even Mordecai Sewall, at age sixty, Samuel and Esther's oldest son, felt a quickening of his pulse, as he always did when the militia had been called out to muster.

Zechariah took in the others. "Our brothers and sisters are in heaven. There is no reason to mourn them. But we should rejoice because they live in glory and the Lord has spared us. Do you know what that *means*, to have been individually spared by the Lord?" Unconsciously he rested one hand on the sidearm at his waist as he strode into the firelight. In the semidarkness, his voice ringing off the cavern walls, Zechariah Brattle looked bigger than anyone remembered him, as if he had taken on a new form. He had, but it wasn't physical, despite the effect the firelight and the sound of his voice was having upon them.

"Friends, Christ started his mission with only twelve, we are forty." He paused and looked again into the faces. Zechariah Brattle had never spoken this way before. It was almost as if the spirit of honest old Reverend Bolton, dead in the attack on Gerizim, had entered into him and given him the power of speech to persuade. He was surprising himself, but he couldn't stop now. "Our survival means that the Lord has something in mind for us. We are going to reclaim our lands and refound our church and reestablish our lives." Zechariah did not know for sure if that was what the Lord really wanted them to do, but it would be a good start. He knew that if there was something else in store, the Lord would reveal it to them in His own good time.

Zechariah now had everyone's full attention. "Pack your things. As soon as it's dark, we're loading into the cars and we're going home."

"Amen!" Abraham Maynard shouted.

"Praise the Lord," ten-year-old Ruth Judah squeaked loudly.

"And pass the ammunition," Comfort whispered, grinning.

* * *

"Comfort and I will walk point; Judah, you bring up the rear. We can switch around. We have that duty because we have the firearms and can employ them immediately if we're attacked. Keep a round in the chamber at all times, safety on. Spencer," he turned to twenty-five-year-old Spencer Maynard, a mechanic, "you drive the lead car. Hanna, you drive just behind him. Keep them moving at a walking pace. If we're ambushed, drive straight off the road, into and through the enemy if you have to, at top speed, and keep moving until you're out of range. You older people—Samuel, Esther, Paul, Sharon—you ride in the passenger compartments— yes, Samuel, you ride inside, don't give me a hard time now."

"Damnit, Zech, you'd think I was an old sack of potatoes, the way you're treating me," Samuel Sewall fumed.

Esther jabbed her husband's ribs. "If he had to share your bed with you of a night as I do, Sam, he'd think you were an old sack of farts!" she cackled.

"Sit up front with me, Sam, you can ride shotgun," Spencer volunteered.

"Well, least there's *someone* in this crowd who respects this old 'sack of farts,' " Sam muttered.

"Children," Zech turned to the young ones, "you'll ride in the passenger compartments too. The rest of you, if there's room, ride inside or on the roofs or walk with Comfort, Judah, and me. The cars will be moving slowly enough that the ride shouldn't be too rough."

"How long will it take?" Nehemiah Sewall, Mordecai's thirty-year-old son, Samuel and Esther's grandson, asked.

"Three days? Maybe longer? We'll have to go slowly because most of the way it'll be cross-country and at night. Amana?" He turned to Amana Rowley, who was a surveyor.

She produced a hand-drawn map of the countryside between their hideout and New Salem. "Three days should do it. I'm pretty familiar with most of the territory between here and New Salem. There are secondary roads we can get on within thirty kilometers of home, and best of all, they run through dense woodland, so maybe we can travel undetected by day, at least part of the way."

"How about it, Zech?" Sharon Rowley asked. "Do the devils know we're here? Are they watching us?"

Zechariah shrugged. "Their technology must be far advanced from ours, so I would assume they can watch us, if they want to. But if they know where we are, then why haven't they finished us off?" He looked up at the ring of faces surrounding the map spread on the cave floor.

"The Lord protects us," Keren Sewall piped up. She was Mordecai and Jemimah's eleven-year-old.

"That's right, Keren," Zechariah said as he folded the map, "but still, we won't take any chances. All right, it's three hours to dark, so let's all try to catch some rest before we move out."

The found the Skinks on the morning of the third day.

At dawn the caravan entered the fringes of a deep forest. This place was familiar to all of them, since on the other side began the lands that had belonged to the residents of New Salem. But because the plants and tree trunks were so thick under the forest canopy, they had decided to park the landcars and complete the rest of the journey on foot. Everyone agreed to continue the trek during the daylight hours.

The forest was the habitat of wild cattle, the descendants of beasts brought originally from Earth by the first settlers. Long ago some of their ancestors had escaped into the forest and thrived there on the native vegetation, which was surprisingly compatible with their diet. But best of all, and this did not escape Zechariah, the animals would provide excellent cover if the devils were using infrared sensors or other devices to detect movement and life in the dense foliage.

The small group was spread out in a column about a hundred meters in length, the fastest walkers matching the pace of the slowest. Amen Judah was bringing up the rear, careful to prevent straggling. Comfort carefully made her way along on the point of the column, twenty-five meters ahead of her father, about the limit of visibility permitted in the dense undergrowth. It was her time of the month, and she felt very uncomfortable in that condition without aid of the necessary sanitary measures, but she forced herself to concentrate on guiding the column.

Zechariah walked ten meters ahead of the others. He was careful to keep his daughter in sight at all times, and Comfort alert to her surroundings. She stopped every few meters to consult her positioning system, a simple navigational device they'd removed from one of the cars. The point man was responsible for keeping the column on the right course, but in the dense undergrowth it was necessary to consult the device frequently.

Several times that morning she had signaled for a halt as she encountered small groups of wild cattle. The first time, she was startled half to death, but even then she had remembered to take the safety off her shot rifle, though keeping her finger away from the trigger until she was sure of her target. The crashing of the beasts through the foliage was clearly audible to the column behind her, and everyone instinctively went to ground until Zechariah gave them the all-clear signal.

Comfort sensed the Skinks before she actually saw them. As the foliage ahead gradually cleared, she signaled her father to halt the column. She crept forward to investigate. Ahead was a glade through which ran a stream. She was not familiar with that part of the forest and she knew that marshy spots abounded throughout the place, yet something was different about the spot, and she sensed it before she could actually see the stream. Checking the safety on her shot rifle, Comfort lay flat on her stomach and crawled slowly forward, cautiously parting the low-growing fronds and branches in front of her until she had a clear view of the stream. Dim sunlight penetrated the glade, but it was sufficient for her to see—nothing. Nothing out of the usual. And then something moved!

It stood on the bank of the stream. It was about the size of a small man, and at first Comfort thought that it *was* another person, and she almost called out to it. But when it turned its head at an angle where she could see its face, she gasped. The face was colored saffron and sharply convex. She could clearly see its pointed, canine teeth, and the sight sent a shudder down her spine. Its legs were bowed, as if from a life of carrying heavy loads. Along its sides there appeared to be scars or ridges like scars. Also running down the creature's side was a stripe, not a different color from the creature's skin but rather a variation in the skin pigmentation that was very noticeable. Beside it on the bank was a pile of equipment which apparently it had taken off temporarily, to relax. The thing stepped into the water and lay there half submerged with its back to her. Comfort's physical discomforts vanished immediately, replaced by the paralyzing knowledge of what the thing before her was. Her heart jumped into her throat. It pounded so loudly she was sure the monster could hear it. She struggled to overcome her fear and slow her racing heart. All her life she had been taught that evil could take a corporeal form, and there was no doubt in her mind that what lounged in the stream only a few meters in front of her nose was a demon.

Three others suddenly emerged from the water. They made squeaking noises as they half walked, half slithered, onto the bank and flopped down in the mud. Slowly, carefully, Comfort let her breath out. They did not know she was there! She offered a silent prayer, and it was answered: she knew what had to be done.

Very carefully, millimeter by millimeter, Comfort slithered backward until the stream bank was out of sight. Silently, holding her breath all the time, she got to her knees and, keeping as low a profile as she could, she crept back toward the column.

Zechariah's own heart skipped a beat when he saw the expression on his daughter's face. Cupping one hand over his ear, she whispered: "Devils! Straight ahead. Three of them."

Zechariah whispered, "Give me your rifle. Then go back

down the line and get Amen. Along the way tell the people
to lay flat on the ground. Not to make a sound. Thank God
we have no infants among us! Go! I'll cover the front."
Zechariah unholstered his hand-blaster and lay flat himself. If the devils came at them, he was ready to rain immediate fire upon them. Moments later Amen, face pale
with fright, joined him. The three huddled in a whispered
conference.

"We cannot go around without being discovered,"
Zechariah said. "We'll go forward to where we can observe
them, and pray they go away without looking back here. If
they do come this way, we'll have to kill them. We have the
advantage of surprise. Take some of this mud and rub it in
streaks over your faces. That'll break up the outline of your
face and make it harder for them to see you if they glance
your way. Comfort, lead us."

Hardly daring to breathe, the trio lay flat under the low-
lying foliage and peered at the devils, who still seemed to be
relaxing in the stream, their backs toward the people. Truly,
the devil's own minions frolicked in the water before them!
A slight breeze wafted in from somewhere. It felt refreshing,
blowing over the backs of the three prostrate people.

One of the devils stiffened suddenly, raising its head and
glancing about warily. It turned around and peered suspi-
ciously into the surrounding foliage. Comfort distinctly saw
its strikingly human eyes, which seemed to be looking directly at her. A nictating membrane closed over them, as if it
were *winking* at her! It gabbled something to its comrades,
who climbed quickly out of the water and began fumbling
with the equipment that lay on the bank. The first one
grabbed something that looked like a long hose and pointed
it in Comfort's direction, but nothing happened and it flicked
some switches.

"Fire!" Zechariah shouted, standing and leveling his
hand-blaster at the quartet. What happened over the next five
seconds seemed to take place in very slow motion. Comfort
squeezed the trigger of her shot rifle, but nothing happened.

She suffered a moment of terror before she remembered to take the safety off. Her father's pistol went *hiss-craack!* Zechariah noted with astonishment how the devil he'd hit with the bolt from his pistol had *vaporized* in a bright flash. And Amen's shot rifle steadily thundered *blam! blam! blam!* The hot casings from his gun flew directly onto the side of Zechariah's head, but he was too busy to notice. The four devils withered under the shots. Large pieces of their bodies splurted into the air as Amen's shot ripped into them.

Then, what was left of the devils bobbled obscenely in the stream. Slowly, the body parts began to drift away from the bank. Comfort let out her breath. She had not fired a shot.

"Father! You killed them!" someone shouted, and Samuel, who had come forward from the column against his mother's express orders, ran from his hiding place down to the stream bank. He looked back up at the three adults standing just inside the fringe of the forest and grinned. He picked up the nozzle device one of the devils had been trying to operate and held it over his head with both arms.

"Samuel! Get back up here! Now!" Zechariah bellowed.

A thin stream of greenish liquid suddenly spit out from behind the foliage on the opposite side of the stream and engulfed Samuel where he stood. He dropped the device he was holding and shrieked in fear and agony as the substance instantly began eating through the back of his head. He whirled around, arms flailing as he tried to wipe the stuff off his back and neck, but the flesh on his fingers began to dissolve. He collapsed, and as he fell facedown in the mud, his horrified father and sister could only watch as the acid ate through the flesh on his back, exposing his vertebrae and ribs.

Four more devils emerged from the forest and waded across the stream. They held the nozzlelike devices in front of them, spurting green streams of death before them. Comfort fired, and fired again and again and again. Each round hit its mark square in the center of the creatures' torsos. At such a short range the effect was terrific—the devils literally flew apart as each load of shot tore into them.

For a brief moment after the shooting stopped, the three stood transfixed on the small rise above the stream bank. Then Zechariah screamed and ran to his son. There was not much left of Samuel Brattle's upper body by the time his father reached him. Even his internal organs had been dissolved into a mass of semiliquid flesh, but his face had remained intact. Zechariah wept and screamed as he held what was left of the boy's face in his hands.

Comfort dropped her rifle and fell to her knees beside her father. She was so horrified by what lay on the ground that she could not find the breath to speak. Only Amen Judah, although shocked profoundly by what had happened, managed to keep his wits. He reloaded his rifle and scanned the forest. All was quiet. "Zach," he said at last, laying a hand on Zechariah's shoulder, "we must get out of here! Zach—*Zach!* We have to get moving!" But it was a dangerously long time before Zechariah Brattle was at last able to pull himself away from what was left of his son.

"Zechariah, the Lord will understand!" Consort Brattle said. Her eyes pleaded with her husband. They stood apart from the rest of the group, who watched them with concern as word of the fight and Samuel's death spread among them.

Zechariah's face was white under the mud streaks, and his cheeks were still tear-stained, but his expression resolute. "We are going to bury our son and give thanks to the Lord for our deliverance."

"But Father, shouldn't we get away from this—this—*terrible* place before we—" Comfort hesitated and then gave up. She looked down at the blanket that covered Samuel's pitiful remains, then turned her head away.

"Zechariah, the people will understand!" his wife said. "We've only just lost our only . . ." Her voice faltered and she could not continue.

Zechariah lay a comforting hand on his wife's shoulder.

"Connie, I am now the spiritual and temporal leader of these poor souls. All my life I have maintained steadfast faith in spite of adversity and told others that tragedy is all part of God's plan, which we must accept without question. I've always believed mankind should look within itself to find the source of God's displeasure. Now that it is I who suffer from deep personal tragedy, am I to run off into the woods in silence? And what of these others?" His arm swept the pitiful group standing some distance apart. "Every single person here lost someone they loved in the massacre. Well, now I can open my own heart to these folks. If I am going to preach—and I think God has given me that duty—I must also practice.

"Comfort, go get Amen. The two of you are excused for lookout duty. Take up positions back along the stream, watch for more of those things. You are right, daughter, we must make haste. As soon as we are done and have buried Samuel, we will move. We'll come back and get him later, after we've settled back into our old homes. And after we have defeated Satan."

"Zechariah," Consort whispered, "at least wash the dirt off your face. You look like a savage."

Zechariah regarded his wife silently for a moment. "No, Connie, I am going to preach as I am, straight from the field of battle. We are the new Children of Israel. We are at war, and our Lord is a Man of War."

Zechariah called the others around him in a tight little circle. "Friends, in a moment I am going to bury Samuel. With my own hands, over there." He pointed to a grove of trees a few meters from where they were standing. He would mark them and later come back to the place and retrieve his son's remains. "I must speak quickly. When I am done, we will move on. We're going on the same course we set for ourselves this morning, across that stream back there and home, to New Salem. You will see the battlefield where Samuel died, and we will take the weapons the devils left behind and use them."

Consort Brattle watched her husband as he spoke. His

beard had grown longer these past days, giving him a wild, prophetic aspect, and his clothes and hands and face were smeared with mud, but as he spoke and as she was carried away by the power of his words, she forgot about his wild appearance.

"A long time ago one of our forebears preached a sermon in the days immediately following the deaths of his loved ones. I want to remind you now of what he said on that occasion: we live in the midst of death. We die daily, but in dying, we draw out the bitterness of death itself. A good man is a strong man who has the strength of character and faith to find consolation in his adversity. But I confess to you now, friends, I wish and pray the Lord would take this cup from me! I do not know if I have the character of that good, strong man. My want of it is perhaps the bitterest dreg in this cup I have been given to drink from. All I can ask of you, dear friends, is that when you yourselves press after this strength of character, that you remember me, and pray for me, that I may share it with you and therewith find my consolation."

The people gazed upon Zechariah Brattle raptly and many wept. "Amen," Hannah Flood whispered.

"And now, friends, I have a mournful duty to perform, and when that is done, be prepared to march!" He drew his hand-blaster and held it above his head. "We are men of war now! And our Lord is a Man of War!"

Consort Brattle leaned on her daughter's shoulder and wept silently. She had never loved Zechariah more than she did at that moment. She was crushed by her son's death but exhilarated by her husband's courage.

And she was very frightened.

CHAPTER
TWELVE

Captain Enkhtuya, commander of Charlie Company, 26th FIST, thought again of how he'd had to reorganize his company. He didn't like it any more now than he liked it when he first got his orders. Two reinforced platoons, consisting of the smaller Marines in his force, would conduct the actual raid inside the cave while the rest of the reinforced company stayed outside for security. He believed that breaking the normal chains of command by shifting his men around according to size would reduce their combat effectiveness. Just as bad—if not worse—he had to stay outside the cave to command the defense. Recon said he was too big to easily fit through the cave. Who ever said being a Marine company commander was supposed to be easy?

He was also unhappy about having to break his company into platoons, each guided by one of the recon Marines who'd investigated the cave, and reinforced with an assault section, to infiltrate to the cave entrance. Together, his 170 Marines were a formidable force; broken into four scattered units, they wouldn't be able to support each other immediately if they ran into a Skink force. Sure, the smaller units were less likely to be spotted by the Skinks than the entire reinforced company if it was together, but he could lose too many Marines if a lone platoon ran into Skinks.

Still, he was a Marine. He had his orders and he'd carry them out. Nobody said he had to like them.

"Sir," Enkhtuya's comm man said, interrupting his disgruntled reverie.

"What?"

The comm man handed him the UPUD. The display clearly showed first platoon, which his command unit traveled with. It also showed the movement of bodies a hundred or more meters off to the platoon's right, headed in the direction of the Haven defenses. Whatever was moving over there didn't show in infrared. He looked in that direction but couldn't see anything; the platoon was in an area just heavily wooded enough that there were few sightlines a hundred meters long.

"Quietly, get down," Enkhtuya murmured into his all-hands circuit as he handed the UPUD back. "Movement right, one hundred."

Almost without a sound the Marines stopped and lowered themselves to the ground. Two men from each squad faced to the left instead of the right to guard against a surprise attack from that direction.

"How many?" Enkhtuya asked.

"Looks like about fifty," the radioman replied.

Fifty. Hardly more than the forty-plus Marines he had. He almost wanted the Skinks—it had to be Skinks—to change direction and come at him. His Marines could score an easy victory against them. But if the Skinks encountered the platoon, his position would be compromised, and that would endanger the entire mission. Enkhtuya gritted his teeth and willed the Skinks to stick to their route.

They kept going. He waited another ten minutes, then reported the movement to Battalion HQ and gave the order to resume the march.

Each of the four units had to stop at least once while Skinks passed by, heading in the direction of the Haven defenses, but all managed to avoid detection. They rendezvoused near the cave entrance.

Captain Enkhtuya lay in the muck on the opposite bank, observing the cave mouth. Next to him was Staff Sergeant Wu, who had guided his platoon.

"Doesn't look like anybody's been here," Wu said after

several minutes' observation. "Time for a closer look." He slithered away from the bank.

A safe distance back, Wu rose to a crouch and moved upstream until he could approach the streamlet out of sight of the cave mouth. Across it, he moved into the forest and zigzagged back, looking closely at the ground and low foliage and stopping frequently to listen. He reached the cave without seeing any sign of Skinks. He spoke into his helmet comm; none of the other recon Marines had seen sign either. Lance Corporal Sonj joined him, and the two entered the cave. Except for small animal tracks, the dirt on the cave's floor looked unchanged from the vid they'd taken when they left after their first patrol. They went fifty meters in before turning around and going back out.

Wu rejoined Enkhtuya and reported. "Looks clear, sir. You can send them in anytime."

"Right," Enkhtuya said, still looking at the cave mouth— it certainly looked big enough for him to get through.

The captain's feelings came through so clearly in his voice that Wu said, sympathetically, "I won't be going in, either, sir. It gets a lot smaller inside. There are spots that are just too tight for me to get through fast." Wu was taller than the captain, but Enkhtuya was wider. He knew the captain would find movment in the cave even more difficult than he had.

Enkhtuya grunted, then spoke briefly into his command circuit. In a moment his infra screen showed him the red splotches of the first of the eighty Marines who were going in. He clenched his jaw in anger and frustration, then forced himself to relax. He whispered, "Good hunting."

Lance Corporal Sonj, the smallest of the recon Marines, led the way. The cave had just as many twists and turns, rises and drops, as the previous time he'd been in it. But movement was faster because they didn't have to pause as often while men struggled with spots that were barely big enough for them to squeeze through. In good time he saw the faint glow of red light in the distance and stopped.

He leaned his head back so Lieutenant Eggers could touch helmets with him. "We're at the final checkpoint," he said when he felt contact.

Eggers, Charlie Company's executive officer, in command of the raid by virtue of being the smallest officer in the company, said, "Let's take a look," and signaled the sapper section chief, Staff Sergeant Larose, to come along. The three padded around the bend to the narrow crack in the wall. One at a time they looked through it. The cavern beyond was still filled with stacks of crates. They didn't see or hear anybody inside. Sonj and Eggers moved beyond the crack so Larose could examine the stone.

The sapper chief's examination only took a couple of minutes. "Better go back now," Larose said when he was satisfied that he could widen the crack without causing the tunnel to cave in. He stood flat against the wall and exhaled to make himself as thin as possible so the others could squeeze past. As soon as they were gone, he began pulling things out of pockets. In a minute he had several pieces of explosive tape strategically placed on the wall. He headed back to where the raiding party waited.

Larose leaned past Sonj to touch helmets with Eggers. "Ready anytime you are," he said.

"Do it."

"Aye aye."

A blast, not nearly as loud as Eggers and Sonj expected, rumbled along the tunnel, raising clouds of dust in its wake. Alarms echoed in the distance.

"Go, go, *go!*" Eggers shouted. He raced up the tunnel, pushing Sonj and Eggers ahead of him. Blind in the dust cloud except for the infra blotches of the two Marines ahead of him, he bounced off the sides of the narrow tunnel as he ran. He would have missed the entrance to the logistics chamber if Larose and Sonj hadn't stopped when they reached it and shoved the Marines behind them through the hole.

Only a few meters inside the chamber, the air cleared of the billowing dust and Eggers was able to see again. He raced to the far side of the vast chamber, looking around as he ran. It was exactly like the rodent's-eye vid he'd studied, save that some of the stacks of material might have been smaller. He could only guess at the distance, but the dim red lights strung out along the main tunnel's ceiling went straight for what looked like more than two hundred meters before turning. A lesser, unimproved tunnel without lights led from the chamber's opposite end. It didn't appear to run straight for any distance. The alarms were much louder inside the chamber, and they all seemed to come from the main tunnel.

On the far side, he stopped and looked back at the Marines who were still pouring through the break in the wall. He didn't have to give any instructions. They'd all studied the vid and rehearsed the raid—they knew where to go. One section from the assault platoon scaled the stacks on the near side of the chamber and set its guns to cover the main tunnel leading into the chamber. The other section did the same on the far side. The gun squads from the blaster platoons covered the lesser tunnel. The blastermen scattered to their assigned positions and started breaking crates open. Before the fighters were all at their assigned positions, the sappers were already placing charges.

New sounds intruded into Egger's consciousness: the whine of motors, the clank of treads, and shouted voices from down the main tunnel.

"Stand by for company, main tunnel," he said into his all-hands circuit.

Throughout the chamber, squad, fire team, and gun team leaders gave hurried last minute instructions to their men.

"Keep them busy, we need a few more minutes," Staff Sergeant Larose said into the command circuit.

In a moment the whining motors and clanking treads were closer, loud enough to drown out most of the shouting voices accompanying them.

"Vehicle coming," reported Ensign Qorn, the assault platoon commander.

"Can your guns hit it?" Eggers asked.

"Can do."

"Do it."

An instant later the chamber was filled with the booming, popping sizzles and brilliant lights of the three big assault guns. Two hundred fifty meters down the tunnel the plasma streams converged on an oncoming mover vehicle similar to the one the recon Marines had seen the supply workers use. If the Skinks who were visible on it flared, their flashes were lost in the incandescence of the blaster streams. The motor whine shrieked and stopped, and the vehicle yawed and swerved sharply. Chunks of white-hot metal broke off when it slammed into the wall. It crashed ponderously onto its side and lay half blocking the tunnel.

"Got it," the platoon sergeant laconically reported.

"Put intermittent bursts down there to discourage anybody else who wants to investigate," Eggers ordered.

"Roger."

The assault gunners began putting one-second bursts of plasma down the tunnel at irregular intervals. The sounds of motors, treads, and voices continued, but nothing more came around the bend. The surface of the rock wall at the bend began to glow, but the plasma bursts weren't sustained enough to make it slag and run.

"We're done in here," Staff Sergeant Larose reported. The sappers had placed half a dozen plasma bombs in strategic points around the chamber. When they went off, they would briefly fill the space with star-stuff, long enough to destroy most of the supplies, and damage what they didn't destroy. The bombs would also set off chemical explosives the sappers had set in weak spots in the walls in the expectation of bringing some of them down.

"Start pulling out," Eggers ordered. "Blastermen, bring your goodies."

The Marines began withdrawing. The dust was much thinner now. The blastermen of the two platoons left by squads, each Marine carrying something from the crate he'd been assigned to open. The assault platoon sergeant led one section into the escape tunnel, followed by the two gun squads with their lighter weapons.

"Set the timers," Eggers ordered.

"Aye aye," Larose replied, then relayed the order to his sappers. When the sappers reported themselves ready, he said to Eggers, "Fifteen minutes." There was little margin for error, but they were almost home free.

The sappers left. Eggers and one assault section remained, one squad keeping up intermittent fire down the main tunnel while the second rigged its big gun to fire automatically—they were leaving it behind to cover their withdrawal.

Suddenly, the chamber filled with the horrifying, ripping sound of a Skink buzz saw from the mouth of the lesser tunnel. The three Marines of the squad firing their gun simply dissolved in a mist of red. Their gun became a cone of debris scattering down the main tunnel; only the tripod mount remained intact.

Eggers drew his sidearm as he dove for the dubious shelter of a stack of crates. The gunner and assistant gunner of the assault squad rigging its gun made it to concealment before the buzz saw let out another *rip* that pulverized the squad leader and gun. Ensign Qorn and the third assault squad were already going out through the break in the chamber's wall when the buzz saw first fired.

"Back," Qorn shouted. "Set up!" The three Marines remounted their assault gun on its tripod, angled toward the lesser tunnel. Qorn bellied toward the edge of the stack he lay behind and peered around its corner. He immediately scuttled backward so fast he felt he must have set a new Human Space record for the reverse crawl—and he was none too fast. The entire corner of the stack he'd been behind went up in a cloud of dust, and the stack beyond it collapsed like a building at nuclear ground zero. He thought fast—he had to get his remaining gun in position to flame the Skinks he'd seen manning the buzz saw. There were four of them; he hadn't seen any others. But how could the gun get into position, aim, and fire before the Skinks spotted the Marines and killed them?

"Qorn, is that you?" Egger's voice came over his helmet comm on the all-hands circuit.

"It's me."

"You got the gun with you?"

"Third squad, yes."

"First squad, who's left?"

The second squad gunner and assistant gunner replied.

Eggers thought fast. He had himself and three other Marines left, aside from the one remaining assault squad— and only one of them was armed with a blaster. The other three carried hand-blasters.

The buzz saw *ripped*, and two more stacks were pulverized—the Skinks were firing randomly, hoping to hit hidden Marines.

"Qorn, how much time does your gun need to set up, acquire its target, and take it out?"

Qorn thought. This was a good assault squad and their gun was already set up. It only needed to be moved into position. "Six seconds from go," he said.

"How much of that exposed?"

"Three." The first three seconds would be movement under concealment.

The buzz saw *ripped* again, sending more stacks to oblivion.

"On my command," Eggers said, "Qorn and first squad, fire at the Skinks. Move fast, fire again, move, fire. Assault squad, while we're distracting them, you do your thing. Everybody understand?"

No sooner had the Marines acknowledged than the buzz saw *ripped* again.

"GO!"

A blaster and three hand-blasters fired almost as one. An instant later the buzz saw struck at the stack from which the first squad gunner had fired, but the gunner had already moved. The four Marines fired again from new positions as the buzz saw shifted its aim to Eggers's former position. The assault squad got its gun into position and was bringing it to bear on the buzz saw when the four Marines fired again. The buzz saw crew was shifting aim to one of those positions when its leader noticed the assault gun and screamed the command to fire at it. He was too late—a heavy stream of plasma engulfed the buzz saw and its crew before they could fire.

Another *rip* echoed through the chamber; a buzz saw firing from the main tunnel.

First squad's assistant gunner was the only Marine in position to quickly return fire. He twisted around on the top of his stack and rose up to sight down the tunnel. His bolt and the buzz saw's *rip* passed each other midway. But the Marine's aim was better—the Skink gunner flared, and the assistant gunner plummeted through the cloud of dust and debris that had been the stack he was on. That gave the assault squad just enough time to move its gun again and fire down the main tunnel. The buzz saw was out of action, and the Skinks moving up behind it were vaporized.

"Get that gun ready!" Eggers ordered.

Qorn set the remaining gun himself. It began to fire down the main tunnel on its own.

"Report!" Eggers commanded.

First squad's assistant gunner was dazed from his fall, but otherwise the remaining Marines were uninjured.

"Pull out, now!"

The Marines scrambled for their exit.

Lieutenant Eggers hesitated for a second, then raced to the lesser tunnel. There were no Skink bodies by the badly damaged buzz saw; he hadn't expected to find any, it was the weapon he was interested in. The buzz saw was too big for one man to carry through the tunnels to the outside, it would even slow down two men. The charred remnants of a bag lay on the tunnel floor next to the buzz saw. What appeared to be a spare barrel for the weapon lay in its ashes. Eggers grabbed it and raced to catch up with his Marines.

They had rounded three bends when the tunnel behind them lit up brilliantly and a wall of heat slammed into their backs. Seconds later the earth rumbled and shook. Rocks fell from the tunnel roof and sides. They ran faster.

Looks like you've got yourself a souvenir, Lieutenant," Captain Enkhtuya said when the raid commander finally exited the cave and joined the command group for a quick debriefing.

"Skipper?" Eggers hadn't brought out the spare barrel, or whatever it was, for himself. He intended to hand it over to the F-2 for analysis. If they could figure out what the weapon was, maybe they could develop a means of countering it.

"You aren't chameleoned anymore." Enkhtuya put a hand on Eggers's shoulder and turned him. The entire back of his uniform was blackened. "What the hell happened to you?"

Eggers twisted his neck and looked at his shoulder. "I guess I wasn't far enough away when the plasma bombs went off. Damn!" If the wave of heat that had hit him when the bombs went off was hot enough to destroy the chameleoning on his back and scorch the material, he was lucky he hadn't been badly burned by it.

Enkhtuya had his comm man raise the battalion and FIST intelligence officers, then listened while Eggers, Wu, and Qorn quickly described what they'd found in the chamber and what they did there. It was a short debriefing. More details had to wait until they were back inside the perimeter. So would mourning for the four Marines killed during those last, manic moments.

"Saddle up, we're moving out," Enkhtuya said into the all-hands circuit. This time they were moving as a reinforced company instead of individual platoons. He hoped they ran into Skinks again—if they did, they wouldn't have to hide; now that the mission was accomplished, they could fight.

The company pulled out in two columns, far enough apart that they wouldn't shoot each other if they ran into trouble, close enough to give mutual support if one had to fight.

*   *   *

Halfway back to the Marine lines, the point man on Charlie Company's left column froze, then slowly lowered himself to the ground.

"Movement ahead," he murmured into his helmet comm. "Coming fast."

Seconds later his squad leader eeled up alongside him. "What do you—" Sergeant Henry began, then changed to, "Great Buddha's balls!"

Skinks, seemingly hundreds of them, were racing through the wetlands toward the Marines across the entire front the Marines could see. Some were on line, others in line. More were in clumps. They weren't assaulting the Marine point, they weren't holding the nozzles of their acid guns in firing position.

"Charlie Six," Henry called over his helmet comm, "Charlie Two-one." He didn't wait for his call to be acknowledged. "The Skinks are withdrawing from Haven and we're in their path." He put his blaster into his shoulder and sighted on a Skink.

"Two-one," Captain Enkhtuya came back immediately, "are they going to pass us?"

"Not the ones right in front of us." He switched to the squad circuit. "First squad, get on line right now!"

"What's their disposition?" Enkhtuya asked.

"All the way across as far as I can see," Henry answered. "We've gotta fight." To both sides he sensed his squad getting into position.

"First squad, straight ahead, volley fire. FIRE!"

Ten blasters fired and seven Skinks flashed into vapor.

"Pick your targets!" Henry ordered, then flared a Skink that was almost on him. A wave of heat washed over him and dissipated. He looked past his sights, seeking another target. Gouts of flame and light danced over the marsh in front of him, Skinks flared by his squad. The Marines had flamed all of the Skinks to their immediate front. He looked to the sides. The Skinks continued the race toward their caves. None of them turned to fire at the Marines who'd just flared their mates. Henry heard loud Skink voices shouting commands—the leaders were urging their troops to continue past the Marines. He saw a shouting Skink and flamed him. The Skinks maintained their course.

Behind Henry the trailing platoons opened fire. As far as he could see to the left, Skinks flared. He looked to the right and saw even more Skinks flaring, caught in a crossfire between the two Marine columns. Then the Skinks were past and the Marines ceased fire.

Captain Enkhtuya agonized for a full seven seconds before deciding that it was more important to return to Haven with the objects they'd taken from the supply depot than to pursue the Skinks and risk running into an ambush or a heavily defended position.

CHAPTER THIRTEEN

Brigadier Sturgeon was silent as he rode through the half-destroyed city streets. Ambassador Jayben Spears, sitting at his side, was also pensive. Their driver was a soldier from an Army of God infantry outfit Sturgeon had borrowed for the occasion. He'd have preferred one of his own men, but due to the recent bombardments, the city streets were choked with rubble and roadblocks, and since this man was a native of the place, he knew how to find the right detours.

"Reminds me of old flat pictures I've seen of Berlin in 1945," Spears said at last. Even after four centuries, the destruction visited upon Nazi Germany during the Second World War was still an icon for the complete devastation of a society, instantly recognizable to all educated people.

"What was that, Jay?" Sturgeon asked.

"The Skinks have done a job on this place," the Confederation Ambassador to Kingdom said. They passed disconsolate citizens picking through the ruins, work crews busy removing the debris from the most recent bombardment, others trying to go about their business in horse-drawn vehicles. While the Skink weapons appeared to fire line-of-sight, the upper floors of all the higher buildings, minarets, and church steeples had been destroyed, as well as all the structures on the hills in and around the city.

Sturgeon shrugged. "My mind is elsewhere." He turned then to Spears and grinned. "We're going to kick some Skink ass, Jay."

"Is that what you're going to tell these bozos?" He nodded toward Mount Temple in the near distance, where the Convocation of Ecumenical Leaders was in session. They had been called before them that morning to deliver a situation report on Brigadier Sturgeon's plan to break the siege.

"Yes, but that's *all* I'm going to tell them."

"You're obligated to tell them *something*, Ted. Me too, if I knew *what*. We're obligated by agreement to treat the Convocation of Ecumenical Leaders with the same respect we'd treat the delegates of any other sovereign government."

"Jay, you know I don't take very well to fools," Sturgeon replied. "Too many times throughout my career I've had to kowtow to goddammed politician fools, and I'm getting tired of it. These religious 'leaders' are some of the worst of the lot. I'm going to talk to these idiots only because I *have* to, and it's going to be short and not too sweet, I can tell you that. You know how they rule this world, Jay. They're about as 'ecumenical' as Heinrich Himmler. That Collegium of theirs is worse than any secret police organization. Christ's bloody piles, Jay, this whole lot of goddammed whining pulpit thumpers disgusts me!"

Their driver, unused to such bold language, lost his concentration and the vehicle nearly rammed into the traffic ahead of it.

"Easy, lad, easy," Spears said to calm the enlisted man's nerves. He glanced nervously at Sturgeon.

"Wish to hell we could deal with this convocation bunch the way we did with those goddammed oligarchs," Sturgeon muttered.

Spears smiled. He remembered with deep personal satisfaction how Sturgeon had handled the oligarchs of Wanderjahr. Yes, the rulers of Kingdom deserved the same kind of treatment. But . . .

The driver pulled into the sally port at the base of Mount Temple, and the pair took the elevator to the council room just below the surface. Fortunately, the Skinks seemed unaware of the importance of Mount Temple. Once their weapons had destroyed all the structures on its surface, they had ceased firing on it except for random interdictory fires that proved more a nuisance than a threat.

All the leaders were assembled, along with aides and other staff. Dominic de Tomas, the Dean of the Collegium, sat by himself near the main entrance. The chairman, Ayatollah Jebel Shammar, nodded at the pair as they entered and gave Ambassador Spears a grimace that passed for a greeting.

"Watch out for him, Ted," Spears whispered to Sturgeon, nodding toward de Tomas.

Sturgeon glanced back in de Tomas's direction. "He's not my problem, Jay. But I'll squash him if he gets in the way."

"Gentlemen, let us come to order," Shammar intoned. Sturgeon and Spears took seats at one end of the conference table.

Sturgeon surveyed the convocation leaders. There was Cardinal Leemus O'Lanners, of the Fathers of Padua, leader of a radical Catholic sect that had established itself on Kingdom about a hundred years before. The sect was best known for its denial of the transubstantiation of the Host. Next to him sat the inimitable Bishop Ralphy Bruce Preachintent, head of the Apostolic Congregation of the Lord's Love and Devotion. Preachintent was best known for a stentorian voice that thundered fundamentalist texts having to do mostly with sin and hellfire.

Then there was the inscrutable Venerable Muong Bo, the chief Buddhist monk on Kingdom. He seldom said much in meetings; probably, Sturgeon thought, because the man actually might have a brain between his enormous ears. Next to him sat Swami Nirmal Bastar, leader of a large Hindu sect whose people still practiced suttee, for which they had been banished from the Indian subcontinent over three hundred years before.

The leaders present did not represent all the sects on Kingdom, only those with the largest membership. The other sects had little say in the governing of the planet and were kept in check mostly by the efforts of de Tomas and the Collegium. He was always present at the meetings, to accept and, seemingly, immediately carry out any assignments the leaders might give him.

Archbishop General Lambsblood sat by himself, a scowl on his face. He commanded the Army of God, and as such, technically outranked Sturgeon, who only commanded two FISTs of Confederation Marines. But when the Convocation had asked for the Confederation's help, it was agreed that the Marine commander would command all of the planet's military forces, and so Lambsblood now had no choice but to accept his subordinate status.

"General Sturgeon," Shammar began, but paused when Sturgeon stood.

"Your Holiness, I am a *brigadier* in the Confederation Marine Corps. The Marine Corps has various ranks of general, but I am a brigadier."

"Excuse me, Brigadier," Shammar apologized quickly. "Brigadier Sturgeon, we—our people, that is—have been fearfully injured by these invaders, and we are now under siege here in the capital city. Under siege in our own capital! Unthinkable! This situation has gone on for days now. When you came here with your forces, you promised to repel the invaders and save our people. But we are on the defensive now. General Lambsblood's forces have sustained heavy casualties. Your forces have sustained casualties. We demand to know how you plan to extricate us from this debacle."

"You must call for reinforcements!" Lambsblood blurted out from where he sat.

"Brothers! *It is the judgment of the Lord!*" Ralphy Bruce Preachintent shouted, rising. The other leaders grimaced and looked at the tabletop. "We have *sinned,* brothers, and the Lord has *allowed Satan* to invest us with *his minions*! I—"

"Brother Ralphy Bruce, *please*," Shammar pleaded. "Be seated. Brigadier Sturgeon must make his report. Brigadier, please take us into your council."

"Your Holiness, gentlemen, General Lambsblood," Sturgeon began, nodding at the assembled personages, deliberately leaving de Tomas out, "I don't need to tell you that the situation is very grave. Our casualties have been heavy, but so have the enemy's. I am going to break his encirclement of the capital and attack him where he is most vulnerable." He sat down.

Ayatollah Shammar gaped at Sturgeon. He remained silent, waiting for the brigadier to continue. When he showed no sign of doing so, he stuttered, "Ah, Brigadier, do you have, ah . . . any, uh, *details* of your plan to communicate to us?" He waved one hand vaguely as he spoke.

"No."

There was silence around the table. The leaders gaped at Sturgeon, not understanding what he meant. "You mean you do not as yet have a plan?" Cardinal O'Lanners asked in astonishment.

"Yes, Eminence, I have a plan," Sturgeon replied.

The leaders looked at one another. Swami Bastar cleared his throat nervously. "Well, share it with us, Brigadier."

"No, gentlemen, I cannot do that."

The leaders gasped and then they all began to talk at once. Finally, Shammar gestured them to silence. "Brigadier, as the representatives of the sovereign government of this world, we *demand* you take us into your confidence in this matter. What are we to tell our people?"

"You may tell your people that we shall defeat the invaders."

"But—But . . . *how*, Brigadier?" Bishop Ralphy Bruce asked.

"He neither knows nor cares!" Archbishop General Lambsblood shouted. "He has used my men as cannon fodder, sacrificing them to save the lives of his own precious Marines!"

"Lambsblood," Sturgeon replied mildly, deliberately ignoring his military rank, "it is *you* who've turned your men into cannon fodder. Before I got here the Skinks were slaughtering your men left and right. At least now they're fighting back, and once my Marines have had a chance to train them in *proper* small-unit tactics, they'll be able to take the initiative away from the enemy. Had you been left in charge here, you wouldn't have an army anymore. And all of you sitting here would be dead now."

Lambsblood was so angry he could only splutter as his face turned a beet red.

"And something else, while we're at it, General. The whole trouble with your army is that you're all so wrapped up in your religious orthodoxies you don't even trust your men at the squad level to have radios!" He leveled a forefinger at the unhappy Lambsblood. "That's criminal! I'll tell you this: that's going to change."

Lambsblood seemed on the verge of having a stroke.

"But—But General, er, I mean Brigadier," Cardinal O'Lanners sputtered, "have you asked the Confederation for reinforcements?"

"I have," Sturgeon answered, "but it's too soon to have received a reply. You all know how long it takes to get messages from here to Earth. We don't have time to wait for a response, much less heavy reinforcements. All I can really do is apprise headquarters of the situation. We are on our own here. So I am going to act on my own and hit the Skinks hard enough to break their hold on this planet."

"That's outrageous!" Bishop Ralphy Bruce shouted. "It'll mean the deaths of everyone!"

Brigadier Sturgeon smiled. "Sir, you are a minister of God. You believe in an omniscient, omnipresent, omnipotent, all-loving God, do you not? You believe in an afterlife, an especially nice one for those who believe as you do. So it strikes me as mighty inconsistent that you're so damned afraid of dying."

The meeting broke into pandemonium. Ambassador Spears thought it was time to intervene. "Gentlemen." He stood. "Brigadier Sturgeon, and he alone, is responsible for the defense of your community now. You have called him away from his duties. He has been kind enough to come here to address you, but he must return to his command post. You will have to accept his prerogative to keep his planning secret until he is ready to put it into operation. You requested the Confederation's help, and you have it. But you will follow our lead in all military matters, and that is it."

Spears sat down. The leaders stared at him with bulging eyes. After a moment Sturgeon spoke again.

"Your Holiness," he said, addressing Shammar directly. "First, before they are finalized, I never share my plans with anyone outside my chain of command. Second, there is the vital matter of security. I do not know what manner of intelligence the enemy might have, but I *do* know that when you men leave here to return to your, uh, respective congregations, you'll tell your closest associates and aides everything you've been told this morning. So I'm telling you nothing. Now, please excuse us; I must be getting back. General Lambsblood." He turned to the apoplectic figure who was still simmering. "Be in my command post in one hour. If you do not feel you can oblige, I will appoint someone else to command your army. If you or if anyone else," his glance took in all the leaders at the conference table, "oppose me in any way, I will take you into custody until my job here is finished." Sturgeon stood, gave the leaders a polite bow and, closely followed by Ambassador Spears, strode out of the room.

As the pair passed de Tomas, who had remained silent during the entire scene, de Tomas stood and bowed deeply at them, a lopsided sneer on his face. Sturgeon ignored him, but Spears could not suppress a grimace of disgust.

In the evening, secure in the fortress that was his headquarters, de Tomas played the recording he'd made of what Sturgeon and Spears had been saying, from the time they got into their car to the time they got out, back at Sturgeon's command post. " 'Christ's bleeding piles'." De Tomas laughed. That was a new one on him. He was beginning to like this Brigadier Sturgeon. They apparently thought alike when it came to the uselessness of religion in running a government. Then he smiled at the brigadier's threat to "squash" him. "No fear of that, my dear Marine commander," he said aloud. "I'll not get in your way. No, sir, my dear Confederation friends! You do your work and then I will do mine. My day is coming." He laughed with real pleasure, and with a flourish as if proposing a formal toast, finished the glass of Katzenwasser '36 he had been drinking.

Back in his billets, the young soldier who had driven Brigadier Sturgeon and Ambassador Spears to the Convocation earlier in the day reflected on the things the brigadier had said in the car along the way. ". . . these religious leaders are some of the worst of the lot," the Marine commander had said. The worst fools, is what he meant. He had never, *ever* heard *anyone* speak that way about the Convocation of Ecumenical Leaders! And he took the Lord's name in vain and was *not* struck by a bolt of lightning! Extraordinary! And he'd said the Collegium, the one institution everyone on Kingdom feared and respected, was "worse than any secret police organization." That's what the brigadier had said! And he'd called them all "whining pulpit thumpers." Those words had literally taken the young soldier's breath away.

These Marines were not like anyone else he'd ever met. They talked freely to everyone, showed no fear of being overheard, and made the most outrageous statements without the slightest fear of correction. And more than that, men only slightly higher in rank than himself were given the most important responsibilities and evidently left alone—*trusted*—by their leadership to carry them out. Such initiative was totally alien to his army, and he marveled that mere enlisted men in the Confederation Marine Corps could be trusted so explicitly. Taking responsibility seemed *natural* to them! And he had never received such good instruction as the Marines were giving the Kingdomite soldiers. Amazingly, it was evident his Marine teachers really wanted him and his fellow soldiers to act as they themselves did.

Deep down inside, beneath a lifetime's religious indoctrination and stringent orthodoxy, a small flicker of doubt burned within that young soldier's soul. He was beginning to like the Marines.

CHAPTER
FOURTEEN

The days following the attack on the Skink supply depot were filled with activity on all sides, but there was little contact between the Marines and the invaders. Most of the activity on the Confederation side wasn't conducted by the Marines, but by the scientists and technicians of Interstellar City and on board the *Grandar Bay*. The raiding party had brought back forty packages from the supply depot. Eleven of them were duplicates, which left twenty-nine different items to identify. The civilian and navy scientists and technicians on the ground and in orbit worked furiously to analyze them. The navy assembled a special engineering team to work on the spare barrel, or whatever it was, that Lieutenant Eggers had captured.

The Confederation forces were excited. The Skinks were decidedly not.

The Over Masters and more senior of the Senior Masters again assembled before the Great Master. No small tables were set between them. No diminutive females moved silently and gracefully among them to serve a steaming beverage. They carried no weapons, not even ceremonial swords. Facing the assembly, the Over Master responsible for defense of the entrances to the underground complex sat cross-legged in front of the Great Master. He was naked except for a loincloth, and a long knife lay on the bare floor in front of his ankles. His face bore no expression. A Large One faced him from a pace to his left and rear. The Large One held a sword, its blade gleaming sharply. The unsheathed sword that lay across the Great Master's crossed legs was a true weapon, not an emblem.

The Great Master glared at the Over Masters and more senior of the Senior Masters; he did not look at the loin-clothed Over Master before him. When he spoke, his raspy voice rumbled and crashed like an avalanche.

"The Earthman Marines attacked us underground!" he roared with the sound of a city toppling earthquake. "The Earthman Marines are not supposed to be able to reach us in our caves and tunnels. Our defenses are supposed to stop them if they attempt to enter our home. They found an entrance we did not know about and destroyed a logistics depot. This should not have happened! This is unacceptable! *This will not happen again!*"

He cast his glare upon the Over Master responsible for defense. Had his eyes been a weapon, they would have reduced that Over Master to his constituent atoms.

"Die," he rumbled, an earthquake's aftershock.

Still expressionless, the Over Master responsible for defense leaned forward, picked up the knife, held its point to the side of his belly, and drew it through the flesh, eviscerating himself.

The Large One a pace to his left and rear brought his sword up and swept it down, severing the Over Master's head from his shoulders. The head bounced off the chest of an Over Master in the front rank and thudded to the floor. Bright blood spurted from the Over Master's neck and splashed onto the nearest Over Masters. None of them flinched, none showed any expression.

"There are entrances to the caves we do not know about," the Great Master said, ignoring the corpse in front of him. "They will be found. They will be defended."

The Over Master newly appointed to command the defenses of the caves and tunnels was given as many Leaders and Fighters as he requested to prowl the land and find previously undetected entrances to the underground complex.

* * *

The cartons and sacks the raiding party brought back were broken open and inventoried. Samples of each item, along with samples of the packaging, were put in a drone and dispatched to Earth. The remainder were divided between the xenobiology team on the *Grandar Bay* and the scientists and techs of Interstellar City.

One carton held shirts, the right size for a young adolescent, but another held some that would have been too big even for the most overweight member of the Interstellar City staff. These were immediately identified. The xenobiologists used the measurements they'd taken of the recovered Skink lower body and determined that the large Skinks stood approximately 2.2 meters tall and massed close to two hundred kilos. Strips of fabric about thirty centimeters wide by two meters long puzzled everybody until an Interstellar City accountant who had once worked as a theatrical costumer wrapped it around his hips and discovered that they were the loincloths the Skinks were sometimes seen wearing. The hats were also obvious. The material closely resembled linen in weave, texture, and feel, but it was not from any plant the xenobiologists could identify.

A small case held ten objects about twenty-five centimeters in length and eight at their widest. At one end was an evident handle. The other was a more or less triangular, shallow-bowled blade. Molecular analysis determined that the components were exactly what they appeared to be; the handle was a flexible polymer of hitherto unknown composition, and the blade was a low grade steel. They decided the object was most likely a trowel for working dirt.

A senior medical corpsman on the *Grandar Bay*, whose hobby was the history of medicine, tentatively identified a carton of metal implements with finely serrated blades as surgical saws—they looked almost exactly like surgical saws he'd examined in a medical museum on Earth. He was more positive in his identification of a small carton of sealed gauze pads with straps extending from each end; he said they were field dressings, the kind of bandages soldiers had carried during the twentieth and twenty-first centuries.

Containers of two different kinds of tablets required further analysis, as did a bottle of a fluid that gave off an astringent aroma.

"Four fingers and an opposable thumb," observed an engineer who examined the contents of a package that contained twenty pairs of gloves made from an unidentified but tough fabric. "That must explain why everything is packaged in units of ten."

Another small carton held forty packets that contained rolls of thread and steel slivers with an eyehole at one end. It caused some puzzlement until a seaman who embroidered for a hobby identified them as implements used to repair torn garments—he called them "sewing kits."

The engineers were excited by a small carton of steel boxes, each of which held twenty short metal sticks with one end enlarged and rough-surfaced. They determined that the sticks were magnesium matches. The construction of the boxes was ingenious; to use them, one flipped up a guard plate on one side and pressed the lever protected by the guard plate. That expelled a match in such a manner that the roughened end scraped against a strike surface and ignited it. The match then continued out of the box and could travel more than a meter before its trajectory began to rapidly deteriorate.

"This must be how they ignite their dead," the Interstellar City chief engineer said. From a safe distance, he'd observed Skinks who were withdrawing from an assault on the Haven defenses setting their dead on fire. He'd wondered how they did it, as well as why. The magnesium matches brought him the how, not the why.

The xenobiology teams were ecstatic. Sixteen of the twenty-nine different items brought back by the raiders were clearly organic, all probably foodstuffs. They got the first clue from the fact that every one of the sixteen types of packages—whether of a clear polymer wrapping that was curiously both brittle and tough, or a metal canister—bore a label made of some paperlike material, each with a picture of something—presumably the contents—in a bowl. This picture label seemed redundant on the items packaged in the transparent polymer. The xenobiologists went to work with a will.

The dry, coppery-colored things sealed in clear polymer looked very much like fish. The different teams, in Interstellar City and aboard the *Grandar Bay,* each rehydrated one and dissected it. Fish analogs, they both determined, though their libraries held no match; the fish-things, they concluded, must be native to a planet outside the Confederation of Human Worlds.

A block of gritty white stuff easily gave up its identity. "Sodium chloride," a *Grandar Bay* tech reported.

"Yes?" Lieutenant Commander Fenischel gestured for him to go on.

"That's it, sir," the tech said. "Common table salt."

"Nothing else in it? No impurities?"

The tech shook his head. "Nope. Very well-refined."

Fenischel blinked. Animal life everywhere needed salt of some sort, but while sodium chloride *was* used by native life on some human-occupied worlds, it was not all that common. He dredged his memory and only came up with half a dozen other worlds where nearly pure sodium chloride was the salt essential to indigenous life.

"Get me a list of every planet where the animals use pure sodium chloride," he ordered. "Mass, diameter, orbit, mean temperature, solar type."

"Aye aye, sir." The tech headed for a library terminal to dig up the information.

Three different varieties of dried leaf, two green and one yellow, were sealed in polymer. They were tentatively classified as analogs of seaweed and leafy vegetables. The same wrapping was used on long, whitish strings that were multiply folded. The strings readily soaked up water and became soft and flexible. They resembled very long noodles.

Canisters in four sizes and two shapes caused a fair amount of controversy. Some xenobiologists and other scientists insisted they were clearly a mechanism for preserving food. Others insisted that, unlike the brittle but tough polymer wrappings, the canisters couldn't be opened by hand or even tooth, and therefore couldn't be used for food preservation because the average person couldn't open them to get at the contents. Their pictured labels, therefore, had to have a different meaning. A petty officer second class on the *Grandar Bay* settled matters when he did a search of the ship's library and found that for a few centuries very similar canisters were used on Earth for food preservation and storage. He even located illustrations of the once-common instruments that were used to open the canisters.

However, that did not explain why the smallest size canister had a lid that was held on by friction. The lid could be twisted off by anyone with a grip of even modest strength. Adding to the perplexity of this canister was the contents—dried leaf—sealed in the ubiquitous polymer.

One of the largest canisters contained what analysis insisted was animal protein packed in gravy.

"If I didn't know any better," Lieutenant Commander Fenischel muttered to himself, "I'd swear this was a cross between a chicken and something else."

Another of the largest canisters revealed tubular animals resembling the eels of Earth. They were packed in some sort of gelatin.

The middle-size canisters held five different types of what had to be animal products. These were impossible to identify except that they were all cut up, sliced or diced, and presumably skinned.

So, the items identified with a fair degree of certainty were foodstuffs. It still remained to identify the leaves in the small canisters with friction lids. Those were thought to be far too fibrous to be digestible. Certainly, humans would have had a problem with them.

One other presumed foodstuff created great excitement, though nobody had a clue to its meaning other than convergent evolution. A white sack, sewn closed, lined with a less brittle polymer, contained what appeared to be grain that looked exactly like rice. Every analytic test run on it led to the same conclusion: but the grain was a variant of rice unknown to the libraries of Intersteller City or the *Grandar Bay*.

"This goes way beyond convergent evolution," Lieutenant Commander Fenischel said in awed tones.

The xenobiology team's senior chief petty officer grinned. "Well, sir, I'll tell ya. There's been speculation for centuries that some Johnny Appleseed went through the universe a few billion years back, planting likely planets with the seeds of life. Then a few million years ago, that Johnny Appleseed or a different one came through again and planted sentient beings on some planets. Stands to reason if that's true, he had to bring the right kind of food for the sentient beings." The Chief Petty Officer beamed. He called the Johnny Appleseed theory "speculation," but he'd believed it since he was an adolescent. As far as he was concerned, this "rice" was proof positive. He'd read all the analyses. These foodstuffs were close enough to Earth norm, right down to the handedness of the amino acids, which he thought not only could a human eat with no ill effect, but thrive on. And he intended to prove that as soon as he could do some pilfering.

"So what does this prove?" Brigadier Sturgeon demanded when he was given the results concerning the items brought back from the raid. "We know the Skinks wear clothes, we've seen them. We already knew they have four fingers and opposable thumbs and that the big Skinks are a lot bigger than we are. We already know they eat food—they're animate, they have to."

"But, sir," Lieutenant Commander Fenischel, who gave the *Grandar Bay*'s report, said in a pained voice, "don't you find it meaningful that their packaging is centuries behind ours, or that they use primitive—" He searched for the term. "—sewing kits to repair their clothing, or primitive bandages to cover wounds?"

Sturgeon snorted. "At their height, the ancient Meso-

Americans were among the most technologically advanced people on Earth, but they never used the wheel or developed metalworking beyond gold ornaments. These creatures have weapons we haven't thought of, and a version of the Beam drive that makes ours look like an internal combustion engine. I need information that will help me keep my Marines alive and let them kill Skinks. What has engineering found out about that spare barrel that was brought back? That might help."

Fenischel looked crestfallen. "Engineering's still working on it, sir."

"When they find out something, I want to know immediately."

Scientists! Sturgeon could barely contain his irritation. Knowing what the enemy ate for dinner wouldn't help him keep his Marines alive or save Kingdom from the invaders.

CHAPTER
FIFTEEN

Jayben Spears was composing a message, perhaps the most important of his long career as a diplomat. He sat deep in thought, his head wreathed in the aromatic fumes of an Anniversario, a gift from Colonel Ramadan's private supply that the 34th FIST's acting commander had brought with him from Thorsfinni's World.

He drew deeply on the fine cigar, held the smoke deep inside his lungs, then let it out slowly. He sighed and closed his eyes in pleasure. The simple things in life are the best, he reflected. Not that savoring Anniversarios was something everyone could afford, but the cost of one was a small price to pay for the delight it gave to a smoker, which lingered long after the cigar had turned to ash.

The cigar was a reward of a kind, a sort of symbol that cemented the relationship between Jayben and the Marines. He had just returned from a briefing at Brigadier Sturgeon's command post, and the brigadier had taken the ambassador completely into his confidence by revealing to him his plan for lifting the siege of Haven. Sturgeon had done this because he knew he could trust Spears. They had been through a very hairy situation on Wanderjahr, and on that occasion Spears had proved to the Marine that he was a man who could be relied upon. Their relationship in the present crisis had only grown closer.

Sturgeon's plan was brilliant, but still, Spears was worried. An old veteran himself, Spears knew the best of plans could easily go awry. The brigadier had asked for massive reinforcements, but the situation was now so critical he could not wait for them, and besides, no response had yet been received from Fargo—nor would one come for a long time. Sturgeon's message to Corps headquarters had been blunt, but he did not know what effect it might have had on the staff back there. "General Aguinaldo will take it seriously, Jay," Sturgeon had said, "but I don't know if he can sell the commandant, and if he does, whether he'll be able to take it further up the chain of command. Anyway, I did what I could. Now it's up to him to do what he can, and it's up to me to make the best of the situation on the ground right here."

"God helps those who help themselves," Spears muttered, then smiled. "Always thought that expression a rationalization for the fact that God helps no one."

Sturgeon laughed. "As luck would have it, Providence was with us."

Now back in his office, Spears considered the day's events. Would the plan work? The worst-case scenario was that it wouldn't and the Skinks would overrun them. Spears did not think that would ever happen with Ted Sturgeon in charge, but he had an obligation as a diplomat to let his own superiors know the situation. If Kingdom went under, the rest of the Confederation must be warned. Jon Beerdmens, chief of the Confederation Diplomatic Corps, was Spears's direct superior, and Spears was obligated by the rules of diplomatic service protocol to address his comments to Beerdmens. But Beerdmens was an idiot! And worse, Spears knew everyone in the Diplomatic Corps considered him to be a superannuated fool given to breaking the rules and acting outrageously. Beerdmens would never pay serious attention to anything he sent him.

Well, I'm not gonna tell him anything about Sturgeon's battle plan, Spears thought, but I'll give the fat bastard both barrels, tell him if he doesn't go to the President it'll be his ass hung out to dry. A beautiful white ash had accumulated on the end of his cigar. He knocked it off and drew deeply on the Anniversario again, the tip glowing a satisfyingly bright orange. He winced. Damn! Thinking about Beerdmens was distracting him from the enjoyment of his cigar. Yes, he'd send the message, but he'd do something else too. The President had appointed him to the job, and although that was merely pro forma, she was the boss and he owed her a warning. He'd send her a separate communication, put fatso on report, because Spears knew that Beerdmens would never go to her based on anything he sent Beerdmens. That way, at least somebody with a brain would be on the case.

"Besides," Spears muttered aloud, "what the hell are they going to do to me? Send me to the Kingdom of Yahweh and His Saints and Their goddamn Apostles?"

Spears sent the message to Beerdmens and then waited a full forty-eight hours before he dispatched the private message to Madam Chang-Sturdevant.

Jon Beerdmens groaned with pleasure and daintily wiped his chin with a napkin. He raised the spoon again and slurped the glutinous concoction with a pleasure as vast as his bulk. All men have their vices, and Jon Beerdmens, Diplomatic Corps chief, had his: eating.

He closed his eyes and sighed deeply, savoring the rich flavor of the soup, crême of Greece, his favorite. When he was in town, which had become almost always, the cafeteria kept a vat of the stuff on the stove so that if he called for some, there'd be plenty of it, piping hot, just the way he liked it. These days he took his soup heavily seasoned with kymchiss, a condiment made from a fiercely aromatic garliclike herb cultivated on Soju. He'd only learned of kymchiss a few months ago when he was introduced to it at a diplomatic function. The stuff fouled the breath and burned like fire when evacuated from the system, but God, did it spice up the soup!

Beerdmens regarded the bowl: only half empty, or rather, half full. He chuckled. Beerdmens fancied himself an optimist. He resisted the strong urge to continue eating and dispose of the soup quickly so he could order another bowl.

There was work to be done. Besides, as he read the important dispatch on his screen, he could make the soup last another ten minutes.

"Excellency," the message began, "I regret to inform you that the news from Kingdom is very bad."

The security classification on the message was Cosmic, the highest degree used in the Diplomatic Corps. During the time he'd been chief, Beerdmens had received only one other such message, and that was to report the abduction of his Ambassador Plenipotentiary, J. Wellington-Humphreys, by the usurper, Marston St. Cyr, on Diamunde. Only Beerdmens and his deputy and heir apparent, who just happened to be J. Wellington-Humphreys, were cleared for Cosmic.

Beerdmens sighed and read on.

IN SHORT, WHAT WE ORIGINALLY THOUGHT WAS AN-
OTHER OF THE FREQUENT INTERNECINE CONFLICTS
AMONG THE VARIOUS RELIGIOUS FACTIONS ON THIS
WORLD IS IN FACT A FULL-SCALE INVASION OF THE
PLANET BY AN ALIEN FORCE KNOWN COLLOQUIALLY AS
"SKINKS." I HAVE LEARNED THAT THESE SAME BEINGS
WERE RESPONSIBLE FOR WIPING OUT A SCIENTIFIC EX-
PLORATORY COLONY ON A WORLD KNOWN AS SOCIETY
437. I HAVE ALSO LEARNED THAT SOME OF THE MARINES
CURRENTLY HERE ON KINGDOM ENCOUNTERED THESE
BEINGS ON SOCIETY 437 AND WIPED THEM OUT. I UN-
DERSTAND THIS IS PRIVILEGED INFORMATION. I CANNOT
REVEAL MY SOURCE, BUT IT IS TRUE.

Skinks, so that's what they're calling them, Beerdmens thought. He read on, his soup momentarily forgotten:

THE MILITARY SITUATION HERE IS CRITICAL. DESPITE
THE PRESENCE OF TWO FULL COMPLEMENTS OF FLEET
INITIAL STRIKE TEAMS, ONE OF WHICH IS THE 34TH—
WHICH YOU WILL REMEMBER FROM THE INCIDENT ON
WANDERJAHR—THE SKINKS HAVE MANAGED TO FORCE
THEM BACK UPON THE CAPITAL CITY, WHICH THEY HAVE

NOW COMPLETELY INVESTED. THE LOCAL FORCES HAVE TAKEN HEAVY CASUALTIES, AND THE MARINES HAVE SUFFERED GRIEVOUS LOSSES AS WELL. DESPITE VERY HEAVY LOSSES OF THEIR OWN, THE SKINK FORCES DO NOT APPEAR IN THE LEAST DIMINISHED. THE LOCAL CONFEDERATION COMMANDER, BRIGADIER THEODOSIUS STURGEON, A VERY CAPABLE PROFESSIONAL SOLDIER, IS CONFIDENT HE CAN BREAK THE SIEGE, BUT I FEAR THAT TIME IS NOT ON OUR SIDE. THE MORALE OF THE LOCAL POPULATION IS VERY LOW.

There followed a detailed summary of the military setbacks. "In conclusion, Excellency," Spears wrote, "I beg you to inform the President at once. I do not know if we can survive here, but I believe what we are experiencing is merely the opening battle of a full-scale attack these beings intend to launch on the human race. The member worlds of our Confederation must be alerted and we must bring all of our military strength to bear in a concerted effort to wipe out these Skinks and eliminate them as a threat to our existence. I must warn you: if my assumptions prove correct and action is not taken immediately, the repercussions are unthinkable."

"He's warning me?" Beerdmens exclaimed aloud. "*He's* warning *me*?" His chins jiggled with indignation. He pounded a hamlike fist on the desk. "Of all the impertinence! That dried-up, useless old fool! I swear, those goddamn Marines have done it again! Fucking jarheads! Fucking—Fucking—glorified bellhops!" he spluttered. He knew what had happened on Society 437. Some semisentient salamanders had risen up against the scientific colony. And now this fool was insisting they were a threat to the human race? Just like the Marines, exaggerating things to make themselves look good, only this time they'd gotten the ear of an ambassador. Spears was a gullible idiot whose brain had gone soft on Marines after the scuffle on Wanderjahr. "Unbelievable," Beerdmens muttered.

He considered sending the dispatch to Wellington-Humphreys, but decided against it. She'd also developed a fondness for the spacegoing bellhops after what had happened to her on Diamunde. He tapped some keys on his console and relegated the message to his private recycle bin. It was best he keep it to himself for the time being. Just think of the panic if that idiot's assumptions were to be made public!

Jon Beerdmens shook his head and lifted the spoon to his lips. Ugh! The soup had gone cold! Additional proof this Spears character was a goddamn jinx.

He ordered a fresh bowl from the cafeteria.

Cynthia Chang-Sturdevant's weakness was ice cream—old-fashioned, fattening, and sinful ice cream. She indulged herself as often as she could, her calendar and waistline permitting. The wonderful dish of delectable Jaskin-Hoggins Hanguk vanilla deluxe she'd just ordered from her servomech was going down very smoothly when her console bleeped that a classified high-priority message was waiting for her. She glanced briefly at the heading. It was Cosmic, and from an ambassador on—Martin H. Luther's proboscis!—Kingdom of Yahweh and His Saints and Their Apostles! She dropped her spoon.

For the next ten minutes Chang-Sturdevant read Spears's assessment, a growing sense of dark despair welling up inside her. "Madam President, on 12/26 Standard I sent this message to his Excellency Beerdmens at the Diplomatic Corps," Spears had concluded. "He does not know I am communicating my assessment directly to you, but I consider it my duty to do so now." She looked at the heading again. The message was dated 12/28 Standard. That meant Beerdmens had had the thing for forty-eight hours and no one over there had bothered to contact her yet? Of course, the Diplomatic Corps was not aware of the measures she had already taken to deal with the crisis. Telling them would be tantamount to issuing a press release. Evidently, word of General Aguinaldo's appointment hadn't reached Sturgeon yet. She wondered briefly what this brigadier had in mind to break the siege. No matter; they'd all find out soon enough.

"Give me Beerdmens's schedule," she asked her console. It popped onto the screen. "The fat bastard's been in town all week," she muttered. So there was no excuse for him not having informed her of his ambassador's concerns. "Okay, send this message to Jon Beerdmens, Chief of the Confederation Diplomatic Corps: 'Jon, get your ass . . .' No, 'Jon, I want you and J. Wellington-Humphreys in my office immediately.' Accentuate 'immediately.' " The message flashed simultaneously on her screen. "Okay, cc my chief-of-staff, add a note to cancel all my appointments for this afternoon, and send it."

She made a face. Those guys are right, she reflected, we are being invaded. Well, Diplomatic'll be here in a few minutes—they'd damn well better be here in a few minutes!—and J. Beerdmens will hike his blubber into retirement. She remembered Wellington-Humphreys well. She'd been through that awful ordeal on Diamunde, from which two enlisted Marines had rescued her. In fact they had been two of Sturgeon's own men! She'd make a good chief of the Diplomatic Corps.

The President of the Confederation of Worlds reached for her dish of ice cream. It had melted into a pool of white slop. "Beerdmens," she laughed out loud, "I'm gonna get you for this!"

CHAPTER
SIXTEEN

Marine Expeditionary Forces, Kingdom, wasn't idle during the time the xenobiolgists, scientists, and techs were examining the objects taken from the Skink supply depot. Somewhere in a remote hold of the CNSS *Grandar Bay* was a supply of equipment that had been superceded by the UPUD—motion detectors and aroma sniffers. Brigadier Sturgeon ordered them issued, two motion detectors and one sniffer to each blaster squad in the two FISTs, and the Marines spent many hours in refresher training in their use. The training was necessary, as few of the Marines had ever used motion detectors with earpieces. Sturgeon insisted on the earpieces—he didn't want to risk losing a man because the Marine was distracted by looking at a visual display on a handheld object.

On the third day, the Marines of 34th FIST took the fight to the Skinks. Blaster platoons, reinforced with two assault squads and an extra communications man, went into the swamps and marshes of the Skink stronghold.

Third platoon, Company L, moved in squad columns on line: first squad on the left; second squad, with Lance Corporal Schultz on point, on the right; the platoon's gun squad in the middle with the command element, where it could reinforce either flank that needed it. The two assault squads that reinforced the platoon, under the command of section leader Sergeant N'ton—a new man with the company—were inboard from the blaster squads, where they could fire to the front, rear, or over the blastermen on their flanks. The platoon also had an extra communications man who constantly monitored an all-hands radio. The platoon's objective was a densely wooded section of marsh to the northeast that was known to contain several cave mouths, some of which were submerged.

Third platoon had experience with submerged entrances to Skink caves. They'd found one on Society 437, entered it, and fought the Skinks inside the tunnel complex that it led to. The Skinks had fought to the death.

Flying animals, native avians, and game birds whose ancestors had been imported from Earth swooped from tree to tree, shrub to bush, cried out their territorial and mating songs. Escaped domestic ducks and geese dipped their heads into the shallow places to scoop food from the bottom. Smaller fliers buzzed and flitted about the ambulatory smorgasbord that moved through their territory, frustrated that they couldn't feast on it—earlier generations of their kind had learned how unpalatable the smorgasbord was, and the knowledge was passed down and spread. Fishy things and water-phase amphibioids scattered in flight from the unknown things that quietly trod their waters. Land-walking swamp dwellers sensed death coming their way and headed for distant parts. The scent of rotten vegetation wafted on the light breezes that moved over the sun-dappled water.

Ten kilometers into the wetlands, Lieutenant Rokmonov called a halt. He spoke into the all-hands circuit.

"We're less than half a klick from the nearest known entrances to the cave system. Squad leaders, show the maps." He paused a moment while the squad leaders transmitted their maps to the HUD displays in each Marine's helmet. The display was real-time, updated by the string-of-pearls. It showed the Marines as red dots in the lower left corner. The irregularly shaped black spots in the upper right quadrant that faded to spreading gray lines and blotches were known entrances and the caves they led to. Submerged cave mouths were circled in bright blue. The men of third platoon had studied the map before they left the perimeter, but

Rokmonov thought it was always a good idea to refresh the Marines' memory of the objective just before they reached it.

"We're going to be methodical about this," he continued. "This is the order in which we'll check out those entrances." He transmitted an overlay that numbered the black irregularities. "We have to assume the cave mouths are guarded. They probably have observation posts out, so squad leaders, make sure everyone with a motion detector or sniffer has it on and it's working." He paused again to give the squad leaders time to check the motion detectors and aroma sniffers. When they reported that the equipment was operating properly, he finished, "We will maintain formation until we are a hundred meters from the first cave mouth or until contact. Then we will move online. Move out."

Lance Corporal Schultz rejected the relatively minor distraction of a motion detector's earpiece, as everyone knew he would. He trusted his own eyes and ears more than any piece of equipment. Corporal Kerr didn't quite trust Corporal Doyle to use it properly, since he knew Doyle was too frightened, so he reluctantly tucked it inside his own shirt and ran the earpiece into his helmet.

Corporal Chan didn't think a sniffer attuned to a particular fish would be of much use in a marsh whose water teemed with fish, so he had no qualms about giving the sniffer to PFC Fisher, his least experienced man. And he got a minor kick from the irony of giving the fish-scent sniffer to a man named Fisher.

Corporal Claypoole had never had the chance to use a motion detector on a live operation, and he really wanted to use it himself. But he had extra responsibilities as fire team leader, so he gave it to MacIlargie, who eagerly plugged it in.

On the other flank, Corporal Dornhofer gave his fire team's motion detector to Lance Corporal Zumwald. He wanted to closely observe the less experienced of his two new men, PFC Gray. Corporal Pasquin had PFC Longfellow carry the sniffer; he felt a need to keep close watch on his new man, PFC Shoup. Corporal Dean was the most comfortable with the man he gave the motion detector to—Lance Corporal Godenov. Yes, Izzy *was* good enough; he knew that.

The marsh's water was surprisingly clear, and it flowed fast enough that little of the rotting vegetation in it had time to settle and completely decompose. About half of the marsh's surface was tussocks and hummocks that rose slightly above mean water level. Grasses grew on them, and reedlike grasses were thick around their edges. Saplings and midsize trees grew on the larger ones. A few trees with buttress roots didn't need the tussocks to stand on. Sight lines in the marsh seldom reached fifty meters. The water's depth ranged mostly from ankle to top-of-thigh. Occasional waterlogged logs and branches littered the bottom of the waterways, and here and there an unseen hole lay in wait to swallow a careless wader. So the Marines trod carefully, sliding their feet along the bottom muck, probing for things that could trip them, holes they could plunge into. The water clouded as they moved. Most of them were experienced and skilled enough that they moved carefully with little or no conscious thought. Those with less experience or skill paid extra attention to where their feet were going. So none of them fell for the three hundred meters that the motion detectors and sniffers were silent.

Schultz lowered himself to a squat in knee-deep water at the same time that Kerr and Godenov reported, "I have movement" and Fisher murmured, "The sniffer's got something." Something splashed out of sight to the platoon's right front.

The Fighters not guarding the entrances to the cave complex or searching for additional entrances were on observation patrol, screening cave entrances throughout the Skink area—all but a few who were sent to harass the Haven defenses. They had been patrolling without relief since late on the day of the raid on the supply depot. The Fighters on patrol didn't walk erect where a sharp-eyed Earthman might spot them; they half crawled, half swam, in the refreshing marsh waters, with only the upper halves of their heads above the surface. Their lungs were collapsed and they breathed through their gills. Leaders supervised the patrolling Fighters. The Masters paid scant attention to the patrolling Leaders and Fighters. They were too concerned with satisfying the Senior Masters, who were intent on obeying the Over Masters in their determination to satisfy the Great Master's command to locate any and all unknown entrances to the cave complex.

As a result, the Fighters, who were only able to grab odd moments of sleep and ate only the unwary local water dwellers they managed to snag on their patrols, were less than fully diligent in their execution. More than one broke surface in chase of a fish creature that leaped for a flying insectoid or to escape the hunting Skink. One did so some sixty meters ahead of Lance Corporal Schultz's advance. A nearby Leader, also fatigued and hungry, was infuriated by this breach of discipline and overreacted.

"Second squad," Rokmonov softly ordered on the all-hands circuit. "Echelon right, form on Schultz. Guns, put one gun on each flank of second squad. First squad, on line facing front, link with the gun on second squad's left flank. Get behind cover."

Before the Marines got into position, a shrill, barking voice shattered the marsh quiet from the direction of the splash. The Marines all instantly went for the nearest cover. For some that meant dropping into the water. They waited tensely, blasters ready, for the Skink assault they expected to come bursting at them through the marsh. The assault didn't come; instead, the shrill, barking voice continued its shouting.

Claypoole listened for a moment, then exclaimed on the squad circuit, "That's a sergeant chewing out his troops!"

"No shit, Claypoole," Sergeant Linsman snapped back. Humor was audible in his voice when he added, "Maybe you *can* learn to be a corporal."

Lieutenant Rokmonov had come to the same conclusion. Excited, he acted on it. "First squad, guns, head for that long dry place," he ordered. He slid his infra shield into place. It showed the two squads advancing toward an elongated islet about thirty meters ahead of them; they advanced more rapidly than they had before. As he followed he murmured additional orders: "First squad, up thirty, maintain visual contact with guns. Assault section, one squad trail second squad, the other squad trail first squad. Five is with you." "Five" was shorthand for Staff Sergeant Hyakowa, the platoon sergeant, whom the new order put in command of first squad and one assault squad. He heard but didn't pay attention to the assault section leader give movement orders to his squads.

The Marines advancing toward the angry voice didn't maintain their line. All of them were still watching their footing on the marsh bottom, and each went at the fastest speed he thought he could go without tripping or falling into a hole. Schultz was the first to reach the islet, Doyle was the last, even behind Rokmonov, who had a later start and farther to go. None of them tripped or fell.

Schultz's heart rat-a-tatted in his chest as he bellied his way up the side of the islet to where he could see across it through the trees and clumps of grass. An amazing sight met his fright-widened eyes and drove away his fear.

Two Skinks, one armed with an acid shooter, stood facing each other in water to their knees. One violently waved his arms about as he shouted in the face of the one with the acid shooter, his flying hands smacking the armed Skink repeatedly in the face and on the shoulders. Small spurts of water shot from the gill slits in his sides with each shout. The other cringed, but was silent and did nothing to ward off the blows. Water slowly dribbled from his gill slits. A quick scan showed Schultz ten more Skinks surrounding the two, at a safe distance from the striking hands. Those ten were mostly submerged. Some had only the tops of their heads exposed, others had heads and shoulders above water—those frequently ducked their heads and gulped water. None of the Skinks seemed to be paying attention to anything but the standing duo.

Rokmonov arrived and took in the scene. He used his UPUD to get a real-time download from the string-of-pearls. Its infra display clearly showed the two segments of third platoon. The two standing Skinks were barely visible as a faint pink spot; the others didn't show. No other red or pink was visible on the display. That could mean no more Skinks were in the immediate vicinity, or that the string-of-pearls simply didn't pick up infrared signals from any others. He placed more trust in the UPUD's motion detector function; its display didn't show any movement he couldn't see for himself.

"Does anybody have movement or scent from anywhere else?" the lieutenant asked on the all-hands circuit.

Nobody did.

"Second squad, guns, pick targets." He paused a moment while the squad leaders assigned fields of fire and the fire team leaders assigned individual targets to their men. "Fire!"

Nine blasters *sizzle-cracked* and the two guns buzzed their rapid-fire *sizzle-cracks,* and all the Skinks flashed into vapor.

"Be alert, everybody!" Rokmonov ordered. He heard the squad and fire team leaders giving the same command at the same instant he did.

The marsh was silent, the constant background of insectoid buzzing was gone. It seemed that even the breeze stopped ruffling through the leaves and grasses.

"Detectors, report," Rokmonov ordered as he studied the displays on his UPUD. He thought the foliage of the marsh would muffle the brief sounds of fire so it didn't carry far, but he knew that sometimes sounds in wooded areas can travel farther than expected. The Marines with the motion and scent detectors reported no suspicious movement or scents. The UPUD was equally negative. But that didn't necessarily mean anything. Hundreds of Skinks could be converging on third platoon beneath the surface of the water.

Rokmonov made a snap decision, one that should draw

any nearby Skinks. "Rat, secure an acid shooter to take back. Collect the rest of them and stack them by me."

"Aye aye," Sergeant Linsman replied. He rattled off orders to his squad. Second and third fire teams crossed the islet to the water where the Skinks had died, while first fire team stayed in position to cover them. The recovery took three minutes.

"Humpf," Claypoole snorted when he dropped an acid gun next to Linsman. "These things are heavy. How do those little bastards carry them?"

"You've got three of them hanging from your arms, Rock," Linsman said. "They carry one in a harness on their backs. That's easier."

Claypoole looked at the two acid shooters he still held and briefly considered trying one on, but the straps looked too short to fit him. He carried them to Rokmonov's position. One hanging from each hand was easier than hauling three had been. He added the two to the growing pile.

While second squad was gathering the acid shooters, Rokmonov studied the UPUD map display. He wasn't looking for any indication of Skinks, he was examining the terrain. The display, in the scale at which he had it set, was detailed enough to show individual trees. He looked up a few times to make visual comparisons between what he could see and what the display showed. He finished annotating the display seconds after the last acid shooter clunked onto the pile.

"Listen up," he said into the all-hands circuit. "We're going into the trees. Squad leaders, here are your positions." He transmitted the map, his annotations marking the trees he wanted the Marines to climb. Neither Rokmonov nor anyone else in the platoon knew if the Skinks would fail to spot Marines in trees, but from time immemorial, ambushers and snipers in trees had been very effective at surprising foes who weren't looking up—and none of the Marines had ever noticed the Skinks looking up into trees as they moved. The Skinks seemed to be oriented downward, toward the depths of caves and water.

The marked trees formed a narrow ellipse about fifty meters on its long axis, less than half that on its short; the nearest marked tree to the islet was thirty-five meters back. Two Marines were to mount each tree. Two trees, one along each long side, were marked for the guns. Two others, again one on each side, were marked for the assault guns.

After allowing a moment for the squad leaders to assign trees to their Marines, Rokmonov said, "Move out."

Claypoole smiled. Lieutenant Rokmonov was going to work out—this was exactly the kind of unorthodox tactic Gunny Bass would have come up with.

"Sir?" Sergeant N'ton, the assault section leader, said on the command circuit. "I can't get my guns up in the trees."

"Yes you can," Rokmonov replied, surprised by N'ton's statement. "Leave the mounts on the ground. The guns can go up." Assault guns in the trees was a trick he himself had used when he was a lance corporal. He was surprised that a section leader didn't know about it.

Minutes later the Marines were all in position. Placing the assault guns was the only tricky part of the deployment. The guns normally fired from tripod mounts; the technique for mounting them in trees was different. Also, an assault squad was three Marines—a gunner who fired it, an assistant gunner who helped the gunner and reloaded it, and a squad leader who spotted for the gun. The squads had to be divided. Rokmonov saw to the assault gun placement himself. He consoled himself with the thought that Sergeant N'ton was new to assault guns.

"Second assault squad," he said when he finally took his own position, "can you see the acid shooters?" The question wasn't necessary—he'd put it where it could see the weapons stack. Second assault squad was on the far side of the ellipse from the islet.

"Clearly, sir," came the response.

"Everybody, get a tree trunk between you and the acid shooters. Second assault squad, rain some fire on those shooters, let's see if they explode or just melt down." Rokmonov knew this wasn't a safe operation. But he wanted to attract Skinks, and he was certain this would bring them. The compressed air tanks might explode if they didn't melt down fast enough to let the compressed air leak out before the pressure ruptured weakened tanks. They might throw fragments a fair distance, which was why he had everybody behind tree trunks—it wasn't likely fragments would reach second assault squad. Exploding pressure tanks could throw acid from the acid tanks. The impregnated chameleons gave the Marines protection from the acid. So did the intervening trunks. Anyway, they were in combat, and combat was inherently unsafe.

The assault gun shrieked, and a line of plasma bolts so close together they looked like a solid stream of star fire angled at the pile of acid shooters fifty meters away. The webbing and nonmetallic supports of the harnesses vaporized almost instantly. An instant later three air tanks *poofed* open, heated and softened too quickly for the compressed air to burst them in an eruption of fragments. The weapons pile, no longer supported by harnesses, collapsed. Metal clanked on metal, breaking through soft spots in another three, *poofing* out more air, flowing acid. The compressed air in another tank burst it, and a ruptured acid tank spun upward, spewing deadly fluid in a gracefully widening spiral. The shock of the explosion weakened the remaining air tanks enough for the overheated gas in them to burst them apart. Metal fragments whizzed through the air, mowed down swaths of reeds, sliced small branches from trees, thunked into tree trunks, splatted into water. Broken acid tanks tumbled into the air, skittered and bounced through the islet's grasses, and threw greenish death into the air, onto the grasses, and into the water.

"Squad leaders, report," Rokmonov ordered. The squad leaders reported almost immediately: no casualties. He huffed out a held breath. His gamble had worked. He hadn't been positive that none of the Marines would be injured. Now to see if the trick paid off.

*   *   *

Five hundred meters away a Master spun toward the explosions that crackled over the marsh. The three Leaders he was supervising also turned and looked. He had been intent on finding other entrances to the cave system. Now he barked a command at the Leaders, who instantly dove underwater and began tearing their Fighters from their search mission. In moments thirty Fighters were arrayed before the Master. Their heads broke the surface only high enough for their ears to clear the water so they could hear the Master's words.

The Master growled commands and pointed toward the source of the explosions. Two Fighters submerged and began swimming in that direction. The Master growled more orders, then he and the three Leaders submerged and purged their lungs of air to free their gills to breathe.

The scene was replicated in two other locations in different directions at different distances. Three groups of Skinks began to converge on the islet on which third platoon had destroyed the weapons. The three groups didn't coordinate their movements. They couldn't. The Skinks didn't dare use radios for communication because of the danger of the Earthman string-of-pearls intercepting their signals and pinpointing their locations.

Guards in four aboveground cave mouths also heard the explosions. The guards had closed-circuit communications with their headquarters. They reported the explosions. Within minutes the Over Master in command of defense of the caves knew about the explosions. He hastily made plans that would send three thousand Fighters sweeping through the area in search of the Earthman Marines who had penetrated so close.

CHAPTER
SEVENTEEN

"I see them!" Lance Corporal Godenov exclaimed.

"Where?" Corporal Dean asked.

Sergeant Ratliff simultaneously wanted to know, "How many?"

"Two of them, approaching the east end of the islet. They're underwater."

"Everybody, look alive," Lieutenant Rokmonov said on the all-hands circuit. "Company's coming, they can be anywhere. Hold your fire, the first ones are probably scouts. We don't want to alert whoever's following them."

Ten meters up in his tree, Dean was surprised at how clearly he could see into the water. At the east end of the islet he saw what Godenov had spotted—two indistinct shapes under the surface of the marsh water. They could have been a couple of large pieces of flotsam, or tightly packed shoals of tiny fish. After several seconds of observation, he made out their kicking legs. Godenov must have seen that motion right away.

As he watched, the two Skinks reached the water on the far side of the islet, where the Skinks they ambushed had been. The scouts flitted about as though examining signs of the one-sided fight. He wondered if there was some taste of plasma or essence-of-Skink left behind in the water. More likely, he thought, they saw fragments of metal from the exploding tanks. Either that or second squad had disturbed the bottom when they retrieved the weapons. After a moment the Skinks swam to the islet and cautiously raised their heads. The tanks of acid guns were visible on their backs, the nozzles in their hands. They quickly scanned the burned surface of the islet and its shattered vegetation, then slid back into the water and swam back the way they'd come.

"More coming from the west," Corporal Dornhofer reported. I see three, underwater."

"Hold your fire," Rokmonov reminded the Marines.

Dornhofer was watching the new trio of Skinks repeat the activity pattern of the previous duo when Corporal Claypoole said, "They're behind us too. I've got two going around my island. I can see back about sixty meters and the water looks darker, like maybe Skinks are in it."

"Keep an eye on the dark area," Sergeant Linsman said. Seconds later he added, "I've got them. He had both his squad circuit and the command circuit open. "Buddha's balls, they're only a couple meters from the base of my tree!" The Marines waited tensely. The Skinks were well within the range of whatever sense they had that allowed them to detect chameleoned Marines, but the aliens passed by without noticing the Marines in the trees above them.

"Their detection sense, whatever it is," Linsman said, "doesn't seem to work between water and air!"

A minute later the three Skinks who came from the west were leaving. They reached the western end of the islet at the same time the two from the south rounded it. For a second it looked as though they were going to fight, but they recognized each other and stopped. One from each team stood and flushed water from his breathing organs. They spoke briefly, then the two scouting teams headed back where they came from.

Claypoole watched the two swim to the darker area of water, where one of them stood. A piece broke off the dark water and rose, becoming a Skink who faced the first one. Water cascaded down their sides. Claypoole couldn't hear any voices, but the two seemed to be talking. They looked exactly like an officer debriefing a scout. After a moment they submerged and blended into the dark patch of water. Claypoole reported what he saw.

"Movement to the east," Dean reported a few minutes later. "They're underwater, a lot of them. I'm counting."

"Hold your fire," Rokmonov murmured. "Remember, there are probably two more groups coming."

Dean watched as a moving darkness under the surface slowly resolved into saffron-colored individual Skinks. They split into two groups. The smaller group, about a dozen individuals, went behind the islet to the area where the Marines had killed the Skinks. The other group, about twice as large, swam to the near side. Dean reported the numbers and disposition.

The Skinks arrayed in what appeared to be defensive positions, except for two, who swam around in the killing zone, examining the bottom. First one of them, then two others, rose from the water. They stood for a moment with their chests heaving. Water cascaded down their sides from their gill slits. They climbed onto the islet. Two of them carried acid gun tanks on their backs, nozzles in their hands. The one who had examined the bottom wasn't armed, unless the pouch on his belt that resembled a holster carried a sidearm of some sort.

"I see them," Rokmonov said. Dean stopped reporting.

The unarmed Skink walked the width of the islet, eyes scanning the ground, while the other two guarded him. He kicked through the charred area where the pile of acid guns had been destroyed, bent down to pick up something, looked at it, flipped it away. He squatted on the near bank and brushed his fingers over a scrape mark left by a crawling Marine. He stood and paced the length of the islet, examining the ground. The marks were there, bent and crushed grass, flattened patches of mud, footprints. It looked to Dean as though the Skink saw every mark the Marines had left behind and understood their meaning. He returned to the center of the islet, where the guns had been destroyed, and peered at the burned ground for a moment. Then he barked something. The two guards rushed into the water, one on each side of the islet. Seconds later all of the Skinks broke surface far enough to expose their ears. The officer—or so he appeared to be—growled and barked at them. He swept his arm in an arc to the south, through the Marine position. The Skinks in the water bobbed their heads in a very human way. *I understand,* they seemed to signal. The officer thrust his hand to the south and gave a final bark. The Skinks submerged and fanned out in an east-west line. The officer re-entered the water.

There was sudden turbulence on the west end of the Skink line.

"I think Skinks are arriving from the west," Dornhofer reported.

"They're moving up," Claypoole reported; the dark water to the south was advancing and resolving into individuals.

"I see someone standing," Dornhofer said.

The officer who had examined the islet stood and waded toward the group that had just arrived from the west. He met an officer from that group.

"How many are there?" Rokmonov asked.

"I can't tell," Dornhofer said. "They're too far away. And some are in shadows. It's hard to make out anything."

"I'm counting," Claypoole said. "More than thirty. Damn, there must be at least forty."

One of the officers briefly ducked underwater. One of the Skinks detached and swam rapidly to the south. Claypoole watched as the messenger intercepted the southern group and gave hand signals to a Skink who wasn't carrying the tanks of an acid gun. That Skink gave a signal that had to mean *Wait in place*, then swam rapidly toward where the other officers were standing, deep in low conversation.

There were more than thirty Skinks in the water thirty-five meters north of the Marines in the trees. Forty or more were even closer to the south. An unknown number, but probably thirty or forty, were not far away to the west. Counting himself, Lieutenant Rokmonov had thirty-five Marines. So far the Skinks hadn't shown much individual initiative in firefights—their troops seemingly needed to be told what to do. And all the officers were together in one place. The Marines could take out the Skink officers and even the odds in a hurry. The big question was: How fast would the Skinks realize the Marines were in the trees and start shooting upward? Most of them were already in range of their acid guns.

The Skink command meeting was breaking up just as Rokmonov shouted, "FIRE!" into the all-hands circuit, and star-stuff lanced into the unsuspecting Skinks.

Third platoon's first gun team fired at the three officers. Two of them flared immediately and the third dove for safety. The assault gun continued firing short bursts into the area the Skinks were in. At the same time, one assault gun squad opened up on the Skinks to the north, its stream of plasma bolts sweeping from right to left along the line of Skinks. The water boiled and steam rose in the gun's wake. First squad also fired, each Marine picking targets ahead of the moving stream from the assault gun, trying to spot and flash Skinks who attempted to flee the gun's plasma.

On the south side of the Marine perimeter, third platoon's other gun and the other assault squad opened up on those Skinks, firing from each end to the middle. The water boiled more ferociously than it did to the north, steam rising thick as blinding fog. Unable to see, second squad held its fire.

"Cease fire! Cease fire!" Rokmonov shouted after less than half a minute. The squad leaders and fire and gun team leaders echoed the command.

The firing stopped. Overheated water still roiled to the north, west, and south of the Marines. Steam still rose. The ambient temperature felt like it had risen twenty degrees.

"Does anybody see anything?"

Mostly, the Marines saw trees emerging from the slowly dissipating steam. Not much of the water surface was visible.

"Squad leaders, report."

There were no Marine casualties. As far as they could tell, none of the Skinks had returned fire.

They listened. The water made noise as it bubbled and

gave off more steam, but all else was silent. Long minutes passed before they could see the surface of the water again. The Marines' fire had been accurate. Few plasma bolts had struck on the tussocks and hummocks that studded the marsh waters, and only a few faint lines of smoke dribbled upward from charred foliage. There was no sign of the Skinks.

Lieutenant Rokmonov reported quietly to Captain Conorado, who gave him revised orders. They agreed that the platoon had enjoyed incredible luck in launching two consecutive ambushes with such success. They couldn't count on it happening a third time. To the countrary, their next contact would likely cause casualties, maybe heavy casualties.

"Saddle up," Rokmonov said when he was through on the radio. "It's a pretty good guess they know we're here now." He suppressed a chuckle. "There's no chance we can reach any of those cave mouths. Here's our new route." He transmitted a fresh overlay to the squad leaders, who gave it to their Marines. The route led back to the Haven defenses but didn't simply backtrack ground they'd already covered. They formed up as before, but in reverse order. Lance Corporal Schultz always wanted the most dangerous position; this time he judged that to be the left rear of the platoon box.

Nobody was willing to argue with Schultz when he said where he wanted to be in a formation when the platoon was in the field against a live enemy.

The Master who dove to avoid the opening burst huddled in the undercut bank of a hummock, only his crown and eyes showing above the water, were hidden in the shadows behind a screen of drooping roots. Where had that helacious fire come from? If Earthmen Marines were on any of the islets he could see, he should be able to discern at least a few of the telltale hollows their invisible bodies made in the grass. They weren't in the water, he was sure of that—the sensors in his sides would have picked up some emanation from their bodies if they were anywhere in the restricted lines of sight along which they would have fired, were they in the water. Nor had he felt their presence when he was standing, conferring with the other Masters immediately before the Earthmen Marines opened fire.

The Master's astonishment was great when he saw the lower branches of trees on a few of the hummocks rustle and he heard the sounds of bodies thudding to the ground. Of course—they had been in the trees! No wonder he couldn't tell where they were! There was a time, centuries in the past, when the True People had put snipers in trees. In those days, well-placed snipers in trees could do great damage to superior forces and tie them down for considerable time, even long enough to mount a counterattack. The Master was surprised that the Earthmen Marines still used such a primitive tactic.

Primitive or not, the tactic had certainly been effective: Two Masters, nearly a dozen Leaders, and more than a hundred Fighters had died. He and five Fighters who huddled in the undercut with him were all that remained. Unless some Fighters from the other groups had managed to get out of the killing zone and fled. But the Fighters were bred to obey orders, to stand and fight, to never retreat. It was unlikely that any fled back to the caves.

What should he do now? If he went back, it could only be in disgrace. He had to go forward. But what could he and five Fighters do against a whole company of Earthmen Marines? It had to be a whole company. The fire that rained down had been too fierce, too intense, to have come from less than a company. He and five Fighters could die, and hope to take an equal number with them. But the Great Master must know that the Earthmen Marines were using primitive tactics. If he did not make that report, more of the Emperor's Fighters and Leaders and Masters of all ranks would needlessly die, and the entire mission to this world might be in jeopardy.

The Master dithered for a few moments, caught between imperatives. Then he decided, and gave a signal. The five

Fighters quelled their fear and swam after him. A strong reaction force must be on its way. He would follow the Earthmen Marines and send the Fighters back, one at a time, to guide the reaction force to where the Earthmen Marines were.

After trailing the Earthmen Marines for a few hundred meters, he was only able to locate one platoon from the company that made the attack. But he knew the rest of the company couldn't be far. He sent the first Fighter back to intercept the reaction force and lead them to this place, where they would be met by the next Fighter he sent back.

Reports from the eighteen platoons in the field flowed into the intelligence section of Marine Expeditionary Force, Kingdom. Brigadier Sturgeon waited for his staff to analyze and make sense of the reports. He couldn't mount a major offensive until he had hard data about the disposition of the Skink forces. He waited patiently.

Archbishop General Lambsblood, Supreme Commander of the Army of the Lord, also waited in the MEF headquarters. But he fumed at the inactivity and what he suspected was the sinfulness of the situation. First this . . . mere *brigadier* had come and wrested away command of the Army of the Lord—*his* army! Then this off-world infidel had placed his own officers in command of the units of his army—over officers far superior in rank. If that wasn't enough, this *brigadier* had then placed lowly *enlisted* men in command of the army's companies and platoons—even to the extent of *sub*-swords in command over acolytes! Now the Army of the Lord was relegated to a purely defensive posture while the infidel Confederation Marines conducted offensive operations against the off-world demon invaders. He wasn't even privy to what was happening in those offensive operations.

He needed to return the Army of the Lord to the field, to *crush* the demon invaders, Lambsblood told himself. Weeks ago Kingdom had needed the assistance of the infidel

Confederation Marines. But that was when the demon invaders attacked where they would with impunity and the Army of the Lord was reeling from their assaults. But the off-worlders had broken the back of the assault; it was now the demons who reeled. The Army of the Lord, Lambsblood was convinced, could now deal with the invaders unassisted.

If it was up to him, he would instruct that dithering idiot ambassador from the Confederation to order the infidel Marines to reembark on their ship and depart the holy precincts of the Kingdom of Yahweh and His Saints and Their Apostles. But those fools of the Convocation were still afraid, and suffered from internal turmoil. They insisted they had made the mistake of sending the off-worlders away once and would not make that mistake again—the Marines would remain to fight the demons to the end.

So Lambsblood waited and fumed.

The platoons of Marine Expeditionary Force, Kingdom, prowled through the two-thousand-square-kilometer area of swamps, marshes, and wetlands where the Skinks were thought to be concentrated. They sent in reports of contact and findings.

Second platoon, Company B, 26th FIST, managed to infiltrate past Skink security patrols and blow three cave entrances before withdrawing ahead of a counterattacking force. They suffered one acid casualty from the only security patrol they encountered during the withdrawal: the wounded Marine had failed to properly seal his chameleons. The Skink security patrol was wiped out.

First platoon, K Company, 34th FIST, reached a major entrance to the cave complex, where they caught security patrols returning to be relieved. They killed eighty Skinks and mined the cave entrance. They suffered one casualty: a Marine stepped on a loose rock and impaled himself on a broken sapling.

Third platoon, Mike Company, 34th FIST, attempted to assault and destroy a cave entrance, only to discover it was guarded by a Skink buzz saw. Three Marines were killed and two others suffered traumatic amputations before an assault gun killed the buzz saw. The cave entrance was successfully destroyed.

First platoon, Company C, 26th FIST, failed to reach the cave entrances that were its objectives. It encountered a presumed Skink reaction force and had to fight its way out. No Marine casualties.

Third platoon, Alfa Company, 26th FIST, intercepted a crew moving one of the buzz saws' bigger cousins, the things that took out aircraft and Dragons. They killed the crew and attempted to bring the weapon back. But the gun was too heavy for them to maneuver through the waterlogged landscape without a vehicle, and Brigadier Sturgeon didn't believe it was safe to send in a Dragon or Hopper to retrieve it. The platoon's attached assault gun squads destroyed it in place.

Many platoons found their objectives—entrances to the cave complex, all of which were guarded—and destroyed them. Other platoons met and fought Skink patrols or reaction forces. They killed the patrols and badly hurt the larger forces before withdrawing, while suffering few casualties of their own.

And third platoon, Company L, 34th FIST, was exfiltrating after having killed more than a hundred Skinks without suffering any casualties of its own.

CHAPTER
EIGHTEEN

The Great Master, clad in the combat armor he had worn in wars on Home when he still fought himself, sat on a commander's low throne in the meeting hall. A sword that had drawn blood in many battles during his long career in service to the Emperor lay across his thighs. His visage was grim as he stared out at the assembled Over Masters and more senior of the Senior Masters. The diminutive female who served him poured a steaming beverage into the delicate cup on the low table by his side, bowed low to touch her forehead to the matting by his feet, then gracefully rose and silently padded away, her eyes cast down on the matting.

Other diminutive females gracefully knelt in front of the low tables between pairs of the Over Masters and the more senior of the Senior Masters and delicately placed two empty cups and a pot of steaming beverage on each. They rose and padded silently away. The Over Masters and more senior of the Senior Masters were unarmed.

The Great Master spoke one word, an iceberg calving off a glacier: "Report." His armor, pressed against his sides, reduced and muffled the rasping through his atrophied gill slits.

The Over Master in command of defense of the caves stood and marched to a point directly in front of the Great Master, within reach of his commander's sword. He knelt and bowed his forehead to the matting.

"Speak," the Great Master commanded, another iceberg crash.

"Lord." The Over Master knelt back on his ankles. "The

search parties have found twenty-seven more cave entrances. Not all of them lead into the complex. The entrances that do not have been destroyed. Those that do are now guarded. The search continues for more."

The Great Master grunted, middle distance thunder, an acceptance of the report and a demand for more.

"Lord, the Earthmen Marines have made numerous probes of our positions. They destroyed a few entrances to the complex, but they failed to penetrate the interior."

The Great Master grunted, thunder less close, a question. He knew about the raids and probes. The purpose of this report was to instruct the assembled Over Masters and more senior of the Senior Masters.

"Lord, in all instances the Earthmen Marines were beaten off with losses. They had none of the worthless soldiers of this mudball with them, or their losses would have been severe. Those Earthmen Marines who have not yet left the area are being harried by our reaction forces and will soon be destroyed."

The Great Master splayed one hand on a thigh and leaned over it. "Have they discerned the pattern?" His voice was a millstone grinding his enemy's bones to flour.

"That is most improbable, Lord." The Over Master in command of the defenses bowed his chin to the matting, his eyes remaining fixed on the Great Master, a signal that his report was complete.

The Great Master sat erect and flicked his fingertips at the Over Master in command of the defenses, who stood and returned to his place.

The Great Master extended a hand and lifted the tiny, steaming cup. He slowly wafted it below his nose and inhaled deeply. A contented sigh rumbled from deep in his chest, a distant landslide.

The less senior of each pair of Over Masters and the more senior of the Senior Masters lifted the steaming pot on the table between them and poured beverage into first his senior's cup and then into his own. All lifted their cups to the Great Master.

The Great Master sipped, and beamed at the exquisite taste. The others followed suit.

"I believe," the Great Master rumbled, a thunderstorm almost upon them, "the Earthmen Marines will digest what they have learned from these probes and devise a plan of attack from them. We will array our forces so that no matter from where the Earthmen Marines attack, we can move to meet them with overwhelming force. The Earthmen Marines will at last meet their greatest defeat!" He tipped the cup to his lips and drained it.

The assembled Over Masters and more senior of the Senior Masters drained their cups as well, then held them up to the Great Master and roared their grateful acceptance of his glorious plan, which would lead them to their long desired and vengeful victory over the Earthmen Marines.

Third platoon had eight kilometers of marsh and other wetlands to slog through before reaching ground that stood above water level most of the time. Then another fifteen to the river, where commandeered civilian boats would meet them for transit back to Haven. The marsh, which was essentially a large, shallow lake studded with islands that took up about half its surface area, made for hard movement. But they were Marines; they never expected anything to be easy. "Join the Marines and see the universe" was one of many recruiting slogans. Most new Marines were shocked to discover the rest of the slogan was, "one step at a time."

Lieutenant Rokmonov didn't need to tell them Skinks might be after them. They knew if their positions were reversed they'd probably be going after the Skinks. Despite the one-sided fights they'd just had, they knew the Skinks were tough fighters, so they thought there was a very good chance they were being followed by a much larger force. As hard as the going was, they made very good time through the marsh—and managed to stay alert no matter how tiring the slogging was. And they knew that a small unit could move much faster than a larger unit. Fast moving and alert, they weren't terribly concerned about any pursuers catching them before they reached the boats and headed back to Haven.

Except for Lance Corporal Schultz. While he recognized that the thought might be nothing more than paranoid delusion, he harbored the suspicion that the Skinks could swim through the marsh faster than the Marines could wade through it.

The Master was becoming concerned. He only had one Fighter left to send back as a guide for the reaction force. It was a kilometer and a half since he last sent a Fighter back, and he hadn't yet detected the reaction force he was sure was behind him. He was certain a reaction force was on its way; one had to be.

He thought about the route the Earthmen Marines were following. It didn't go straight: it zigged and zagged at odd times and for varying distances. But when he straightened the route out in his mind and compared it to what he remembered of the map, which was a great deal—Masters were bred to remember such things—it was clear to him that the Earthmen Marines were headed toward a specific area at the edge of the marsh. There were many directions they could go from there, but the marks they left in their path would be clearer on dry land than in the water.

He instructed his remaining Fighter on what to tell the commander of the reaction force, then sent him back. Once the Fighter was gone, the Master stopped trailing the Earthmen Marines and headed straight for the section of marsh edge he thought his quarry was headed for. He found a hiding place and waited.

Most of the Marines of third platoon were relieved to step back onto dry ground. Even though they still had almost twice as far to go as they'd already traveled, their footing would be more secure—and the Skinks couldn't hide as effectively on land as they did in the water.

Lance Corporal Schultz wasn't relieved at leaving the

marsh. He was acutely aware of the fact that he'd been afraid ever since the day on the *Grandar Bay*, en route to Kingdom, when he realized the Skinks were waiting here. He'd been feeling more and more paranoid since operations began on the benighted world. So at first he wanted to attribute the unease he felt on reaching the end of the marsh to that paranoia, and he hesitated to say anything. But his combat sense finally overcame his uncertainty.

"Somebody's watching," he said on the squad circuit.

"Where?" Sergeant Linsman asked.

"Don't know. Close."

"Is it an ambush?"

"Don't think so. Scout, maybe."

Linsman relayed Schultz's suspicion to Lieutenant Rokmonov. Though Rokmonov had been with Company L for long enough to know Schultz's reputation and to trust his observations in the field, he hadn't worked with him enough to consider him nearly infallible when he said the platoon was under observation.

"Keep alert," Rokmonov ordered. "Third platoon, step it out." The Marines increased their speed.

Schultz walked backward, turning his head to the front only often enough to maintain contact with Corporal Kerr and to make sure he wasn't backing into a major obstacle. Kerr spent half of his time walking backward as well. Schultz was glad Kerr was with him. Kerr was a sound Marine—and he had a motion detector.

The Master watched as water slid down from nowhere along the edge of the marsh. His skin crawled at the eerie sight, and his genitals wanted to crawl inside his body, but he knew what it had to be—water running off the legs of the invisible Earthmen Marines. His heart jumped when he saw something in his peripheral vision—it looked like a leg. But when he looked straight at it, all he saw was water slowly dripping through the air. Puzzled, he let his eyes go out of focus and flicked them from side to side.

There! The invisible Earthmen Marines *could* be seen!

Don't look directly at them, but to the side; don't try to focus. They were indistinct, but their shapes could be discerned. No matter what else happened, this information had to get back to the Great Master. He almost left right then, but he remembered, *this* Earthmen Marine platoon and the rest of the company it was joining had to be destroyed. He watched as they melted into the forest.

Before he climbed onto the shore, the Master waited only until he was sure they had actually moved on and didn't simply move into an ambush position. He went along it for a distance and placed a series of markers, then trailed after the Earthmen Marines. That many were easy to follow; a footprint here, a snapped twig there, a random noise up ahead. He left deliberate markers of his own for the reaction force to follow. It was nearly inconceivable that the Fighters he'd sent back had failed to intercept a reaction force and lead it to him.

Schultz faced front and in a few rapid steps reached Kerr. He touched helmets with his fire team leader.

"We're being followed," he said. Conduction carried the words from his helmet to Kerr's. No one else could hear them.

"How many?" Kerr asked. He kept walking. Schultz faced backward and kept pace with him.

"Don't know. One. Maybe two."

"Scouts."

"Yes," Schultz agreed.

Kerr looked to Corporal Doyle. He didn't believe Doyle ever looked back to make sure he, Kerr, was still in contact. That was an infantry skill he'd probably never developed. He grimaced. He was going to have to teach Doyle how to function in a rear point under the worst possible conditions—on a live operation. But not at that moment.

"Let's get him," Kerr said.

Schultz grunted. That's what he wanted to do. Kerr looked for a place they could safely lay in wait. Schultz spotted one first, a screen of bushes that grew along the side of a ripple in the ground. In the ripple, behind the bushes, even if the Skinks had infrared vision, the follower or followers probably wouldn't spot them. Careful to leave no sign that they broke off from the body of the platoon, Kerr and Schultz made their way behind the brush in the ripple.

Little more than a minute later the Skink crossed their front about forty meters away. He rushed from tree to tree, cautiously using every bit of cover and concealment available. His skill and furtive movement hid him from the front, which was why they hadn't seen him earlier, but not from the side. The Skink wasn't carrying the tanks of an acid gun on his back. Kerr and Schultz glanced toward each other, their eyes glittering unseen behind their chameleon shields. Did that mean he was an officer? He wasn't carrying a sword, so maybe he was the Skink equivalent of Marine recon. If so, where there was one, there were more. They waited and watched. After two more minutes, they didn't see any other Skinks, nor did Kerr's motion detector pick up anyone else.

Kerr touched helmets with Schultz. "Let's get him," he said again.

They got to their feet and chased after the Skink. The Marines' use of cover and concealment was every bit as good as the Skink's, maybe better. The sensors on his sides didn't detect them until they were twenty meters away.

The Skink spun around. They weren't as close as they wanted to be, but Kerr and Schultz put on an extra burst of speed. Had he been human, the expression on the Skink's face would have shown shock mingled with fear. He groped at the pouch on his belt, but Schultz crashed into him before he could bring the weapon to bear and it spun out of his hand. The Skink thudded to the ground, and Schultz landed on him heavily and knocked out all his breath. With his lungs half collapsed, the Skink's gill slits opened and his gills fluttered in a vain attempt to extract oxygen from the air. By the time he was able to gasp air, his arms were firmly trussed behind his back and a line ran from his wrists to a loop around his neck. If he attempted to reach out with his head to bite, the loop would tighten and cut off his air.

Schultz retrieved the weapon the Skink dropped when he hit him, examined it, and handed it to Kerr. "Projectile," he said.

Kerr looked at it and blinked. The weapon looked exactly like images he'd seen of centuries-old slug-throwing automatic pistols. "I guess if you've got a five-fingered hand with an opposable thumb, there are only so many ways you can design a handgun," he said.

Schultz made no reply, not even a grunt. That was obvious to him.

Kerr toggled the command circuit on his helmet comm. "This is Two-one. We've got a prisoner," he reported.

"What?" Linsman asked, astonished.

"Hammer said we were being followed. We dropped back and got a prisoner."

"Third platoon, hold up, defense to the rear," Rokmonov ordered into the all-hands circuit. "Two-one, how many are there?"

"Only the one, Six."

"Get the prisoner to my location."

Rokmonov was standing under a tree when Kerr and Schultz arrived with the Skink. He had his shields up and an arm exposed to make it easier for them to locate him. The two raised their shields as well.

Rokmonov stared at the Skink for a long moment. The Skink stood with its eyes cast down. As far as the lieutenant knew, this was the first time anyone had seen a Skink so close without being in hand-to-hand combat with it. This had to be an astonishing example of convergent evolution. The Skink's face was sharply convex, but he'd seen a human or two with faces just as curved. There was something odd about the shape of the outer corner of the Skink's eyes, but otherwise its eyes looked uncannily human. Aside from the legs being bowed, the rest of its body was so close to the human norm that it didn't matter. Given its small stature, from a modest distance, dressed right, it could easily have passed for a half-grown human adolescent. Rokmonov shivered. A bunch of these things disguised as children could penetrate deeply into defenses and cause a lot of damage, kill a lot of Marines and civilians.

"Do you understand English?" Rokmonov asked, then corrected himself. "Do you speak a human tongue?"

The Skink made no reply.

"Look at me when I'm talking to you."

The Skink kept its gaze down.

"The xenobiology boys are going to have a ball when we get back with this. What do you think he was doing?"

"Probably scouting for a reaction force," Kerr said.

Schultz nodded.

"But they aren't right behind us?"

Schultz shook his head.

"Then let's stay ahead of them." He signaled to the assault gun section leader. "Sergeant N'ton, take the prisoner." Into the all-hands circuit: "Third platoon, move out."

Third platoon resumed its movement; only five kilometers to go.

"The next time you two birds pull a stunt like that without telling me," Linsman snarled when he reached them, "the Top gets whatever's left of your asses when I'm through with you. You did good, but if you'd been wrong about there only being one scout, you probably would have been killed, and you would have put the rest of the platoon in jeopardy. Close it up," he added to Corporal Claypoole. "I'm changing position so I can keep an eye on these two."

"Aye aye." Claypoole and MacIlargie hurried to close the gap between them and second fire team. Linsman fell in behind them. He walked backward to make sure Kerr and Schultz resumed their positions in the formation.

Less than a kilometer behind, a reaction force two hundred strong was closing the gap. Normally, the Leader commanding the reaction force would not move so rapidly through enemy territory, but he had scouts well out to the front and both flanks, so he was sure he would not blunder into an ambush. The Fighters and the Leaders who were junior to him in the force were the largest command he'd ever had—and he wouldn't have it if the Master who had commanded hadn't tripped and torn up a knee when he decided to cross an islet instead of swimming around it. He intended to make the most of the opportunity. He would, of course, have to give up command to the Master he was trailing when they reached him, but simply bringing the force up so expeditiously would gain him recognition, perhaps sufficient recognition to gain the promotion to Master that he so eagerly wanted.

In a low growl, he urged his Fighters, "Faster."

Several hundred paces later a forward scout came to him with a report that was both ominous and exhilarating: the scouts had found signs that the Master had been captured. Yes, they were sure he was captured and not killed. There was no sign of the scorching, which would have been evident if the Master had been shot by one of the forever guns. More than that, they found a footprint that had to be his a little farther along.

The report was ominous in that none of the True People had previously been captured by the Earthmen Marines. Being captured was a most terrible disgrace; it was ominous because it meant the Earthmen were very, very alert; they would not be caught completely unaware. But the report was exhilarating in that with the Master taken, the Leader wouldn't have to give up command. Surely, he would be promoted to Master now!

"Faster!" he commanded.

Third platoon was still nearly a kilometer short of the river where they were to rendezvous with the boats when Schultz said on the squad circuit, "Someone's behind us."

"How many?" Linsman asked.

"Can't tell."

"Is there just one? A battalion? Give me an idea."

"Maybe one, two. More behind."

"Are you sure about more behind?"

"No."

"You're guessing?"

"Educated guess."

Linsman relayed Schultz's report to Rokmonov. This time Rokmonov was more willing to accept Schultz's word that someone was following them as something to be acted on.

"Pick it up," he ordered.

The Marines sped up.

The point fire teams could just glimpse the river through gaps in the trees when a *crack-sizzle* and a flaring Skink announced that Schultz finally had a target worth shooting at.

Rokmonov and the squad leaders began shouting orders. First and second squads fell into line in a shallow curve with its concave face toward the river. The two guns of the gun squad were set in the middle of the blaster squads. The assault guns were set up with one behind each squad.

"Does anybody have a target?" Rokmonov demanded on the all-hands circuit when he didn't see the flashes of flaring Skinks answering the *crack-sizzles* of the Marine fire. "Cease fire, cease fire!" he ordered when nobody reported targets. "Squad leaders, detector report."

All four motion detectors reported movement. The scent detectors also picked up fishy smells that didn't come from the nearby river. Schultz's terse statement that the Skinks in front of first squad outnumbered the whole platoon was given equal weight.

"Give me range," Rokmonov ordered.

The motion detectors showed Skinks moving in depth fifty to a hundred meters out, just beyond sight lines, spreading into assault formation. Schultz said they were closer, behind cover.

Rokmonov considered the reports. The motion detectors put the Skinks at the extreme range of their acid shooters. According to Schultz, others were within their range. If they had buzz saws, the range of their acid shooters didn't matter. He decided and gave orders.

On command, the blaster squads began putting out volley

fire, aimed to graze the ground until it glanced off about thirty meters distant. On impact, the plasma bolts might fragment and throw a shower of fire in a spreading arc forward; otherwise they'd ricochet, some high, some low in the direction of whatever targets might lay beyond. The guns began firing bursts in a wide arc, also aimed at the ground thirty meters away. The assault guns fired in sweeping arcs deeper into the forest, on a trajectory no higher than a meter above the ground.

The fire was met by flashes from flaring Skinks. The disciplined shouts of officers and sergeants giving orders came from the forest. The assault guns fired bursts toward the voices. There was a flare, and sudden silence in that quadrant.

Voices shouted again and greenish streams of acid arced toward the Marines. Most missed, but some spattered on chameleons. The assault guns were out of range of the acid shooters.

Another command rang through the forest, and a hundred or more Skinks leaped to their feet and charged the Marine line, spraying acid as they ran.

The Marines fired as fast as they could at the running forms, and the forest shade glared like bright sunlight with the flashes of hit Skinks. But there were too many of them, and they were too close for the Marines to get them all before they closed.

Momentarily dazzled by the flash from a Skink he flamed at close range, Corporal Claypoole didn't see the other Skink racing straight at him. That Skink gripped the hose of his acid shooter and swung the nozzle like a mace at the place his side sensors told him the Marine's head was. The blow glanced off the side of Claypoole's helmet and the point of his left shoulder. Instinctively, he rolled to his right—into the path of the charging Skink. One foot slammed into the top of his helmet and the other clipped his already bruised left shoulder as the Skink flipped over him. Claypoole spun about, ignored the pain of his shoulder, and lunged at the Skink, which was already pushing back to his

feet and drawing a large knife. The two collided and Claypoole landed on top. He used his superior weight to pin
the Skink to the ground and hammered a fist into his face.
The Skink shrieked and bucked, but Claypoole was too
heavy for him to throw off. The Skink thrust the knife at
Claypoole just as Claypoole's hand found a death grip on the
Skink's throat and squeezed. Something crunched inside the
Skink's neck and he dropped the knife. His hands clutched
at his mortally injured throat but couldn't force it to open to
allow air to reach his starving lungs. The Skink's gill slits
opened and tried to extract oxygen from the air.

Claypoole rolled off, shook the remaining stars from his
vision, and looked for the blaster he lost when the Skink's
running feet hit him.

Corporal Dean had an easier time with the two Skinks
that converged on him. He lunged between them and rolled
to his feet, turning around to face them as he rose. One
Skink dove at the same instant Dean moved, and was
sprawled on the ground where he'd been. The other had
leaped over his diving partner and was already turned
around, facing Dean, turning the nozzle of his acid shooter
toward him. Dean shot faster and the Skink flared. Then he
shot the other, who was scrambling away. He spun around,
looking for more targets.

Corporal Doyle wasn't looking for targets. He screamed
as he fired wildly at the charging Skinks. A weight thudded
heavily on his back and his screams cut off with the air that
was knocked out of his lungs. He let go of his blaster and
scrambled to his feet, free of the weight. He spun and saw a
Skink staggering to regain balance. Wide-eyed with fear,
Doyle screamed as he raised his hands high above his head
and brought them down, clenched together, onto the Skink's
unprotected neck. The Skink dropped like a rock and didn't
move again.

Lance Corporal Schultz shuddered as he jumped to his
feet and slammed his blaster crosswise into the faces of two
charging Skinks. Their feet flew out from under them and

they crashed to the ground. Schultz kicked one in the head hard enough to shatter bone in the skull, then leaped onto the other with both feet, crushing the Skink's chest. His heart hammered inside his own chest as he used his blaster to batter other charging, shrilling Skinks.

The Leader commanding the reaction force didn't grapple with any of the Marines as he sped through their thin line. His objective was one of the assault guns that was still mowing down his Fighters. He had his projectile sidearm in his hand and fired twice before he realized he was wasting his ammunition until he was closer or stopped to aim. He stopped firing and kept running. Ten strides from the assault gun, he sensed an invisible Earthman Marine and fired again. He heard a cry and the fall of a body, and before he could fire again, a shout caught his attention. He looked toward it and was horrified to see the Master he'd been trailing bound ignominiously to a tree. The sight of a Master so disgracefully treated was too great for him to bear. He fired again toward the assault gun, which was rapidly turning toward him. There was a cry of pain, and then the gun swung uncontrolled. He jammed his sidearm back into his holster, grabbed at the assault gun and spun it until the back end was in his hands. It had two grips with a plate on a swivel positioned between them. The arrangement was constructed for hands bigger than his, but he could reach. He pointed the assault gun at the captured Master and pressed the swiveled plate. The Master flared, but the Leader never saw the flash—a bolt from Sergeant N'ton's hand-blaster vaporized him as he pressed the thumb plate trigger.

The fighting didn't last much longer. Thanks to Schultz, the Skinks took too many casualties before they began their assault. Someone shrilled an order, and the few Skink survivors of the melee began to retreat, flaming their fallen companions as they fled. None of them reached the cover of the deep forest before the Marines flared them, but they had done their job—only charred spots remained on the ground where dead and dying Skinks had lain.

When they were sure the Skinks were gone, the Marines gathered their casualties and moved to a new defensive position on the river bank. The boats arrived soon after.

The squad leader and gunner of the second assault squad weren't the only Marine casualties, though the gunner was the only Marine who died. Sergeant N'ton suffered first and second degree burns when the prisoner he was guarding flared. First squad's Corporal Pasquin, Lance Corporal Godenov, and PFC Gray all suffered knife wounds, as did second squad's Sergeant Linsman, Corporal Doyle, Lance Corporal MacIlargie, and PFC Little. In the gun squad, only Lance Corporal Kindrachuck was injured. None of the Marines suffered wounds from the acid shooters.

Third platoon had no further contact on its return to Haven.

CHAPTER NINETEEN

The headquarters of the Collegium crouched in the shadow of Mount Zion. Since the hill gave it some protection, the complex had sustained no damage from Skink bombardments. In any case, most of the facilities were housed safely underground, as befitted de Tomas's secret agendas.

Years before, when he had taken over as dean, de Tomas embarked on a major construction project to expand the facility, renaming it Wayvelsberg, after a medieval European fortress he'd read about that had impressed him. He designed the main entrance to the building after the portcullis of an ancient castle, except that the massive doorway was framed on each side by a huge bas relief of knights in armor, each of which stood fifteen meters high. Armed officers of the black-uniformed Special Group always stood guard just inside the dimly lighted entrance hall, which was draped in heavy tapestries depicting the Collegium's logo: a silver goshawk perched on golden lightning bolts. All of this gave the visitor the impression he was entering a dungeon. For many visitors, that was just what Wayvelsberg was, and if they emerged alive, they were never the same again afterward.

Behind the portcullis there was a courtyard paved with flagstones so that when a visitor's escorts marched him across it, their footfalls echoed sharply from the surrounding walls. In the center stood the statue of a horseman with a hawk, wings outstretched for flight, perched on one outstretched arm;

the other arm's massive mailed fist rested on the hilt of a
sword. On the figure's head was the royal crown of Heinrich
I, studded with precious stones; on bright days, the sunlight
glinted off them. Those passing through who were not preoccupied with what might await them in the chambers deep
below the surface of Wayvelsberg often noted a striking sim-
ilarity between the facial features of the stone Heinrich and
the dean of the Collegium.

The visitor on this occasion was none other than Archbishop General Lambsblood, commander of the remains of
the Army of God, still fuming from the dressing down
Brigadier Sturgeon had given him during the Convocation of
Ecumenical Leaders. His escort guided him down one of the
many gloomy corridors that led off the courtyard to an elevator bank. Once inside, it seemed to take a long time for
them to reach the subbasement where de Tomas kept his
working offices, which, in contrast to the atmosphere on the
surface of the complex, were ultramodern and brightly lit,
bustling with clerks and officials of the Collegium, who
stood politely aside as Lambsblood was marched down the
corridors to de Tomas's office suite. His escorts ushered him
into a waiting room and, saluting smartly, left him there to
wait for de Tomas.

The general was impressed. The waiting room was more
like a book-lined private study than a place to cool one's
heels. The furniture, covered with genuine leather, was a bit
heavy for the general's personal taste, but it blended well
with the ceiling-high bookshelves stuffed with hundreds of
volumes printed on paper. Casually, Lambsblood inspected
the spines, and after looking at a few of them, gasped in surprise. They were forbidden volumes! Obviously confiscated,
he concluded quickly. One caught his eye, a thin, leather-
bound volume with bright gold lettering: *The Rubaiyat of
Omar Khayyam* in the English translation by Fitzgerald.
Lambsblood had heard of that volume of salacious poetry by
the apostate Khayyam, but had never seen an actual copy. He
was alone and the room was dimly lighted from widely

spaced lamps. He was just pulling it from its place between a volume of Lord Chesterfield's letters to his son bound in buckram and Hogarth's etchings when—

"Thank you for coming on such short notice, Archbishop General," a voice boomed from behind him. Lambsblood started and whirled around, his face turning a dark crimson. There stood Dominic de Tomas, dressed in the black uniform of the Special Group, a golden goshawk on each lapel. "Interested in English literature?" De Tomas grinned, nodding at the shelf of books behind the general.

"Ah, well, um, confiscated items, I presume?" Lambsblood stuttered.

"Yes, Archbishop General," de Tomas replied, still grinning. "Some from the public library system, but most from the private collection of J. Benton Pabst, Master Librarian to the Ecumenical Council. Do you know him, perhaps?"

"Uh, yes . . . yes, I do. Haven't seen him in a while, though," Lambsblood answered nervously. There were rumors about Pabst . . .

"Nor will you be seeing him again." De Tomas grinned unpleasantly. "Please be seated." Grateful to be dismissed on the matter of the books and the late Master Librarian, Lambsblood plopped down in one of the leather armchairs. The cushions hissed as his weight gently settled into them. "All the books you see in here, General," de Tomas took in the shelves with a sweep of his arm, "are, as you say, 'confiscated.' But I did not burn them as we usually do with such filth. I have the works of all the ancient philosophers; Bertrand Russell, Ayn Rand, Norman Vincent Peale, terrible filth. But I keep them here on display because you must know your enemy, yes, General? Cigar?"

Lambsblood took the humidor offered and selected a cigar. "Anniversarios!" he exclaimed quietly. "These must cost a fortune," he said as he cut the end of his. He leaned forward as de Tomas offered a light.

De Tomas lit a cigar too, and they both smoked for a few moments. "Archbishop General," de Tomas continued, "I know you are spending valuable time here and you're anxious to get back to the front, but I have something to discuss with you. We both know that a successful soldier must know his enemies. Do you know who yours are, Archbishop General?"

Caught off guard by the blunt question, Lambsblood hesitated and then blurted, "Brigadier Theodosius Sturgeon!"

De Tomas smiled cryptically. "Yes, I was there at the meeting, when he insulted you so grievously. That was uncalled for. But Sturgeon will leave here one day and we will be faced with putting our world back together again. Let me put it to you this way: When that time comes, who will be your friend?"

Again Lambsblood hesitated. He shrugged. Whatever his failings as a military commander, he had always followed his orders to the best of his ability. He never thought like a politician.

"Archbishop General," a strong note of iron in de Tomas's voice now, "I want to show you something." Lambsblood's armed escort, responding to some secret signal de Tomas had evidently triggered, came back into the room. Lambsblood stood as de Tomas got up, gesturing that he should follow the escorts. The four of them returned to the elevators, aromatic cigar smoke trailing behind them, and descended rapidly to another floor. "This is the deepest level of Wayvelsberg," de Tomas said as they exited the elevator. "It's where we conduct our interrogations. One is in progress just now, and I would like you to sit in on it."

Lambsblood was ushered into a small soundproofed room. The one-way glass looked into an interrogation chamber where a middle-age man lay naked, strapped to an operating table. His body was covered in a sheen of perspiration. A technician dressed in white stood on the other side of the glass. He put a question to the man on the table, something about the Koran. Lambsblood could not quite hear the man's answer, but then the technician threw a switch on a console in front of him and Lambsblood jumped involuntarily as the man on the table screamed in agony. This went on for ten minutes. Lambsblood's cigar had gone out by the time the man on the table was fed feet first into a blast furnace.

"Archbishop General, it is time you were getting back to your command," de Tomas said, clapping Lambsblood heartily on the shoulder.

"Why—Why . . . ?" Lambsblood croaked. His clothing was soaked with perspiration and he felt sick to his stomach.

"I want you to know that you have a friend and ally in me, General," de Tomas answered. "I support and reward my friends. My enemies, well . . ." He gestured toward the interrogation chamber where the technician was busy cleaning things up. "That business with Sturgeon—forget it. It will clear up by itself and you will get back the command of your armies. I will be calling on you soon."

De Tomas shook Lambsblood's hand. Somewhat dazed, Lambsblood allowed his escort to take him back to the surface. On the way up he reflected on what de Tomas had told him, especially, "you will get back the command of your armies." Yes. The Dean of the Collegium was a powerful man on Kingdom. His powers exceeded even those of the army commander and the Council of Ecumenical Leaders. This fact was so well understood that Lambsblood had never even bothered to ask what the man on the table down there had been accused of, that his life should be ended so horribly. The Archbishop General had just assumed the man had committed some terrible heresy and deserved what he got.

De Tomas's next guest proved not to be as educable as General Lambsblood.

"I do not approve of your methods," the visitor announced as soon as de Tomas entered the room.

"A cigar, Reverend?" De Tomas offered him the humidor, ignoring the remark. He knew very well what his visitor thought of the Collegium.

"I don't engage in that dirty habit," the guest replied curtly, waving the humidor away.

"A seat, then?"

The Reverend, as he was known to members of his sect,

sat. "I want to know why you felt it was necessary to get me here personally, Dean. I have important business to attend to. This is a time of crisis, and change is in the air."

De Tomas nodded. "Change," he repeated. "Sometimes that can be a good thing. Your sect has long advocated change in the way the Convocation does its business."

"Yes. I wonder why you haven't made any of my people 'disappear' because of our opposition to the Convocation." The Reverend was a small red-faced man with orange-red hair, which many suspected he dyed. His small, almost elfin features disguised a monumental ego combined with a powerful intellect. Born into a society where the benefits of genetics were loudly denounced, one of his legs was several millimeters shorter than the other, forcing him to wear one shoe with a built-up sole. While the sect he led was not the largest of the many to be found on Kingdom, it was one of the most vocal, and people listened to what its leader said. He had a deep and powerful voice that could mesmerize even those who disagreed with him.

"Mind if I smoke?"

The Reverend waved a hand indicating he did not care. De Tomas took his time lighting up. He blew a large cloud of smoke into the space separating them. The Reverend winced and waved it away.

"I could have crushed you a long time ago," de Tomas announced.

"Yes. So why didn't you?"

"Because I happen to agree with you."

The Reverend was not prepared for this degree of frankness. "You do?" he asked hesitantly.

"Yes. And change is in the air. This invasion changes everything. We have suffered terribly. The entire City of God sect, for instance, was wiped out."

"Yes, I can see the tears forming now in the corners of your eyes," the Reverend replied cynically. They both laughed.

"I have studied the military situation very carefully," de Tomas said, "and while I do not know the precise details of this Brigadier Sturgeon's battle plan, it is evident to me that he is devising a master stroke to break the siege here and expel the invaders. These creatures are powerful and ruthless, but I do not believe they are as smart as we humans. They have suffered enormous casualties bringing about this siege. I do not believe they are very good strategists. The Marines will break this siege, and then . . ."

The Reverend leaned forward, interested now. "And then?"

"And then we will have to go about rebuilding our world. We will have to restore the people's faith in themselves. Changes will have to be made in how we do things here."

"Precisely how?"

De Tomas hesitated. He looked into the Reverend's eyes. There was interest there, ambition too, vast ambition. How far would that take the man? Would he be a rival? Yes, de Tomas concluded. But not for long. He smiled. "Consolidation of decision-making authority," he replied.

The Reverend leaned back. "How do I fit in?"

"I need a spokesman," he responded. "I need a propaganda minister."

The Reverend did not respond at once. "When?"

"Soon. I will let you know."

"My dear dean, you are planning to overthrow the Convocation, that is very clear to me. That is treason. What makes you think I won't run to the Convocation and warn them?"

"That is a very stupid question, my dear fellow. Do you care for a demonstration?" De Tomas's voice was hard now.

"No!" the Reverend answered quickly. "You can count on me." They shook hands.

Several other guests visited Wayvelsberg that day. Two of them were never seen again. By the time Dominic de Tomas retired to his private rooms to enjoy a quiet bottle of Katzenwasser '36 before bed, he was ready to move.

He toasted Brigadier Sturgeon. All he needed now was for the Marines to do their thing.

In person, Dominic de Tomas's handsome face radiated goodwill, and this often fooled people. But his eyes were cold, expressing an extraordinary degree of intelligence, but utterly devoid of humanity. Sympathy, much less love, were not qualities he possessed or even understood in others; he didn't even "like" anyone in the ordinary sense of that word. There were people he tolerated because they were useful to him, but he didn't have a friend in the world. He didn't need any, and if he had any, he wouldn't have known what to do with them.

Naive people, seeing the books in his library, thought de Tomas must be a cultured man, a person who appreciated art and ideas. In fact those volumes represented all areas of human endeavor. Personally, de Tomas found books meaningless things. His "library" was there for a special purpose: de Tomas monitored his visitors carefully, to see their reaction to the bound volumes. Depending on what interested a visitor, a lot could be learned about them; because he understood that anyone who entered the library and was not impressed by the books shared some of his own traits, and so had to be dealt with carefully; those who showed any interest in them, as apparently Archbishop General Lambsblood did, were vulnerable because they could be distracted. Lambsblood, for instance, had an interest in the venal. That was useful to know, because if the Archbishop General's ego was not sufficiently big to be used, his weakness for the flesh could be exploited when the time came.

The men recruited into the Special Group had been selected because they possessed some of the same traits as de Tomas, and during their rigorous training program those who resisted indoctrination were eliminated. Ruthlessness was ingrained into them. By the time their indoctrination was finished, they believed completely that Dominic de Tomas was their infallible leader and that everyone who came into the clutches of the Collegium were the worst enemies of the state, people who deserved degradation and punishment.

His men were far from goons, however. De Tomas insisted

they be free of bad habits, literate, educated at least through secondary school level, and have no criminal records. While horrible tortures and beatings of prisoners were routinely conducted, they were executed only on higher orders, and anyone who exceeded his authority was severely disciplined. De Tomas realized that sparing selected individuals was good propaganda—it spread fear of the Collegium in general and of the Special Group in particular. And those spared could be counted on to cooperate in any way necessary.

The members of the Special Group were highly trained, devoutly dedicated men armed with the latest weapons and technology and sworn personally to Dominic de Tomas. Their zeal and ruthlessness more than compensated for their relatively small numbers. Furthermore, de Tomas had organized a vast system of informants throughout the sects on Kingdom—people, not only former victims of the Collegium, who, for the right price, were willing to betray even members of their own families. But Dominic de Tomas's goal had never been to enforce orthodoxy among the sects, although he wanted people to believe as much. From the beginning of his selection as dean of the Collegium, a position he had occupied for years before the Skink invasion, he had been quietly consolidating his hold.

The authority of the Collegium spread everywhere on Kingdom. The media and the schools, when not run directly by the Collegium, were heavily monitored, so that news and school curricula were subject to its direction. Thus, millions of people, regardless of their religious convictions, were convinced Dominic de Tomas was a brilliant leader who had everyone's best interests at heart. His portrait hung in many homes and people admired him as the one man who could hold their world together. Most of the members of the Convocation of Ecumenical Leaders concurred, looking to de Tomas to keep not only their own sects in order, but the others as well. Those who did not fall for this carefully engineered propaganda—such as the neo-Puritans, the Anabaptists, and the Scientific Pantheists—were not powerful enough to oppose either the Collegium or the Convocation, and where de Tomas was not able to penetrate their congregations and eliminate their leadership, he was content to wait. He would deal with them when he had all the reins of power in his mailed fist.

CHAPTER
TWENTY

"Good afternoon, Commodore," Brigadier Sturgeon said.

Commodore Roger Borland looked at the main hatch into the bridge of the *Grandar Bay* and grinned at the Marine. "Welcome aboard, Brigadier. Come on in." He gestured toward the vacant commander's chair, which stood next to his own.

"Thank you, sir." Sturgeon took the three steps to the chair. He sat and looked at the display Borland had been gazing at. An arc of Kingdom filled the lower quadrant of the large screen. The terminator was visibly advancing along the planet's surface. Above the planet, stars speckled the heavens.

"I never tire of that view," Borland said softly. "The sight of an inhabited world from orbit, with the stars in the firmament above, stirs something positively atavistic within me."

"It is a magnificent sight," Sturgeon agreed.

"It is a most potent reminder of how far we have come since our ancestors first gazed upon the stars and wondered what they were," Borland said. "And how much farther we have to go before we can visit them all."

Sturgeon chuckled. "And after the Milky Way, other galaxies?" It wasn't quite a question.

"I'd love to know the answer to that, but I never will."

The two watched the screen for a few moments, the silence broken only by the bips of the instruments and the susurration of voices of the crew members who monitored them.

"But you didn't come all the way up here to join me in stargazing," Borland said in a firm voice. "You came because I have something less philosophical to show you."

"That's true, but a spell of stargazing is good for the spirit."

"If you will come with me, Brigadier."

"I am at your service, Commodore."

They stood, and Borland led the way off the bridge. A bos'n's mate third stood ready nearby with a shipboard runabout. The two boarded it and the bos'n drove away without instructions.

"I think you're going to get quite a kick out of the briefing Engineering has prepared for you," Borland said when they were under way.

"I expect so. Your message inviting me up was intriguing." Sturgeon shook his head. "Unfortunately, it didn't offer a hint as to the nature of the 'great discovery.' "

"I think you'll grasp the reason for the mystery fast enough."

They didn't bother with small talk for the remainder of the eight-minute ride. They dismounted and Borland led the way into the engineering wardroom.

"Attention on deck!" one of the engineers shouted when he saw the commodore.

"As you were," Borland said to the engineers, who were scrambling to their feet.

Five officers and three chief petty officers were in the wardroom. There was also a petty officer second class, but Sturgeon didn't recognize the rating symbol on his rank insignia. Four of the officers had been sitting in a conversation group in a corner of the room. The other officer and the chiefs stood in front of a table, while the petty officer third worked on a trid unit. They all stood easy; only the PO third returned to what he had been doing.

"Gentlemen, you probably recognize this Marine with me as Brigadier Theodosius Sturgeon, commander of Marine Expeditionary Forces, Kingdom," Borland said. "But I'll treat the entire department to a party if he has any idea of your names, so," he turned to Sturgeon, "I will make introductions. Commander Foderov, head of the Engineering Division."

"Pleased to meet you, Brigadier," Foderov said. He bowed

slightly as Sturgeon shook his hand. The other engineering officers did as well. The chiefs grinned but didn't bow—despite his rank, they recognized Sturgeon as a fellow working man.

Engineering Mate Second Class Goldman beamed when Sturgeon shook his hand. "Sir, I helped modify an armored vacuum suit for one of your Marines at Avionia," he said proudly. The navy officers exchanged glances; they didn't know anything about Avionia.

"So, you're the one? I got a good report about you," Sturgeon said, giving Goldman's hand a squeeze.

Goldman managed not to grimace at the strength in Sturgeon's grip. "Yessir."

"Better be careful. Sometimes, when we Marines think a sailor is good enough, we take him from the navy."

Goldman grinned weakly. He had no desire to go into harm's way with the Marines. The navy was so much safer. The officers and chiefs chuckled nervously; they suspected Sturgeon was serious.

The other introductions went quickly and then Sturgeon turned to Borland. "You and your officers didn't hear any of that business about Avionia. I'm not even cleared to know it, and it was my people."

The commodore cleared his throat. "Well, gentlemen, we are here for a purpose," he said, changing the subject. "Brigadier, Engineering has a program for you."

"Sir, if you will sit here." Foderov indicated a chair. Borland and the other officers sat in chairs to its sides. The chiefs remained in front of the table, blocking Sturgeon's view of the object on it. Coffee and biscuits were at Sturgeon's chair. Goldman worked controls on the trid unit, the wardroom's lights dimmed, and a display resolved above the unit.

A planet revolved under a scattering of stars. When Sturgeon looked at the planet's pattern of white, blue, and green he recognized it as Earth. A large, tubular object moved into view, its long axes aligned with the revolving planet. With nothing to use as a measure, Sturgeon couldn't judge its size, though he had the impression it was somewhat larger than an Essay.

"Sir," Commander Foderov said, "half a millennium ago humanity was still restricted to one world, fragmented into a plethora of nation states, and wracked with wars. The most powerful of those nation states, the United States of America, developed a weapon of devastating power. This weapon, called a rail gun, used electromagnets to project an inert chunk of metal at ten percent of the speed of light. On impact the kinetic energy of the projectile was tremendous. Inexpensive munitions could be used to knock out armored vehicles." The display changed to a massive, early twenty-first century armored vehicle speeding across a plain. It was struck by what appeared to be a bolt of light from above and the display momentarily whited out. When it cleared, only a crater in the ground remained. "A rail gun could destroy power plants with one shot." The display changed again, to an industrial-looking structure that Sturgeon assumed was an early twenty-first century power plant. A flash of light speared down onto it and the display whited again. When it cleared, bits of wall were left standing around a steaming crater.

"Rail guns," Foderov continued, "were excellent at taking out large, hardened targets." The trid moved rapidly through a series of displays: a ship at sea lost its entire middle third and sank; an armored tunnel entrance was demolished; a mobile artillery piece vanished, leaving only a crater to mark where it had stood; the main building of an industrial complex went the way of the earlier power plant; some sort of surface-to-orbit vehicle was sundered into a ball of debris. After a few more examples, the display returned to the cylindrical object in orbit.

"But the rail gun had major problems," Foderov said, resuming his narrative. "It required huge amounts of energy, it took so much time to reload and aim that it required up to half an hour between shots. And it was big, so big that it wasn't readily usable on the planetary surface—it could only be used from orbit, which created additional problems. Crews had to be rotated and resupply runs made—not for energy, though, an orbital rail gun got its energy from early, primitive solar cells. The crew and supply runs could be vulnerable to interception." The trid displayed a rising rocket disintegrating as it was struck by beams of coherent light from the planet's surface. "As you saw in the demonstrations, the rail gun was a point weapon—it needed precise data on a target's location. It took too long to reload and aim to be effective against an armored formation, and was even less effective against infantry. No one ever figured out how to make a small, mobile rail gun that could be reloaded and aimed rapidly. By the middle of the twenty-first century the device was abandoned. Second." He addressed the last to Goldman, who turned the lights back on and the trid off.

"Sir," Foderov said, "the Skinks figured it out. That is the barrel of a rapid-fire, mobile, rail gun." He gestured, and the three chief petty officers moved from the table so Sturgeon could see the object it held, the barrel Lieutenant Eggers brought back from the Skink supply depot.

What am I supposed to do with that? Sturgeon wondered. Maybe the navy had some ideas of what he could do with the information that would save the lives of his Marines. He asked.

"It uses large amounts of energy," Foderov said. "We're working to determine whether it radiates an energy signature before it fires. Unfortunately," he looked at the barrel, "we don't have a power source for it. We know what kind of leakage and signatures the twenty-first century rail guns gave off, but we don't know about this."

Borland broke in. "The Surveillance Division is analyzing the records of the actions in which we suspect the rail guns were used. Once we get that data identified and isolated, the string-of-pearls can monitor for the signatures, and the *Grandar Bay*'s lasers will be able to knock the rail guns out before they fire."

Sturgeon cocked an eyebrow; he doubted the navy would be able to knock out more than a fraction of the rail guns before they fired. But any help was better than none. "How long will it take to identify and isolate?"

"I put S and R on it as soon as Engineering identified the rail gun. Actually, I had expected them to have it in time for this briefing."

"Let me know as soon as they do. We'll coordinate a trap for a rail gun."

"I look forward to working with you on that."

"Now I need to return planetside. I have a war to run."

As he strapped himself into the webbing in the Dragon that would ride an Essay back to Kingdom's surface, Sturgeon reflected that while it was nice to know what that hellacious weapon was and that the navy was working on a way to counter it, that knowledge did nothing for him right now. He felt the trip to orbit had been a waste of time and effort; the navy could have transmitted the same information to him in a secure message less than fifteen words long.

A message, not much longer than fifteen words, arrived shortly after his Essay landed outside Interstellar City. S&R had identified and isolated what they believed was the radiation signature of a rail gun. The *Grandar Bay*'s Laser Gunnery Division was anxious to utilize its skills and weapons to start taking them out.

Previous operations had identified four entrances to the underground complex that were guarded by rail guns. The Marines' Dragons had barely been used, since they had proved to be so vulnerable to the rail guns in the Swamp of Perdition. Sturgeon decided to sacrifice one to test the *Grandar Bay*'s Laser Gunnery Division. He assigned the job to 34th FIST and coordinated with the navy.

This is crazy, Corporal Claypoole told himself for the umpteenth time since Captain Conorado and the captain from FIST operations met with third platoon to brief them on the mission. How many divisions do the Skinks have out here, and we're one lousy platoon?

He heard the rumble, muted by intervening trees, of Dragons about half a kilometer to the west. The Dragons Claypoole heard were empty; the crews that drove them and, if the opportunity arose, would fire their guns, were safe in bunkers in the Marine encampment outside Interstellar City. The civilian engineers in the off-worlder colony had worked round the clock for more than thirty-six hours to design, construct, and install remote piloting systems for three Dragons. They were much chagrined that Brigadier Sturgeon hadn't allowed them time to field-test the systems—he insisted the operation be set in motion at the earliest possible moment. Maneuver for the Dragons was just a touch slower than normal, and the guns' response time would also be a tad laggardly because the commands radioed to the Dragons were relayed by the string-of-pearls.

Corporal Claypoole toggled on the fire team circuit. "Wolfman, got anything on your mover?" In his infra he saw Lance Corporal MacIlargie wading through the marsh ten meters to his front, but he couldn't see the motion detector attached to the front of Wolfman's chameleons. MacIlargie moved a bit gingerly. The wound he'd received a few days earlier was still sore.

"Only us and the Dragons, Rock," MacIlargie answered. "Not even any animals."

"You didn't look at it," Claypoole complained.

"I'm listening to it."

"Look at it. How do you know you're hearing it right?"

MacIlargie made a noise that Claypoole translated as *asshole*, but he pulled the motion detector off his chest and flipped up the cover to look at the display. "It still only shows us and the Dragons," he said.

"What scale?"

"What?"

"What scale are you looking at?" Claypoole sounded annoyed.

MacIlargie expelled a breath. "One klick." The detector showed all movement in a one square kilometer area.

"Increase scale, show ten klicks." Claypoole sounded nervous.

MacIlargie looked around. "Someone that far away isn't going to run into us."

"Check it anyway!" Claypoole ordered in a rising tone.

"All right, all right." MacIlargie made the adjustment. "Still only shows us and the Dragons."

"You're sure?"

MacIlargie stopped and turned toward his fire team leader. "You want to look at it yourself? What's the matter, Rock? You're acting like somebody's grandmother." He held the motion detector out where the display was visible to Claypoole.

"Cover that!" Claypoole snapped.

The display vanished as MacIlargie snapped the chameleoned cover shut. Muttering to himself, MacIlargie faced front and resumed his movement. He touched the controls on the motion detector and returned it to the one klick setting.

Claypoole wasn't the only Marine in third platoon who was on edge. The last time the platoon had been there, it was one of eighteen platoons in the wetlands; this time it was the only one. And last time there wasn't a big, inviting target nearby like the three Dragons half a klick away.

Lance Corporal Schultz, on point as always, paid a lot more attention to his right front and flank than he did his front or left. The Dragons and their noise—he knew they were there to draw the Skinks' attention—were to his left. He knew the Skinks didn't need to be close to hit the Dragons; they had weapons that could take them out from a distance. He was afraid that when the Skinks fired, they'd fire from the right—through him. The Skinks would use that big gun, the big brother of the buzz saws, to hit the Dragons. He'd seen what was left of a Dragon after it was hit by one of those things in the Swamp of Perdition. Something with that much striking power could atomize a man and maybe not even notice it hit something. He knew it was a line-of-sight weapon and that it had a totally flat trajectory, just like the blasters did. Whatever its range, it was more than half a klick. If it fired from the right, Schultz knew he was right in its path. So he watched to the right more than to the front or the left. If the Skink gun was in that direction, maybe he'd sense something and have time to hit the deck before he got pulverized. And maybe geese migrated north in winter.

Corporal Doyle would have been catatonic if only Corporal Kerr would let him lay down on one of those nice bits of dry land that edged above the water all over the place. But no, Corporal Kerr kept on him about moving ahead and maintaining contact with Schultz. Why did he have to maintain contact with Schultz? He didn't *want* to follow Schultz. Schultz always went places that were dangerous. Doyle didn't want to go anyplace dangerous; he was supposed to be a clerk. It was some kind of horrible *mistake* that he was out in that marsh following Schultz in a mad search for Skinks and their monstrous weapons. All his eliminatory sphincters would have let go and emptied his bladder and bowel, except that they were already empty—they gave out when the orders came down for third platoon to accompany the Dragons, and he hadn't been able to hold anything down since.

"Keep moving, Doyle," Corporal Kerr said on the fire team circuit. Kerr was secretly glad Doyle was in his fire team. Doyle's fear and his constant need to be reminded to pay attention were the only things that distracted Kerr from the motion detector he carried. Somewhere inside, Kerr knew that if he was glued to the motion detector, he could well miss something else and get killed because of it. Still, he listened too hard to the motion detector and looked at its display far too often. He tried not to flash on the Siad horsemen—*horsemen!*—who had almost killed him on Elneal. The Skinks were far more deadly than the Siad could ever have been. Kerr strained to break his concentration on the motion detector. He knew he had to give his own senses and his hardearned combat savvy a chance to keep him alive.

At the rear of the platoon column Corporal Dean was keenly aware of how Company M had been mauled by Skinks who hid in the water and didn't attack until the Marines had passed them. He and Lance Corporal Godenov walked backward, looking forward only often enough to keep from tripping over objects in their path. PFC Quick, his third man, had a tough job. Quick had to keep contact between them and the rest of the platoon, to make sure they didn't get separated. Quick also monitored the motion detector. Maybe he should have had Godenov walk drag and had Quick back here with him, Dean thought. Godenov was more experienced and could handle both jobs better. But Quick was good too, and Dean wanted those experienced eyes watching the rear with him. Godenov was more likely than Quick to spot something subtle. Maybe the next time they stopped he'd switch them around. But there was no way the Skinks were going to hit third platoon, Company L, the way they hit M Company. Nossir!

Staff Sergeant Hyakowa wondered what had happened to the Skink patrols that third platoon and so many others had run into a few days earlier. He didn't think it was simply luck that kept the platoon from encountering patrols—the Dragons should have been a magnet for Skink security. Unless the Skinks had something else in store for them. He communicated this thought to Lieutenant Rokmonov, but otherwise kept his concerns to himself.

CHAPTER
TWENTY-ONE

Brigadier Sturgeon sat at a console in a corner of the MEF operations center, out of the way of his staff. They were monitoring everything: the movement of the Dragons, of Company L's third platoon, and of the sensors in third platoon's area of operation. He'd chosen the area for the mission precisely because it had been seeded with a full array of sensors. His staff was in constant communication with the *Grandar Bay*'s string-of-pearls monitors and Laser Gunnery Division. The displays on his console and the earpiece he wore kept him in constant touch with everything that was happening—or not happening, as it was turning out.

Third platoon and the Dragons had been out there for hours. They'd already passed within range of several known entrances to the underground system without incident. They would have to turn and begin the arc back soon. Why weren't the Skinks taking the bait? Sturgeon wondered.

"Mudmen, this is Skyboy," a voice said over the string-of-pearls circuit. Sturgeon held his earpiece tight. "We've got the signature you've been waiting for. Details coming."

Sturgeon saw the coordinates and the location appear on a map. A suspected rail gun was a kilometer and a half north-northeast of the Dragons. If it was giving out a signal, it was probably ready to fire.

"Locked on," came another voice. The Laser Gunnery Division was ready.

The air seemed to crackle, and Schultz, about to step around the end of a long, narrow hummock, dove into the water behind it instead. Behind him the rest of the platoon also went for cover. The concussion wave from the eruption of a Dragon half a kilometer away rippled the water and shook the trees around third platoon. The fans on the surviving Dragons raced faster, louder, and they shot off in evasive movements. Dean raised his head to look forward and saw a lance of light slash down from the zenith to strike somewhere ahead of third platoon. Something exploded where the laser hit.

"Signature silent," the string-of-pearls reported.

Cheering burst out in the Marine operations center. Officers and NCOs congratulated each other, slapped each other's backs, shook hands.

Brigadier Sturgeon didn't join in the celebratory reaction. How many more of those things do they have? was the question on his mind. Killing one gun wasn't enough cause for celebration. He sidestepped the chain of command and radioed directly to third platoon.

"Patch me into the all-hands circuit," he ordered. When he was on, he said, "This is Brigadier Sturgeon. We just lost a Dragon, but that was deliberate. There was nobody on that Dragon, no Marines were lost. In return, we killed one of the Skink main guns. Now we know how to kill them when they're ready to fire. I want you to go in farther and see if you can get more of those guns to expose themselves. Good hunting. Sturgeon out."

He looked across the room to where the crews of the Dragons sat at their control stations. All nine Marines were looking back at him. They hadn't joined in the celebration: it didn't matter to them that no Marines were injured when the Dragon was destroyed—that Dragon was one of theirs. He got up and walked over to them.

"This time let's see if you can kill one of those guns before it gets another Dragon," he said softly.

The nine Marines smiled grimly at him. "Yessir," one of them said. "Where do you want us to go?"

He told them, then went back to his console and told the string-of-pearls monitors what he wanted them to do. The cheering and backslapping stopped and everybody returned to the job that needed to be finished.

The Dragons stopped evasive maneuvers and sped across third platoon's trail as though they were cutting and running. But they were headed on a course that would expose them to more cave entrances that might be guarded by rail guns. Third platoon rose and followed along a parallel route. The Dragons stopped behind an islet that stood high enough to shield them from the suspected Skink positions and waited for the infantry to catch up. Third platoon went past the islet on its other side, closer to the entrances. The Marines stayed in the water, crouched to present the smallest possible targets for Skink gunners. When they were less than two hundred meters from the cave entrances, they stopped and waited for the Dragons to come forward.

"Rail gun signature detected," the string-of-pearls monitors reported.

The Dragon crews immediately directed their vehicles into evasive maneuvers, and the gunners oversaw downloading of the targeting data from orbit to their guns.

"Damn!" one of the drivers swore. The slap he gave his console sounded like a gunshot in the command center.

"Dragon One down," the Dragon One commander said with a leaden voice.

"Not your fault," the Dragon One crew chief told his driver. "The relay took too long." There had been a slight time lag between when he gave the commands and when the commands reached the Dragon. That lag could have been long enough to keep the Dragon in the line of fire of the rail gun.

"Dragon Three, locked on," the gunner of the remaining Dragon said calmly. Its gun was able to maintain a lock on its target no matter how violently the vehicle maneuvered.

"Fire," the Dragon Three crew chief said, just as calmly.

Unseen in the command center, the Dragon spat a ball of plasma at the rail gun that had just taken out its partner.

"Signature gone," the string-of-pearls monitors reported. "New signal up. Locking on." This time the *Grandar Bay* didn't download targeting data; it was the Laser Gunnery Division's turn. "Signature gone," the ship reported to the Marine command center.

Mere seconds separated the three explosions: the one that demolished one of the two remaining Dragons was quickly followed by two more a couple hundred meters east of third platoon. A moment later Lieutenant Rokmonov ordered the Marines to move out—east, toward the location of the explosions.

Lance Corporal Schultz halted and lowered himself when he saw the devastation through a break in the trees. Tendrils of smoke still rose from a patch of charred vegetation in the middle of a small hummock. The hummock was covered with tumbled and shattered trees and brushes, and broken vegetation floated in the water around it. Here and there sunlight glinted off something metallic. Nothing moved except the rising smoke and small fragments of foliage in the breeze.

Corporal Kerr observed the scene from a few meters away. "Doesn't seem to be anybody alive there now," he reported. "I don't see a cave entrance."

"Wait for me," Rokmonov replied. A moment later the lieutenant was with Kerr and Schultz. He watched for a minute, then said, "Let's check it out."

Kerr and Schultz rose to a crouch and quickly crossed to the destroyed area and a short distance beyond it. Corporal Doyle reluctantly went with them. The three Marines examined the ground around the charred area and the water surrounding the hummock.

"All clear," Kerr reported.

"Five, set a perimeter," Rokmonov said on the all-hands circuit as he went to join the fire team on the hummock.

"Aye aye," Staff Sergeant Hyakowa answered. He began issuing orders to the platoon. The Marines moved into positions around the hummock, leaving Rokmonov and the comm man alone to examine the hummock.

Fragments, some of them metal, studded the ground in the charred area. More fragments were flung about the hummock. It was obvious that the Dragon's plasma cannon had destroyed the Skink weapon. But what had it been doing sitting exposed in the open? And why hadn't any of the many patrols the Marines and Kingdomites sent out found one before?

Hyakowa joined Rokmonov and quickly wondered the same thing. "Rat, give me Claypoole and Mac," he said.

Claypoole's toe caught on something just inside the charred area and he almost fell. "What?" he squawked, and knelt to see what had tripped him. His probing fingers found a hard ridge about a centimeter high and a couple millimeters wide. He brushed at it, clearing ash and dirt away to expose several centimeters of the ridge.

"Look at this!" He raised his chameleon shield so the others could see his face and kept brushing at the edges of the visible ridge, lengthening the exposed area. By the time Rokmonov and Hyakowa joined him, he could see about thirty centimeters of the ridge. It was uniform in height and slightly arch. He did a quick mental calculation and concluded that if the arc continued it would probably make a circle.

"Buddha's blue balls," Hyakowa said softly when he saw the arc. "How deep does it go?" He dropped to his knees and began digging with his knife along both sides of the ridge.

"Mac, get over here," Rokmonov told MacIlargie. "See that? Help Claypoole clear it."

"Mohammed's cocked eye," MacIlargie whispered when he saw the metallic ridge. He dropped and began clearing it in the opposite direction from Claypoole.

"It goes down about ten centimeters on the inside of the arc," Hyakowa said. "It seems to be the side of a dish." He dug away from the ridge.

"Rabbit, give me a fire team," Rokmonov said.

Sergeant Ratliff sent his third fire team.

"See this?" Rokmonov said when Corporal Dean and his men joined him. Dean whistled. "See if you can find more of it. One of you dig in the middle." Rokmonov indicated the narrow trench Hyakowa was digging from the ridge toward the center of the charred area.

"Izzy, dig here," Dean told Lance Corporal Godenov when he and his men were near the middle of the charred area.

"Right." Godenov began digging with his knife.

Dean and Quick went to the opposite side and probed with their toes until they found the ridge, then started clearing.

The digging soon revealed that the ridge did indeed make a circle, and the circle was the lip of a dish about four and a half meters in diameter. And MacIlargie made another discovery.

"I found a cable!"

"The rest of you keep clearing," Rokmonov said. He signaled Hyakowa to come with him.

The top end of the cable Godenov found was fused from the heat of the plasma ball that had destroyed the rail gun. The bottom end went through the metal dish under the dirt.

"Hammer has an uncomfortable feeling," Ratliff reported on the command circuit.

Rokmonov considered for a few seconds, then spoke into the all-hands circuit, "Let's check out the other one, then head in. Everybody, look alive, there are probably Skinks nearby."

The *Grandar Bay*'s laser had been even more destructive. More than half of the dirt from the "dish" was gone, which clearly was a constructed platform for the rail gun. Unlike the platform hit by the Dragon's plasma gun, this one was depressed from the surrounding ground far enough to expose the edge of a retracted lid that would slide into place when the rail gun was belowground. Rokmonov understood why none of the patrols in the area had ever found one.

*   *   *

Now that he knew how to locate and kill the rail guns that had grounded his aircraft and kept his armor out of action, Brigadier Sturgeon put his staff to work drawing up new operational plans. He even brought Archbishop General Lambsblood into the planning—the Army of the Lord would have a major role to play in the upcoming offensive.

Lambsblood was elated. De Tomas had been right; the business with Sturgeon was clearing up, and command of his army returning to him! He shuddered when he recalled what he had seen in the lowest level of Wayvelsberg. Perhaps he wouldn't need Dominic de Tomas as a friend in the future. De Tomas was a powerful man, a dangerous man. After the demons who now infested the countryside were banished back to the hell from whence they came, perhaps something could be done about—

No, now was not the time to think such thoughts. The Collegium had eyes and ears in too many places. Sometimes, Lambsblood thought de Tomas could read thoughts.

The commander of the Army of the Lord was given an extensive briefing on the latest findings. He had never heard of rail guns, but was thoroughly impressed by the presentation on the history of the weapon he was given by the Confederation Navy. The daring displayed by the Marines in locating rail guns and the inventiveness and close cooperation displayed by them and the Confederation Navy in destroying three of them made him wonder if they had known about the rail guns earlier and weren't admitting as much. He grew eager as Brigadier Sturgeon outlined the plan of operation.

In his excitement about being the main thrust, he failed to wonder why Sturgeon had relegated his own forces to such a minor, supporting role. Nor did it occur to Lambsblood that the supposedly complete briefing he was given was in fact somewhat less than fully complete.

Phase one of Operation Exorcism was designed to reduce the number of rail guns in the Skink arsenal. The Army of the Lord sent two battalions of remotely controlled Gabriel armored fighting vehicles into the wetlands where the demons were concentrated. During the one day it took for the rail guns of the demons to consume all of them, the Gabriels and the *Grandar Bay* killed at least 150 of the rail guns. Phase one was declared over on the second day, when not a single rail gun made its presence known.

The Great Master sat on his commander's throne, his face expressionless. No females hovered in the background, ready to serve steaming beverages to the assembled Over Masters and more senior of the Senior Masters. No cup or graceful vase with delicate flowers sat on the low table by his side—not even the low table was there, nor were there tables between the kneeling Over Masters and more senior of the Senior Masters who knelt in their rows before the Great Master. The Great Master wore his battle armor once more. The battle sword that had drunk blood in so many battles lay across his knees, one hand wrapped tight around its hilt.

The Over Master in command of the defenses stood in front of the Great Master, not facing him, but with his right side to the Great Master. He held his battle sword, both hands on its hilt, its point on the matting between his feet. His subordinate, the Senior Master in command of the greater rail guns, knelt with his back to the Great Master. Both of them were clad only in loincloths.

"The Earthmen have done us a great damage!" the Great Master said, his voice a breaking storm. "Greater damage than when they raided one of our supply depots. They did it because no one saw the damage being done and kept our greater rail guns hidden, where they would not be destroyed. This is unpardonable dereliction! There is only one course that may be taken."

The Great Master's slitted eyes flicked to the Over Master in command of defense, flicked to his sword, flicked to the Senior Master in command of the greater rail guns. The Over Master in command of defense bowed deeply, raised his sword above his head, and brought it down on the extended neck of the Senior Master in command of the greater rail guns. The Senior Master fell forward onto the matting, his spine cleaved almost all the way through. Blood gushed from the wound, and the Senior Master's mouth opened and closed as though he tried to speak. The Over Master raised his sword and brought it down again. His aim was true, the head rolled clear. The Senior Master's body spasmed once, twice, lay still. More blood flowed.

The Great Master looked dispassionately at the corpse, then spoke one word to the Over Master in command of defense, the closing of a crypt door: "Die."

The Over Master in command of defense reversed his sword, held it by the blade, with the point against his abdomen just below his ribs, and fell forward onto it. An involuntary gasp escaped his mouth as the blade went deep, severing major blood vessels and carving vital organs. He took long minutes to die.

The Over Masters and more senior of the Senior Masters who knelt before the Great Master remained silent and expressionless during the proceedings. None dared remind the Great Master that it was he who had authorized such profligate use of the greater rail guns.

CHAPTER
TWENTY-TWO

Three light-years from Kingdom, the starship SS *Fundy's Tide*, a commercial freighter, popped out of Beamspace. Navigation went to work immediately to find out exactly where they were. As soon as Navigation was oriented, the location was passed to Helm, who then aimed the starship toward a nearby planetary system. The inertial drive kicked in and the *Fundy's Tide* began the Space-3 portion of its transit to the uninhabited world known formally as Society 362. A dozen years or so earlier, the Bureau of Human Habitability Exploration and Investigation had abandoned Society 362 as unsuitable for human colonization. The scientists and technicians who declared it uninhabitable had dubbed it "Quagmire." BHHEI had left an array of video, audio, seismic, and atmospheric recorders behind.

Ten years after the abandonment of Society 362, the Explored Worlds subcommittee of the Congress of the Confederation of Human Worlds, as part of an investigation of possible budget irregularities of BHHEI, decreed that a survey be made of all planets the Bureau had investigated and determined were unsuitable for human colonization. BHHEI had few ships of its own; it mostly relied on contract ships, commercial vessels it could charter or book space on. As all of BHHEI's ships were engaged in the exploration of other worlds, it put to bid contracts for shipping companies to make stops at the eight hundred or so worlds it had explored and abandoned. In most instances, starships could simply drop out of Beamspace long enough to go into orbit around the world and signal the recorders—such as those the

BHHEI had left on Society 362—to upload the data they'd collected.

In the normal manner of governments, the contracts went to the lowest bidders, which meant in most cases the contracts weren't very lucrative, which in turn meant they were low priority. So, quite naturally, the survey took longer than anticipated. Even though starships regularly ported at the Kingdom of Yahweh and His Saints and Their Apostles, none of the shipping companies that made those runs had a BHHEI contract. Thus, it was two years before a ship owned by low-bidder Southern Seas Cargo and Freight, a minor player in interstellar trade, made a voyage that took it in the vicinity of Society 362. The small payment from BHHEI for this side trip was expected to be the biggest chunk of the profit for the voyage.

Navigation between stars isn't a precise science. No matter how exactly a Beamspace course is plotted, the reentry point into Space-3 can be off by several light-minutes. Since reentry inside a gravity well would destroy a starship, reentry points were always plotted with a great enough margin of error to guarantee that the ships would reenter Space-3 outside a gravity well. The *Fundy's Tide* reentered Space-3 eight days' travel from Society 362.

On orbit minus seven, the radar section reported a difficulty with its equipment.

"What's the problem?" the captain asked.

"It's reporting an object approaching us at point one C," Radar said.

The captain couldn't think of anything that could travel at .1C in Space-3. "Find and fix the problem," he said.

"Skipper, according to the diagnostics, there's nothing wrong with it."

"There must be something wrong, nothing moves at point one C in Space-3."

"Ah, it's heading straight for us, Skipper. Collision course." Radar's voice had a rising edge.

"Where's it coming from?"

"It's coming from the direction of Society 362."

The captain considered this for a few seconds. Just because nothing traveled at .1C in Space-3 didn't mean nothing was on a collision course with the *Fundy's Tide*. "Course deviation," the captain said to Helm. "Move us ten kilometers to the left."

"Aye, Skipper."

The *Fundy's Tide* was out of the path of the object when it went through the space the starship would have been in had the captain not ordered the course deviation. Every instrument that tracked or observed the unidentified object insisted that it was traveling at an unbelievably appreciable percentage of the speed of light. Nobody had any idea what it was or how it might have attained that speed.

On O–6, or six days prior to orbit, radar reported another .1C object heading toward the starship from the vicinity of Society 362.

Once more *Fundy's Tide* sidestepped.

"The navy has a starship at Kingdom, doesn't it?" the captain asked Communications after the second object passed harmlessly by.

"Sure does, Skipper. There's some sort of war going on there. Hey, they've got Marines and everything!" Communications had wanted to enlist in the Marines but failed the physical and so joined the Merchant Marine as a way to "see the universe."

"Good. I want to send a drone to Kingdom. Two messages, both telling about those point-one-C objects. One message goes to the Confederation ambassador. Tell the ambassador that if another object comes toward us at that impossible speed, we're aborting this mission. Second message to the navy: tell them if they've got something in orbit here, they should put up warning signs for starships that might come nearby; those things are dangerous. Add that if the objects aren't theirs, they should send someone to check out the situation."

Shortly after sending the drone, the captain said, "Radar, are you picking up any ships in orbit around Society 362?"

"Checking, Skipper."

It was nearly a half hour, standard, before Radar completed its check and had sufficient resolution on the returned signals. "Skipper, there are several blips. None are transponding identification signals."

"What kind of information do the blips give?"

"One seems to be about the size of a Ragnorak-class vessel. The others appear to be smaller."

The captain thought long and hard about that; Ragnorak was the civilian cruise ship version of the Confederation Navy's Crowe-class amphibious battle cruiser. He asked, "Could they be navy, testing a new weapon?"

"Yessir, could be."

"Communications, try to raise them, tell them they're endangering a civilian freighter."

No object came toward *Fundy's Tide* at an impossible speed on O-5, five days before the planned orbit. Neither did a reply come from the ships in orbit around Society 362, so the crew spent the day in idle and unproductive speculation about what the objects were and who was in orbit. The captain ordered Communications to send another drone to the navy at Kingdom asking about the ships in orbit around Society 362.

On O-4, Radar picked up another object.

"That's it!" the captain said. "Abort, we're getting out of here. Damn navy!"

Navigation began plotting the next jump while Engineering spun up the Beam drive engines and Helm sidestepped the oncoming object.

That was when Radar shouted, "More objects! We have to jump now!" Helm tried desperately to sidestep the next object, but it was too close, and the Beam drive engines were still warming up. Long before they reached jump power one of the objects struck *Fundy's Tide* and it disintegrated, spilling its atmosphere, cargo, and crew into the cold vacuum of space.

The hop from Society 362's system to Kingdom was short, only three light-years, and Beamspace transit took hardly more than twelve hours, standard. As soon as it jumped back into Space-3, the drone began transmitting a *Come get me* signal. It checked the stars and headed toward the one that showed a large disk. En route, it searched for and found its destination planet, and adjusted course for it. After two days it closed on the fast frigate CNSS *Admiral J. P. Jones*, the *Grandar Bay*'s sole escort ship, which had been sent to intercept it. The *J. P. Jones* transmitted the appropriate command sequence, and the drone fired breaking rockets to match velocity with the starship, which scooped it up. The *J. P. Jones* then returned to Kingdom at flank speed. Four and a half days after being dispatched, far too late to have any chance of helping *Fundy's Tide*, the drone gave up its messages to *Grandar Bay*'s Communications Division.

The message, addressed to "The Ambassador, Confederation of Human Worlds," was sent unopened planetside on the next Essay.

The message addressed to "Confederation Navy in orbit around Kingdom" went to Captain Maugli, the *Grandar Bay*'s executive officer. The XO was extra busy coordinating the activities of the starship's departments because of the campaign to kill the rail guns and didn't have time for routine messages from merchant starships, so the message sat in his in-tray for a couple of days. When the XO finally had time to read it, he had to check Society 362 in the *Handbook of Inhabited and Known Planets* to see what and where it was. The entry said little more than it had been investigated by BHHEI and abandoned a dozen years earlier. There was no mention of a current survey that would visit the planet. He decided the message was possibly a hoax and put it aside to deal with later. In Maugli's defense, he was exhausted and only half awake when he read the message.

Ambassador Jayben Spears, on the other hand, was wide-awake when he read the message addressed to him.

The ambassador was already waiting in Sturgeon's office when the brigadier got there from the operations center.

"Good morning, Jay," Sturgeon said. He waved at a chair.

"Good morning yourself, Ted," Spears replied, and sat down.

"Ah, thank you," Sturgeon said to a lance corporal who knocked at his door. "Bring it right in." The corporal carried in a tray with a pot and two mugs, which he set on a side table. "I'll pour." The lance corporal left. "Real coffee," Sturgeon said to Spears. He poured both mugs full and handed him one. "If you want to fancy it up, you'll have to do it yourself."

"Black is fine," Spears said, and sipped. His eyes lit up. "Much better than I expect to find on this godforsaken world."

"A gift from Commodore Borland. He gave me a whole kilo."

"That's one thing about the navy—in some ways they go first class. You're looking well, Ted. You're having success against the Skinks?"

Sturgeon nodded. "We've been knocking out their heavy weapons. I should be able to use my air assets again. And I've got something cooking to flush them out of their caves."

Spears raised an eyebrow, but Sturgeon didn't tell him anything more. "Ah, yes. Operational need to know, and I don't need to know. But you'll tell me afterward how you did it?"

"I will. Now, you wanted to see me."

"Something I think you should see. It may affect your future plans." He pulled a folded sheet of paper from an inner pocket and handed it over.

"Another movement in congress to disband the Marines? They've been doing that for centuries." Sturgeon unfolded the sheet of paper and scanned it. Then he read it again.

SS FUNDY'S TIDE
Southern Seas Cargo and Freight
Katishaw
"We Treat Your Goods Like Our Cargo"

TO: AMBASSADOR, CONFEDERATION OF HUMAN WORLDS, THE KINGDOM OF YAHWEH AND HIS SAINTS AND THEIR APOSTLES
FROM: CAPTAIN, SS FUNDY'S TIDE

DATE: JANUARY 15, 2456
RE: SOCIETY 362

Sir,

Under contract to the Bureau of Human Habitablity Exploration and Investigation, *Fundy's Tide* is approaching Society 362. Twice, once on day seven prior to orbit and again on day six prior to orbit, an unidentifiable object has approached this starship from the vicinity of the above planet at a speed that is an appreciable fraction of C. Each time, this starship had to deviate from its plotted course in order to avoid a possibly catastrophic collision with said unidentified object.

By this letter I serve formal notice on the Confederation of Human Worlds that should this happen again, I will abort this survey visit to Society 362 until such time as I have been assured such approach is safe.

Sturgeon looked at Spears. "Sounds like a rail gun."

"My thoughts exactly."

"What and where is Society 362?"

"It's an exploratory world, abandoned as unsuitable for colonization some years ago." Spears hesitated. "It's only three lights from here."

Sturgeon looked into the distance for a moment, then said, "When I get a chance, I'll have Commodore Borland send a drone to Earth with messages for Aguinaldo and the Combined Chiefs. Also any messages you want to send."

"Thank you, Ted. I'll prepare my messages." Spears put his mug down and stood. "I know you're busy, so I won't take up any more of your time. But I thought you should see that."

"You're right, Jay. Thanks for showing it to me." He escorted Spears out of his office, then went back to retrieve his mug. He hadn't yet drunk any of the coffee, and real Earth coffee was too good to let go to waste.

Operation Slay Demons got under way. Four divisions of the Army of the Lord went north by west of Haven, got on line in close order, and advanced to the east, through the Skink-infested wetlands. The divisions were screened by a line of remotely controlled vehicles disguised as Gabriels. Archbishop General Lambsblood was confident that if any of those Skink horror weapons the Confederation had identified as "rail guns" opened fire, the *Grandar Bay* would destroy them before they could do significant harm to his army.

Brigadier Sturgeon wasn't as sanguine; he expected the Skinks to use buzz saws. Nobody knew if the string-of-pearls could detect them fast enough to neutralize their effectiveness. If the big guns weren't deployed, his Air could deal with the buzz saws. He instructed his FIST commanders to arm their Raptors with Jerichos and have all of them on the ready line. The Hoppers and Dragons all stood by to take on Marine infantry. All recon and scout-sniper teams were in the wetlands observing Skink positions that weren't in the Army of the Lord's line of advance.

The Army of the Lord advanced into the wetlands following its screen of dummy Gabriels. The string-of-pearls tracked them and relayed their movements to the operations center of Marine Expeditionary Forces, Kingdom. Sturgeon watched intently as the two lines, separated by two hundred meters, grew raggedy. Either Archbishop General Lambsblood wasn't paying attention to the data being relayed to his command center, or he didn't feel it was important for his army to maintain formation. The lines began to fragment as some elements moved faster than the elements to their sides, or fell behind because of obstructions. In some places, fragments of the infantry line closed the gap with the fake Gabriels ahead of them; in a few places the gap between screening vehicles and trailing infantry widened. Elements began drifting, so gaps grew between adjacent elements, and some moved behind others.

"Sir," Commander Usner, the operations officer, said. "Should I contact the local C-cubed and advise them to dress their lines?" He was asking if he should advise Lambsblood's Command, Control, and Communications Center to get their lines back in order.

Sturgeon shook his head. "I want the Skinks to jump at that bait." Sturgeon thought that even after working with and being trained by the Marines, the Kingdomite soldiers would fare poorly against the Skinks no matter how well they maintained formation. And he believed the Skinks would attack them earlier if they were in disarray than if they were in good formation. Further, he suspected that Lambsblood would ignore any recommendations from the Marines.

An element in the right center of the vehicle screen was the first part of the advance to reach known entrances to the underground complex. It passed them unmolested. So did the infantry that trailed those vehicles. More elements approached entrances.

"Three," Sturgeon said to Usner.

"Sir?"

"Contact Kingdom C-cubed. Recommend that they hold up and dress their lines. Tell them why."

"Aye aye." Usner picked up the handset of the open land line to Lambsblood's command center.

Sturgeon continued to watch the display from the string-of-pearls. He swore to himself when he saw the foremost elements stop in place and wait for others to come up, instead of pulling back to straighten the line. He silently swore again when the Kingdomite army resumed its advance into the wetlands before everyone caught up.

"They're going to be in the middle of it," Usner murmured.

"I know," Sturgeon said. He turned to his link to the two FIST commanders. "When you get the launch command, I want those Raptors in the sky immediately and locked into the string-of-pearls."

Brigadier Sparen and Colonel Ramadan answered that their Raptors were ready to launch and their missile guidance systems were already locked in. Minutes later the launch command came.

Sixteen Raptors, all the Marines had, lifted into the air and headed in flights of two to designated locations just outside the wetlands. Data flowed into their guidance systems

as they flew, so that when they arrived on station they were
ready to fire—and they did. They turned around to return to
base and rearm with another load of Jerichos before their
first volleys struck. Ten minutes later they were back on station firing second volleys.

While the Raptors were on their first sortie, waiting infantrymen scrambled aboard Hoppers and Dragons. They
waited for the command to move out.

Symbols showing lines of fire and probable points of origin appeared on the main display in the Marine operations
center—points that were probably buzz saws. Some of the
Skink buzz saws were too close to friendly units to risk firing Jerichos at them; others weren't. The latter were the aiming points for the missiles. Holes began to appear in the
Kingdomite lines as units were wiped out. Symbols indicating lines of fire and points of origin blinked off as Jerichos
struck home. More symbols vanished when the *Grandar
Bay*'s lasers opened fire on the point targets. Marines in the
operations center overheard panicky radio transmissions
from units of the Army of the Lord—Skinks were pouring
out of the ground, popping up from underwater in ever in-
creasing numbers.

"Launch the infantry," Sturgeon commanded.

Hoppers hopped into the air and headed for the wetlands;
Dragons roared onto their air cushions and sped toward the
marshes.

The Raptors, already reloaded after their third sorties,
headed out to launch even more Jerichos. This time the Jerichos were aimed at the southern end of the Skink area,
where the Marine infantry was going.

CHAPTER
TWENTY-THREE

The Hoppers played it safe, flying as low as the squadron commanders dared while keeping as much of the little high ground between their flight paths and the Skink positions as possible. They landed more than five hundred meters from the nearest position. The Marines of 26th FIST's infantry battalion began debarking even before they touched down. Thirty-fourth FIST's infantry entered the area on Dragons and pulled right up to their objectives.

The infantrymen of 34th FIST raced out of the Dragons into a landscape shocked silent by the devastation. It looked like the chunk of the Swamp of Perdition where Jerichos broke the buzz saw ambush that had done so much damage to them early in the campaign. All the grass on the islets and the reeds on their fringes were gone, leaving only a residue of ash. The larger trees were reduced to charred, smoking spikes rising from desiccated ground; smaller trees were simply gone. So was the water where it had been shallow. Bare ground visible through the ash and charring was sere and cracked. At every step ash rose and fried dirt crunched underfoot. Entrances to the underground were clearly visible as burned pits, many with dried and crumbling edges.

There were no Skinks.

By platoons and squads, the infantrymen of two FISTs poured into the gaping entrances to the Skink stronghold. The entire lighting system in line of sight of the entrances was knocked out. Blast and fire damage from the Jerichos was clearly visible for the first fifty to a hundred meters inside the tunnels and chambers. Beyond the first bends in the tunnels, the Skink lighting systems still worked. No Skinks were encountered for more than two hundred meters, though there were random scorch marks near dropped weapons and other gear, which may have been all that remained of Skinks struck by heat waves from the blasts. The Marines went deeper along wide tunnels before any of them encountered a live Skink.

Lance Corporal Schultz, on point for third platoon's Bravo unit, padded swiftly along a three-meter-wide tunnel. On the other side of the tunnel, Corporal Kerr was almost level with him. After the first fifty meters, the tunnel never went for more than twenty meters without a turn. At each turn they paused while Kerr used the motion detector to check beyond it.

Staff Sergeant Hyakowa, in command of the Bravo unit, positioned himself behind Kerr and opposite Corporal Doyle. The data stream from the string-of-pearls couldn't penetrate into the caves and tunnels, and radios could not reach from one unit to another, so each squad or platoon was on its own underground. An inertial guidance system kept Hyakowa's HUD up to date, and Bravo unit's route and first objective were clearly marked on the HUD. They were to join the Alfa unit at the first objective.

The gun team came next, followed by the rest of second squad. Corporal Claypoole and Lance Corporal MacIlargie, frequently looking behind them, brought up the rear.

"We don't need to watch behind us, Rock," MacIlargie objected when Claypoole told him to "check our six." "Nobody there but the swamp."

"There could be hidey-holes. Skinks could come in from the swamp," Claypoole said. "We watch our six."

MacIlargie grumbled, but not much, and looked to the rear almost as much as he watched where he was going. Between them, Claypoole and MacIlargie kept an almost constant watch behind Bravo unit.

They were just four bends from the first objective when Schultz murmured to Kerr that he sensed something. Kerr's motion detector also picked up something ahead of them, but it didn't seem to be around the bend where they'd halted.

Hyakowa moved forward and touched helmets with Kerr. "Let me see."

Kerr pushed the motion detector toward Hyakowa. The platoon sergeant flipped up the lid and studied the display.

"First fire team, listen up," Hyakowa said into the command circuit. Schultz and Doyle acknowledged while the others of Bravo unit listened in. "Someone's moving around the next bend after this one. We don't know who it is. I'll take a look here to verify we're clear, then—"

"Already did," Schultz said.

"You looked?"

"It's clear."

"All right. The four of us will advance to the next bend. Kerr, I want you on the inside of the bend. Hammer, outside, but out of sight. Doyle, behind Schultz. I'll be with Kerr. On my command, one of us will look. Got it?"

They rogered.

"The rest of you, hold your positions; I want space if we have to pull back in a hurry. Taylor, get your gun ready to cover us. Use your infra so you know we aren't in your line of fire if you have to shoot. Got it?"

Corporal Taylor, the gun team leader, acknowledged.

"Second fire team, use your infras, be ready to support. Third fire team, watch the rear."

Claypoole and Corporal Chan acknowledged.

"Let's do it."

The four Marines moved silently around the corner and took positions at the next bend, twenty meters farther along. Hyakowa, still holding the motion detector, stuck close to Kerr.

Kerr listened to the motion detector's earpiece, Hyakowa looked at its display. Hyakowa spoke softly. "There's less movement than before, but it's in the next straightaway."

"That's how it sounds to me," Kerr agreed.

"Hammer, are you close enough to see anything?"

"A shadow. Wait." Schultz lowered himself to his knees and leaned forward onto his left hand. He held his blaster ready in his right, then stretched forward.

Simultaneously, he pulled back and pressed the firing lever on his blaster. The tunnel wall centimeters from his head burst into rock dust. The chattering roar that filled the tunnel told the Marines the Skinks had a buzz saw set up around the corner.

Kerr stuck his blaster around the corner and fired blindly. Schultz flattened himself and stretched out his right arm to point his blaster down the next length of tunnel and fired away. Brilliant light flared and the buzz saw's roar stopped. Schultz scuttled forward to where he could see.

"No Skinks," he said, and bolted to his feet to sprint the few meters to the buzz saw.

Hyakowa slapped the motion detector against Kerr, who took it and replaced it in its holder.

"Come on, first fire team!" Hyakowa ordered, and pushed Kerr ahead of him.

Nervous sweat washed over Doyle as he followed.

There were scorch marks on the floor, walls, and ceiling of the tunnel near the buzz saw, showing where Skinks had flared, but the weapon didn't seem to have suffered any damage.

"Everybody up," Hyakowa ordered. He turned the buzz saw around to face away from his Marines and knelt to examine it. "Allah's pointed teeth," he murmured. "This looks almost like the firing mechanism on some twenty-first-century machine guns I saw in the Marine Corps Museum on Carhart's World. Heads up, everybody." He took hold of the two handles in the rear of the weapon and pressed his thumbs on the swivel plate between them. The buzz saw ripped, and the wall of the tunnel at the next bend powdered. He pulled his thumbs back almost instantly, but the burst was still long enough to plow a gouge several centimeters deep in the wall. He examined the weapon more closely. Except for the oddly cased barrel, it looked remarkably similar to the ancient machine guns in the museum. The box on the side of what appeared to be the receiver assembly had to be the ammunition container, he decided. How many rounds did it hold? Two more canisters sat on the floor nearby. There was nothing that resembled a safety—unless it was, *yes*! Another plate slid out from in front of one of the handles hooked into a recess in front of the other handle and covered the thumb trigger to keep it from being accidentally depressed.

"First fire team, cover the next bend. Chan up." Hyakowa continued to examine the buzz saw. In a moment he had the receiver cover raised and the ammunition container detached and open. Inside, the receiver didn't look like anything he'd ever seen before. The container was filled with uniform metal bits. They didn't look particularly aerodynamic, but he guessed at the speed they were propelled, they didn't have to be. There was no obvious mechanism for feeding them into the receiver. He pulled one out and weighed it in his hand. It felt lighter than ten grams.

"First fire team, get back here." He lowered his infra to make sure the three Marines got behind him. When they were out of the line of fire, he reattached the container, closed the receiver cover, and shoved the safety plate out of the way. He tapped his fingers against the trigger plate and a short burst shot from the buzz saw's muzzle.

"Chan, did you see everything I did?" Hyakowa asked as he replaced the safety.

"Yes."

"Show me." He moved out of the way. He watched the receiver cover rise and the ammo container lift off, then re-attach and the cover close. The safety slid out of the way and the trigger plate depressed briefly. A burst powdered more of the facing wall.

"We're in business. Chan, you've got the buzz saw. Have each of your men carry one of those ammo containers. Let's move out."

Third platoon's Bravo unit resumed its advance into the depths of the Skink stronghold.

*   *   *

The Great Master received reports of the battle in his command center. The reports were all negative. Nearly all of the heavy guns that could take out Earthmen aircraft and armored vehicles were destroyed. The advance of the Earthmen scum army of this mudball to the west of the underground complex had been stopped, but at the cost of too many weapons and Fighters for the defense to hold for much longer. Earthmen Marines were inside the complex, advancing against scattered and disorganized resistance from the south. The mission to draw the Earthmen Marines into a decisive battle had succeeded. But yet again, the True People had failed to defeat the Earthmen Marines. *He* had failed.

He summoned his second in command and major subordinate commanders to meet him in his quarters. They arrived and bowed respectfully. The Great Master sat cross-legged on a mat on the floor, wearing a simple robe. They waited for him to speak.

"I have failed," the Great Master said at length, his voice chalk crushed underfoot.

The few Over Masters who attended him stood silent, their heads bowed.

"Send the rovers against Haven to draw the Earthmen back," he said to the Over Master in command of defense, his voice a rasp on wood. "Prepare defenses for when the Earthmen Marines return.

"Get a message to the Grand Master Commanding," he told the commander of communications, his voice the sigh of a breeze through an ancient forest. "Tell him we need the ship.

"Take command," he ordered his second in command. "Return Home with the survivors," his voice a mouse gnawing a hole in a silo's side.

"Now leave me," he said, his voice sand running through a glass.

The few Over Masters who attended the Great Master bowed again, not as deeply as when they arrived, and filed out of his quarters. A Large One remained behind.

"You know what to do," the Great Master rasp-whispered to the Large One, who bowed deeply in appreciation of the singular honor he was being granted.

The Great Master opened his robe and shrugged it off his shoulders. He reached under his thigh to pick up a knife that had lain there out of sight and raised it before his misted eyes. Slowly, he lowered the knife and turned it until its point rested ever so softly against the side of his abdomen. He held it there for the time of two rasping breaths, then plunged it in and slashed it across with the same fervor he had cut through the bodies of foes when he was a young Master at war.

The Large One bent over the Great Master and took the knife from his trembling hands. Then he gripped his commander's head with one hand and bent it back. He sliced the Great Master's throat to the bone. When the Great Master's eyes glazed, the Large One flamed the corpse.

The Marines hadn't entered the underground through all of the entrances on its southern fringes; there weren't enough platoons and squads. Nor did they have enough Dragons to cover the entrances the infantry hadn't used. And there were many, many more entrances in the wide gap between the fringes where the Marines went underground and the western fringes where the Army of the Lord fought its terrible battle. Many of those entrances were large enough for smallish vehicles to use. Small armored vehicles began to trickle out of the larger cave and tunnel mouths; entrances the Marines hadn't used, entrances between the Marines and the Kingdomites, entrances deeper within the Skink stronghold. None of the vehicles sought out the Dragons standing watch on the southern fringes, none assaulted the Army of the Lord to the west. Instead they struggled through the waterways, heading southwest, toward Haven. The going was difficult for the vehicles because they were designed for travel on dry land and had only limited amphibious capabilities.

The string-of-pearls spotted them almost as soon as the first one moved from the darkness underground to the light of day.

Brigadier Sturgeon got the report from the *Grandar Bay* and saw the speckling on the large situation map that indicated the vehicles. He swore under his breath. Where had those things come from? Why hadn't the Skinks used them before?

"Get me a visual on one of those vehicles," he ordered.

In seconds an image from one of the many surveillance devices planted by the Marines came up on his console. A tank trundled past the device. It seemed sluggish, though he thought that might have been because of the marsh. The tank tapered in steps, front and back, to a cupola on the top. The barrel of a weapon sprouted from the front of the cupola. Using the Skink who was half out of the top of the cupola for scale, Sturgeon was able to tell its size—less than half that of a Dragon. When it climbed out of the water onto an islet, he saw it moved on two pairs of treads, one fore, the other aft.

He looked at the large situation map. The speckles of the armored vehicles seemed to all be moving toward Haven.

"Get me an ID on that weapon," he ordered Commander Daana, the intelligence officer. By the look of the barrel, he suspected it was an acid shooter. If it was, Marine artillery and aircraft could do the attackers severe damage. But if it was a rail gun . . . The Haven defenses were thinly manned by two understrength Kingdomite infantry divisions that would be shattered by the three hundred or so small tanks headed toward them. He needed his infantry. But most of the platoons and squad were out of touch inside the Skink stronghold.

"Two, send recon and the scout-snipers in to get the infantry out, we need them here," he ordered Daana.

"Aye aye, sir," Daana answered. He passed the order to his comm men. A moment later he said, "Sir, I have an ID on those weapons. Acid shooters. The Skinks used those tanks in several attacks during the course of the original invasion. According to the ambassador's records, they're pretty nimble." He looked at an image on a console. The vehicles didn't seem nimble in marsh. On the large situation map, speckles began blinking out as the *Grandar Bay*'s lasers picked them off. More flowed from underground. The small tanks started to join together in formations.

Another report came in from the *Grandar Bay*.

"An object, possibly a defensive missile, just launched from the Skink complex. It jumped into Beamspace before the Laser Gunnery Division could fix on it."

"That's impossible," Daana said. "Nothing can jump into Beamspace from inside a gravity well!"

"I know that," the *Grandar Bay* replied, "but all the signatures it kicked out said it was doing it anyway."

"Then it probably destroyed itself."

"We're hoping that up here. If it didn't, we don't even know in what direction to look for it." The *Grandar Bay*'s comm officer sounded very nervous.

"Two," Sturgeon interjected, "the recordings recovered from Society 437 showed Skink shuttles moving in and out of Beamspace inside a gravity well. It might be impossible, but they do it anyway."

Before Daana could reply, the *Grandar Bay*'s comm officer spoke again, this time with evident relief. "We picked it up again, it made a course adjustment. It's not a defensive missile, it's heading out-system!"

Sturgeon squeezed his eyes shut to block the sudden pain he felt. He remembered the message Ambassador Spears showed him from *Fundy's Tide*. Society 362, only three light-years away, almost positively had Skinks. That launch was probably a drone heading for Society 362, a request for reinforcements. Three light-years. Not quite twelve hours, standard, travel time in Beamspace—assuming the Skinks traveled in Beamspace at the same rate as human ships. Given the Skink ability to move in and out of Beamspace within a gravity well, the only question was how fast reinforcements could board ships. If they were already on board, it was conceivable that more Skinks could arrive in just over twenty-four hours, standard.

"Where's my infantry?" he growled.

The infantry was assembling by platoons and companies in six predetermined locations, one per company, within the Skink stronghold. Of the thirty-five units from the two FISTs—which ranged from reinforced platoon down to reinforced squads—that entered the massive cave and tunnel complex, only sixteen had contact with Skinks. Eleven had captured buzz saws, and seven of the eleven had figured out how to work them. The four that hadn't figured it out were quickly shown. Marines were always armed and deadly; now they were better armed and more deadly.

Company L assembled in a large chamber that had matting on the floor and a low dais at one end. A chair with a low seat, oddly elegant despite its lack of ornamentation, stood on the dais.

The two units of third platoon were jubilant at rejoining. They admired the buzz saw each had captured. Each group was only slightly disappointed that the other had figured out how the weapon worked, and neither was able to show off its superior skills.

"Listen up," Captain Conorado shouted. He had his helmet off so his men could see him. Everyone except the few who were assigned to watch the entrances to the chamber looked at the company commander.

"Don't think we've got this fight won yet," Conorado said sternly. "All we've done so far is clear a few entrances to this complex. You've seen the maps, so you have an idea how big it is. We've barely gotten inside. There's a lot more fighting ahead of us. Some Marines are going to die and some will be crippled before we're finished. I want as few of those dead or crippled Marines as possible to be from Company L." He transmitted the current situation map to the platoon commanders and platoon sergeants. His voice lost its harsh edge and he continued. "Here's where we are and where we're going next. Show it to your people."

Throughout the chamber, Marines clustered around their squad leaders to study the maps they projected into the air.

Conorado checked the time. Lacking communications between companies, the operation was being coordinated by the clock.

"Rest up a bit," he said. "We're moving out in one-four minutes. Any questions?"

"Send more Skinks!" Corporal Dean shouted.

"Don't worry about it, Dean," Conorado said above the laughter. "We've got quite enough of them ahead of us."

The two Marines of a scout-sniper team, breathless from running, arrived less than two minutes before Conorado gave the order for Company L to move out.

"Company L!" he shouted. "New orders. We are withdrawing. The Skinks have launched an armor attack on Haven."

Armor. The word shot through the Marines like a jolt of electricity. Most of them had fought in the campaign on Diamunde, the first war in centuries in which heavy armor was used in combat. They shuddered when they remembered the monster vehicles that had been so hard to kill and had killed so many members of the company. That war had been fought by six FISTs and an entire army and was supported by navy Air. Even then, the outcome had been in doubt for weeks. Here, there were only two FISTs, no army backing them up, and no navy Air in support.

Armor! Christ on a crutch? It was more like Buddha's blue balls locked in Mohammed's pointed teeth!

CHAPTER
TWENTY-FOUR

Free from worry about rail guns, half of the Marine Raptors stopped firing Jerichos at the Skinks battling the Army of the Lord and took flight after the armor, which began massing as soon as it left the wetlands. The small tanks were nimble enough to avoid most of the point-target missiles the Raptors fired. The Marines quickly shifted back to Jerichos and found them very effective against the little armored vehicles.

Artillery, Marine and Kingdomite, began pounding the Skink armor as soon as it got in range. As imposing as they looked to men on foot, the Skink tanks' armor was thin, and so highly vulnerable to area-denial munitions. Between the Jerichos and the artillery, they died by the dozens. The survivors fled back for their underground homes, reaching the marshes and swamps, only to encounter the Marine infantry. The captured buzz saws simply shredded the tanks. The guns of blaster platoons and the bigger guns of the assault platoons easily burned through the thin armor with long bursts and vaporized the crews. Blastermen who evaded detection found that a fire team that concentrated its three blasters' fire had enough power to burn through the thin armor at the backs of the tanks. Almost none of the tanks of the Skink counterattack made it back underground.

"Now I know why they didn't use their armor against us earlier," Brigadier Sturgeon said. He wondered what other surprises the Skinks had in store. That futile attack had to have been a diversion. But a diversion for what?

He ordered the infantry to return to Haven. He made sure Commodore Borland understood the situation the same way he did, then composed messages to dispatch to the Combined Chiefs, Commandant Tokis, and Assistant Commandant Aguinaldo to travel in the same drone Borland was using to send messages to the Combined Chiefs, the Chief of Naval Operations, and the Minister of War.

The staffs of Marine Expeditionary Forces, Kingdom, and the two FISTs worked on defense plans. They assumed the worst—that Skink reinforcements superior in number to the original Skink invasion force were on their way.

All Raptors returned to base to preserve the remaining Jerichos. The Hoppers, with less effective area weapons, replaced the Raptors in support of the Army of the Lord on the western fringes of the Skink stronghold. Marine artillery was moved into position and added its support. It wasn't long before the Skink resistance completely collapsed. Sturgeon ordered Archbishop General Lambsblood to return his divisions to Haven.

Lambsblood was furious. He wanted to pursue the demons into their Hades and expel them back to the hell they had come from. Unwillingly and protesting, he complied with Sturgeon's orders. Twelve hours after the collapse of the Skinks' western resistance, the badly battered divisions that had participated in that assault were integrated into the Haven defenses, which looked a great deal different from how they had earlier.

Twenty-four hours and thirty-seven minutes after the Skink drone launched, a starship the size of a Crowe-class Amphibious Battle Cruiser popped out of Beamspace into orbit within visual range of the fast frigate CNSS *Admiral J. P. Jones*. The *J. P. Jones* was so surprised by a starship entering Space-3 that deep in a gravity well, it didn't immediately take defensive action. By the time it did it was too late—missiles fired by the Skink starship had already been fired and were closing on the *J. P. Jones*. The *J. P. Jones* got off one shot from its laser battery before the incoming missiles destroyed it. The debris cloud left by the fast frigate began its slow expansion.

The *Grandar Bay*, in orbit on the opposite side of Kingdom, was shocked by the abrupt arrival of the Skink starship in orbit and the destruction of the *J. P. Jones*. Battle stations were called immediately and the *Grandar Bay* prepared to defend itself. But the strange starship didn't attack. It dropped shuttles that popped in and out of Beamspace on their way around the globe to the Skink stronghold.

The Marines gritted their teeth. Those so inclined prayed to whatever gods they believed in. They did whatever they could to prepare themselves for a fight they expected would be fiercer than any they'd ever been in before.

The Soldiers of the Lord weren't told about the arrival of the Skink starship and the impossible descent of the shuttles. Lambsblood was too afraid of panic in the ranks and mass desertions.

The first shuttles touched down in the wetlands. On the *Grandar Bay*, the Laser Gunnery Division locked on targets and fired.

"What do you mean, missed?" demanded the gunnery officer.

"The targets are still there," the senior chief petty officer who was the gunnery chief said. "Must be a glitch in the aiming program."

The gunnery officer checked the visual, radar, and emissions displays. The lasers had fired at an array of six shiny shuttles on the ground. The six shuttles were still there, apparently intact and unharmed.

"Run diagnostics on the computer and debug the program," the gunnery officer ordered. "And while you're at it, fire another salvo at those shuttles."

"Aye aye," the chief said.

The gunnery officer watched the displays as the lasers fired the salvo. He nodded to himself. The cloud of mist that rose from the ground made it obvious that the lasers hadn't missed. Then he watched in utter astonishment as five shuttles rose above the mist and blinked into Beamspace. When the mist cleared, he saw one shuttle still sitting there. He adjusted his visual display to show the shuttle in the highest resolution possible. The resolution wasn't fine enough for him to be certain, but it appeared that the shuttle's ramp was down and that there was significant charring around the open ramp.

"Missed again, sir," the gunnery chief said.

"Show me." His display flicked to another view, and he saw six shuttles rise and blink out. He adjusted the resolution and could just make out evidence of laser damage in the bit of marsh he looked at. He located another half-dozen shuttles and watched while tiny dots representing Skinks boiled out of the water and onto the shuttles. The shuttles rose into the air and blinked out.

"They aren't bringing in reinforcements!" he exclaimed. "They're pulling out. Get me the bridge. Watch the targets. Try to shoot when their ramps are down."

While the Laser Gunnery Division was struggling to kill the Skink shuttles, *Grandar Bay*'s Orbital Missile Division struggled to kill the Skink starship. But every time the starship launched a flight of shuttles, it blinked into Beamspace, only to return at a different place to recover a flight of shuttles. Each time it returned to orbit around Kingdom, it launched two salvos of missiles of its own. One salvo, aimed at the string-of-pearls, knocked out satellite after satellite. The other went at the *Grandar Bay*, which couldn't jump into Beamspace to get out of the way. The Laser Gunnery Division was diverted from its attacks on the shuttles to defensive fire against the Skink orbital missiles. None of the Skink missiles got through the laser fire.

The debris from the destruction of the Skink missiles was another matter. Each destroyed missile burst into a cloud of fragments. Some of the debris plunged into lower orbits and burned up in Kingdom's atmosphere. Other bits lost part of their velocity, and their orbits decayed until they also burned up in the atmosphere. Detonating warheads imparted enough velocity to some fragments to send them upward at escape velocity, and they disappeared into interplanetary space. But there were chunks that continued on their original trajectories and peppered the hull of the *Grandar Bay*.

All nonessential compartments on the side of the *Grandar Bay* facing the missiles were evacuated, secured, and their atmospheres pumped out. The Damage Control Division went into red status. The *Grandar Bay* was double-hulled to reduce the chance of catastrophic interior rupture. Vacuum-suited sailors worked swiftly in the tween'ull space between the starship's outer and inner hulls to patch holes. Fortunately, few of the fragments struck the *Grandar Bay* with enough kinetic energy to pierce the inner hull.

Then a warhead that failed to detonate went unrecognized into a parabolic orbit that put it on a collision course with the navy starship. By the time the tracking system realized the fragment coming at the *Grandar Bay* was a warhead, it was only a few hundred meters away. The close-in guns, designed to destroy oversized hunks of space debris or hostile shuttles attempting to board the starship, had trouble hitting a target as small as the warhead, and it was less than two hundred meters away when it was finally hit and detonated. The tiny fragments that hit the *Grandar Bay* were negligible.

The Orbital Missile Division stopped trying to fix on the Skink starship and send targeted missiles at it. Instead it launched salvos of missiles armed with proximity-attraction fuses in the hope that the Skinks would reenter Space-3 close enough to one of the missiles for it to divert to the starship and hit it before it could jump back into Beamspace. One finally did get a lock. The Skink starship's jump back and the missile's explosion were so close together that the *Grandar Bay*'s computers couldn't tell if the missile hit it or not.

Whichever, the starship didn't return. No Skink shuttles were planetside. It was conjectured that it might not have returned because its evacuation mission was over. The *Grandar Bay* sent Essays into the debris cloud left by the *Admiral J. P. Jones* to search for survivors. Only sailors who were already in vaccuum suits when the starship was hit could possibly have survived. There were a few, but precious few.

Brigadier Sturgeon immediately summoned his two FIST commanders and Archbishop General Lambsblood.

His orders to them were succinct: "Brigadier Sparen, Colonel Ramadan, prepare your FISTs for immediate embarkation on the *Grandar Bay*. I believe I know where the Skink starship went. We're going after it. Archbishop General, there may still be Skinks underground. You have the best maps of the Skink complex we have available. Send a division to search it thoroughly and root out any Skinks who remained behind."

Lambsblood slapped his open hand on the tabletop. "NO!" he bellowed. "You are only trying to sacrifice the Soldiers of the Lord. Send your Marines underground. They have been in the tunnels, they know how to search the caves. If the Soldiers of the Lord go into the bowels of the earth, they risk everlasting damnation at the talons of the demons below!"

Sturgeon waited for Lambsblood to finish, then said in a deceptively calm voice, "Archbishop General, you heard my orders for my Marines. The invasion here is over. We are going in pursuit of the enemy. Mopping up any remnants of their forces is your responsibility. And, if I remember correctly, yesterday you argued strongly against pulling your army back to Haven because you wanted to pursue the Skinks into their caves."

Lambsblood ignored Sturgeon's reminder of what he'd said the day before and focused instead on the Marines' departure. "No! By all that's holy, I know what you are up to. You wish to weaken the Army of the Lord. That has been your objective on every assignment you have given the Army of the Lord since you arrived on Kingdom. Our casualties have been horrendous. We are already too weak to perform all of our normal duties."

Sturgeon held up a hand to cut him off. "Your casualties dropped dramatically once my Marines started training with them and leading them. Your casualties when the Skinks launched their major assault against the Haven perimeter were severe, but without my Marines, the Skinks would have totally wiped out your defenses and captured Haven. Yes, you suffered badly in Operation Slay Demons. *They would have been less if you had stopped when I told you to!* But no, you had to keep going until the Skinks could hit your fragmented forces from all directions.

"Archbishop General, the severe damage your army has suffered has been the result of incompetent leadership, inadequate training on your part, and poor tactics. The only thing I could have done more than I did to save your army was to dismiss you and your entire officer corps!

"Now, we are leaving to pursue the invader and destroy their ability to launch another invasion. If any Skinks remain on Kingdom, finding and neutralizing them is your responsibility. Any harm that comes to the people of Kingdom from any remaining Skinks who aren't hunted down is on your head."

Furious, Lambsblood blustered, but couldn't find anything coherent to say. He finally stood so abruptly that he knocked his chair over, then he stormed out.

"Well spoken, Ted," Ramadan said when the Kingdomite commander was gone.

Sturgeon's only reply was an annoyed growl.

"How soon will the navy be ready for us to board?" Sparen asked.

"I don't know. I haven't told Commodore Borland what we're going to do."

Brigadier Sturgeon caught a shuttle to the *Grandar Bay* to tell Commodore Borland what he wanted in person. The commodore received him in the captain's dining salon. The room was lined with what looked like real mahogany wainscotting; painted portraits of ships and navy officers hung on its walls. They sat at a table covered by a white linen cloth with a damasked pattern. The coffee and cake service settings and napkin holders before them appeared to be sterling silver. The coffee a steward poured into china cups, Sturgeon was sure, was from Earth-grown beans. He thought of the Flag Clubs he'd been to on brief visits to Headquarters, Marine Corps, at Fargo on Earth, and other major Marine Corps and navy bases. The captain's dining salon appeared to be as richly appointed as any of them. The navy does take care of itself, he thought. He didn't recognize the flavor of the cake.

"They killed the *Jones*," Borland started. He was obviously shaken by the loss of the fast frigate; it was rare for a Confederation Navy starship to be lost in orbital battle. "That ship had a crew of two hundred officers and men." He shook his head. "We only found seventeen of them alive." He straightened up and forced the pain from his face; the Marines had suffered far worse casualties. "But that's my problem, not yours. You had something you want to discuss with me."

Sturgeon nodded. "I'm sorry for your losses, Roger, I truly am." After a brief pause, he gave the reason for his visit.

The commodore had two reasons for saying no.

"My starship took hull damage during the Skink evacuation," was the first. "We need repairs, the kind we can only get in a navy shipyard."

"Is the *Grandar Bay* crippled?" Sturgeon knew it wasn't.

"Crippled? No. But the outer hull was breached in numerous places. The patches are intended as temporary expedients, not as permanent repairs. We need a shipyard for that."

"But those temporary repairs will hold long enough to make a trip all the way back to Earth, plus a three-lights' side trip, won't they?" Again Sturgeon knew the answer.

So Borland hauled out his second reason. "I have messages from a civilian starship approaching Society 362—"

"Ambassador Spears showed me his message from

Fundy's Tide. I know about what may have been a rail gun that fired on the ship."

Borland cocked an eyebrow at Sturgeon. He hadn't known that the ambassador also received a message. Then, "Did you know the *Fundy's Tide* hasn't been heard from since?"

Sturgeon hadn't known.

"Did the ambassador's message mention the flotilla of unidentified vessels in orbit around Society 362?"

This was the first Sturgeon had heard about the orbiting ships.

"And that one of them appeared to be the size of a Crowe-class Amphibious Battle Cruiser?"

"A Mandalay-class ship is the same size as a Crowe."

"Yes, it is," Borland agreed. "But it doesn't have the same armament. What if that Skink ship does? And I don't have my escort anymore." They both took for granted that the ships in orbit around Society 362 were probably Skinks.

"How many ships do the Skinks have in orbit at Society 362?"

Borland shook his head. The *Fundy's Tide* message hadn't given a number, it only used a plural.

"What's the range of your lasers?"

"They're defensive weapons, Ted. They can take out planetside missile launchers. They aren't designed for ship-to-ship combat in interplanetary space."

"How about your missiles?"

Borland shook his head. "Defensive. Not much good for use outside planetary orbit."

"You've got some sharp engineers on board, Roger. Can they modify the lasers or the missiles?"

The commodore had to smile. "I've got the best engineers in the navy, Ted. But no matter how good they are, Society 362 is so close there isn't enough time to modify anything."

Sturgeon smiled back, but his was a crooked grin. "You're right, Roger. It's Marines who do the impossible in a day or two, not the navy. I'm sorry for your losses." He began to stand.

"You sit your ass right back down there, Marine!" Borland planted a fist on the table and leaned over it. "Now hear this and hear it well! A Mandalay-class starship isn't supposed to go in harm's way without at least a destroyer division in escort," he said harshly. "That's graven in stone in NavRegs. I did have one, lone, fast frigate. Now I don't even have that. If I take the *Grandar Bay* to Society 362 and we find the reported flotilla, if I survive I won't need the pension the navy won't give me because I'll be spending the rest of my life at hard labor in a maximum security brig! It's not a matter of what I want to do, or a matter of what my engineers can do. It's NavRegs.

"Goddamn!" He sat back and pounded his fist on the table. "I'd love to head for Society 362 and get those bastards. But I can't, you have to see that!"

Sturgeon said nothing, merely watched Borland, who was obviously thinking hard about the situation. After a long moment he asked a question to nudge the commodore.

"Who knows about the contents of that second message?"

"Me and my XO." He began drumming his fingers on the tablecloth and drifted back into thought.

Sturgeon let him think. The Marine might have been in command of operations as long as they were on Kingdom, but he knew that when the two FISTs boarded, command transferred to Borland.

Borland snapped back to the here and now and pressed a button out of sight on the bottom of the tabletop. A white-coated steward opened the salon door and stepped inside.

"Get Captain Maugli for me," Borland said.

"Aye aye, sir." The steward quietly closed the door behind him as he left.

Borland killed some time by putting out another silver setting and refilling the cups.

Maugli, the *Grandar Bay*'s executive officer, entered the

dining salon almost immediately after Borland resumed his seat. "You called for me, sir?"

"Yes I did, number one. Sit down, Zsuz. You've met Brigadier Sturgeon."

"Yessir." Captain Maugli sat at the third setting but didn't touch the coffee or cake that waited for him.

"How'd you like to go after the Skinks?"

"I'd love to, sir, but NavRegs . . ." He lifted a hand and turned it over.

"NavRegs say we can't knowingly go in harm's way without an escort. You know the regs better than I do. What do they say about finding ourselves in harm's way?"

"You mean if we go someplace where we have no reason to expect trouble and find it? That depends on the mood of the court of inquiry," the ghost of a smile crossed Maugli's face, "and on the success of the mission."

"I believe we received a message from a civilian freighter approaching Society 362, something garbled about high velocity objects coming at them from the plane of the elliptic?"

"Yessir, I believe we did." Maugli's smile became less ghostly. "Terribly garbled, though. The drone that carried it must have run into something in Beamspace that scrambled it."

"And that civilian freighter hasn't been heard from since, has it?"

Maugli's smile was now a grin. "Nossir, it hasn't. And I do believe Communications will verify that."

"So it's possible, even likely, that the civilian freighter was crippled?"

Maugli nodded.

"What do NavRegs say about going to the rescue of civilian shipping?"

"Providing that such a diversion does not interfere with an essential military operation, a rescue is top priority."

Borland turned to Sturgeon. "Brigadier, would you say operations planetside have reached a satisfactory conclusion?"

"Commodore, I would say all that's left planetside is some minor mopping up that's best left to local forces."

"Well then, Brigadier, I request you embark your Marines. Number one, begin preparations for transit to Society 362. We have a ship to avenge, er, find."

Commodore Borland had his engineers working on modifications to the *Grandar Bay*'s weaponry before Brigadier Sturgeon touched down planetside. Borland wasn't concerned that this would look suspicious to the court of inquiry he'd face if he survived; most of the advances in modern navy navigation, arms, and other systems were made by starship officers and crews who played with them during their long hauls in Beamspace, when most of them had nothing else to do. He needed lasers that would be effective at ranges far greater than geosynchronous orbit, and he needed missiles that could lock onto and hit targets at one astronomical unit. Without them, the *Grandar Bay* could be destroyed with all hands before it got close enough to use its weapons, or have to abort the mission before it accomplished anything.

A Mandalay-class Amphibious Landing Ship, Force, was designed to carry a reinforced FIST, so the Marines of the 34th and 26th FISTs were cramped in the *Grandar Bay*, but not as cramped as they might have been—both had suffered casualties and were understrength. The *Grandar Bay*'s deck crew worked round the clock to jury-rig enough racks for all of them. Hot racking—Marines sharing a bunk in shifts— would have worked for a trip inside a planetary system, but everyone needed to be securely strapped in for jumps into and out of Beamspace. The first phase of transit to Society 362 was the three days it took the starship to get far enough out of Kingdom's gravity well to safely make the jump.

After a few minutes less than twelve hours in Beamspace, the *Grandar Bay* made the jump back to Space-3. Navigation had cut it close, maybe too close—they were only two and a half days' travel above the plane of the elliptical, almost directly due north of Society 362. Minutes later emanations were detected from three ships in orbit around the destination planet. One was the size of a Crowe. The other two were destroyer size. On the face of it, the *Grandar Bay* was likely outgunned. More worrisome, though, was what the nearby gravity well was doing to the starship.

CHAPTER
TWENTY-FIVE

The pain was a constant companion, like existing permanently in a sheet of white-hot flame.

He was immobilized, not with straps and chains but by the effects of some drug. He couldn't move his head, so his field of vision—blurry at best—was restricted to what he could make out just above where he lay. In the few lucid moments when his entire being was not being consumed by pain, he could make out dark shapes looming and flitting about the edges of his vision. He supposed they were images of his tormenters. In those brief moments of relative respite, he could remember who he was and how he'd gotten into that living hell. Then too, he heard screaming that was not his own, so he knew he was not alone. In those few moments of relief, hatred and defiance welled up within him and he thought the most foul curses to hurl against his tormentors. But such thoughts were followed immediately by the all-consuming pain. He realized the monsters who were holding him knew what he was thinking at such times, and they did not like it. And then there were the voices: they whispered insistently, telling him horrible things, asking him disturbing questions, demanding answers, cajoling him to cooperate. They were not couched in language but consisted of thoughts somehow dropped into his brain, wet and slimy like gobs of spittle. They were somebody else's dirty mental images, from the brain of someone who hated him and who could somehow enter his consciousness, overriding any attempt he made to block the intrusion. He could not remember afterward precisely what was asked or what he answered, but he knew he answered, and that disturbed him greatly. Clearly his interrogators were not satisfied with his answers because the pain continued.

When the other mind withdrew from his momentarily, giving him back some control over his own thoughts, he concentrated on remembering who he was and how he'd gotten to that place. Through the haze of the pain, he vowed: You will *not* break me! I will defy you even if it kills me!

If death was the only way he could get out of there, he'd gladly accept it. But goddammit, he wanted to live!

Zechariah remained by his son's grave after he'd given the others orders to resume the march. He had even ordered Consort and Comfort away. He had to be alone for a while. He could catch up when he was ready.

At length he got to his feet and looked about. They could find this spot again, he thought, when things got back to normal, or even if they didn't, and remove Samuel's remains to a more fitting resting place. He stood over the freshly turned earth and listened carefully. He heard no sounds at all above the furtive rustlings of forest creatures and insectlike lifeforms. That was very good because it meant that the refugee column was proceeding in almost total silence. Fortunately, there were no infants among them and even the youngest of the children were cooperating in the noise discipline Zechariah had imposed on their movements.

Nehemiah Sewall was walking point, one of the alien acid rigs strapped to his back. He held the long, flexible, hose apparatus loosely in one hand as he cautiously threaded through the undergrowth, stopping every few meters to check his direction and survey what lay ahead. Ten meters or so behind him and ten meters to the right flank of the column, Comfort Brattle provided flank security, her shot rifle at the ready. On the left flank Amen Judah did the same. Behind them, at the head of the column, two of the younger men, equipped with acid-throwers, watched for Nehemiah's signals; at the tail end two more, similarly armed, provided security and watched for Zechariah to rejoin them.

They had tested the devils' acid-projectors before putting the rigs on. The mechanisms were easy to figure out. The rig was mounted on a packboard with shoulder straps, and consisted of two tanks—one large, painted green, and the other somewhat smaller and painted russet. The colors were muted, to blend in with the foliage native to that hemisphere. The larger of the two containers held the acid, and the smaller held the compressed-air propellant. A single hose ran from a coupling between the tanks, up under the user's arm and to a nozzle assembly that looked something like the muzzle of the shot rifle Comfort was armed with. The nozzles were about .75 caliber. By depressing a lever behind the nozzle, a thin stream of the stuff could be projected a good fifty meters. The special gloves the devils used to protect themselves against back spray would not fit human hands, but in the equipment bags they'd recovered from the dead devils there were different-size shields that could be fitted behind the nozzles to serve the same purpose. Each acid tank bore writing in characters that were indecipherable, just lines and squiggles, but the analog gauges were easy to read: they indicated all the tanks were full. The units were light, and although the straps were not designed to fit the human body, they fit it well enough even when the refugees moved through heavy undergrowth. The tanks were also durable: several had sustained hits from the shot rifles when their owners had been killed, but none of the bullets had penetrated the metal.

The refugees had gone from being a frightened and desperate gaggle stumbling through the wilderness to an armed and alert force that had drawn blood in its first encounter with the devils and was ready for battle. Nehemiah held up his hand. Through the foliage about twenty meters ahead of where he crouched, he could see that the trees thinned out, and the forest ended in a vast, hilly plain. His heart jumped. He knew they were about maybe thirty kilometers from New Salem. He motioned the others forward, and soon everyone crouched nearby under the cover of the trees. Without being told to do so, the armed security detail had taken up positions on the group's flanks. The sun shone brightly on the plain, but they were in deep shade back under the trees.

Zechariah came up and crouched beside Nehemiah. "Good work," he said, clapping the young man on his shoulder. He caught Comfort's eye on the far edge of the group and smiled. "Gather 'round," he told the others in a low voice. They scrunched in closer, making a rustling sound in the undergrowth. They were like so many furtive animals hiding from larger predators, but now he saw something else in their eyes: determination and alertness. "We can't cross there in the daylight," Zechariah said, nodding toward the open plain on the other side of the trees, "so I say we camp right here until nightfall and then start out." The others murmured their assent.

"How long will it take us to get home?" Sharon Rowley asked.

"Let's take it in easy stages. The Shelomoth River is about ten kilometers from here, if memory serves. We can make it there with plenty of darkness to spare."

"That's right!" Joshua Flood exclaimed. "I've fished and hunted there many times. The river bottom is thick with cover. We can hide there until tomorrow night."

"Yes," Samuel Sewall chimed in. "And no more than twelve kilometers beyond the river are the Sacar Hills. When I was a boy, we grazed sheep there. I remember some caves we can use to fort up during the day."

"Thank the Lord for the wild cattle," Susan Maynard said.

"Amen," someone replied. They suspected that if the devils had infrared surveillance in operation, they might not be able to distinguish between a group of slowly moving humans and the many herds of grazing cattle that inhabited the plain, the descendants of animals released many generations ago by early settlers in the region.

"All right, then," Zechariah summarized, "tonight we head for the Shelomoth; tomorrow the Sacar Hills; and the third night should bring us home."

The one thing on everyone's mind, which needed no discussion, was that sooner or later someone was going to miss the devil patrol they had wiped out.

"Our casualties have been enormous since Operation Rippling Lava commenced, and you want me to worry about a mere eight Fighters?" the Over Master roared. "Our forces are closing in on the enemy and you are worried about a lost patrol?"

The Senior Master shuddered and bowed even lower before his commander. The security of the interrogation center was his responsibility, and he had sent the patrol on a reconnaissance of the area, as much to look for more prisoners as to discover any potential threats. It was his duty to inform the Over Master of the overdue patrol.

"Send another patrol, then, to look for the first," the Over Master continued.

"Most respectfully, Lord, I have not the resources to do that and provide security for our operations here," the Senior Master replied.

"Then forget about the missing Fighters! Wild beasts must have gotten them."

"Most respectfully, Lord, the local wild beasts are herbivores, herd creatures, very stupid, most unlikely to attack anyone."

"Enough!" the Over Master bellowed as the Senior Master quivered even more, wishing desperately he could burrow into the floor. "When the eight are found, execute them! I will not have our Fighters dawdling about in the woods. Besides, our work here is almost done. The Great Master has sent word to terminate the interrogations. We are preparing for the final push. Besides, we have gotten all we are going to get out of these useless Earthmen prisoners. They have been reduced to the level of idiots anyway, if they ever had much intelligence to begin with. Revive those who have survived. They may still be useful to us as laborers. When we evacuate this site, do with them what you please. That is all."

The Senior Master respectfully bowed his way out of the

Over Master's presence, the eight missing Fighters completely forgotten. As to the remaining prisoners, they would be left behind to starve in the wilderness because the Senior Master was resolved not to waste a single drop of acid on such pond scum.

The Brattles huddled together on the riverbank just above the turbulent waters of the Shelomoth, dozing fitfully under their blankets. The other refugees clustered nearby. They had arrived just at first light and spent the daylight hours trying to catch up on their sleep. Since their food supply was running low, several of the men and boys had spent the morning catching edible animals in the river while Joshua Flood explored up the riverbank, looking for a fording spot. He returned at dusk and shook Zechariah from a doze.

"I have found it, Mr. Brattle. It was just where I remembered. The water flows over a rock outcropping but we can make it across on foot if we're careful."

Zechariah shook himself and awoke Comfort and Consort. They stretched and gathered up their things. The others were likewise stirring. When it got full dark, Zechariah had them all line up in a column, each person holding on to the shirt of the person in front of him, and took a head count. At his command, Joshua led the way, guided by starlight. Crossing the river was difficult but they all eventually scrambled up the opposite side over a low bank. Once everyone was up, Zechariah took another head count and then, each person still holding on to the one in front, they moved over the plain again. The going was very difficult.

They came in view of the Sacar Hills just as the stars were dimming in the sky. Joshua, in the lead, mounted a small rise and was the first to see them. He froze and instantly ordered everyone down. Zechariah came running up, doubled over to make as small a target as he could. He did not have to ask Joshua what he'd seen once he peered over the ridge. About a kilometer away the hills rose in a low ridge about two hundred meters high.

"Heavenly Father, it's their camp!" Zechariah gasped. At

the base of the ridge a collection of what looked like temporary structures formed a compound, well-lighted from some
unseen source and bustling—with the devils! Fortunately,
the grass all around where they lay was about a meter high,
so they had adequate cover, but it was obvious they could go
no farther that night.

Zechariah crawled down the length of the column, in-
forming everyone that they would have to go to ground
where they were and try to stay hidden until dark. "Conserve
your water," he whispered. "It'll be a hot one today, and
there is no more water between here and New Salem." He
ordered those carrying weapons to join him with Joshua.
"Spread out in the grass to the left and the right, no more
than an arm's length from the person next to you. Keep a
sharp lookout. We'll take turns watching while the others
sleep. If God wills it, we can stay hidden here until dark. If
not and they spot us, we'll take a lot of them with us. But
God is with us."

The day dragged on endlessly, and as the sun rose, the
heat under the grass became stifling. Even so, following
Zechariah's orders, they used their water sparingly. They had
filled the bottles at the river and the water was tepid and
tasted of mud, but at least it was wet.

In mid-afternoon Joshua nudged Zechariah. "What is it?"

"I've been watching for some time now, Mr. Brattle.
There are *people* down there!"

Zechariah peered through the tall grass. Yes! "Oh, dear
God, they're using them as beasts of burden," he whispered.
Then to the others, "Stay still. Do not move. Not a sound
from anyone!" Off to his left he heard Comfort sobbing quietly. He rested his head on his arms as Joshua watched him
nervously. The people were carrying various unrecognizable
objects from one of the caves to what appeared to be a flying machine. Little devils were acting as guards, but it was
too far away to see what condition the humans were in. The
figures staggering under their loads were clearly men, and
the weariness of their movements was evidence of abuse or
exhaustion.

"There is nothing we can do," Zechariah said. "We shall stay hidden here until dark and then move on. Do not mention this to the others until we're safely home."

"It looks like they're leaving, sir," Joshua said.

"Yes, I pray to God that they are," Zechariah answered. "Now, Josh, you get some sleep. I'll watch. Take your eyes away from that sight. Empty your mind of it. We must survive."

That day seemed to drag on forever.

Exhausted and starving, but spirits high, they reached New Salem just before dawn on the third day. Zechariah had maintained strict discipline during the trek, demanding from each person the utmost in self-control, and such was the force of his personality that he had gotten it. Now they all lay flat on a slight rise above the town, waiting for the sun to come up.

New Salem was deserted, and in the days since they had abandoned the place wild cattle had invaded it. In the dim predawn illumination they could clearly make out small groups of the animals bedded down along the streets and in the yards of the abandoned homes. But nothing else stirred down there. "If they're all we have to worry about, we have no worries," Consort Brattle whispered to her husband.

"I can see our home!" Comfort whispered. Zechariah put his arm around her shoulders. There were tears in her eyes but she gripped her shot rifle tightly before her, ready to bring it into action. In those desperate days that lay just behind them, his daughter had become a soldier. He wondered idly what kind of man Samuel would have been had he lived, but he put that thought out of his head as soon as it came to him. No use going down that path. Samuel was with God. Comfort would be his staff now.

The sun broke over the horizon. "It'll be a clear day," Zechariah said. The others along the ridge murmured softly among themselves as they watched the sky lighten. Gradually the rays touched the roofs of the houses, throwing the yards and streets into dark shadows, but as the sun climbed, these faded too, revealing New Salem, a bit shabbier after being abandoned, but otherwise undamaged. When the sun was full up over the horizon, Zechariah stood. He drew his hand-blaster and held it over his head. "Friends, let us go below and take back our lives!" he shouted, starting down the ridge. Despite their weariness, the others raised a loud cheer and followed him down.

Suddenly, Zechariah felt better than he had in days. The fatigue seemed to flow out of him, to be replaced by exuberance. They were *home* at last! They had met the enemy and defeated it and avoided detection, and if they must make a stand, at least it would be in defense of their homes. He lifted his voice in an old, old hymn, and the others, experiencing the same rush of elation at having survived the ordeal, took it up. Their voices echoed through New Salem's empty streets. The wild cattle, alarmed at the villagers' approach, stirred and then rumbled off into the surrounding fields, leaving piles of dung steaming in the early morning sunlight.

But in his heart Zechariah Brattle knew it would be a long, long time, if ever, before they would take back their old lives.

CHAPTER
TWENTY-SIX

The pings, metallic groans, and sharp cracks that reverberated throughout the *Grandar Bay* almost drowned out the alarm klaxons and the huge ship shook violently. An electrician's mate in the radar department had overridden the timers on the clasps of his transition harness so they would release the instant the jump was completed. The shaking threw him from his couch into a power block. The pain in his shoulder had time only to force the beginning of a scream from his mouth before his head slammed into the same power block. His scream cut off when the concussion knocked him out. The ship's shaking tossed him about then slammed him into more hard-surfaced and sharp-edged equipment. He was the only casualty.

Commodore Borland and the bridge officers and crew struggled to gain control of the ship and smooth its passage into Space-3 while Navigation worked feverishly to calculate a course that would use the force of the destabilizing gravity well to stabilize the ship. In the engine rooms, crews struggled valiantly to modulate the inertial power plant to counter the shakes of the ship. The chief-of-ship roared commands to the deck crews, whose men always made jumps wearing vacuum suits. Most of the deck crews shuffled unsteadily on magnetic shoes to the tween'ulls to repair patches broken loose by the violent shaking. Other deck crews answered calls to repair damage wherever the violent shaking had broken things loose.

Elsewhere, officers and crew who weren't involved in

bringing the ship under control or repairing damage stayed strapped down in their jump couches. Those who had duty stations during jumps did what they could to operate their systems while strapped in. The Marines in their compartments remained locked in their jump webbing. Here and there voices rose in prayer and supplication to whatever gods the praying crewmen and Marines thought might give a damn about what happened to them.

Over a period of minutes that seemed much longer to the officers and sailors working on controlling the ship, and longer yet to the crew and Marines strapped helplessly in place, the bucking starship was calmed down. The Marines were kept strapped in to keep them out of the way while the ship was hurriedly inspected and all damage categorized, repaired, patched, or ignored.

The Radar Division aimed detectors at Society 362 and searched the electromagnetic spectrum around it. Passive instruments picked up emanations and fed them into computers for analysis. The computers spat out their results: three ships in orbit, no weapons activity discerned, no active search pings. Neither were the ships broadcasting ID signals.

Commodore Borland ordered the course set not to Society 362, but sunward, to use stellar radiation to mask the *Grandar Bay*. The ships in orbit would pick up signals from the *Grandar Bay*'s maneuver, but wouldn't be able to track it once it was in the stellar background. Or at least they *shouldn't* be able to; nobody knew if the Skinks had detection capabilities well beyond those of the Confederation.

Shielded, they hoped, by local stellar radiation, the *Grandar Bay* approached at half speed, to have as much time as possible to gather intelligence about what awaited. They still detected only three ships in orbit. None had been found orbiting on the other side of the planet. The Lagrange points were unoccupied as well. The *Grandar Bay* trained its optics on the orbiting ships.

"That's the one from Kingdom!" shouted the astronomy

mate second class who manned the optic focus. "It's got the same markings."

"How can you be sure?" the astronomy chief asked as he peered at the ship on the main display. "Those markings aren't all that sharp."

"Take a look here," the second class said. The chief joined him and looked at the second class's personal pocket computer. "I captured enough images off the string-of-pearls during the fight to give me the whole thing," the mate said. "When I got this ship focused," he nodded at the display at his station, "I called up my image and matched 'em up. See?"

The chief carefully compared the live image on the station display with the image on the mate's comp. The markings looked the same.

"Look at that." The mate pointed at a fuzzy spot of the hull shown on the live image. "That looks like damage."

"Could be," the chief agreed. "Could be. Let me borrow this." He snatched the mate's comp and headed for the astronomy officer.

Three hours later they could make out considerable damage to the large starship's hull and what must have been repair modules crawling over the damaged area. One of the smaller ships had left orbit and jumped. Shuttles were transiting between the ships and surface.

"I don't know how that ship survived the jumps with that much hull damage," the astronomy officer observed.

"Triple hulling, reinforcing beams between hulls, some kind of inert stuffing in the tween'ulls," said the astronomy chief. "It's expensive, but it can be done."

"I guess they think the expense is worth it."

"The way they attacked out of nowhere, I expect they have the kind of experience that tells them they need it." The chief had never been able to bring himself to believe that just because humanity hadn't had any contact with alien sentiences—before the Skinks—meant that there weren't any. He knew that when two species tried to occupy the same ecological niche, they fought until one fled or was wiped out.

An hour later the optics showed the remaining smaller ship well enough to determine that it was not a destroyer or other fighting ship but an amphibious landing barge.

The Skink ships weren't in geosync orbits; the Crowe-class ship was higher than the landing barge. If there were satellites in orbit, they were not transmitting data. Every time the Crowe-class ship's orbit took it behind Society 362, Commodore Borland had the *Grandar Bay* adjust orbit. He wanted to be in maximum effective laser range when the alien ship appeared above the planetary limb. Provided they didn't maneuver, he would know exactly where to expect the Skinks to appear. Also, if they knew the Confederation ship was approaching, they wouldn't be sure exactly where it was, if the *Grandar Bay* adjusted its orbit.

"Movement in the pods," Radar reported just before the Skink ship disappeared below the horizon. Several protrusions on the hull of the ship had been tentatively identified as weapons pods. "We've been pinged."

"Adjust," Borland ordered. The helm made a prearranged course adjustment to throw off the aim of weapons that might fire at it when the ship reappeared. The *Grandar Bay*'s weapons weren't in range yet, and Borland hoped they were still outside the Skinks' range. He took it as a positive sign when the Skink ship didn't fire when it reappeared. More shuttles rendezvoused with it. An hour later it dropped below the horizon again.

The next time it appeared, it would be in range of the *Grandar Bay*'s modified lasers. The orbit after that, the Crowe-class ship would be in range of the Confederation ship's missiles.

"Lasers, prepare to lock on the pods," Borland ordered. The *Grandar Bay* made another course adjustment, a fairly large one. Minutes ticked away. The smaller ship dropped below the horizon. The *Grandar Bay* adjusted vector again. It would see the Skink ship from south of its orbit; its previous maneuvers had all been from the north. "I always did want to command a cruiser," he murmured. The Skink ship blipped on the limb of Society 362.

"Locking," the Laser Gunnery Division reported.

"Locking," Borland acknowledged.

"Receiving emanations similar to the rail guns from the ship," Radar reported.

"Fire now," Borland said calmly.

The *Grandar Bay*'s lasers fired at the Skink ship, which was less than its own diameter above the horizon. In the visual display, puffs rose on its surface; some on the pods, some near them.

"Rail emanations ceased," Radar reported.

The Skink ship fired its inertial drive and moved out of orbit, tangential to the *Grandar Bay*. If it stayed course, it would be in range of the missiles in less than half an hour. Borland ordered the Orbital Missile Division to lock on and prepare for launch. The lasers fired another salvo. More puffs appeared on the surface of the Skink ship. Shuttles that were rising to rendezvous turned about and headed planetside.

"Vector on enemy ship," Borland ordered. That would cut down the time before he could launch missiles. He checked the time; the smaller ship should have reappeared. It hadn't. The larger Skink ship accelerated. The *Grandar Bay*'s lasers fired again. More puffs, too many.

"Missiles launched," Radar reported. "Receiving pings. Enemy missiles locked."

"Fire defensive missiles," Borland ordered. "Maintain course." He badly wanted the big Skink ship that had killed the *Admiral J. P. Jones*, and kept his attention fixed on it so he didn't see his defensive lasers kill the missiles fired at the *Grandar Bay*.

But he wasn't going to get the Skink ship; it jumped. One second it was on a closing vector, the next the very fabric of space-time seemed to be rent. The *Grandar Bay* shuddered. Then the Skink ship wasn't there.

Borland shook himself. He'd never before been that close to another ship making the jump into Beamspace.

"Damage Control, report."

"Damage Control, checking," came the reply.

"Put us into geosync orbit," Borland ordered the helm while he waited for Damage Control to report. "Radar, find out what happened to the small Skink ship."

"Bridge, Damage Control. Only minor breakage of loose objects. Appropriate crews are cleaning up. Chief-of-ship has his teams inspecting for hidden damage."

"Thank you, Damage Control." Borland switched his comm to the all compartments channel and pushed the bosun button.

A whistle sounded throughout the ship, followed by a carefully modulated, computer-generated female voice saying, "Now hear this, now hear this . . . All hands, now hear this . . ."

"This is the commodore," Borland said after the voice called for attention. "The enemy has departed Society 362. Well done, everybody. Especially the Laser Gunnery Division and the engineers who worked to modify the lasers. The major Skink ship suffered possible damage before it jumped. That is all."

He stood. "Officer of the Watch, the bridge is yours. I will be in my quarters. My compliments to Brigadier Sturgeon. Ask him to join me."

"Aye, sir. The bridge is mine. The commodore's compliments to Brigadier Sturgeon."

In his quarters, Borland opened a bottle of Corsican Special Reserve cognac and set it on the table next to two snifters. Sturgeon arrived a moment later.

Borland greeted the Marine, poured cognac into the snifters and handed one to Sturgeon. "Were you able to follow that action, Ted?" he asked.

"Yes I did, Roger, and with great interest. I've witnessed very few naval battles." Sturgeon smiled. "This was the first battle I'd ever seen in which an amphibious ship attacked enemy shipping."

"Then you understand why I feel the need for a celebratory drink."

"I do indeed." They clinked glasses. "To more victories."

"Thank you."

They sniffed and sipped. The cognac delighted their palates and flowed easily down their throats. They enjoyed the sensation for a moment, then sipped again.

"Sit, please." Borland waved a hand at two captain's chairs arranged at a small table. They sat and put their snifters down. "You saw the big one get away."

"With what appeared to be significant damage, yes."

"We don't know where the smaller one went."

Sturgeon cocked an eyebrow.

"It didn't come back around, so it must have jumped. But we didn't detect any drive emanations."

Sturgeon nodded. "And there are still Skinks planet-side."

"That seems a reasonable assumption. At least the crews of those shuttles that turned back are still down there. We know they didn't launch again—their landing area is still in view. There could be more Skinks planetside, possibly a lot of them."

"Then I should take Marines planetside and root them out."

Borland nodded. He picked up his snifter and held it out. Sturgeon picked up his and they clinked.

"There's another thing we have to consider."

"I know. Where did the Skink ships go when they left orbit here?"

"Our mission was to stop the fighting on Kingdom. We did that, but now we're here."

"And the Skinks might have decided to take advantage of our absence and returned to Kingdom."

"That's not likely, but we have to consider it."

"I'd like the ground commander's view of splitting his forces."

"Land 34th FIST here and you go back to Kingdom with 26th FIST, just in case. Come back if the Skinks aren't there."

"Thirty-fourth FIST will be isolated."

"FISTs are accustomed to fighting alone, unsupported. Let's do this thing."

The two commanders wished each other good hunting, and glasses clinked again.

"High speed on a bad road," was what the Marines called their method of planetfall. They boarded Dragons that were nestled by threes into the bellies of Essays and strapped themselves firmly in. The Essays were forcibly ejected from the starship transports, gathered in formation nearby, then headed planetside. Most planetfalls made by the Essays were relatively sedate affairs—the shuttles went into deteriorating orbits that normally spiraled them around a world three times from the top of the atmosphere to touchdown. Not when they landed Marines, though. With Marines aboard, the Essays aimed almost straight down and kicked in the afterburners. The initial forces vibrated the Essays and their embarked Marines wildly. As the atmosphere thickened, the vibrations turned to shaking, then rattling, and finally rolls so violent it felt like the Essays would tumble and crash. Anyone who had not been firmly strapped in returned to orbit with the Essay—and hoped he lived long enough to reach the starship's hospital.

Essays carrying Marines took not much longer to go from the top of the atmosphere to the surface than the same trip took a meteorite. This was deliberate, done to reduce the time of entry and the exposure time to planet-based defenses. Since Marines made planetfall via "high speed on a bad road" when making planetfall on any world, no matter how friendly, many Marines suspected the real reason was to make the trip so unpleasant they would be in a killing mood when they got where they were going. Whatever the real reason, when it seemed that a catastrophic deceleration encounter with the surface was inevitable, the Essays leveled off and extended stubby wings and their flight paths became speed-eating spirals. When the Essays' speed dropped enough, drogue chutes popped out of their rears to further slow them. At the end of the rough ride, the Essays set gently down—usually at sea, over the horizon from the nearest landmass.

The science and technology expedition that had investigated Society 362 a dozen years earlier nicknamed it "Quagmire" for good reason. It had no dry ground; it was covered in a tremendous thickness of mud. The Marines of 34th FIST who made planetfall on Society 362 didn't come down on an oceanic surface—Quagmire didn't have any oceans since it was too wet for an ocean basin to form and hold. Every time one began to develop, the sides collapsed and filled it in. There were rivers all over the planet. They ran into other rivers and into lakes that grew into temporary ocean basins. The only variations in the weather forecast anywhere on the planet were how low the overcast was and how heavy the rain was coming down.

High speed on a bad road to get *here*? the commander reflected. The Marines of 34th FIST would truly be ready to spill blood.

When decoys sent planetward failed to draw fire, the landing force was launched. The Essays touched down twenty kilometers from the area where the Skink shuttles had launched and returned. The Dragons roared off the Essays and charged through a dripping forest of tall, widely spaced trees held up by spreading buttress roots. Secure in their webbing in the bellies of the Dragons, the Marines couldn't see what the Dragon crews saw—the damnedest indigenous fauna they'd ever seen. Most of them, large and small, were hexapods. That wasn't as weird as the fact that none of them had heads! The Dragons were going so fast over the unknown and potentially treacherous landscape that the crews couldn't spare enough attention to notice the snouts that projected from high in the chests of the hexapods, or the eyestalks that popped up and down on their shoulders. They certainly didn't notice that the man-size creatures with torsos that reared up above the middle pair of legs carried spears.

The spear-bearing headless centauroids, eaten by curiosity and driven by anger, scampered after the Dragons. They couldn't scamper and clamber nearly as fast as the Dragons rushed, but they never had to stop and back up and go around an obstruction. They dropped behind, but even so, they reached the island of the murder-monsters close behind the strange new monsters.

And these new monsters were the strangest of all the monsters they'd seen. Or not seen, but that was a question for the shaman.

The hunters hunkered in the deep shadows beneath the roots of the forest giants, hid behind boles in the crooks of mid-size trees and watched a more amazing battle than any of them could ever have imagined. In the middle of the great island in the great river where they had established their base, the murderous monsters who enslaved and killed so many of the people lay or crouched behind the very hard nests that moved. They sprayed their evil acid at the near end of the island. The hunters watched the near end of the island very closely. The monsters they saw there—they were invisible, but rainwater sluiced over otherwise unseen forms—threw balls of lightning at the monsters that sprayed acid! Monsters they couldn't see except for the holes they made in the rain throwing balls of lightning. It was incredible, but were these monsters less believable than the monsters who murdered people and worked them to death? Or less believable than the other monsters who were there half a lifetime ago, who left behind so many strange and wonderful objects before departing for reasons knowable only to them?

"We live in interesting times," one of the hunters said. He was just giving voice to what was on the minds of many of them. Mature hunters were chilled by the thought. The younger hunters were excited by it.

The battle between the evil monsters who sprayed flesh-eating acid and the invisible monsters who threw balls of lightning was fascinating. Especially when one of the murder-monsters was struck by a lightning ball—it vanished into a larger ball of lightning! The hunters watched spellbound. They didn't know anything about the monsters they couldn't see, but they hoped they'd win this battle since they hated the murder-monsters.

CHAPTER
TWENTY-SEVEN

Kilo Company was stuck on the downstream end of the four-kilometer-long island. The constant rain was leaching the acid retardant from their chameleons—which they discovered when three of them went down with acid wounds—so they couldn't just get on line and move through the Skink positions. And the Skinks were firing from behind massive vehicles, and so didn't have to expose themselves to fire. The Marines had put concentrated fire on the vehicles in an attempt to slag or even melt them. But the vehicles were too big, too hard, and the rain kept dissipating the heat anyway.

Neither were the Dragons much help for flanking maneuvers. The flora on the sides of the river was too dense for them to get through without burning their way, and too wet to burn without plasma fire. The Dragons had attempted to swim the river itself to flank the Skink positions, but the Skinks had some bigger acid shooters that could reach across the river. Concentrated fire from the acid shooters had eaten through the armor of one Dragon and sent it to the bottom. Two others were damaged.

Company M sat in its Dragons half a klick downriver, waiting for orders. It couldn't come up to help Kilo Company because there wasn't enough room on the end of the island. Company L was dismounted and advancing through the growth fifty meters deep from the left bank of the river, but the foliage was thick and tangled, and the ground slippery and soft. The going was hard, and it would be a while before they got to a position to pour flanking fire on the Skinks.

*   *   *

Corporal Claypoole put his right foot on yet another knee-high buttress root and stepped up. The bark under his boot sloughed off and he yelped as his foot slid and his knee turned in a way it wasn't supposed to. He yelped louder when the twisted knee slammed against the root.

He dropped his blaster and swore, "Buddha's sweaty balls!" He massaged the injured joint with both hands.

"More like Christ on a crutch," Lance Corporal MacIlargie said. "I think you just got an idiot stripe. You're bleeding."

MacIlargie sloshed close and picked up the dropped blaster. "It's a good thing for you Staff Sergeant Hyakowa didn't see you drop this," he said. "Or I'd be the new fire team leader and you'd be following my orders."

Claypoole snarled and snatched the blaster back. "I'm fire team leader, Boot," he said as he stood erect and lifted his injured leg over the root. He flinched as he put his weight on the leg, but the knee held as he lifted his left leg over. "Don't you ever forget that."

"Sure thing," MacIlargie said. He wished Claypoole could see his grin behind the chameleon screen.

"Close it up, second squad," Sergeant Linsman said on the squad circuit.

Muttering to himself, Claypoole limped after the rest of the squad, careful not to step on any more roots.

Lance Corporal Schultz, on the point, didn't make any missteps. He'd never before been in a forest quite like this one, but he'd been in enough rain forests that he didn't find it a totally alien environment. It reminded him more of the swamps of Kingdom than of rain forests. He stepped over roots rather than around them, and put his mass over his lead foot before applying all of his weight to it. He took care to walk on an automatic level; all his senses were directed outward. So far as the Marines knew, all of the Skinks were on the island, pinned down by Kilo Company. But that didn't mean there weren't any on the land on this side of the river.

He kept himself oriented by listening to the sounds of the battle that raged on the island—the company was too far inland to see the water through the trees.

It was slow going in the forest. Captain Conorado followed between third and first platoons with a truncated command group: himself, Gunnery Sergeant Thatcher, Corporal Escarpo on comm, and a fire controller from the artillery battery. He didn't think he'd have any use for the artillery controller except as an extra blaster—if the battery had managed to clear enough trees forward of their position to fire, he was sure they'd already be firing in support of Kilo Company. By the sounds of the battle on the island, he judged the command group was nearly parallel to Kilo Company's position. When Company L advanced far enough that second platoon was slightly to the rear of the Skinks, he'd call a halt and change formation—third platoon would form a defensive arc upstream and inland, with first platoon doing the same from the opposite direction, while second platoon moved closer to the river to fire into the Skinks. Nobody knew whether there were more Skinks somewhere; when Company L joined in the battle, the Marines had to be prepared to fight in all directions.

The battle didn't seem to favor either side. Fewer of the murderous monsters were turning into lightning from the lightning balls thrown by the invisible monsters, and no more of the invisible monsters were being killed or injured either. The chief hunter left the other hunters where they watched the fight and clambered upstream through the trees. He went in search of a way he and his hunters could tip the tide in favor of the invisible monsters.

At its upstream end, well above the fighting, the island grew close to the far bank and the water ran slowly over a shallow bottom. When he was sure none of the monsters were looking in his direction, the chief hunter slithered into the river and swam to the shallow channel. Once there, hunkered low, he crawled onto the point of the island. There were many, many—the chief hunter's vocabulary didn't have words for the things—many *things* on the island. So many that the fight at the downstream end wasn't visible through them, and the lightning thrown by the invisible monsters couldn't get through them. A hunter could lie in ambush here safe from sight and injury. But lying there wasn't good enough; it was not possible to reach the murder-monsters, to injure or kill them.

The chief hunter moved closer, flitting from one *thing* to the next until at last he came to where he could extend his primary eyestalks around the corner of a *thing* and see a murder-monster. It was within the casting range of his spear. A six of spears lay in their quiver on his back. Without conscious thought, one came to his hand. It would be so easy to kill one of the murder-monsters from here. He hefted the spear, then lowered it. No, before he killed a murder-monster, he needed to bring more hunters, enough that they could do serious damage to the murder-monsters and tip the battle in favor of the invisible monsters. He returned to the water by the same route he'd come. A short while later he was back where the other hunters watched the battle.

"Is there any change?" the chief hunter asked.

An older hunter extended his dorsal eyestalks and aimed them at the chief hunter, his primary eyestalks remained fixed on the battle. "None," he told the chief hunter. "They remain with neither able to gain advantage."

"We can reach casting distance behind them unseen," the chief hunter said to all. "Those who want to kill a murder-monster, join me." Without waiting for replies, he turned about and clambered back upstream to where he would enter the flowing water.

Each of the hunters had lost at least one family member or close friend to the murder-monsters; some had lost many. All wanted vengeance. None remained behind to watch the battle from safety.

*   *   *

Captain Conorado couldn't fully trust his UPUD to tell him where he was, relative to the Skink positions on the island, since the *Grandar Bay* hadn't strung a complete string-of-pearls. He judged the company's position as much by the sound of the fighting as by the UPUD. When the UPUD's display and his ears agreed that second platoon was beyond Kilo Company, he called a halt.

"Take new positions," he ordered.

The platoon commanders and platoon sergeants of first and third platoons began directing their squad leaders to get their Marines into position. They hadn't rehearsed the maneuver, but everyone knew where he was supposed to be relative to the Marines on either side.

Conorado watched what movement he could see on his UPUD, and listened to the orders given over the command circuit. When first and third platoons were in position, he ordered, "Second platoon, advance to the river."

Before second platoon reached the bank, the forest a half kilometer upstream erupted with the impact of a barrage of missile impacts.

"Get Battalion, ask if that was ours!" Conorado ordered Escarpo. "Second platoon, continue to the river."

Before either could obey the orders, the roar of landing shuttles sounded from the area of the missile impacts.

When second platoon reached the river, they saw the Skinks rapidly withdrawing from the island.

The hunters were paddling across the river, completely submerged except for their dorsal eyestalks and snorkeled nostrils, when the shock waves from the explosions slammed through the water and violently buffeted them. As one, they stopped, paddling enough to keep from being swept downstream. Most of them extended primary eye-stalks to look at the chief hunter for guidance—none had ever experienced a buffeting like that.

The chief hunter was aware that the other hunters watched him, waiting for instructions, but he paid them no attention for the moment. He had no more idea than they did what caused the monstrous explosion. Before he could tell them whether to continue or retreat, he needed to know whether it was a threat. Maybe the murder-monsters could tell him what they were doing? He aimed his dorsal eyestalks beyond the middle of the island, toward where the murder-monsters battled the invisible monsters. He was too low, there were too many *things* in the way, he couldn't see to where they were. Then new vibrations came to him, conducted from the air through the water. He rolled to one side and raised himself to expose a tympanum. A roaring sound grew, a roaring he had heard before—the strange nests that took the murder-monsters to beyond the sky! He rolled back and lifted enough to aim his primary eyestalks in the direction the sound came from. *Yes*, he saw several flying nests rapidly descending toward the forest upstream and inland from the top of the island. Were more murder-monsters coming?

He looked back at the island and saw the murder-monsters racing toward its end; some were almost at it. The flying nests must be coming to take them beyond the sky! This could be the only chance the hunters had for vengeance. He signaled the hunters and swam rapidly toward the shallow channel. They could reach it before all the murder-monsters crossed it.

"Third platoon, the Skinks are withdrawing. Move upstream on line. Fast! Cut them off," Captain Conorado ordered as soon as second platoon reported the Skinks' retreat. "Try to cut them off." He turned to Corporal Escarpo. "Report to Battalion, the Skinks are withdrawing." Escarpo had already relayed a message from Battalion—the missiles that erupted in the forest were not theirs. The Skinks had a ship up there, so it had to be the smaller one that had vanished while the *Grandar Bay* was fighting the Crowe-type ship. The missiles had to have been fired by it to clear a landing zone for the shuttles he heard coming down. "Second platoon, fire on them. First platoon, catch up with third platoon."

"You heard the man," Lieutenant Rokmonov ordered. "Let's cut them off. *Move, move*, MOVE!"

Third platoon scrambled, slipping and sliding over roots and through mud. First squad struggled to catch up with second squad and get on line with it. They batted wet foliage out of their way instead of going around or ducking under. This was not the time for stealth.

Lance Corporal Schultz was the first to spot the Skinks. He threw his blaster into his shoulder to fire at one, but didn't shoot. "What the . . . ?"

The first of the murder-monsters was already across the shallow channel when the hunters reached the top of the island, and the last were approaching it. The chief hunter pointed, and the hunters surged onto the tip of the island. Their mid and hind limbs powered them forward into the trailing monsters, and they crashed against their smaller foes and bowled them over. Their spears stabbed into the bodies of the monsters, and the monsters screamed in agony as death rattled through them. The monsters were so intent on flight and so surprised by the attack of their former slaves that none of them fought back immediately. That delay cost them their lives.

The chief hunter shrilled a command, and the hunters raced into the shallows to fall on the fleeing murder-monsters from behind.

A Leader ran behind his Fighters, harshly barking at them, exhorting them to run faster—the shuttles wouldn't wait long, and they had to get to them before they lifted off. *Run, run, run,* he barked, *faster, faster, faster.* The Fighters ran as fast as they could through thigh-deep water. When the Leader stopped barking, only one Fighter, who had a genetic defect that afforded him more intelligence than all other Fighters, wondered why. He turned his head to investigate and his eyes bugged at the sight that met them: a mob of the local creatures, the semisentients the True People used as slave animals, milled among the Fighters behind him. The creatures knocked the Fighters and Leaders down and stabbed them as they foundered in the water! The river flowed red with the blood of Fighters and Leaders.

The Fighter pushed himself harder than any Leader or Master had ever pushed him, and got ahead of his fellow Fighters just before they reached the far bank. He barked commands at them—*stop, turn around, and fight!* The other Fighters hesitated; he was a Fighter like them, not a Leader. But he barked orders as a Leader or even a Master might bark them, so they stopped and turned around to see the unthinkable. At the command of the Fighter who gave orders like a Leader, the other Fighters unslung nozzles and pointed them at the creatures who were starting to charge toward them. The Fighter barked *FIRE!* and they sprayed their greenish fluid at the charging creatures. Several of the creatures fell, screaming in agony, pawing at the acid that ate into their flesh. The others dove into the water and swam away from the streams of acid.

Then the *crack-sizzle* of Earthmen Marine forever guns came from their left flank. The Fighter with the genetic defect barked more orders, and the Fighters with him fled from the forever guns, racing to catch up with the others. He didn't go with them. Instead he dove into the shallow channel and swam to the point of the island, where he had seen bodies of Fighters and Leaders sprawled dead on the ground. He crawled to shore, barely below the sight of the Earthmen Marines on the bank. The bodies lay close to each other, so he didn't need to waste any time pulling them together. He lay near one and took the fire maker that months earlier he'd taken from the corpse of a Leader on the Earthman world called Kingdom. He used it to flame the body. Moving quickly, he touched fire to more bodies. The heat of the flames nearly touched him off, though he rolled away each time. Satisfied that all were burned or would burn, he dropped the tanks from his back and dove into the river. Underwater, he swam rapidly upstream for a short distance before climbing the bank. As he went he saw a few of the local creatures watching him, but none approached.

On land again, the inexplicitly intelligent Fighter raced through the forest toward where he heard the *crack-sizzle* of Earthmen Marine forever guns firing at the soldiers of the True People.

Lance Corporal Schultz only hesitated an instant when he saw the headless centaurs spearing the Skinks. Other Skinks had already made the bank, and he shifted aim and fired at them. His first bolt missed, his second was met by the flash of a flaring Skink. Corporals Kerr and Doyle fired almost as soon as he did, then the rest of second squad caught up, along with the gun attached to them, and they all fired into the forest. Lights flashed among the trees where Skinks flared. The flashes had stopped by the time first squad caught up.

"Third herd, MOVE!" Lieutenant Rokmonov roared on the all-hands circuit. Third platoon scrambled through the forest in pursuit of the Skinks, firing as they went. Occasional flashes showed they were hitting the Skinks.

"*What?*" Corporal Claypoole screamed when he looked up into the trees and saw a roughly man-size creature skittering through the branches five or six meters above. He shook his head and looked again, using his light-gatherer and magnifier shields. The—The *thing* undulated on six legs and didn't have a *head*! No, it wasn't running along the branches on six legs—one limb ended in a hand, and that hand held a *spear*! He dropped his infra into place—the thing showed as brightly as a man, not dim like a Skink. In his peripheral vision he saw MacIlargie raise his blaster.

"Stop!" he shouted at MacIlargie. "It's not a Skink!"

"What is it?" MacIlargie shouted back, his quavering voice indicating how shaken he was by the strange creature.

"I don't know, but I think it's chasing the Skinks."

The Marines followed, but the Skinks were more agile in the drenched forest. Before the Marines came in sight of the clearing made by the missiles, they heard the roar of the shuttles launching.

"Third platoon, hold up," Captain Conorado ordered. "First and second platoons, link with third."

It took another five minutes for Company L to link up and form a defensive position. During that time, Lieutenant Rokmonov joined third platoon's second squad in looking at the strange sight in front of them.

"Skipper," Rokmonov said on the company command circuit, "I think you should take a look at this."

A dozen creatures stood in the trees ten or so meters ahead of third platoon. They stood on roots and branches, grasped branches with crudely formed mid-limb paws, gripped with a hand on a forelimb, held spears in their free hands. Their bodies folded upward at the joint of the mid-limbs, similar to the centaurs of ancient myth. They didn't have heads.

"My God," Conorado whispered.

"What are they?"

"I don't know. There wasn't anything about tool users in the BHHEI reports on this planet."

"They have eyestalks sticking out of their shoulders," Rokmonov said softly.

"Yes." As he watched, one of the headless creatures retracted its eyestalks and extended a second pair from alongside the snout that projected forward from between its shoulders.

"They look almost like they can see us."

"Yes," Conorado agreed. He raised all shields and watched as the centauroids focused on his face. He turned his head to Rokmonov. "They don't see us," he said. "They see the rain running over us."

"We're invisible men."

"More likely invisible monsters. Everybody," he said on the third platoon all-hands circuit, "raise shields. Let them see your faces. Don't point any weapons at them."

One of the creatures swiveled his eyestalks along the line of Marines; his gaze seemed to pause at each of them. Then he dropped down out of the tree he was in and lowered his forebody with his hands supporting his weight. When his muzzle almost touched the mud, he extended his dorsal eye-stalks at the Marines and spoke. His voice came in grunts, clicks, and whistles.

"I wonder what he's saying?" Rokmonov murmured.

"He's probably thanking us for helping to drive the Skinks away."

The creature pushed himself back up and climbed into the tree. He grunted, clicked, and whistled to his companions, then all of them clambered through the trees to the shallows and headed for the island. Conorado alerted Kilo Company.

Intensely curious, Claypoole climbed a tree to watch. The creatures ignored the Kilo Company Marines, who were still at the downstream end of the island, and went straight to a long shed, which they broke into.

"What are they doing there, Rock?" Conorado asked.

"Holy . . . They're leading more creatures out of the shed. Jesus Mohammed, they look sick. Some of them can't walk by themselves. The guys who chased the Skinks, they're carrying a couple of the others." He paused to see what the creatures would do next. "They're heading for the river and getting in. I lost them, they're underwater. No, wait, some of them are bobbing to the surface. It looks like some of the healthy ones are holding sick ones up where they can breathe. They're at the other side now, getting out of the water." He looked down at his company commander.

"Skipper, remember what you did on Avionia? I think we just did the same thing here." On Avionia, Conorado had freed the sentient aliens who were being held as research animals by a senior scientist.

Conorado nodded, he believed he was right about the centauroid thanking the Marines for helping drive the Skinks away—it looked like the Skinks had been using some of them as slaves. That was confirmed when the Marines searched the camp.

The shuttles docked in the amphibious barge-type starship and the Skinks filed off, to be led to the troop holds by crew members. An Over Master stood in the entrance to the passageway from the docking bay and studied the passing Fighters. He saw one without a weapon and stopped him.

The Over Master stared at the Fighter for a time. "You're the one," he said.

The Fighter said nothing. He stood, head bowed, before the Over Master. He wondered if he should dread this encounter. Losing a weapon in combat was sometimes punished severely.

"Your unit's Leader was killed. Instead of continuing to follow his last order, you saw the threat from behind and assumed a Leader's position. You gave new orders to the other Fighters in your unit and fought off the slaves who were attacking. Then you fired our dead so their helixes would not be left for the Earthmen Marines to discover."

"I am the one," the Fighter said, his head bowed.

"I remember you. You did a similar thing sometime back on the Earthman planet, assumed a Leader's position when your Leader was killed."

The Fighter said nothing, just stood with his head bowed. If he was ever going to be promoted to Leader, this was his best chance.

"Your unit should have been destroyed each time after your Leader was killed. Instead, this time, you led your unit in a fight that saved our withdrawal and brought your unit here. Before, you accomplished a part of our mission that would not have been accomplished had you not assumed a position above yourself, one for which you were not bred."

The Fighter knew these things. He was patient. The Over Master would decide what to do when he was ready—that was the way of Over Masters.

"Look at me and tell me if you are the one."

The Fighter looked at the Over Master. "I am the one."

The Over Master stared at the Fighter. In all his years of service to the Emperor, he could not think of another instance of a Fighter assuming a Leader's position on his own initiative. Fighters were not supposed to *give* orders, they were bred to *obey* orders. He should kill the Fighter now, before he usurped authority again. But the campaign had cost the lives of too many Leaders and Masters of all ranks. It would take a great deal of time to train enough new Leaders, and train and promote new Masters of all ranks.

"You know who I am?"

"Yes, Over Master."

"When the ship is safely away from here in nether-space, come to my quarters. When you leave my quarters, you will no longer be a Fighter, you will be a Leader."

The Fighter was elated. "I will," he said, and bowed lower.

"We shall see." Fighters were not allowed in the area of the ship where Over Masters were quartered. If this Fighter could manage to reach his quarters without being detained and executed, he deserved to become a Leader.

The Skinks did not return to the Kingdom of Yahweh and His Saints and Their Apostles. The Marines, two weeks later, did. From there they headed back to Thorsfinni's World and Camp Ellis.

Ambassador Jayben Spears was ecstatic about the news of the headless centauroids.

"I'll get this off in a diplomatic pouch immediately," he crowed to Brigadier Sturgeon. It's about time those hidebound bureaucrats at Behind got a thumb in their eye!"

CHAPTER
TWENTY-EIGHT

Senior Stormleader Errik Romer had been a soldier most of his life. He had served in the armed forces of several member worlds of the Confederation and was widely known as a highly respected military professional. His many decorations for bravery under fire attested to that. At loose ends between wars, and hankering after a challenging position that would give him an opportunity to exercise the full range of his military talents—he was an excellent administrator and logistician, in addition to his proven competence on the battlefield—he had accepted Dominic de Tomas's offer to help him organize what became known as the Special Group on Kingdom.

De Tomas's success with the Special Group was due in large part to Romer's organizing and administrative abilities. It was he who oversaw the recruitment process so that the SG obtained only the most highly qualified individuals, and it was under Romer's guidance that the SG's training program evolved into a mechanism for totally successful indoctrination of SG recruits.

The members of the Special Group and the Lifeguards seldom fraternized with the civilian population. Their police and security duties prescribed that they remain aloof from the people they might have to arrest and execute. And so, when off duty, they spent their leisure hours engaged in sports and physical conditioning or in their private service clubs. At Wayvelsberg, the Black Order Bistro served the leisure-time needs of the officers. Romer spent most of his time there, often staying until the early morning hours, drinking, singing, and playing cards with the other officers.

No one outside the Special Group was allowed in the place, and in keeping with de Tomas's deep-seated but secret animosity toward clerics and organized religion in general, the Black Order Bistro was decorated exclusively with murals of famous battles and the portraits of famous generals. Over the door, inscribed in burnished gold lettering, were the words: "Struggle Makes You Free," and over the bar, "As We Grow Pitiless and Hard in the Struggle for Power, We Also Grow Pitiless and Hard in the Struggle for the Preservation of Our Race—Adolf Hitler."

Group singing was a common pastime in the bistro, especially the signature song of the Special Group, "When All Others Are Unfaithful, We Shall Remain Loyal," and "Raise the Flag!"

RAISE THE FLAG! OUR RANKS ARE TIGHTLY CLOSED!
RAISE THE FLAG! THE TRAITORS ARE EXPOSED!
THE STORM MEN MARCH WITH QUIET, STEADY TREAD,
WE MARCH AS ONE, THE LIVING AND THE DEAD.

Dominic has *never* been a soldier," Romer had remarked one night, relaxing with his lieutenants, called stormleaders, or simply "leaders." "Goddamn chicken farmer," he muttered. "Would've failed at that if his mom hadn't bought him out," he added with a snort. "And this," he gestured wildly with one hand, "is not soldiering! *Pfagh!* I'm the only real soldier here!"

At those informal gatherings, Romer always referred to de Tomas by his first name, which he never would dream of doing in person. Behind *his* back Romer's officers called him "Six-Bottle Romie," because his capacity for Wanderjahrian vintages on these occasions extended to the consumption of six bottles before he had to be led off to his quarters. That night, he had been well into his fifth. "I have plans, boys," he went on, noisily wiping his moist lips with the hairy back of a hand, "and I don't mean commanding the group for the rest of my days either." He winked broadly at the young officers sitting around his table. "No!" He pounded the table loudly, startling them. "Dominic's going to come out on top of these goddamn godfreak fanatics, you see, and when he does—" He paused and leered drunkenly at the young men. "I will take command of the goddamned Army of God!" He nodded gravely, as if the decision had already been made.

Romer put his arm around the young man sitting to his right and hugged him in the effusive manner of drunks. "Ain't that right, Mikey?" he rumbled. "We are goin' places, m'boy. You stick with ol' Romie," he took in the others with an unsteady wave of his hand, "and you'll all go with me."

"Are you ready, Herten?" Dominic de Tomas asked Overstorm Leader Herten Gorman, assistant commander of his Lifeguard Battalion.

"Yes, my leader." Gorman bowed from the waist.

De Tomas had formed the Lifeguards as a special unit under his personal command. Like the SG, they swore total allegiance to de Tomas, but unlike the SG, which often moved far afield in its police duties and was directly commanded on those occasions by Senior Stormleader Romer, the Lifeguards remained always within de Tomas's immediate control.

"You must strike swiftly and mercilessly. I want the traitors killed with as little fuss and publicity as possible. Get them all before the sun rises. Here is the list. He handed the Overstorm Leader a list of about thirty names, all ranking members of the Special Group.

Herten took the list. He knew all of them. He had once been an Overstormer, a rank equivalent to captain, in the Special Group, before de Tomas had selected him for promotion to the grade of Overstorm Leader, the equivalent of lieutenant colonel, and the position of assistant commander of his bodyguard, the elite of the elite.

"I want Romer brought alive here to Wayvelsberg, Herten."

De Tomas had decided that it was time to clean house, to move against the sects when the off-worlder Marines were gone and the Army of God was preoccupied with mopping up the alien invaders.

An insistent pounding on his door awakened Romer.

"I'll get it," Romer's personal bodyguard said.

Romer stretched. It was just past midnight. He heard loud voices in the entryway and then a cry of pain and heavy boots stomping up the staircase outside his bedroom. He snatched his sidearm from a holster fitted to his side of the bed and leveled the muzzle at the doorway, which was suddenly filled by the figure of Herten Gorman. He lowered the pistol but did not reholster it.

"Good morning, Overstorm Leader." Gorman bowed. Behind him, Romer saw several shooters of the Lifeguards crowded in the hallway.

"Good morning to you, Overstorm Leader. What is the meaning of this intrusion?"

Gorman eyed the pistol in Romer's hand. "No need for that," he said, nodding at the gun. "Dean de Tomas requests your presence at Wayvelsberg, sir, and I have come to escort you there."

"At this hour? With armed guards? De Tomas could have called me personally if he wanted to see me." He raised the pistol.

A stormer behind Gorman fired. The blast hit Romer's right arm and sent the pistol flying. Before he could even react to the trauma of the injury, Gorman and his men were on him.

When he awoke he was in Wayvelsberg. "I have *never* been disloyal to you, Dominic!" ex–Senior Stormleader Errik Romer shouted. Through the haze of pain from his throbbing arm, he discovered that he lay securely strapped onto a conveyer. An open furnace door yawned above him. "Nooo!" he screamed, his voice rising to a high falsetto when he realized what was about to happen to him. *"Nooo!"*

"My dear Errik," de Tomas crooned, "you have always talked too much. Now you shall have an opportunity to exercise your vocal cords in another way. Oh, meet your replacement." He patted the grinning Herten Gorman on the shoulder. On both of Gorman's collars the single gold lightning bolt of an Overstorm Leader had been replaced by the two golden lightning bolts signifying his new rank, Senior Stormleader and commander of the Special Group.

Gorman signaled a technician to start the conveyer rolling.

Romer shrieked as his hair caught fire, filling the room with an acrid stench. He continued screaming as the flames licked at the sides of his head. De Tomas held up his hand, and the technician stopped the conveyer for a moment to allow the flames to consume the flesh on the top of Romer's head. Romer shrieked and screamed and writhed at the straps holding him firmly on the conveyer. De Tomas gestured, and Romer slowly proceeded deeper into the maw of the raging oven. Romer fell silent at last as his shoulders disappeared into the flames. De Tomas nodded, and the conveyer rolled the body swiftly into the oven, the iron grate slamming shut with a clang.

"You are merciful, my leader," Senior Stormleader Gorman commented as he accompanied de Tomas out of the torture chamber.

"How is that?" de Tomas asked.

"You fed him in head first instead of feet first," Gorman replied dryly.

De Tomas snapped his fingers. "My mistake!" He laughed. From within his tunic he withdrew another list. "Now, Senior Stormleader, I want the people on this list arrested before dawn and brought here for interrogation."

Gorman glanced at the list and raised his eyebrows.

"Is there a problem?" de Tomas asked.

"Nossir. I will have it done. But these people are all rather highly placed clerics in the sects."

"Not so high, Senior Stormleader, not so high. See to it."

Senior Stormleader Gorman smiled.

*   *   *

Providence Warwick was a peaceable man, as befit the descendant of Quakers. Although his sect was very small in comparison to the more mainline churches on Kingdom, he was well-known and respected because he practiced what he preached: nonviolence and the love of all men.

It was way past the middle part of the night before Warwick reached his temporary home in Haven, very late for a man of Warwick's abstemious personal habits. But he had been invited to a dinner hosted by Ambassador Spears in Interstellar City, and the evening had been protracted and enjoyable, as much as anything could be in these perilous times. Jayben Spears was such a congenial, cosmopolitan, and fascinating person that any meeting with him was a pleasure. Tonight they had eaten well and talked of many things. While he had consumed none of the alcohol offered that night, he was so happy that he might have appeared drunk to a casual observer.

"The bastard's three sheets to the wind," the Storm Leader whispered acidly to the Shooters who stood beside him. They watched Warwick fumble with the key pad to his door. "They're all alike," the officer muttered, "full of God in the pulpit, full of shit all the time. Take him and his family as soon as he gets the door open."

"Mr. Ambassador! Mr. Ambassador!"

Jayben Spears sat up groggily. It was Carlisle Prentiss, his chief-of-station. "What the hell?" He looked at the time. "What is it, Prentiss?" Prentiss did not wake people up without a reason.

"Something very strange going on in town tonight, sir."

Spears grunted and rubbed his eyes. "This damned place is always strange, Prentiss. What's so out of the ordinary?"

"Jim Chang, one of our communications technicians? He's, ah, well, he's shacking with a girl who lives in Haven, sir."

"Contrary to all regulations and diplomatic protocol, but go on, Prentiss." Spears knew about Chang's love life, but he hadn't done anything about it because he despised the Ecumenical Council's rules against fraternization, and besides, the girl was devastatingly beautiful. If the Council were to find out and declare Chang persona non grata, he'd stand up for the man.

"She lives in the same street as Providence Warwick. At about 0330, Special Group men arrested him and his family. I thought you should know. And there's more, sir."

"Let's have it." Spears was fully awake now.

"The Collegium's been arresting other people, I don't know how many, but it seems they're all second-echelon personnel in the various sects. It looks like de Tomas is making a move, sir."

Jayben Spears's guts turned to ice. He knew very well what the Collegium did to people brought to Wayvelsberg. He began dressing. "It's my fault, Prentiss. I should have warned the Council earlier."

"But that is not our business, sir. This is an internal domestic affair. They would not have believed you anyway."

"When have I ever minded my own business? But yeah, I don't have a leg to stand on as the Confederation's figurehead down here. Well, get the car. We're going to visit all of these birds right now, I don't care what time it is. Goddamn," he said as he slipped on his shoes, "that de Tomas is brilliant, isn't he? Half the people are celebrating the end of the invasion, and the other half's attention is on the mop-up. All the Army of the Lord forces are engaged in the mopping up, and the goddamn Ecumenical Council of Leaders is useless now anyway, so who'd miss them?"

Spears stood. "Prentiss, you drive. Let's take the mountain to Mohammed. Heigh ho!"

Bishop Ralphy Bruce Preachintent did not look the same in the early morning light as he did in Council meetings or when he was preaching to his flock. His face was haggard and drawn and without his immaculately groomed pompadour, set aside for the night. Strands of scraggly reddish hair lay plastered to his head like chunks of pumpkin pie.

Spears realized that the man must carefully prepare himself each day for his ministry, like an actor before going onstage. Alone like this in his private apartments, Ralphy Bruce was a mere shadow of his pulpit self.

"I don't believe it," he said after Spears had briefed him on what de Tomas was up to. His voice sounded weak and unsure. "Dominic follows the guidance of the Ecumenical Leaders," he added, as if reassuring himself. Secretly, he was delighted. The Quakers were a nonconforming, interfering lot of troublemakers. High time the Collegium had a chat with people like Warwick.

"Bishop Ralphy Bruce, I assure you that you are in grave danger. I strongly recommend you seek refuge with me in International City," Ambassador Spears said at last.

The conversation went on for a few more minutes, until Spears was sure he was wasting his time and excused himself. "Prentiss, Cardinal Leemus O'Lanners is next. Maybe he'll listen to reason."

Cardinal O'Lanners was at breakfast when Ambassador Spears was ushered into his presence. The cardinal offered Spears a seat and a plate, but he refused politely. The breakfast table was heaped with food and wine cooling in buckets. Spears marveled that any man could eat so much at one setting, but judging from O'Lanners's girth, apparently he did.

"Breakfast, Mr. Ambassador! Most important meal of the day!" the Cardinal enthused. "Sure you won't join me?" When Spears refused, O'Lanners went back to devouring a mound of eggs. "Well, have a seat and some coffee, then," he said, waving a free hand at a chair while scooping up a rasher of bacon with the other hand.

"Your Eminence, I have news of the gravest importance. I believe you are in very serious danger," Spears began, and told him of Warwick's arrest.

"I bet he deserved to be arrested!" O'Lanners roared happily, pouring himself a glass of wine and gulping it down. He patted his lips with a napkin and burped gently. "Excuse me!" He chuckled. "Yes, old Warwick's been a pain in the ass for years, Mr. Ambassador. About time the Collegium talked to him."

"Eminence, I'm afraid he wasn't the only one," and Spears told him of other sectarians who'd been arrested.

O'Lanners waved a hand dismissively. "All radicals," he said. Privately, he was overjoyed. At last de Tomas was cracking down. He made a mental note to have his secretary send a memo to all his parishes to take up the long-banned proselytizing efforts. There might soon be some more souls looking for salvation. "You mustn't interfere, Mr. Ambassador, or be particularly concerned. The Collegium has the authority to detain apostates of all kinds, and that's all de Tomas is doing, I assure you."

"Eminence, I strongly urge you to come back to Inter-Stellar City with me, now, and seek sanctuary in my embassy."

"*What*? *Me* seek sanctuary?" O'Lanners roared, leaning back and laughing heartily. "No need of that, Mr. Ambassador. And now, sir, you must excuse me while I prepare for my postprandial devotions." He arose from the table and waddled out of the room.

The other interviews had the same results. The members of the Council of Ecumenical Leaders did not believe they were in danger from the Collegium.

Spears was slumped down in his seat as they drove into the embassy compound. "Fools," he sighed, "all fools, Prentiss. They think these arrests are godsends for their own sects, ridding them of the competition, you see."

"And now what do we do, sir?"

"We have done what we can for those idiots, Prentiss. Now we're going to do something for *us*. We're going to my office and we're going to break out that bottle of bourbon the staff gave me for my birthday and we're going to get drunk."

CHAPTER
TWENTY-NINE

"Archbishop General, are you still with me?" de Tomas asked. They sat in an anteroom on Mount Temple, minutes before the Convocation of Ecumenical Ministers was to start its momentous session. Archbishop General Lambsblood hesitated. "*Are* you?" de Tomas repeated, looking coldly at the commander of the Army of the Lord and thinking, The vacillating coward, he thinks he can defy me.

"Archbishop General," de Tomas went on calmly, "let me remind you of some things. Those men in there"—he nodded toward the chamber where what was left of Kingdom's entire religious leadership was already assembling—"betrayed you. It was *they* who asked those *off-worlders*," de Tomas spit the words out like an epithet, "to come here, and it was *they* who agreed, almost without protest, to put Brigadier Sturgeon in command of your forces. Therefore, it is *they* who are responsible for the slaughter of your army. *They* let the Marines use your men as cannon fodder. And don't forget the day Sturgeon insulted you in their presence, called you a coward in front of them, and *not one* voiced an objection!

"I shall not remind you," de Tomas continued, "of what I do to my enemies or of what we agreed to that night at Wayvelsberg. Conversely, I do not need to remind you how generously I treat my friends. Your army is virtually destroyed and it must be rebuilt. Look at this."

He passed a sheet of paper across the table to Lambsblood, who picked it up. On it de Tomas had written a figure. Lambsblood looked at de Tomas questioningly.

"That, my dear Archbishop General, is the current strength of my Special Group. Senior Stormleader Gorman," he nodded at Gorman, who sat to one side of the little room, his legs comfortably crossed, fingers drumming silently on a tabletop, "has been conducting an assiduous recruiting and training program that was started by his predecessor, who died recently of accelerated natural causes. My Special Group is the only viable combat force left on Kingdom. I repeat, your army has been severely depleted and must be rebuilt. I will do that. How would you rather live, taking your orders from those fools," he nodded again to the Great Hall, "or from me, your friend and benefactor?"

Where did he get all those men? Archbishop General Lambsblood wondered. Is he lying? Then he said, "I am with you, Dean de Tomas," and held out his hand.

"I am no longer 'Dean.'" De Tomas smiled, taking Lambsblood's hand. "You will now call me 'Leader.' The Collegium is dissolved."

"Dissolved?" Lambsblood repeated in astonishment. "But there has *always* been a Collegium."

"Yes, but not after today," de Tomas answered airily. "I will have no time anymore for this religious sectarianism. I am into politics now. One more thing, Archbishop General—read this, it will be announced as one of my first proclamations." He handed Lambsblood a sheet of printed material:

FOR SPECIAL POLITICAL TASKS, WHICH CAN BE ASSIGNED TO THE SPECIAL GROUP (SG) BY THE LEADER: (A) THE SG WILL FORM AN ARMED STANDING MILITARY FORMATION CONSISTING OF THE STRENGTH OF THREE REGIMENTAL EQUIVALENTS AND ONE INTELLIGENCE DEPARTMENT UNDER THE DIRECT COMMAND OF THE LEADER. *THERE WILL BE NO ORGANIZATIONAL CONNECTION TO THE ARMY OF THE LORD IN PEACETIME.* (B) IN CASES OF NECESSITY UP TO 25,000 MEN OF THE SG CAN BE MOBILIZED FOR THE USE OF THE POLITICAL POLICE. (C) IN TIME OF WAR IT IS AGREED THAT MEMBERS OF THE SG WILL BE

PLACED AT THE DISPOSAL OF THE ARMY OF THE LORD,
BUT UP TO 25,000 MEN WILL BE HELD BACK FOR THE
PURPOSE OF STRENGTHENING THE POLITICAL POLICE. (D)
IN PEACETIME THE MEMBERS OF THE SG WILL BE PRE-
PARED FOR THEIR WAR TASKS. (E) IN BOTH PEACE AND
WAR, THE SG AND THE ARMY OF THE LORD WILL FUNC-
TION UNDER THE DIRECT ORDERS OF THE LEADER,
TRANSMITTED TO ALL RANKS BY THE APPROPRIATE SUB-
ORDINATE COMMANDERS.

Lambsblood relaxed. "This is brilliant!" he exclaimed,
though not fully grasping what it meant.

De Tomas smiled. It *was* brilliant. With this proclama-
tion, he would create two independent but competing military bodies, both totally subordinate to the person of the
Leader. That would assure that no one in either organization
would get any ideas about usurping power for himself. It
also left open the door for the eventual takeover of the Army
of the Lord by the SG. Finally, it legalized a powerful and
vastly expanded police force to search out and eliminate any
political opponents who might arise in the future.

"All your men, Archbishop General, like the SG, shall
swear their oath of loyalty to me personally, although in day-
to-day operations and in the execution of orders they shall be
subordinate to you as the army commander."

"Yes, Leader, that is wise," Lambsblood said enthusiastically. "Let me be the first to swear that oath!" He held up his
right hand.

"Not at this moment, Archbishop General; we will have a
formal ceremony for that purpose later." De Tomas laughed
and stood up. "I hear the Convocation gathering. It's time we
three went out and took our places. Are the men ready, Senior Stormleader?" Gorman nodded and snapped to attention. De Tomas paused and then laughed again. "We shall
now take our places, and then . . . then we shall take their
places!"

*   *   *

"Prepare yourself for a huge ration of nonsense," Jayben Spears muttered to Carlisle Prentiss as the two sat in the rear of the Great Hall. "The leaders are going to announce an end to the emergency and no doubt give themselves all the credit for defeating the Skinks."

"No doubt," Prentiss agreed. He nudged Spears. "There's de Tomas, Lambsblood, and that other one, Gorman. Do you think de Tomas is ready to make his move?"

Spears glanced at the seats along one side of the Great Hall that were reserved for ministers and other government functionaries. "Not here, Prentiss. Too public. De Tomas is the kind who strikes in the night. Try not to laugh when old Shammar makes the announcements."

Despite the arrest of many sect leaders, the Great Hall was nearly filled to capacity. Many minor functionaries and community leaders had been invited to hear the special victory announcement. But Spears still smarted over the events of that terrible night when the Special Group had arrested the sect leaders, especially the foolish and self-interested rejection of his warnings afterward by the five men who now sat smiling on the leaders' dais.

Ayatollah Jebel Shammar, the presiding leader of the session, called for order, and instantly the Great Hall was plunged into silence. "Brothers! I thank you for your attendance at this auspicious occasion! Allah has smiled upon us, brothers! We called this convocation to announce officially that the demon invaders have been expelled from our world! The military forces under the command of our dear brother, Archbishop General Lambsblood, with assistance from the Confederation Marines, have broken the back of the invaders and they have fled in confusion. We hereby proclaim a Worldwide Week of Thanksgiving. You may all now repair to your homes, your churches, your mosques, and give thanks to heaven for our salvation! You may now, in the confidence of your faith, proceed with the rebuilding of your lives and cities and the further propagation of your—"

The steady tramp, tramp, tramp of marching boots filled

the cavernous hall as two long lines of heavily armed black-uniformed men of the Special Group filed in and took up positions along either wall, forming a cordon around the assembled leaders and their guests. The leaders on the dais sat with their mouths hanging open in astonishment while the guests whispered and gestured among themselves. Some thought the SG a guard of honor, others a special ceremonial formation to honor the veterans of the recently concluded war. None grasped what was about to happen.

Except Jayben Spears. "Good God, Prentiss, I was wrong!" he gasped.

Ayatollah Shammar looked to de Tomas, who rose and strode purposefully to the center of the stage on which the dais stood. A dozen SG men detached themselves from their positions along the side of the hall and marched to stand behind the leaders.

"Fellow citizens!" de Tomas began, addressing the assembly. "While the valiant Archbishop General Lambsblood's Army of the Lord was fighting the demon invaders, *these men*," he gestured at the leaders, "were enriching themselves from the spoils of war, diverting vast sums from the public treasury into their own pockets, cheating the faithful members of their sects of their rightful emoluments and perquisites!"

Leader Nirmal Bastar jumped up and began to shout something in protest but was slammed back into his seat by the SG man standing behind him. The audience was too astonished to react.

"I have conducted a full investigation, the details of which will be fully disclosed to the world in the coming days," de Tomas continued. "I hereby arrest these men on the charge of treason and illegal speculation." People in the audience began to shout, some in protest, others in anger. De Tomas allowed them to call out for a few moments and then signaled Senior Stormleader Gorman.

"*Be silent!*" Gorman ordered. At his command, each SG man roared, "ARRRAH!" and leveled his rifle at the crowd, which instantly subsided into its seats.

"With firmness in the right as God gives us to see the right, I am reluctantly assuming, temporarily, the mantle of government," de Tomas went on. "In the coming days, working with your cooperation, we shall establish a council to conduct the affairs of government on our world. Until then I am imposing a dusk-to-dawn curfew in the city of Haven. This is necessary because certain lawless elements of our society will no doubt try to take advantage of the current situation. The men of my Special Group shall deal with them. In addition—" He paused dramatically. "—We have reason to believe some of the demon aliens might still be alive and hiding in caves and swamps. Have no fear. Archbishop General Lambsblood and his troops will find them and wipe them out.

"Fellow citizens, friends, Kingdomites!" de Tomas went on, raising his arms. "Leave this hall now in an orderly manner, in peace, as the Great Buddha, the Prophet Mohammed, and your Lord and Savior, Jesus Christ, would have mankind live and love one another, and in the complete confidence that your lives are safe and your affairs unimpeded in any way! Return to your homes! Tomorrow I shall address the entire world and we shall all march forward, arm in arm, toward peace and reconstruction!"

Reluctantly at first, as if only partly absorbing what de Tomas had just announced, people began to stand. After a few moments, as the true impact of what de Tomas had said sunk in, they began filing in an orderly manner toward the exits.

SG men seized the five leaders and hauled them to their feet. Manacles were placed on their wrists.

"Goddamn *hell*!" Jayben Spears cursed quietly. He began elbowing his way through the crowd toward de Tomas, who stood on the dais giving his lieutenants orders. "De Tomas!" Spears shouted. "A word! A word!"

"Should I throw him out?" an Overstormer asked.

De Tomas shook his head. "Mr. Ambassador!" He turned and greeted Spears affably. "I thought I saw you sitting way back there." He gestured for two enlisted SG men to help

Spears up onto the dais, but Spears shook them off angrily and mounted the stairs on his own.

"De Tomas, I'd like a word with you in private, please," Spears gasped, out of breath not from the exercise, but because of his anger.

De Tomas nodded toward an alcove off to one side. He reached out to take Spears by the elbow, but the ambassador shook off the hand with a snort and stomped off into the alcove. There, he turned and faced de Tomas. "You fuck! You rotten shit! Do you think I don't see what you're doing here!" Spears began.

"My, my, Mr. Ambassador, such language from a diplomat!"

Spears caught his breath, controlling himself. "You are nothing more than a murderer, de Tomas, and you are creating a police state here."

De Tomas only shrugged. "Kingdom has always been a police state, or hadn't you noticed?"

De Tomas's easy cynicism and calm further infuriated Jayben Spears. "You bastard!" Spears hissed, shoving a forefinger into de Tomas's face. "You have gone too far now, and I am going to—owww!" De Tomas reached out and seized Spears's wrist, squeezing it in an iron grip. He easily forced the older man backward and down onto a small settee set in one corner of the alcove.

"Now you listen to me," de Tomas said, letting go of Spears's wrist. "This is an *internal* affair and you have no authority here. Furthermore, Spears, don't take that high and mighty tone with me. You Confederation government people have always put your interests before those of the member worlds, and you personally, Spears, despised those fools out there, despised everything about this world. If you had your way, you'd have disposed of the leaders a long time ago. Now my advice to you is to get your ass back to Interstellar City and keep it there."

Spears, massaging his wrist, glared up at de Tomas. "I'm filing a report on you," he gasped, "and I'm recommending a police force be sent here to restore order to this place." But even as he said it, Jayben Spears knew his threat was a hollow one. De Tomas was right—he despised the Kingdomites, and what was happening now was a purely internal affair. Even if the Confederation dispatched a fact-finding mission to Kingdom, de Tomas could easily handle their inquiries.

"A report on me?" De Tomas laughed. "Be my guest, Mr. Ambassador! But be assured, *I* am filing one on *you*, and you shall be removed subsequently from your post."

"Mr. Ambassador! Mr. Ambassador!" someone shouted. It was Carlisle. Two SG men were restraining him.

"Release him!" de Tomas said, stepping aside to let Spears out. "The Ambassador and I have concluded our discussion." He smiled and bowed at Spears.

"What happened to your wrist?" Prentiss asked Spears as they rode back to Interstellar City.

"Nothing," Spears answered, then hid his bruised hand inside his coat. They drove in silence for a while. "Prentiss, you know what has just happened, don't you?" Prentiss nodded. Spears sighed. "I should never have accepted this assignment. I'm powerless to do anything now but file reports that will be ignored. I think I've reached the end of the line."

"He did that?" Prentiss meant Spears's injured wrist.

"Yeah, I think he broke the goddamned thing," Spears said, taking his hand from his coat. "I'm lucky he didn't haul me off to Wayvelsburg. Be warned: don't shake your finger in de Tomas's face, Prentiss."

Carlisle pulled over and stopped the landcar. All around them, up and down the street, which had been mostly cleared of rubble, people were celebrating. "They don't know what they're in for, do they?" Carlisle asked.

"Oh, they don't care, Prentiss. The lives of ordinary people in a dictatorship are seldom affected by the politics of tyranny, so long as they have their bread and circuses. These people are used to obeying somebody, whether it's their mullahs, their priests, their whatnots. A man like this de Tomas will have them believing he's a god in no time."

"Do you really believe that, sir?"

Spears looked at his station chief. "Nah. That's just the way I'm feeling right now."

"Sir, I want to tell you, you are the bravest and most principled man I've ever served under. I wish you'd stay on here. I really do."

Spears looked at Carlisle. "Well, thank you, Prentiss," he replied, his voice husky. "I—well, let's go back to the embassy and have a couple of drinks and we'll think about it."

Carlisle smiled and moved the car back onto the street.

"Goddamn, Prentiss," Spears said, holding up his wrist, flexing his fingers experimentally. "I guess it's not broken after all. Probably just sprained. Now I really do owe that sonofabitch payback!"

The assembled ministers were slaughtered in the Great Hall where they sat, gunned down by the men of the Special Group, and then the hall was sealed. The five Ecumenical Leaders, however, were taken back to Wayvelsberg and executed slowly in a soundproof chamber, hung from hooks in the ceiling of the room until the life wheezed out of them. The proceedings were filmed as each man struggled for breath at the end. The bodies were burned afterward.

There would be no public trial of the leaders. In the events that were to come on the world known as the Kingdom of Yaweh and His Saints and Their Apostles, no one would ever notice.

CHAPTER
THIRTY

"Are we ready, my dear Gorman?" de Tomas asked.

"We are, sir," the Senior Stormleader replied. He had never seen de Tomas in such a jovial mood. The coup had been a total success—surprisingly easy, in fact—but that was not the only reason the new ruler of Kingdom was so excited. He was about to make his first public address. Until then, few Kingdomites had known much about Dominic de Tomas personally, although every child knew what the Collegium stood for and what it did. But all that had changed. He was confident that they would not only come to know him well, but love him.

When de Tomas had announced his intention of making a public announcement of the coup, Herten Gorman had been opposed to the idea. "Do you think that is wise, ah, I mean necessary, sir?" he'd said. The thought of de Tomas going on camera before the entire world struck him as ludicrous, possibly even dangerous to the success of their recent coup. His sallow complexion and saturnine features marked de Tomas for what he really was—an inquisitor and an assassin. Like most such men, he was not photogenic.

"And why, my dear Herten, do you think a public address on this most auspicious occasion would be unwise or unnecessary?" De Tomas smiled sardonically.

"Well . . ."

"I want you to meet someone." At a signal, the door to an outer office opened and a trim young female walked in followed by two more young women. "Senior Stormleader Gorman, meet Gelli Alois and her assistants."

327

Astonished, Gorman rose, bowed politely, and took the young woman's hand in his. "Charmed, I am sure, miss," he said, brushing his lips lightly over the back of her well-manicured hand. She smiled up at the senior stormleader coquettishly. Gorman, even out of uniform, was a handsome man.

"I am charmed likewise, Senior Stormleader. These are my assistants, Miss Rauber and Miss Madel." The two women bowed.

"Ladies, set up your equipment and start to work. Herten, these ladies were lately special assistants to that miserable pulpit thumper, Ralphy Bruce Preachintent. They were his makeup artists. They now work for me. Ladies, you may commence."

Before Gorman's eyes the three women began the transformation of Dominic de Tomas. They were done within the hour. As they stood back, admiring their work, Gorman could not resist clapping his hands enthusiastically. Even in the comparatively dim indoor lighting of de Tomas's den, his face glowed with radiant good-natured charm, so skillfully had the women applied their powders and rouges; his hair had been trimmed neatly and restyled carefully to reduce the length of his jaw, which ordinarily gave him a distinctly horsey look. The roseate glow of his skin actually made him look younger and vital, and brimming with good spirits.

"Well, what do you think?" de Tomas asked at last.

"I think they should go to work on me next," Gorman answered, and they all laughed. The way Gelli Alois tossed her head and winked at the senior stormleader, it was clear that she would like the opportunity to show him what she could do.

The hour had arrived. In the foyer, camera crews were setting up and technicians bustled everywhere. De Tomas was going to make his broadcast right in front of Heinrich the Fowler—the ancient unifier of the Germanic peoples revered by the Special Group as their hero.

De Tomas was in a jolly mood, joking with the technicians. Once again, Gorman was surprised. He'd never seen de Tomas like this. People were actually responding to him as he moved among them, joking with one person here, slapping another on the back there, asking questions about the broadcast equipment, bantering and making small talk. He remembered de Tomas in the torture chamber and wondered how anyone could achieve and maintain such a contrast as his leader was demonstrating just then.

Then Gorman realized that de Tomas lived in two worlds he carefully kept apart. One was the world of his fantasy—Dean of the Collegium and, now, the supreme political power in the world, where he was endowed with unlimited power to shape and change, where his will held sway over that of everyone else who came within his sphere. In the other world, de Tomas was the avuncular, cosmopolitan man of the people, charming and witty, sincere, the arbiter of all the problems of the "little" people of the world, a man to be respected and loved, but mostly loved. Gorman smiled. He had no doubt now that de Tomas would convey his public image with complete success. The only question was, which of his worlds was the fantasy and which the real?

De Tomas took his place behind the ornate, old-fashioned desk that had been brought into the foyer. Gelli Alois and her assistants fluttered around him, making minor adjustments to his makeup. At last he nodded to the technician in charge, who called for silence. At a nod from his leader, Gorman came to attention and shouted, "Ah-TEN-HUT!" The Lifeguards who had been standing at parade rest around the walls of the foyer crashed to the position of attention. All was silent in the great hall. "One, two, three," the chief technician whispered, then pointed a rigid forefinger at the Special Group bandleader. The stirring first bars of Franz Lizst's "Les Preludes" echoed throughout the vast chamber. Then, as the music died away, Dominic de Tomas began to speak.

"My friends," he said gravely, "I have the most momentous news for every man, woman, and child in the world." As de Tomas spoke, Gorman slowly became convinced that his leader meant every word he was saying, though he knew he should have known better.

"Our glorious military forces, under the brilliant leadership of that valiant old soldier, Archbishop General Lambsblood, have succeeded at long last in expelling the demon invaders from our world. The demons are in full retreat and our forces are pursuing them.

"You have suffered greatly since these evil creatures came here. Many have died, and our towns and cities have been laid waste. But now it is time to rebuild. We always knew in our hearts that they could break our walls but never our spirits.

"But some things in this world have now changed forever. For the better. I have the sad duty to announce to you that yesterday evening, in my official capacity as Dean of the Collegium, I was forced to arrest the entire Ecumenical Council of Leaders." Here de Tomas paused dramatically. "After a long investigation, incontrovertible proof was obtained—and I tell you this with the greatest sadness—that our leaders were to a man engaged in an unholy conspiracy to profit personally from our terrible misfortunes. Each was enriching himself from money made from black marketeering and illegal off-world currency transactions while hampering our military forces' operations against the enemy!" His voice had risen almost to a shout and the veins stood out on his forehead. He paused again, as if taking control of himself. "All the facts of this investigation will be made public in due course, and you will be able to judge for yourself the degree to which our leaders have betrayed us."

De Tomas carefully folded his hands in front of him, visibly taking a deep breath. "I was forced to move with the greatest speed to end this conspiracy. I did that on my own initiative, but in your name and on your behalf. I have been reluctantly forced now to take the reins of government into my own hands. That is the last thing I ever wanted, but it has to be done. I am not a politician. I am not a leader. And I will wear the mantle of this awesome responsibility only until I can pass it to someone more capable.

"Therefore, I announce formally and officially that the Collegium is hereby dissolved. Henceforth each sect will run its own religious affairs according to its own tenets without interference or oversight from my government. You will render unto that government only that which it is due, and you may practice your religion as you see fit."

Standing in the shadows off to one side, Gorman smiled. They wouldn't need the Collegium to control the people anymore. The schools, the media, and social organizations would take care of that. Soon each sect would be isolated from the others, and de Tomas could then deal with them individually. He did not care what they believed, only that they obey, and obey they would once their livelihoods depended on it. Already members of the Special Group and the Collegium's bureaus were actively gathering in the reins of finance and industry. With peace restored and money to be made, the bankers and industrialists had proved so far only too cooperative.

"I will announce my cabinet in the next few days," de Tomas continued. "After that I shall present to you a new constitution written to guarantee your religious and personal freedoms so that never again can corrupt government rule this world."

Again de Tomas paused. An expression of humble submission and sincere gratitude crossed his face. He looked steadily into the camera. Watching on a monitor, Gorman felt a catch in his throat. De Tomas looked so *honest* and . . . *saintly*—the reluctant hero, called to this momentous act by a sheer sense of duty!

"Now, my friends, I must be about your business. We will have frequent talks like this as the next weeks come to pass. I wish now that you all return to your homes and start to rebuild your lives. Until we meet again, God bless you, and good night."

It was a very short speech for a man who had just succeeded in seizing absolute power on an entire world. Unlike dictators before him, such as Adolf Hitler, Benito Mussolini, and Denon Irondequoit of Kanitarons, Dominic de Tomas had no need of lengthy speeches. Those other megalomaniacs had agendas to pursue that required the cooperation of their people, so it was necessary for them to persuade as much as it had been to usurp. De Tomas had no agenda beyond the seizure of power. He would extend that power through the instruments at his disposal—the Special Group and its affiliates, and Archbishop General Lambsblood and the Army of the Lord. Whoever did not cooperate would be destroyed. He did not need to persuade anyone to agree with him.

"Why that mealy-mouthed, phony, lying sonofabitch!" Jayben Spears raged. He and his staff were watching the broadcast from their offices in Interstellar City.

"He's pulling it off brilliantly, though," Carlisle Prentiss remarked.

"Yes, all the more dreadful," Spears sneered. "How the hell did they make him up to look so . . . so . . . ?"

"Human?"

"Yes. You've seen him close up," Spears went on, unconsciously massaging his wrist. "It's amazing, Prentiss. We can take the human body apart and put it back together again like new but the only treatment for a sprained wrist is to apply ice packs and wrap it in a goddamn elastic bandage." He grimaced and turned back to de Tomas. "He looks like death warmed over. But here he is on this worldwide hookup looking like—like some tanned and athletic vid star!"

"Well, regrettably, sir, he's pulled something off on us. The preliminary reports we're getting from the outlying districts is that people are more interested in putting their lives back together than in what happened to the Ecumenical Leaders. Besides, the Collegium's been a part of the scene in this world for so long now people automatically assume whatever it does is perfectly legitimate. The average man in the sect apparently thinks if the Collegium drags someone off in the night, especially if it's someone from another sect, well, that person must have deserved it."

"Yes, yes," Spears said, "and so far as the 'man in the sect' is concerned, the high mucky-mucks in the Convocation are as remote from his daily life as any lay politician from the man in the street anywhere else in Human Space. Well, Prentiss, this is *it* for me."

"You mean you're resigning, sir?"

Spears looked hard at his chief-of-station before answering. "Hell *no*, Prentiss! I'm not resigning." He held up his wrist, the one de Tomas had sprained. "Not now. I owe that sonofabitch. No, I'm staying right here, and I'm opposing that bastard in every way I can. He can complain about me all he wants to. I can outwrite the bastard in my own dispatches. The only way they're going to get me off this world is feet first or by presidential decree, and I guarantee you, with what Ted Sturgeon and I will have to say about Mr. Dominic de Tomas, the old girl will want to keep me right where I am." He raised his glass and toasted Prentiss. "I have not yet begun to fight."

Carlisle sighed inwardly. I'd better contact the commander of the Marine security detail, he thought. The old boy's going to need all the protection he can get from now on.

"You were absolutely brilliant, my leader!" Gorman enthused, alone with de Tomas.

De Tomas smiled and nodded. "Thank Miss Gelli and her maidens for that, Senior Stormleader."

"Sir, messages have been coming in from all over the world, congratulating you on your bold action, your integrity, your . . ." He held up a sheaf of telegrams from government officials and church leaders, those too far down in the chain to have been earmarked for elimination, praising de Tomas's performance earlier in the evening. "The people are behind you!" Gorman was nearly in tears, he was so happy.

"Yes. Well, if anybody is *not*, we know how to handle them, eh?" De Tomas laughed. "But Senior Stormleader, I have a special request of you," he went on, very serious now.

"This is a matter of some delicacy and I entrust it to you exclusively. You are to tell no one. Is that clear?"

"Of course, my leader! I stand ready for your orders!"

"Ahem. Senior Stomleader, I need companionship."

Gorman hesitated an instant before responding, " 'Companionship.' Yessir."

"I have devoted my life to my people," de Tomas mused, looking off into space. "I have had no personal life, no family, no friends. I think now I must have a—consort." He looked straight at Gorman.

"Ah, yes, my leader, a 'consort,' surely. Naturally."

De Tomas nodded, speaking almost to himself. "She must be young. I do not want a woman old enough to have been corrupted by those around her." He held up one finger. "She must be healthy, Senior Stormleader—mark that, healthy." He held up a second finger. "She must *not* be a religious zealot." He held up a third finger. "She cannot, of course, be married. A widow would do, but she cannot be married." He held up a fourth finger. "And finally, Senior Stormleader, she must be comely. Do you know what comely is, Senior Stormleader?"

"Yes, my leader, comely." Gorman thought fast. "Comely like, ah, Miss Gelli, my leader? Miss Gelli is comely, very comely. Ah, yes, and so is Miss Madel," he went on quickly, mentally kicking himself that he'd mentioned Gelli first.

"Yes, yes, yes," de Tomas waved a hand, "but I have other things in mind for Miss Gelli and her assistants, Senior Stormleader." Gorman felt a wave of relief pass over him. *He* had something in mind for Miss Gelli too. "But you are right, she is comely. I want a woman as comely as she, Senior Stormleader. So there you have it."

"Yes, sir. Ah, have *what*, my leader?"

"I want you to find this ideal woman for me, Senior Stormleader!" de Tomas said as if talking to an idiot. "In your travels, in your discussions, in your business as the commander of the Special Group, I want you to find a woman who fits my requirements and bring her to me here at Wayvelsburg. I will interview her. If she turns out unacceptable, bring another, and so on. Until you find just the right one for me."

"My leader, consider it done!" Gorman bowed deeply from the waist. But inside he seethed at the thought that elevated to command the Special Group, he was now to be his leader's procurer.

EPILOGUE

The Brattles sat comfortably around the fire in their living room. It had taken them several days to reestablish themselves in their old home. The men had spent most of that time gathering in the stray livestock—the few that had been left behind in the rush when the community moved to Gerizim—and the animals were now secured in the barns. New herds would be bred from them in time, and in the spring—it was winter now in this hemisphere—crops would be planted and the community would also take root again and thrive.

None of the City of God survivors knew anything about the war against the Skinks or what had happened in the world since their sect had been attacked. They had known, of course, that the Confederation Marines had landed, and they also knew that the ministers of their sect were of the opinion the Marines had come to further oppress them. But since the disaster at Gerizim, the survivors had given no more thought to the off-worlders, or if they had, they would have been glad to see them.

Outside, a violent sleet storm raged in the night. In the flickering firelight Zechariah was reading aloud from the twenty-seventh chapter of Deuteronomy, when someone shouted. The words were carried away by the wind, but Zechariah looked up. "Who could that be?" he asked, reaching for the gun that was always close by these days. Comfort shifted the barrel of her shot rifle so it covered the door. The voice came again, accompanied by pounding on the door. Cautiously, Zechariah got up and opened it. Hannah Flood, accompanied by a blast of frigid air, stumbled inside.

"The night is aptly named after you, Hannah," Zechariah said, his weak attempt at humor lost in the blast of sleety air that accompanied the woman. She stood gasping for a moment.

"Zach, come to the meetinghouse at once! Strangers have arrived! Oh, the poor souls, you should see them!"

Without a further word Zechariah slipped into a waterproof and stepped out into the darkness. Comfort followed, her shot rifle slung beneath her slicker. The three trudged down the street to the meetinghouse, its windows dimly aglow through the tempest. Inside, several villagers stood around three prostrate forms, two men and a woman, stretched out on the floor. Someone had taken off the rags they'd been wearing and wrapped them in warm blankets, but still, their faces were blue with cold and they shivered uncontrollably.

"They came to our home," Esau Stoughten explained to Zechariah, "and we brought them here, but they need a doctor, Zach, look at their bodies." He pulled the covers off one of the men. Comfort gasped. The outline of the man's ribs showed plainly through his pallid skin, as did his pelvic bones, and his cheeks were sunken in like those of an old man. "They are all like this," Esau explained, "and look at their poor feet." He drew back the covers farther, to expose the man's feet, which were torn to shreds. "They have walked a long ways, and in this weather, without shoes, only those pitiful rags." He nodded at the sodden pile of clothes in one corner.

Zechariah knelt by the man. "Can you hear me?" he asked. The man's teeth chattered but he nodded. "Where are you from? What happened to you?" He noticed the man's body was laced with scar tissue, some of it very fresh but most of it from old wounds.

"Sk-Skin-Skinks," the man whispered, shaking his head. "Monsters," he croaked.

"Oh, dear God," someone exclaimed.

Zechariah remembered the humans he'd seen hauling loads at the demon encampment on their way back to New

Salem. "Skinks" is what this man called them? If they came from there, the monsters would be looking for them, would follow them, and would come to New Salem. Well, so be it, he thought. Then: "We must take them to our homes and care for them. I'll take this man. Come, let us move them, and quickly."

Two days passed and the demons did not come. The Brattles cared for their guest around the clock, Comfort and Consort feeding him nourishing broth and keeping him warm under a pile of quilts. Shortly after getting him into a bed, he lapsed into a feverish coma. He stayed that way during those two days, sometimes muttering incomprehensibly and groaning but otherwise unresponsive.

Early in the morning of the third day, Comfort dozed by his bedside, her Bible lying open on her lap. "Are you an angel?" a voice croaked, startling the young woman fully awake.

"Oh! Are you all right?" she said, kneeling by the man's bedside. She lay a hand on his forehead. The fever was gone.

"I feel terrible," he rasped, a weak smile on his lips. He gazed up at Comfort for a moment. "Who are you? Where am I?"

"My name is Comfort Brattle and you are in my father's house in New Salem," Comfort answered, pouring him a glass of water. She held it to his lips and he drank thirstily. Some slopped onto his chin, and Comfort gently wiped it away with a napkin.

"Th-Thank you, Com-Comfort," he managed. "Comfort? What a beautiful name." He smiled again. "You are an angel," he sighed. His eyes began to flutter.

"What is your name, sir, and who are you?" Comfort asked. The man's eyes began to close. She shook him. "Who are you?" she asked again.

The man opened his eyes. "I am . . ." He hesitated as if trying to remember who he was. "I am—call me—Charlie, Charles—call me—dear God—*I don't remember my name!*"

It's the 25th Century, but the Marines are still looking for a few good men...

STARFIST
by David Sherman and Dan Cragg

Book 1
FIRST TO FIGHT

Stranded in a hellish alien desert, stripped of their strategic systems and supporting arms, and carrying only a day's water ration, Marine Staff Sergeant Charlie Bass and his seven-man team face a grim future seventy-five light-years from home.

Book 2
SCHOOL OF FIRE

On Wanderjahr, nothing is as it seems, not even the animal life, and everyone has an agenda. The Marines are drawn deeper into the politics of a world where murder, terror, and betrayal are the accepted methods of government.

Book 3
STEEL GAUNTLET

After the resource-rich planet Diamunde is seized by armed forces of a corrupt industrialist, the Confederate Marines face their most desperate battle yet against the mechanized forces of a bloody usurper.

STARFIST
by David Sherman and Dan Cragg

Book 4
BLOOD CONTACT

When a scientific team exploring an obscure planet fails to make its regular check-in, the Marines of the Third Platoon are sent to investigate. They prepare for a routine request operation, but find a horror beyond description....

Book 5
TECHNOKILL

A terrifying secret hidden on an alien world, an evil coterie of ruthless masterminds, a murderous battle of cunning and deadly skill with the fate of the Human race in the balance. It's time to send in the Marines.

STARFIST
by David Sherman and Dan Cragg

Book 6
HANGFIRE

Six agents have died hideously trying to penetrate the crime families behind a vast empire of pleasure and debauchery on Havanagas. Now, it is up to the Marines to break this cycle of death and destruction.

Book 7
KINGDOM'S SWORDS

While slogging through the planet Kingdom's fetid swamps, the Marines are attacked by powerful unseen weapons that can destroy half a platoon with one shot. Third Platoon's orders are to penetrate deeper into the jungle hell and face the danger like Marines...

In paperback from Del Rey Books.
Available wherever books are sold.

Visit www.delreydigital.com— the portal to all the information and resources available from Del Rey Online.

- Read sample chapters of every new book, special features on selected authors and books, news and announcements, readers' reviews, browse Del Rey's complete online catalog, and more.

- Sign up for the Del Rey Internet Newsletter (DRIN), a free monthly publication e-mailed to subscribers, featuring descriptions of new and upcoming books, essays and interviews with authors and editors, announcements and news, special promotional offers, signing/convention calendar for our authors and editors, and much more.

To subscribe to the DRIN: send a blank e-mail to join-ibd-dist@list.randomhouse.com or sign up at www.delreydigital.com

The DRIN is also available at no charge for your PDA devices—go to www.randomhouse.com/partners/avantgo for more information, or visit www.avantgo.com and search for the Books@Random channel.

Questions? E-mail us at delrey@randomhouse.com

 www.delreydigital.com